Sweetly Scandalous

A WILLOW CREEK NOVEL

By Jacqueline Winters

Stay Scandalous ♡

Jacqueline Winters

ISBN: 978-1-943571-02-4 (print)
ISBN: 978-1-943571-00-0 (Kindle)
ISBN: 978-1-943571-01-7 (ePub)

Editor: EJ Runyon
http://www.bridgetostory.com
Copy Editor: Brenda Letendre
Cover Design: RBA Designs
http://designs.romanticbookaffairs.com
Formatting: Michelle Josette
www.mjbookeditor.com

Prologue

Down the street, a familiar horn honked, announcing Travis' impatience. Allie Jordan gathered her envelope clutch purse and took a deep breath to still her shaking nerves. From her upstairs bedroom window she watched the red and white striped pickup pull into her driveway. She wondered how soon into their evening she should tell him it was over.

She tried catching a glimpse of his face, to gauge his demeanor. But it remained hidden by the sun visor's shadow. She should hurry. Any further stalling would only aggravate what was sure to follow her shattering announcement. She'd have to gamble he wasn't in a mood to shove her down a flight of stairs.

Dashing through her room, Allie accidentally knocked a paperback from her nightstand and bent to pick it up. For a brief moment, she debated shoving the romance novel into her purse. Another honk; she decided against it. Travis hated her reading those books. Tonight, she didn't need any help setting him off.

The horn blared again, twice this time. Allie fumbled down the stairs.

Travis Meyers hadn't always been this way. Before his father left town, Travis was normal. Popular, even. He'd had a hardworking reputation. And at parties, girls crowded Allie to distract her so one of them could try seducing him. But he'd always fight his way through the web of girls back to Allie's side. Travis was loyal if nothing else.

Before Allie could make her escape out the back door, Pam Jordan called out from the living room, yelling above the noise, "When will you be home?"

Still, he held down that horn.

"When I am!" Allie called back, pushing through the screen door and letting it slam shut. The last thing she needed: Mom badgering her about a curfew. Travis hated it. Thought it was demeaning for an eighteen-year-old.

Allie hopped into the passenger seat, catching a quick glimpse of Travis' gray eyes. They gleamed with something she couldn't pinpoint. The wafting of cologne he rarely wore invaded the cramped cab. The faint trace of a smile came at her when he leaned in for a kiss.

"Took long enough."

Travis wrapped his hand around her neck as his kiss deepened, stubble scraping against her cheek. She tried kissing him back like she meant it. But any sparks that once flickered had died months ago. When he stopped being so sweet and considerate. The first time he shoved her back a couple of feet with his palm.

She hoped her kiss felt convincing.

Travis pulled back, his face inches from hers. His gray eyes studied her expression. Allie felt her heart pound. Fear that he'd figured her out. Forcing a smile, she asked, "What are we doing tonight?"

"I've got something special planned." He yanked the truck into reverse and pulled back in the opposite direction she'd expected.

"Where are we going?"

His unkempt blond hair was its usual unruly mess. A style that'd only made half the senior girls try to steal him from Allie. She wished one of them had succeeded.

Allie assumed it would be a ride to the old farmhouse. The one his mother acquired after the messy divorce. His father's childhood home. It'd been empty for decades, but Travis considered it a special place. One he dreamed of fixing up and living in some day with a large family.

"Out to dinner." Travis reached for her hand and squeezed it at a stop sign. "If you don't mind a date?"

Swallowing, Allie plastered a smile on her face. "Sounds great."

Travis turned onto the highway and sped away from the small town of Willow Creek, Nebraska. "You'll be graduating soon."

"Just a few weeks." Allie's voice fought to keep an even tone. It'd been weeks since they'd engaged in small talk.

She longed for the old Travis. The one the town admired for his unwavering work ethic. The one who opened doors for her. The one who had ambitions and a noble reputation. Since his dad's departure, however, Travis had receded into himself. His temper flared at unexpected moments. In the past few weeks, things had escalated. All the more reason to end this tonight.

"You still planning to go to Lincoln?"

When it came to talking about the future, every spoken word was a landmine. "Yes."

"You really want to run track in college, Allie?"

Pleading eyes met hers. *Does he really want me to stay in town?* She considered gushing over how much she loved track. How the rush of those short sprint races gave her an almost euphoric high. Instead, she settled with, "I do."

"It's going to be a lot of work, you know. And you might not be good enough. Such a big school." Rough fingers grazed Allie's bare shoulder. "You might just sit on the sidelines the whole time."

Allie bit her tongue. *Where is this going?*

She knew there'd be more competition, sure. As a freshman at University of Nebraska Lincoln, she'd have to work twice as hard just for the chance to compete in their college meets. That didn't frighten her. She'd broken two high school records that had stood for thirty-two years. And if she performed well at the district meet next week, she'd have a full-ride scholarship, too.

But she didn't mention any of that. "I know."

"Why don't you stay closer to home? The community college has sports. And you'd only be half an hour away. Instead of three."

Allie should've stopped herself, but her words escaped before she thought. "Why don't you apply too? There's still time."

The truck jerked to a halt. Dusk fell over the empty fields on either side of the road, no cars visible for miles. Travis shackled her arm, his fingers digging into her skin. "You know that's not what I want," he spat through clenched teeth. "You telling me I should've gone to college three years ago instead of staying here to work? You calling me stupid?"

Allie shook, her curled hair bouncing off her cheeks. "No. I'd never do that."

If she cried, he might hit her. She bit the inside of her cheek, and through the sting told him, "You're not stupid. I just thought you might like—"

The ringing of his cell silenced her, bringing both of them back to the reality that they'd stopped in the middle of the highway. Fingers prying her arm free, Allie glanced to the side mirror, spotting a car in the distance, gaining on them. Travis floored the gas, reaching for the phone tucked in the ashtray.

At the next gravel road, he jerked off the highway and stopped. Shoving his door open, he slid from the truck. He never wanted Allie hearing his conversations lately.

But he'd left the truck's rear sliding window open this time. She caught, "I can't tonight."

Allie contemplated running. But with the nearest farmhouse over a mile away and the cornfields barren of tall stalks this early in the season, there was nowhere for her to go where he wouldn't find her.

She was fast, but Travis would catch her.

Instead, she listened to his conversation drifting through the window with the uncomfortably warm breeze.

She heard, "I'm not fucking doing it, that's why."

Travis paced, crunching gravel beneath his heavy steps. "I got something important to do. Call someone else." Travis pounded his palm against the side of his truck, rocking Allie in her seat. "Yes, she's with me." A pause. "I want double, then." Travis' head disappeared from the side mirror; he'd leaned down.

When he stood, he chucked a large rock into the empty field. "Fine. But I want my cut tonight."

Allie trembled when Travis climbed back into the truck. He leaned over her, causing her breath to hitch. Instead of touching her, though, he reached for the dusty glove box. Opening it long enough for a glint of fading sunlight to catch the gleaming metal barrel of a gun.

Chapter 1

Five years later...

Allie peeled her sweaty cheek from the pages of her latest romance novel, *Forbidden Pleasures*. Norman's leash sat piled beside her blanket in the grass. Eyes failing to open, her lusty dreams and comfortable blanket lulled her back to sleep. Last she remembered, she'd left Rance and Bianca in a stable with arms and legs in a tangle.

A whisk of air shot over her head, forcing her eyes to flutter open. Reality sank in; she'd fallen asleep during her dog's naptime.

Norman!

Lifting from the quilted blanket, her hair slipped across her forehead, and she pushed it back. She caught sight of her black German shepherd pawing at his red Frisbee near the edge of the grass, where the dirt track began. A yawn escaping, Allie wondered how her dog had thrown his own toy.

Norman nosed the Frisbee off the grass enough to grip it with his teeth. He shot away from her, toward a stranger standing next to the goalpost on Willow Creek's only football field.

Allie's first instinct was panic. She pushed off the grass, prepared to leap in pursuit of Norman. By breed, her dog was protective, not always friendly with people he didn't know. Before she got any farther than her knees, Norman dropped his Frisbee at the man's feet. A man she'd never seen.

A gorgeous man.

The Frisbee shot through the air, away from her this time. She rubbed her eyes. Allie glanced down at her book resting on her blanket, then back to the man's nice rear. Had he jumped from the book's pages?

As the stranger turned back toward her, Allie glimpsed a sleeveless shirt hugging defined muscles. Slipping off his sunglasses, his green eyes met hers. When he sent a sexy smile her way, Allie feared a melted puddle might be all Norman would find of his owner. *Rance?*

Am I dreaming? She hoped she was. She had to be.

Everything around her looked too real to be a dream, though. The green football field at the very edge of town stood outlined by a dirt track. A wall of trees to the west, the brick school building to the east.

"I hope you don't mind."

"Mind?" *Why would I mind? Isn't this the part where you ravish the damsel on the blanket?* "I'm surprised he didn't maul you."

Norman dropped the Frisbee at the man's feet again. Her dog tossed her a quick glance, reserving most of his focus for his new friend. Strange. He wasn't one to warm to strangers quickly, especially without Allie introducing them first.

"I wasn't too worried. Dogs love me."

Allie sat up. *I'm sure they do. Along with cats, zebras, and tiger sharks.* Stretching out her legs, Allie tried sorting out if she was or wasn't dreaming. And if she were about to be taken advantage of on this sunny Sunday morning, or not. "Well I'm glad he didn't bite off a limb. The town's a little short on doctors at the moment."

His smile caused Allie's stomach to fill with drunken butterflies. She had to remind herself she didn't know him. In a town as small as Willow Creek, that was enough reason to be suspicious.

She watched him dip to grab at the toy and launch the Frisbee again, muscles flexing with each motion. Allie suddenly felt thirsty. "I haven't seen you around here before." Reaching for her bottle of water, she took a swig.

"Just moved here."

"How did you sneak in like that?" A hand snaked through his dark brown hair, mesmerizing her for a second. She was imagining how that hand might roam over other places. On her body. *Get a grip, Allie!* She took another drink of water. She hadn't heard rumors about anyone's arrival lately. Someone moving to Willow Creek, population 783—now 784—should've spread through town faster than a prairie fire.

"Got in last night, actually." He seemed to be waiting for the wind to aid his throw before he hurled the Frisbee again. Once Norman shot off after it, the stranger took a few steps closer to Allie's blanket. "I'm Nick. Nick Bryant."

"Hi, Nick." Glancing at the novel face-down on her blanket, Allie's heart began pounding. She considered telling Nick her name was Bianca, like her book's heroine. But in a town this small, it'd take no time at all for him to discover the lie. "I'm Allie."

Norman trotted toward them, red Frisbee flapping in his jaw.

"Welcome to town," said Allie in haste. His attention less on the dog's toy, Nick eyed her romance novel. She jumped up and began stuffing her sweatshirt and water bottle into her tote bag, burying the book.

"Thanks."

She expected Nick to give her dog a simple pat on the head, but he knelt down and ran both hands over Norman's ears. The book slipped from her hands. A grasshopper shot away from under it as it tumbled at her feet. "Norman, I need the Frisbee."

"Here." Nick reached out, Frisbee in hand. "I hope you don't mind me playing with your dog. It's just that you were sleeping, and he brought me the Frisbee. He's pretty insistent."

"Not at all," said Allie. *How did that bugger get off his leash?* Kneeling down, she folded her blanket and shoved it into her tote. "Saves me the trouble."

"Must've been a boring book to put you to sleep."

Allie felt her cheeks redden, thankful her back was turned. She wasn't about to admit her secret to a stranger. Even if he was so alluring it made her shaky. Not everyone knew she read romance novels by the truckload. Only her best friend Kim had any clue her bedroom closet was stuffed from floor to ceiling with them. "It's actually a very good book."

Nick laughed, his smile distracting her. Sexy. *Why can't he be Rance? So I could tackle him to the ground...* Spotting the leash a few feet away on the grass, Allie hopped up to grab it.

"So good it put you in a coma? I think he jumped over you at least three times."

"Really?" Allie hadn't gotten much sleep last night. Her blog followers expected a book review today. And Norman hadn't allowed her to sleep in. "I was up late." She'd die before she'd admit she stayed up half the night following Rance and Bianca in a crazy whirlwind of sexual tension.

Discovering the book upside-down on the grass, a mixture of relief and panic flowed through Allie. If he didn't know the topic, he obviously hadn't seen the cover. The one that featured a woman with a ripped bodice and a shirtless, chiseled man.

Allie felt the urge to run. She didn't know this man. And no one was around to help, should things turn awkward. At eight-thirty on a Sunday morning, most of the town was several blocks away, packed into one of two churches.

And Norman had proved a useless guard dog.

Standing, Allie added, "We'll get out of your hair. I'm sure you came out here to run?"

He nodded. "That's the plan."

She'd love to stay and watch this man run laps. And fantasize a little. But she needed to leave before he pried more about the book she still held onto.

"It was nice—"

Norman rolled over in the grass in front of Nick, all fours shooting straight up in the air. *So much for a quick getaway.*

The lifting sun formed beads of sweat along her neck, warning Allie that another hot Nebraska day was coming. "Some guard dog," she muttered. "We should really let you get in that run before the heat—"

"I've run in worse," said Nick, wrestling with her dog. "Norman's a great dog, by the way."

Allie shot him a look. She hadn't mentioned her dog's name.

"It's on his tag," he read her mind.

Well, duh Allie!

Another question caught her off guard. "What's your book about?"

"It's a mystery," she improvised, watching the steel bleachers in case they decided to move. "Really fascinating."

The look Nick wore warned her he'd be asking more, but she cut him off.

"Norman needs to get home. He's a wimp without air conditioning after nine." Allie held out the leash, still confused with the easy way Norman played with Nick. Like they were old buddies.

He scanned the empty track field. "I should get that run in."

Allie clipped on Norman's leash. She felt like sprinting home the few blocks. If she stayed another thirty seconds, she'd be acting like Bianca. And those acts weren't appropriate to do with a stranger in public. "Have a nice run."

"I'll see you around?"

Allie let out a laugh. "In a town of less than eight hundred people, you'd have trouble avoiding me." As dumb as the words felt leaving her mouth, Nick laughed.

His smile weakened her resolve to head home despite every instinct telling her to run as fast and as far away as she could. This Nick Bryant, a man who'd seemingly hopped right out of a romance novel, was surely trouble.

"See you later, then." He took off in a jog around the dirt oval.

It'd been a long time since Allie felt such instant attraction to a man, and never for a stranger. Such attraction, she'd learned the hard way, was a one-way ticket to heartbreak. Had she not been reading a steamy scene before drifting into an unplanned nap, she'd surely have her heart rate under control.

"We need to work on your guard dog skills," She chided Norman.

Two blocks later, she chanced a look back toward

the track field. A blur of white disappeared behind the cover of the brick school building. "Too bad it wasn't a dream."

She passed the square house on the corner, the empty porch swing swaying with the morning breeze. Her neighbor, Ed Mullins, was either at church or downtown at the local café drinking coffee with the other elderly townsmen. In fact, they were probably talking about Nick right now. If anything happened in town, that group was the first to know.

Allie smiled, already plotting to bring over a beer to butter up Ed later. A sure way to hear the latest gossip about this Mr. Bryant.

Next door to Ed, Allie admired her cute little home with its blue-gray siding, crisp white shutters, and covered front porch. One of the several homes in Willow Creek that her mom owned, it felt like a cottage. It'd been the first home her mom had renovated after the accident that claimed Allie's dad.

Digging keys out of her tote, she automatically glanced over her shoulder before unlocking the front door. Most residents of Willow Creek didn't bother locking their doors at all, especially just a for quick Sunday morning jaunt. But Allie felt safer for doing it, reassured that no unwanted visitors could be waiting in her living room.

Tote slipping from her shoulder, she threw the door open. She jumped, eliciting a squeal that frightened Norman. "Amanda!" The leash fell from her hand. Norman seized the opportunity to leap over the end table between the couch and recliner toward Allie's younger sister.

Amanda hopped up off the couch, prepped for Norman's overbearing greeting. "Hello to you too."

"How'd you get in?"

"I know where you keep the spare key, duh. You know that."

"That's for emergencies only." Despite the six-year gap, Amanda stood an inch taller than Allie. A pair of skintight khaki capris accentuated her long legs.

Allie forced deep, calming breaths into her lungs. The spare key. Hidden in a secret compartment under a purposely loose porch board; she'd told Amanda about it. How Ed had built that contraption two years ago when he caught her picking out new hiding spots every couple of weeks.

"Chill." Amanda fell into the middle of the couch. "I put it back, jeez. It's not like anyone saw me."

Allie doubted that Amanda had been as incognito as she claimed, but she dropped it. Travis was still in jail, not lurking in the shadows watching Amanda for the location of spare keys. She changed the subject. "You going to church or something?" But the clock on the wall told Allie church services were halfway done.

Amanda shook her head.

"You're kind of dressed up." Her sister wore a fashionable silky tank and a dressier pair of sandals. "And awake before noon."

"I'm here to talk to you about something."

Kicking off her shoes at the door, Allie plopped in the recliner. She hadn't missed how her sister avoided her probing.

Amanda fell back onto the couch and slid a can across the coffee table. "I got you a Dr. Pepper."

"From *my* fridge."

"And I carried it all the way to your living room for you. You're welcome." Amanda shoved her hands beneath her thighs. "I have a wonderful idea, Al."

Cracking open the can, Allie raised an eyebrow. Those infamous words had preceded several disasters throughout their childhood. Many had gotten them both grounded. "Never a good sign."

"C'mon, Al. Just hear me out."

"Fine."

"Let's go to California this summer."

Allie shook her head. "Vacations cost money, Mandy-bear."

"Really? I totally thought they were free. And don't

call me that!" Her sister grabbed a pillow off the couch, preparing to launch it. Instead she set it on her lap, dropping her elbows as anchors. "I'm serious, Al. How fun would that be? Me and my only sister walking along sandy beaches, visiting Hollywood Boulevard, stalking celebrities…"

The impractical idea was about to end. "And just how are you planning to pay for your half?" Amanda didn't have a job, nor would her aspiration to sleep away half the summer allow for one. "You don't think I'm paying your tab?"

"I'm working on it." Amanda patted Norman's head. "So will you think about it?"

"What's *really* in California, Amanda?"

"You mean besides sunshine, hot shirtless guys, beaches, and celebrities?" Amanda hopped up off the couch. "What else do you want?"

How about my spare key left alone? "A *good* reason to spend that much money. Do you have any idea how expensive it is out there?"

But Amanda wasn't having it. She darted for the front door. "Gotta run, Al. I'm heading to Norfolk."

Allie bit back the urge to ask what was in Norfolk on a Sunday morning. She needed to finish those last fifty pages of her book so she could crank out a blog for her readers. Amanda didn't know she even had a blog.

"Don't spend all your money."

"This isn't over, Allie. We're taking a vacation whether you like it or not."

Emptying her can of pop, Allie pushed out of her recliner. *There are worse things to be threatened with.*

Once Amanda left, Norman charged into the kitchen, claws clicking along the vinyl tiles. He lapped up water as she disconnected her laptop cord from its usual plug beside the buffet table.

A worn envelope Allie kept beneath the laptop caught her eye every time she lifted her computer, no matter how much she tried to ignore it. Which was the purpose of its placement. He'd been locked up almost two years when the letter with Travis' unmistakable scrawl had wormed its way into Allie's mailbox from the Lincoln Correctional Facility.

But it drove the point home, creating a daily mantra: *leave Willow Creek before Travis Meyers is out on parole.*

In that moment of self-preservation, California didn't seem like such an awful idea.

Carrying her romance novel and laptop out onto the shaded deck in her backyard, she tossed her book onto the patio table. A vacation would have to wait. Allie didn't spend money on things like that. Since the day the letter arrived, she'd only spent money on the necessary things. She saved every other penny for her permanent departure from Willow Creek.

Eager to let reality slip away, Allie set her computer on an adjacent patio chair. She dropped into her cushioned porch swing, flipping to the steamy scene in the stable; the spot with her sweaty cheek mark on the page. Norman shot out his doggie door seconds later.

She'd have these last fifty pages read within the hour. Then came the fun part. Writing the blog. Sharing her love of romance novels with an online community of appreciative readers. Ones who didn't belittle or chastise her for reading such books.

Allie had no delusions about romance novels and reality. Their lines didn't cross. But she enjoyed slipping into fantasy worlds that promised dreamy, sexy heroes, and stubborn, strong heroines. And a few hundred easy pages of nail-biting sexual tension. Always a happy ending.

So unlike reality.

Chapter 2

A large, wet nose hovered an inch above Allie's face. "Norman!" Reaching out her sleepy hand, she scratched behind his ears. With a few sloppy licks, her seventy-five-pound dog showed his appreciation.

Releasing an exaggerated yawn, Allie sat up against the headboard of the spacious bed. She slapped her buzzing alarm clock but missed the snooze button. A worn paperback copy of *Desiring the Enemy* somersaulted to the floor.

Before she could hit the clock again, the bright red numbers registered, elevating a level of panic in the seemingly calm morning. Ripping her covers away, she darted the few feet to the bathroom and cranked on the shower.

Only moments later—dressed in an acceptable outfit and her dog fed—she flew out the door and into the already-humid morning air.

If she hadn't before, Allie certainly appreciated the tiny size of Willow Creek this morning. The town comprised just over a square mile of area. A stray cat shot off in fear as Allie sprinted the short two and a half blocks, scattered with houses and various sized yards, to the hospital.

She dashed toward the alley as one of Willow Creek's oldest residents waved from his front porch. "Good morning," she called over her shoulder, zipping by.

Slipping through the gap at the back door, her foot caught. She stumbled across the threshold, threw out her hands and squeezed her eyes shut, bracing for the inevitable fall. *So much for being discreet.* Instead of smacking the cold tile floor as expected, she fell into a crisp shirt covering a firm chest, nearly swallowing what might be a nice silk tie.

"Are you okay?"

Cheeks blazing, Allie realized this shirt held a man inside.

"I'm fine." She broke free of the arms supporting her, dusting herself off as if she'd actually fallen. "Thank you fo—" Looking up, she failed to finish her sentence. "Hi, Nick."

Emerald eyes locked with hers. Then he grinned. "You weren't kidding about this small town stuff."

Any words she might've squeaked before were lost now. Her surroundings faded around her as Allie envisioned a steamy scene from yesterday's novel.

"Hope you and Norman made it home all right?"

Allie nodded, reality crashing back. Reminding her she was already a few minutes late. "I have to get clocked in. It was nice to see you again." The urge to run returned, lest he remember her reading her romance novel at the track.

What are you doing in the back of the hospital, Mr. Bryant?

Passing the kitchen, her empty stomach rumbled in objection at the alluring aroma of bacon and biscuits. But being three minutes late, Allie sighed and scurried to the time clock instead. No time to swipe any scraps now.

"Good morning," greeted Suzy Holmes, the senior ward secretary at Willow Creek General Hospital. Blonde, silvering hair brushed her shoulders. "Don't worry, she hasn't been by yet."

Still catching her breath, Allie fell into her rolling chair behind a rounded counter that served as both their desks and the front desk for patients and family members. "Have I missed anything?" Allie asked automatically. Behind the half circle, a doorway opened to the nurses' station, the chatter of a few nurses spilling through.

"Just a couple of memos for you to type up for Lesley. Needs them right away, of course."

They shared a knowing look. Lesley was Lesley Jamison, CEO; the hospital administrator; notorious for demanding things last minute. Insisting nothing could possibly be more important. Chastising anyone who dared contradict her emergency requests.

Allie'd rather be at home reading her latest romance novel than answering phones and prepping doctors' charts. But reading didn't pay the bills.

Just one more year, then I'll be somewhere far away from Cruella.

Suzy reached for a case folder. "I hope you can read her handwriting—she wrote in kind of a hurry."

The abundance of inked scrawls left little white space on the note, indicating they'd been scribbled in urgency. "I'll manage." The normally curly cursive writing was smashed together in some places and drawn out in others. Once Allie made sense of it all, the computer keys clicked like tap dancers beneath her quick fingers.

The daunting click of heels made Allie stiffen. "And here we have our administrative staff," said a voice she'd been expecting. The head cheese. It was enough to keep her from looking up.

Lesley often went out of her way to make sure Allie felt unappreciated. The woman could hold a grudge longer than most people could remember what they'd done wrong in the first place. Like it'd been Allie's fault Lesley's son had ended up in jail. She focused on typing, glancing every so often at the mess of notes.

"Suzy Holmes has been with us for several years now," Lesley continued. "She's the senior ward secretary and a great asset, as you'll soon learn. You'll come see her in the mornings for your charts once you have hospital patients."

Suzy looked up long enough to nod a quick acknowledging greeting and shake hands.

"Shall we continue, Doctor?"

"You forgot someone."

Allie's heart pounded in recognition of the southern drawl. *You've got to be kidding me.*

"Oh. Well, this is Allie Jordan, another ward secretary. Ladies, this is Dr. Nick Bryant."

Doctor Nick Bryant. Nurses would surely be running patients' wheelchairs into walls with such a distraction.

Lesley continued, "He's Dr. Rowe's replacement."

"We've actually already met." Nick's hand extended toward Allie from the higher counter he was now leaning against.

As Allie's eyes traveled from that hand to his white lab coat, she was momentarily hypnotized by his smile. How could she be expected to get any work done with a hot doctor roaming the halls?

"Shall we continue *now*?" Lesley asked, her icy gray eyes targeting Allie.

"Of course."

Once Nick and Lesley were out of sight, Suzy finally hung up the phone. "Looks like someone's a little distracted." Her gold-rimmed glasses slid to the end of her nose, just above her crooked smile, and her eyes lit up with amusement.

"Huh?"

"Unless you meant to type an entire page of the letter *t*."

Allie might as well have typed out: *Smiles that sexy should be outlawed.*

Holding the delete key, Allie determined she wasn't distracted so much as caught off guard by *Doctor* Nick Bryant. He might've mentioned he was a doctor while he was lulling her dog into a belly-rubbing coma yesterday.

She hid her smile behind a bottle of Dr. Pepper. At least she'd have nice scenery at work for her last year in Willow Creek.

The outdoor air, though thick with humidity, was calming compared to the claustrophobic feel of the restaurant as Nick stepped outside. The lineup of questions he'd just been subjected to had sucked away most of the oxygen. He had feared he'd be an outcast who'd have to work hard at gaining trust and friendships in such a small, tight knit community. Instead, three nurses had insisted Nick join them for lunch at Willow Creek's only restaurant, The Saber Saloon. They hadn't given him the option to decline before they were pulling on his arms, heading out the back door of the hospital.

An early afternoon meeting with Lesley Jamison gave Nick an excuse to slip out of the restaurant a few minutes early and walk the two short blocks back on his own. He felt grateful that the three nurses, whose names eluded him, had talked over each other, giving him very little opportunity to answer most of their prying questions.

Where are you from?

Gotta be somewhere down South with that accent.

Any children? Oh, you're not married? How is that even possible?

At this rate, the town would uncover all of his secrets by the end of the week. He'd simply wanted a chance to start fresh. To move on from his failed marriage. Forget it ever happened. *Easier to do if half the staff doesn't bombard you with personal questions.*

Back in the hospital, Lesley stood waiting by the front desk, shuffling through a red folder of papers. Approaching her, Nick surmised that she must be in her early forties. With her perfectly curled auburn hair, expensive beige dress, and black heels, it was obvious to Nick that appearance meant a great deal to Lesley Jamison.

"Dr. Bryant." Lesley plastered a smile on her face, but it didn't reach her eyes.

"Ms. Jamison."

"We haven't had a chance to discuss particulars." Lesley tossed an impatient glance at the clock. "Suzy, have you heard from Dr. Montgomery yet?"

"He'll be here in twenty minutes."

"Good." She yanked a couple of papers from her folder, shoving them at Suzy without explanation. "Dr. Bryant, why don't you follow me to my office. Suzy, page Dr. Bryant when Dr. Montgomery arrives." There was an arrogant edge about Lesley as sharp as her stiletto heels.

Trailing behind Lesley, he noticed the empty rolling

chair beside Suzy. It'd been a happy coincidence that the girl he'd found asleep in her novel, Allie, also worked at the hospital. The idea that he'd get to see her smiling face on a regular basis suited him. Meeting her had been one of the more positive experiences since his move from Georgia, unlike the trip getting up here.

During his trek to Willow Creek he'd received a speeding ticket in Tennessee, spent three hours in a torrential downpour on the side of the road in Missouri, and had not one but *two* flat tires.

When Nick closed the door behind them, Lesley motioned for him to take a seat. Her spacious office was immaculate, like her precisely applied makeup. Everything in its neat, tidy place. An oak desk featured a granite surface that glimmered in the sunlight. Nick suspected the nameplate, reading *Lesley Jamison, Hospital Administrator,* was gold. Even her silver pens looked expensive.

"Care for coffee?" She filled a ceramic mug from an espresso maker that appeared more expensive than most appliances.

"No, thanks."

Slipping gracefully into her plush leather chair, Lesley said, "Let's get right down to it, shall we?"

Nick nodded. Lesley Jamison was one of the few people in Willow Creek who was aware of the extent of his arrangement.

"As you know, Dr. Rowe and I called in a few favors to fast-track your state medical license. Willow Creek has been without its own doctor for almost a year, and we couldn't afford to wait much longer."

"I appreciate—"

"Favors come with a probationary period. As I'm sure you discussed with Dr. Rowe."

"I did." Nick had met Dr. Herbert Rowe in Florida. Though their encounter was completely coincidental, meeting the man had given Nick an opportunity to start over. One he didn't care to screw up.

"No one in Willow Creek, besides myself, the hospital Board, and you, Doctor, are to know of this trial period. If the town caught wind that you may not last longer than ninety days, it'd not be good for any of us. Whether you want to be or not, you're our knight in shining armor."

Nick studied his folded hands in his lap. *No pressure here.*

"For three months, you'll work for the hospital. Dr. Rowe's downtown office is undergoing renovations through September, so the façade will be easy to uphold. This gives the Board time to assess your skills." Lesley wrapped manicured fingers around her mug, taking a slow sip. "Ensure you are a good fit for the town. Dr. Rowe is relying on our recommendation before he'll agree to sell you his practice at the end of the summer."

Less than two months earlier, Nick had discussed these terms with Doc Herb in a bar. They hadn't changed, but hearing them from Lesley Jamison's mouth gave them more gravity. *Probably want to stay on her good side.* Nick nodded. "That sounds about right."

"Good. Any questions?"

After discussing weekly schedules, Lesley added, "There are a total of four doctors in the surrounding area, to include yourself. As I'm sure you can understand, a hospital this size cannot afford to staff its own doctors and specialists, so we grant hospital privileges to those individuals to come in when we need them."

He'd never been to a hospital this small before. One that offered only a single story with two wings; one for hospital patients and another for long-term residents. One of the nurses at lunch had mentioned there were fewer than twenty patient rooms.

"You won't have your own patients for a couple of weeks." Lesley folded her hands in her lap. "Until then, I'd like you to work with the doctor on duty to get a handle of the routine. I imagine things run a little slower around here than at a city practice."

"I'm looking forward to the change of pace."

"I should mention that the *Willow Creek Journal* will want to interview you."

Willow Creek, though friendly, seemed much more interested in Nick than he'd bargained. Swallowing a silent groan, he wondered what questions they'd ask. What all they'd try to dig up. He'd dodge that interview for as long as possible.

"On behalf of the hospital Board, and the town of Willow Creek for that matter, I'd like to welcome you, Dr. Bryant. We're certainly glad you're here."

As Nick thanked Lesley, he heard his name over the loudspeaker.

"Ah, Dr. Montgomery is here." Lesley motioned toward the door. "Follow him on rounds. He's the only one with hospital patients. Once that's finished, you're free today. Just have your phone handy in case there are any emergencies."

Nick had his hand on the door when she spoke again, "Let me know if there's anything you need."

"Certainly."

At the reception desk, a tall man in a lab coat with a mop of white hair and square-rimmed glasses stood reading charts on a clipboard. As Nick approached, the man removed his glasses and extended his hand toward

Nick. "Dale Montgomery. Nice to meet ya."

Shaking his hand, Nick said, "Nick Bryant."

"You're good to go, Doc." Suzy placed a clipboard on the counter. "Only two today."

Dr. Montgomery skimmed through the clipboard's charts. "Should be a quick tour."

Nick tried not to stare at the half-empty bottle of Dr. Pepper that sat beside Allie's wrist. Her chocolate-colored eyes remained locked on her computer screen, fingers furiously typing. Trying to think of something to say to draw her attention to him, he took in the sight of her wavy chestnut hair falling past her shoulders, the lines of her maroon shirt distracting him.

"Where's my charge nurse?" Dr. Montgomery's question shook Nick from his daze.

Forget about it. The last thing you need is to get mixed up with a local before the divorce is final. Before you know if you're staying.

"In Room Sixteen."

"Well, let's get to it. Agnes Wilson had gallbladder surgery yesterday."

Following Dr. Montgomery down the south wing, Nick appreciated how the man had referred to his patient by name. In Savannah, nurses rushed him in and out of appointments because the waiting room was always overflowing. He never had more than a few minutes with any patient. Certainly not enough time to remember names.

Everything about this opportunity in Willow Creek felt right. All he had ever desired in becoming a doctor was to make a difference to each and every one of his patients. To give them overabundant attention and care. To remember their names when he saw them on the street.

He just had to survive the first ninety days.

Chapter 3

Tossing keys onto the kitchen counter, Nick released a deep breath; one he felt he'd been holding in all day. Partly, he'd been consumed with meeting the staff at the hospital, scarcely able to find a single minute alone until now. But he mostly felt relief that nothing else had gone wrong.

Not since the hot water heater quit working halfway through my morning shower.

He lingered in his kitchen, unwilling to face the overwhelmingly vacant feel of the new four-bedroom home. New to him, anyway. *Guessing this interior hasn't seen much updating since the early nineties.* He hadn't grown used to the spacious living room; the one larger than the entire first floor of his former condo. Scarcity of furniture only magnified the emptiness.

Even the TV, when it worked, echoed off the high ceilings.

Pushing away thoughts of empty houses, Nick threw open the fridge, contemplating dinner. It didn't help that the shelves were just as bare as the home. Before departing Georgia, his sister had packed him a box of food. What remained were a carton of eggs—useless with his lack of cooking skills—a mostly empty jar of pickles his niece and nephew had determined he *had* to have, and a half gallon of milk he'd picked up in Norfolk on Saturday night. "Guess I'll need to run to the store soon."

He decided on pickles. Heaven knew he couldn't scramble eggs to save his life.

Reaching for the jar, he heard a chime echo throughout the massive living room. The doorbell. Odd considering his house didn't have any immediate neighbors. Doc Herb's old house sat on top of the town's only hill, behind the school. The one road that ended at his driveway didn't connect with any other homes.

A petite, elderly woman in a spring blue sun visor and light matching sweater stood on his front porch, holding a towel-covered baking dish. "Hi, Doctor. I'm Ruby Rowe. But most folks call me Aunt Ruby." Two skinny arms draped in blue cotton shoved the dish at Nick.

The dish felt cold to the touch, like it'd just come out of the refrigerator. "Thank you. Are you related to Doc Her—"

"Cousin of mine." Aunt Ruby spun around to leave. "Bake at three hundred and fifty degrees for forty-five minutes."

Halfway down the steps, Nick called out to her, "It's very kind of you—"

"Don't read into this any, honey. It's just a runza casserole."

"What's a runza?"

"Nebraska thing. You'll love it."

"Thank you," hollered Nick, amazed at how quickly Aunt Ruby power walked to her Buick.

He watched the woman back out of his driveway and speed down the lone road. The one that put almost a quarter mile between him and the rest of the town.

After slipping the casserole, as ordered, into a preheated oven, another ring echoed. This one different than the doorbell. The ringing landline phone displaced Nick as he stared dumbfounded through the doorway of the kitchen. The shrill noise bounced off the high ceilings until he shook himself out of his trance, remembering that very few people had this number. *Maybe it's an emergency.*

"Dr. Bryant speaking."

"Hey, baby brother."

Nick stiffened. He wasn't sure he could stomach another lecture tonight. "Miranda."

"Who else would it be? It's not like I gave out your number to she-who-shall-not-be-named."

"How are you?"

A child squealed in the background. "Hallie, I'm on the phone." Miranda apologized. "You know I'm fine. The reason I called was to see how you're doing."

"I just got home, actually." Nick heard theme music. One of the many children's movies he'd watched during the nine months he'd stayed with Miranda's family. He already wished he had both his niece and nephew curled up with him on the couch watching *Toy Story*.

"Home," Miranda repeated. The words seemed to leave a funny taste in her mouth. "How is Nebraska treating you?"

"You mean other than the sudden drastic lifestyle change?" He walked toward double doors he'd spotted his first night in the home. Peeking behind sheer curtains, the sunset tempted him outside onto the deck. "It's nice here. Very friendly town. A little old lady just brought me a casserole." Already, a wonderful aroma he couldn't identify filled the house. Whatever runza casserole was, he was certain he'd savor every bite.

"You sound better than I expected."

Nick decided against mentioning the hell he'd gone through to get to Nebraska. She'd only use it against him. Turning the door handle, he contemplated an answer. He settled with, "I am."

Miles beyond the deck, fields were filled with young corn, beans, and alfalfa. He couldn't peel his eyes away, captivated by the endless expanse of the slightly rolling, almost flat landscape. Dusted with scarce patches of trees, it made Nick feel small and insignificant.

"I'm glad," said Miranda, but she sounded distracted. Insincere. He heard muffled scolding. He'd been gone less than a week, but already the sting of leaving resonated. He'd become so accustomed to her family and the noise. His giant house seemed eerily quiet.

"I'm back," said Miranda. "Movie's going now, so they should be in a trance."

Leaning on his deck's railing, Nick could see the rooftops of nearly every home on the west side of town. He almost said *I miss you guys*. But Miranda would worry about him, probably try to convince him to come back to Georgia. And that, he just couldn't do. Not yet. "How have they been?"

"Hallie asks at least five times a day when Uncle Nick is comin' back." A heavy sigh fell from the opposite end of the line. "Joey hasn't quite figured it out yet." He waited, not taking the bait. "I just wish you'd picked somewhere a little closer to Savannah."

Nick swallowed a sigh. They'd had this argument continuously since he announced his choice of Nebraska. "I can't argue with the hand fate dealt me."

Miranda sputtered a laugh. "You go to Florida to look for a job, then come home announcing you're moving out to the Midwest. Yeah, fate is wonderful." Another squeal in the background. "Hallie, stop throwing animal crackers and watch the movie."

"It's what I've always wanted," reminded Nick. "To be a family physician in a small town."

"There are plenty of small towns in Georgia. Several of them close enough to family, and still far enough away from *her*."

He wasn't sure what lengths Dana would go through to find him. But the closer to home he was, the higher the chance she'd get bored with her new lover and come crashing back into his life. "I haven't committed to staying here, you know. I've got ninety days to prove myself. And at least as long before the divorce is final. I'll reassess things then."

"I'm holding you to that."

"I know." Nick pushed himself off the deck railing, surprised when the section that had supported his weight snapped and tumbled onto the lawn below. *Well, up until now nothing else had gone wrong today.*

"What was that?"

"Squeaky door. Nothing."

If he confessed to one unlucky occurrence, he feared he'd spew them all. Shot water heater, blown breakers, shattered light bulbs. Miranda had an effortless way of drawing every last detail from him. He'd always thought she'd make a good lawyer, but to her being a mother had a much higher appeal.

Deciding to rescue the broken railing later, Nick headed back inside. Hand on the doorknob, he caught sight of a barn to the north, nestled in a patch of overgrown trees. It shouldn't seem so out of place. But the barn had hidden itself behind unruly tree branches, long grass, and its bland, gray color.

"I mean it, you know. In three months we're going to have a serious talk. Don't go buying a new practice without consulting me."

"I need to check on that casserole. It's almost done."

Ear-splitting screams shot through the phone. "I gotta go," muttered Miranda, no doubt annoyed at the timing. "Joey launched a toy truck at Hallie."

Relief washed over Nick, knowing the grilling session was over. At least for tonight.

In the kitchen, the emptiness hit him like a kick in the stomach. He felt conflicting urges to run five miles, down a bottle of whiskey, or curl up on the couch and cry himself stupid. This two-story, four-bedroom giant was intended to house a family, not a masquerading bachelor. Nick nearly lost himself to the agonizing reality that the woman he loved had uprooted his entire world.

Whiskey seemed the least destructive option.

Pouring himself a small glass and dropping in an ice cube, he squeezed his eyes shut. Nine months ago, he'd been sure he and Dana had a great marriage. But now, his wife was back in Savannah, probably sleeping in *his* bed with his former best friend.

Soon to be ex-wife.

Nick took a swig of whiskey, blocking the horrid memories of that day. The tangled arms and legs, the wafting of sex in the air, the blaring AC/DC covering moans through the half-opened bedroom door.

Setting an empty glass on the counter, he waited for the agony of it all to settle over him. He'd been running from the awful reality for nine months, and expected to see Dana's face, her perfectly styled blonde hair, ocean-colored eyes, and wicked smile still flash through his mind. Regardless how he'd tried refusing to process the pain. Maybe it'd be better to face the painful emotions now and get it over with.

Instead, the memory of Allie Jordan face-down in a

romance novel pushed its way in, conjuring unexpected laughter. Laughter that died only when the oven timer beeped minutes later.

Gripping the casserole dish with potholders, Nick smiled, remembering Allie's embarrassment. Like she'd been caught doing something inappropriate. She'd tried to hide that paperback so many times it'd become entertaining.

Dishing a large portion of steamy casserole onto his plate, he tried not to question why Allie even crossed his mind. All he wanted was a chance to start fresh and focus on his work. He'd sworn off women for the foreseeable future. *Never found one who hasn't cheated on me.*

Nick cleaned his plate and filled it with a second portion. He'd identified hamburger, cheese, cabbage, and something with a little spicy kick in this wondrous casserole. He contemplated calling Aunt Ruby and ordering a month's supply, offering to pay whatever she wanted if only she'd send more.

After dinner, Nick tried the TV again. But just like the last time, it blew the breaker. He wanted to get angry, but when the breaker had blown Sunday morning, he'd been convinced to go for a run. He remembered Doc Herb mentioning the school football-slash-track field just a short walk from the house, through a mass of maple trees.

It was the sight of her large black dog running toward him that had caused alarm that morning. Then he spotted Allie, curled up on her blanket. At first he'd worried that the dog felt the need to protect the sleeping girl. Instead, Norman had charged him with a wagging tail and a Frisbee clenched between his teeth.

He knew Allie and Norman weren't at the track tonight. He'd already walked the trail through his trees and found the field empty. Instead of another run he didn't feel like taking, Nick backtracked to the barn.

The two-story outbuilding once had been white, but most of the paint was now chipped away, leaving it a dull gray that blended into the overcast sky. Nick yearned to revive the sad-looking structure.

A long two-by-four held the large center door shut. A smaller door off to the side provided easier access. He expected to find it padlocked, but the rusted metal lock dangled open.

From the state of its exterior, he felt certain he'd discover piles of junk, maybe bales of moldering hale, an ancient tractor, and, if he was lucky, some neglected furniture in need of restoration. But with the luck he'd had so far, he didn't count on it.

Swinging the door open, the scent of stale sawdust greeted him. Feeling along the wall, Nick's fingers found a light switch and he flicked it on. The bright glow revealed a thick coat of dust on every surface. Cabinets and counter space lined the side walls. The back wall displayed built-in shelves designed specifically for holding various sized pieces of wood. Tingles of excitement coursed through him at the sight of a dining table on its side in the middle of the room, missing two legs. *Something I can fix.*

He threw open some of the cabinet doors, discovering neatly organized tools, varnish, sanding blocks, and paint. *Everything I'd need to build or restore furniture.* The meticulous interior was a contrast to the neglected shell hiding this wondrous secret workshop.

A built-in ladder caught Nick's eyes from across the room. Curiosity pulled him up to the loft.

Up on this level, a large window drew in the setting sun, just peeking out from behind masses of clouds, its rays falling across a large architect's desk. He approached it, noticing that like the cabinets downstairs, the surface, aside from a thick layer of dust, was bare. He opened the top drawer, discovering a sketchbook and set of charcoal pencils. Flipping through the pages, he found blue prints for several pieces of furniture, including the unfinished dining table.

Though Nick didn't build furniture like Doc Herb obviously had, he enjoyed refurbishing old pieces. Setting the sketchbook back in its drawer, he felt truly excited for the first time in months.

Well-respected doctors don't scuff up their hands. Dana's belittling voice echoed. Nick clamped his hands over his ears, forcing her taunting words away. Anger simmered; he knew what came next. The recurring nightmare shoved its way in before he could block it.

It'd been a clear, sunny day. He remembered that detail above all else. Sunlight, which had felt so promising, was little more than a mockery. It cast an almost fairytale-like glow on Everdeen Street, their favorite neighborhood in Savannah. They were scheduled for an exclusive sneak-peek showing in just two hours.

Surprising his wife with the news that the house they'd admired was coming on the market by the end of the week had seemed like the perfect start to an amazing day. One that'd mark the beginning of their future together. But coming home earlier than planned hadn't boded well...

Nick jumped up from his living room couch, refusing to let the horrid memory get the best of him. "No!"

He fled thirteen hundred miles to escape that agonizing day. He would not allow it to break him down now.

Marching to the kitchen sink, he filled a glass of water and chugged.

Doc Herb had pulled a couple of favors for Nick and left him with some crucial advice. "You may meet some resistance in Willow Creek if the wrong people find out you're going through a divorce. Best you keep that detail to yourself until it's done or the Board might decide you don't fit the bill."

Nick had no qualms keeping his impending divorce a secret. Even though he'd been able to avoid Dana in Savannah outside of meetings with lawyers, he hadn't been able to avoid their friends and their looks of pity. He didn't want anyone feeling sorry for him. Those heartbreaking looks only reminded him that he'd failed.

He was through allowing Dana to carelessly toss his dreams to the side, like they weren't good enough for her ideal lifestyle. She'd wanted him to become a surgeon. "That just sounds so much more prestigious than a simple physician, doesn't it? A surgeon. Now that's a title I could toss around at parties."

Willow Creek was his chance at a fresh start. He'd be damned if he'd let Dana take this away from him too. As long as he kept this a secret, he might stand a real chance at moving on from his past. A past he wanted nothing more than to forget.

Chapter 4

"Can you fix it?" Allie raised her hand, shielding her eyes from the sun's setting glare. During the last heavy rain, the gutter on the front of her house had produced a waterfall right onto her front steps. The gutter had sagged ever since, and she was worried that she'd be replacing all the gutters on the front of her little house.

Ed Mullins looked over his shoulder from the middle rung of the ladder. "Just needs a couple screws, is all."

"Any kind?" asked Allie, not wanting Ed to come down from the ladder if he'd only be going right back up. For a man of seventy-five, he was still in pretty good shape. But he limped from time to time on an irritable knee.

"Outdoor woodscrews. Got a couple in my bag down there."

She dug out the longest screws she could find. "These?"

"Yep."

The whine of the drill made conversation impossible. It gave Allie more time to ponder how she'd ask Ed what he'd heard about Nick without sounding desperate for information. The hospital had buzzed with excitement, nurses already fighting over next week's shifts just to be paired with him.

"There, good as new." Ed passed down his drill, then dismounted the ladder. She tried to keep her nervous eyes focused on anything else. *Don't want to insult him.*

They'd been neighbors for three years. Allie's first night in her house the breaker in the kitchen blew, and she didn't know what to do. She'd had no choice but to knock on Ed's door, and he'd come to her rescue without question.

He folded his ladder and set it against the side of the house. "I'll take that beer now."

She always kept a fresh stock of his favorite in her fridge. She'd come to think of him more as a grandpa than merely a friendly neighbor. Her only surviving grandparents had retired to Arizona five years ago, and she hardly saw them.

Rushing inside, Allie popped the lid off a bottle of Miller Lite, retrieved a Dr. Pepper for herself, and snagged a treat for Norman. Returning to her porch, she found Ed eased into a chair, Norman at his feet. From the top stair, she rested her back against a thick column.

A June bug dropped onto the wood planks, near Norman's front paws. She focused on Norman's insect chase, allowing Ed to enjoy his beer before she probed him with questions.

"I heard it's supposed to storm in a couple of days." Nebraskans loved to discuss the weather. It wasn't just polite conversation, but a staple. A safe segue into any conversation.

"All day Thursday," Ed said.

When the June bug took flight, Allie tossed Norman his treat.

"Farmers will be happy." Ed readjusted his worn cap. "Crops are thirsty."

Cracking open her Dr. Pepper, she took a swig. Down the street, two women power walked along the curb. A fly buzzed above Norman's head. The dog chomped at the air, missing it by an inch.

"I suppose you've heard the latest," said Ed.

She sat up straighter. "What do you mean?" Norman plopped down on the porch next to Allie, chewing on the remainder of his treat, fly forgotten.

"All anyone can talk about is the new doctor. Doc Bryant. Surely you've seen him at the hospital?"

"I did. Seems like a nice guy. Very polite." *Did I mention he should double as a romance novel cover model?*

"Word is he's a southern city guy," said Ed. "'Course, I'm sure you picked up that accent of his already. Folks are relieved to have him. But a little suspicious."

"Suspicious?"

"City doctors're used to makin' a lot more money. Seems a little off he'd give all that up, move out here where the pay's so much less. Makes folks think something maybe happened at the city practice."

"You don't think something bad, do you?" Ed's words held a certain gravity that forced her to consider his scenario.

He shrugged, taking a swig of beer. "Just tellin' ya what folks are sayin'."

"What's your opinion, Ed?"

"Hard to say. Haven't met the guy." With another swig of beer, he set the bottle on his dirty denim knee. Allie suspected he'd been gardening before she burdened him with her sagging gutter. She'd offer to help him pull weeds, but he always turned her down. It was something sacred to him; something he and his late wife had done together.

She didn't know what to say regarding the new doctor. *Seems quite a financial sacrifice, leaving a city practice for one in a tiny Midwestern town.*

"Rumor's also flyin' that this doctor is single." Ed took another pull of his beer. "Thirty-one and no wife or kids. Mark my word, if any of the crazy women in this town have any say, he'll be married off within a year."

Allie smiled, remembering the nurse who'd literally walked into a wall watching Nick down the hall. She'd be surprised if some of the women in Willow Creek weren't already conspiring to leave their husbands.

"You gettin' in the line too, Allie?"

"Line?"

"Yeah, the line outside the doctor's front door. I heard it's so long that it starts in his driveway, runs all the way down that long road of his, and stops somewhere near Wilkerson's." Ed laughed. "Better hurry if you want a shot. Don't tell me you weren't eager to hear he's not got a wife and six kids."

Heat rushed into her cheeks. "No point in me competing. I'm gone in less than a year, anyway."

Ed waved a hand through the air. "Oh, right. You're moving someday." His teasing lacked conviction. Allie had stopped getting upset a long time ago. He seemed to think she'd stay in Willow Creek forever. Because she enjoyed his company, she didn't argue.

Ed finished his beer, then stood. "Well, little lady, it's time I get home. Evenin' news is about to come on."

"Thanks again, Ed. For everything."

Norman darted inside, tail wagging as he trotted in search of his favorite stuffed squirrel. Toy in tow, he plopped down on the couch and punched the squeaker with his nose.

Dropping Ed's empty beer bottle in the trash, she was about to settle on the couch with a new romance novel when her cell phone blared her favorite song. Allie rushed back to the kitchen to answer it. "Kimmie!"

"Hey, Al. Whatcha up to?"

"Ed just fixed my gutter."

"That sounds exciting."

Deciding to leave out her ulterior motive, Allie said, "Better than the eave of my roof rotting." She glanced toward her laptop, resting in its usual spot. Travis' prison letter was hidden beneath its weight, but not from her mind. "I'd rather save that money for moving."

She thought she heard Kim laugh. Instead, a coughing sound came through the receiver.

"You choking?"

"Yeah, sorry." Kim heaved a deep breath. "Where you moving this week?" Kim coughed again. "I mean— where is it you're moving again?"

"Newport has a certain appeal to it," Allie said, ignoring the jab in Kim's question. She had changed her mind a few times about *where* to move. But not when.

"Rhode Island? I thought you were heading to Ohio." Kim chomped on gum. "You know, the whole affordable thing. Good neighborhoods and walking trails for Norman."

Allie swallowed another drink of pop. "I started looking for something else. Turns out the winters suck, and Cincinnati's crime rate's a little higher than I bargained." She set her mostly empty can on the coffee table. "Newport just has this charm to it. Right on the water. Sailboats everywhere—what could be more romantic than that? Perfect blog-writing city if you ask me."

"Right."

Hopeful to change the subject, Allie asked, "How's work been?"

"Which job?" Unlike Allie, Kim worked three jobs. She saved every penny she could squeeze for her floral shop fund. Kim even had a tidy strategy that included a polished five-year business plan.

"Any of them." Allie carried her empty can into the kitchen.

"I'll fill you in on all of them next week."

"What's next week?"

"I'm coming to Willow Creek for a little visit. I have an impossible weekend off. I'm not asking anyone how that happened, just fleeing Norfolk before someone notices I'm not on the schedule."

"I'd be running too, if I were you." The tapping of claws on vinyl announced Norman's trot through the kitchen. He disappeared through his doggy door, into the fenced backyard.

"I'll be staying with you next Friday night," said Kim. With anyone else, Allie would've felt imposed upon. But Kim had been her best friend since the summer before kindergarten. She'd shown up on Allie's doorstep, inviting her to jump on her trampoline. They'd been inseparable ever since.

"I'll make cupcakes."

"And we'll eat them all!"

Allie fought a yawn, but it escaped anyway. "Kim, I better let you go. I'm falling asleep at the table, and I still have a hundred pages to read."

"You should really do something with that blog, Allie."

"Like what?"

"You have thousands of followers."

"Well, like four."

Romance novels had been an escape earlier in life, when Travis went from being the doting boyfriend to the possessive, jealous one. After that transformation, her crowd of friends dissipated, as Travis considered them a threat.

"Four thousand romance novel lovers who rely on you to tell them what's good and why."

"It's never been about the followers, Kim."

Back then, she'd read her romances in secret. The first time Travis caught her with one, he'd been furious. She forced the memory away.

"Maybe not," said Kim. "But you have followers whether you meant for that to happen or not. You owe it to yourself to do something bigger now."

Because of Travis, the blog had started as an outlet. Allie inhaled romances by the dozens and longed to share her excitement with someone. *Anyone.* She'd even started a journal once, but feared he'd find it. Instead, she went online where writing a blog allowed her anonymity. "I'd love to sit around all day reading books and blogging about them. But c'mon, Kim, that doesn't quite pay the bills."

"We'll chat more about it next week."

Her dog shot into the kitchen from the doggie door. "Looks like Norman's ready for bed too."

He was already curled up on his blanket at the edge of the bed when Allie stepped into the bedroom. She slipped into pajama shorts and a tank. Sifting through the pile of paperbacks on her nightstand, Allie wondered what Kim meant by turning the blog into something more. *Blogs don't work that way.* It's not like she would charge her followers a fee for reading each post. Even if she were willing to do that, in a week she'd probably go from four thousand followers to none.

Slipping under the covers, she lost herself in the pages of *Treasure of Passions.* She'd left Maximus, a pirate, and Samantha, a runaway duchess, in a heated fight after their carriage, destined to take them to his ship, broke down on a deserted road.

Allie preferred her romance novels to reality. She could safely bet that Maximus, pirate or not, would never harm Samantha to create a diversion for his own getaway should they be caught.

But Maximus wasn't Travis. The bad decision that put all of Allie's plans for the future out of reach. "Hard to get a track scholarship on crutches," she muttered.

As the pages flew, Maximus began to deviate from the blond, blue-eyed hero his author dictated into a doctor Allie conjured in her own head.

Her bitterness for Travis dissipated by the time the rain came pouring down in the story's next chapter. The two characters were forced to take refuge inside their broken-down carriage, waiting for help to arrive. The hero's blond darkened to mahogany in her mind's eye as she yawned, his sapphire eyes now taking the color of clear, bright emeralds.

Chapter 5

Wilkerson's Grocery on the corner of Main Street and Sixth was a small store crammed into two buildings. Half a century before, the owner, Kim's grandfather, had purchased the second building to accommodate expansion. He had a majority of the common wall demolished on the ground floor, leaving up just enough to maintain structural integrity.

Allie stood in the second portion of the store, staring at cake mixes, when Rachel Jamison stepped into her aisle. Turning her back, she hoped she hadn't been spotted. The woman had hated her since high school, though Allie never quite figured out why.

"Baking a cake?" Rachel asked as she strutted by, her lush blonde hair flowing several inches past her shoulders. "You know how many carbs are in one of those boxes?"

No, Ice Princess, but I'm sure you're going to tell me.

"Hi, Rachel." Allie knew she hated her addressing her by her first name, like they were equals. But she didn't have to call her Coach anymore.

"There's a fresh shipment of fruit, you know. Mr. Wilkerson said it came in just this morning. So much healthier than cake. And it won't put on the pounds."

Allie bit the inside of her lip. Since graduation, Rachel hadn't been able to hold volleyball over her head anymore. But she still had to think about her sister. Nasty words begged for release. Amanda could get a scholarship with her talent. Allie wouldn't risk Rachel benching her out of spite.

"I've got a rambunctious dog that helps keep off the pounds just fine."

Rachel laughed. "I was just teasing you, you know."

She refused to meet Rachel's sapphire eyes. Eyes that made most men fawn over her.

"I hope you're enjoying your summer, Allie," Rachel said.

The two hardly talked more than a few seconds. Just enough for Rachel to dish out an insult and sashay on her way. Assessing her possible agenda, Allie answered, "I am. And you?"

"I love my students, but I'm looking forward to some time off." Rachel twisted the glimmering bracelet on her wrist. "Time enough for me to get to know the new doctor, don't you think?" She patted Allie on the shoulder and continued down the aisle, turning a corner.

She shouldn't care. The last thing she needed was a reason to stick around this small town. Nick was nice to look at. *And dream about.* But eventually she was leaving, and he was staying.

Still studying cake mixes, debating between confetti, chocolate, and red velvet, another voice startled her.

"I would go with the chocolate, myself."

"Hi, Nick," said Allie. "Doctor Bryant," she corrected herself, aware Rachel might be an aisle or two over. She smiled at him, daring to meet his green eyes. She regretted it the moment he smiled back.

"Nick is perfectly fine for a grocery store."

Her stomach felt like butterflies were competing for gymnastics in the Olympics. The steamy scene from last night's romance played in her mind—the one where the hero looked a little too much like Nick. Since his arrival in town a couple of weeks ago, most of her romance novel heroes held strong resemblances to him, despite the authors' best intentions.

"It's pretty quiet for a Friday afternoon." Nick glanced around the deserted aisle. "I'm used to standing in line so long my frozen food thaws."

A whiff of expensive hairspray hit Allie's nose just as Rachel came rounding back into the cake aisle, retracing her steps as if there were anything there she'd actually add to her basket.

"You must be Dr. Bryant," said Rachel, stopping. Allie felt her stomach tighten. It was one thing to declare her intentions to her, but it was another to flirt right in front of her like she wasn't even there. "I'm Rachel Jamison, high school English teacher and volleyball coach."

Nick took the outstretched hand as they exchanged typical pleasantries.

Allie wanted to throw a box of red velvet cake mix. *Maybe the carbs will scare her away*. Instead, she pretended to scan her options, listening to Rachel telling Nick all about herself and asking the usual small town questions. Thanks to Ed, she already knew the doctor wasn't married and had no kids, but when Rachel asked where he was from, her ears perked up.

"Savannah."

"I thought I caught a southern accent." Rachel patted his arm playfully. Allie averted her eyes. "What on Earth brought you all the way to our neck of the woods?"

"The opportunity to work in a small town."

Sounds rehearsed. Allie waited for more, hoping he'd elaborate.

"Well, it was a pleasure to meet you, Nick. May I call you Nick?"

In her mind Allie shouted, *No!* But of course he'd have to oblige, considering he'd just told Allie she could moments before.

"Have you decided on a flavor yet?" He asked as she watched Rachel slip around the corner to the checkout counter.

"Still debating. Stuck between red velvet and chocolate."

"Special occasion?"

"You ask a lot of questions." Allie smiled, less bothered by his string of questions tonight than she'd been when they first met. Of course, she wasn't trying to hide a romance novel from him this time. "My best friend is coming over tonight. I haven't seen her in a few weeks. Her parents own this store." She didn't know why she was rambling. "Cupcakes are kind of a tradition with us. Even if they are chock full of carbs." She hadn't meant to let that last part slip out either.

"You don't look like a couple of cupcakes will do any harm," said Nick, smiling that sensual smile, threatening to turn Allie into a puddle. "How's Norman?"

"He hasn't made any other best friends since he met you, if that's what you're wondering," teased Allie. As much as she longed to continue talking, Kim would be arriving in just over an hour. She still had to whip up supper as well as bake cupcakes. "Well, I think I'm going with good ol' chocolate."

"Good choice." Nick shoved his hands into the pockets of his black dress pants. "Is there a home improvement store around here?" The curious tilt of Allie's head prompted him. "I need to repair some deck railing."

"Two blocks south, across the street. Meyer's Hardware Store."

"Thanks. Do you know where I'd find the steaks?"

Allie pointed. "All the way in the back corner."

He stepped closer to her, placing a friendly hand on her bare arm. "Maybe I'll see you and Norman at the track sometime?"

"Maybe."

She fought a smile that threatened to stretch her cheek muscles into agony. Nick turned the corner down another aisle as she released a breath she'd not recalled holding. *It's just a harmless little work crush. Just a crush. Nothing more.* Half the women in town, married or not, had a crush on Nick. *Dr. Bryant.* It didn't mean anything, despite the crazy tingling sensation his touch had left behind.

Nick was unpacking groceries when he realized how distracted Allie had made him. *Might've been a bad move to snub a local teacher.* Nothing else could explain buying canned pumpkin and canned spinach—items that would do little more than collect dust in his cupboards. He had no clue how to bake a pie. And he'd hated spinach since the age of six, when he spent the night sleeping at the kitchen table for refusing to finish his mother's mushy spinach casserole.

His urge to stop by Wilkerson's on the way home seemed odd to him too, in retrospect.

He'd received enough casseroles to last him a month. Every evening, at least one woman showed up at his doorstep. Last night it'd been an older one named Mary with her fifteen-year-old granddaughter. Nick had been a little uncomfortable with the way the young girl kept undressing him with her eyes.

Most of the casseroles sat in his freezer now, but he'd been craving something other than water and milk to drink. And then, there Allie was. He shook his head, knowing he'd need to get his mind off Allie Jordan. His little irrational crush could only end badly. Just because he refused to let his past stir up negative emotions didn't mean he was ready to start a new relationship. He'd best focus on making a solid impression on the town before he worried about women.

All the more reason to distract himself with manual labor.

Although he'd intended to repair the deck railing, Nick had discovered paint scrapers in the garage. A sure sign that giving the old barn a facelift would be a more productive and longer-lasting distraction. He'd yet to call Herb to discuss the woodworking shop, fearing that conversation would jinx his chances of staying in Willow Creek. But even if he were forced to pack everything up in three months, leaving behind a freshly painted barn certainly wouldn't hurt the resale value for Herb.

After warming some of the tuna and noodle casserole in the microwave, Nick changed into older clothes and headed toward the barn. It might take all weekend to scrape off the paint, but it'd keep him from thinking of his former life in Georgia. *Or Allie.*

Laying tarp along the front edge of the barn, Nick felt the first beads of sweat trickle down his neck. Nebraska was more humid than he'd expected.

As the paint chips scattered from his intense scraping, he couldn't help but recall Rachel Jamison's earlier question about moving to a small town. He'd have to face that question in a few days when the local paper interviewed him. Lesley hadn't let him out of that one, even when he tried to tell her he wasn't interested in the recognition.

"Nonsense," Lesley had said. "You're already a local celebrity. And the entire town's curious. Better to give them your story than have them making up their own. Just remember what you're not at liberty to discuss."

He scraped with more vigor, a large patch already cleared and ready for a new coat of paint.

The hospital Board knew that Nick had run into Doc Herb, but it was among the many secrets he was forced to keep until his probation period ended. Herb had phoned in a personal recommendation the morning after they met. Nick had been in Florida, promising his sister he'd interview at a couple of small hospitals there.

He felt a little guilty not telling Miranda that instead of interviewing, he'd taken a detour to Daytona Beach.

He'd spent the past eight months living with his sister and her family, listening to her advice day in and day out. He needed some time to himself. Time to decide what was next in his life. To think about what *he* wanted instead of what everyone else wanted for him.

Nick had visited Daytona Beach once before, when he was twelve. On a weekend Miranda spent at a summer camp, his mother had taken him with her on a mini vacation. The entire drive, his mother gushed about her love of the town—the boardwalks, beautiful beaches, and amazing piers. It was the last beach trip they took together before she got sick.

The smell of the ocean mixed with the flavor of mint chocolate chip ice cream haunted him; one of his last pleasant memories of his mother before cancer deteriorated the happiest woman he'd ever known. It was only natural that he'd gravitate back there during this life crisis.

Nick dismounted the ladder, carrying it a few feet to the right. Wiping the sweat from his brow, he leaned it against the barn.

It had been his first night in Daytona Beach, and he thought it'd take the full week to sort everything out. Content to sit in a sports bar with a basket of wings and a beer watching the Braves, he hadn't expected his life to change so quickly.

That morning, his lawyer had informed him that Dana finally agreed to the settlement. It didn't make much sense to him, why she fought the terms. Most of the money was hers anyway, and Nick wasn't asking for more than he rightfully earned. Pocket change in comparison to her inherited family fortune.

Climbing the ladder, he recalled the bartender's words. "Something eatin' at ya?" Herb, he was soon to learn. The retired doctor from Willow Creek, Nebraska.

He really just wanted to enjoy the game and some spicy buffalo wings. But Herb offered him an opportunity to get everything off his chest. *I'll never see this man again*, or so he'd believed. By the time Nick admitted he was on a secretive trip to figure out what to do with the rest of his life, Doc Herb was smiling.

"You find my pathetic life amusing?"

"What if I were to tell you I could make all your dreams come true tomorrow?"

Nick laughed. "Are you my fairy bartender?"

The smile faded from Herb's face, a serious expression replacing it. "I just might be."

Fate had intervened that night as Doc Herb described an opportunity for Nick to do what he'd always dreamed of doing: become a small town doctor. Without a complaining wife to nag that such a position was beneath him or would embarrass her in front of her friends.

Telling his sister had been another matter.

A dusting of lightning bugs illuminated the fields as

the horizon pulled down the sun. Nick kept scraping, ignoring the ache in his hands.

"Where?" Miranda's hands posted firmly on her hips, like she was ready to put him in timeout with Hallie. "You can't be serious, Nick. Nebraska?"

"It's the perfect setup, Miranda." He slid a beer out of the fridge. "It's like a trial run."

"Do explain."

He rattled off the terms of his probation period. "Besides, I can't buy a house before the divorce is final. If I did, Dana could claim interest and stop the process. And we'd be back to square one. Just like I can't sell the practice here until *after* the divorce." It'd be just like her to cause trouble before the divorce was finalized. Nick knew he needed to get as far away from Dana as possible.

"Doc Herb has a house in Willow Creek," Nick explained.

"Doc Herb?"

"Yeah. It's a place he's been saving for the new doctor. A doctor the town's been looking for, for a year. He's willing to let me stay there until the time is up. That way, if it doesn't work out or I want to come back to Georgia, I'm not stuck trying to sell a house." He took a swig of beer. "I just can't tell anyone in Willow Creek about our arrangement."

"But you've told this man, this *Doc* Herb, that you're planning to come back to Georgia, right?"

Not exactly.

He took another swig of beer. "Would you be mad if I wanted this to work out? You know I've always dreamed of being able to remember my patients' names. Their stories. What're the odds that my dream's handed to me on a silver platter?" *In a bar while watching the Braves,* Nick almost added. But he hadn't admitted to Miranda that he'd skipped his interviews in Florida altogether.

She shoved a drawer closed. "We have plenty of small towns in our home state in need of that very thing."

"I need some time away, Miranda. I'm sorry. But everything here is a reminder of my failed marriage. Of my wife *cheating* on me with my closest friend."

Miranda had nothing to say to that, so a month later she let him go.

An hour after the horizon swallowed the sun, Nick descended the ladder. Rolling up the tarp to catch all the paint flakes, he smiled. In his frenzy, he'd scraped every inch of old paint away.

"One side down, three to go."

Chapter 6

Sloppy Joe mix simmered on the stove as Allie sat hunched over her kitchen table, immersed in another romance novel. She'd started reading it today on her lunch break and had a hard time breaking away even to run to the grocery store.

Just eighty pages shy of the end, Allie heard a pounding on her front door. Norman bolted from the kitchen.

She quickly absorbed the chapter's last paragraph, dismayed that the lovers were quarrelling. When she looked up, Kim stood in the doorway with a bundle of fresh flowers clamped in one hand. With the other, she patted Norman on the head.

"Hey Al!" Kim threw her arms around Allie's neck. She stood a couple of inches taller than Allie, and her short blonde hair brushed the edges of her cheeks, most of it hidden beneath a white sun hat.

"Beautiful flowers!" Allie fished an empty vase from the cupboard above the fridge. "What kind are they?"

"Irises." Kim dropped the bundle into the vase. "Gram insisted I bring you some since they're in bloom." With quick work, she arranged floppy purple petals, placing the yellow spots flapping outward. She'd turned the handful of flowers into a beautiful centerpiece.

"Sit down," Allie said. "I'll get you a plate."

"You read my mind. I'm starving." Norman nudged Kim with his nose, begging for more attention. "Hey there, Norm. I brought you a treat!" Kim fished a packaged knee bone out of her backpack.

Allie slid a readied pan of cupcake batter in the oven, set the timer, then prepared two plates. While she busied herself scooping the mixture onto a couple of toasted hamburger buns, Kim asked, "What's new in the life of Allie Jordan these days?"

"Same old stuff," Allie said.

She almost spilled the plot of her latest read, but she'd always spared Kim that long-winded enthusiasm. Though Kim was the only person who knew how much she loved her happily-ever-after stories, she didn't share that love. Not like Allie's blog followers. "Mostly working and reading. And some baking in between for the Legion's bake sale."

"How's the blog?"

Allie moved to the table, setting down both plates. "Great!" It was too late to curb her enthusiasm. Her last post had generated so many comments that she'd barely managed to read them all. "It's nice having a group of people just as excited about these books as I am."

"Group?" Kim shook her head, dumping a pile of chips on her plate. "You call *four thousand* a group?"

Allie shrugged, and tried again. "A bunch?" She retrieved two cans of Dr. Pepper cooling in the fridge.

"You need to look into making this a thing." Kim pointed the top half of her bun at Allie. "A real thing." She picked up Allie's latest read, scanning the cover. The one that featured the bare sculpted chest of a firefighter, his open jacket fluttering in the wind. "There's got to be a way to make money from this."

"It's not like I can charge people to read and comment on the posts, you know."

"No, I agree." Kim set the book back on the table. "I'll keep thinking. But you should too. When you're this passionate, there's always a way to turn it into something."

The two ate in silence for several minutes. "Did I tell you Amanda wants me to go to California with her?"

"You should do it, Al."

JACQUELINE WINTERS

Will Allie take a chance on her own happily ever after, or WILL HER PAST PROVE THAT NOT ALL SCARS HEAL?

Sweetly Scandalous

Romance novel enthusiast ALLIE JORDAN has a closet secretly stacked full of STEAMY BODICE-RIPPERS and a past relationship gone wrong.

Her vicious ex, Travis, demeaned her love of her favorite books, leaving Allie to seriously doubt the existence of HAPPILY EVER AFTERS beyond their fictional pages. One unfortunate night, Allie falls victim to his rage. Years later, with Travis behind bars, the scars he's left behind still haunt her. Only through her anonymous—but quite popular—blog does Allie share her excitement of SEXY HEROES AND STUBBORN HEROINES.

When DOCTOR NICK BRYANT arrives in Willow Creek looking like he might've jumped right from the pages of one of Allie's LUSTY BOOKS, she can't seem to stay away. And with Nick's past, she probably should.

With Nick harboring secrets of his own and Travis nearing parole eligibility, will Allie take a chance on her own happily ever after, or WILL HER PAST PROVE THAT NOT ALL SCARS HEAL?

"It's too expensive." *Not the reaction I was expecting.* "The amount I'd spend in a week on a vacation for two is enough to get me through an entire month without a job somewhere else."

Kim shook her head, taking a deep swig of pop. "You've been talking about leaving Willow Creek for three years."

Automatically, Allie glanced at the buffet table against the far wall. "Because that's been my plan. For three years. Since that letter arrived."

The silence grew tense between them. Kim's can came crashing down on the table. Even Norman jumped. "You've got to stop letting that stupid letter control your life." Kim crammed a chip into her mouth. "Do you think it was anything more than an empty threat? I mean, how much can Travis Meyers really do from behind bars?"

"But he'll be out next year," said Allie. Norman, convinced all was well, returned to gnawing on his new bone.

"Has he written any letters since?"

Allie shook her head. "You remember reading it. It said he wouldn't."

"I just don't get why you have to run away."

Anger flashed red hot in Allie's cheeks. "He could've killed me, Kim. Forgive me if I'm a little afraid of him."

She shoved her chair back, yanking plates from the table. "If I don't want to be within five hundred miles of him when he's free." Dropping empty plates into the sink, she said, "Maybe it's stupid being afraid he'll actually *kill* me this time, but I am."

"Al, calm down. I'm on *your* side, remember?" Kim emptied her can of pop. "But, do you really *want* to move? I mean, it's not fair that he can still bully you like this after all these years."

Allie fell back into her chair, growing tired of this conversation. "Yes. Of course. Can't stay here all my life, can I?" She wanted to lighten the mood before they filled the whole night with tension. It'd been weeks since they had an evening to hang out like this. "Let's talk about anything else."

"Okay."

Suddenly, Allie knew exactly how to lighten the mood. "There's a new doctor in town."

"Yeah?" She didn't seem too interested.

"He's *hot*, Kim. I mean like he walked right out of the pages of one of my books."

Kim's interest renewed. "Single?"

"Surprisingly, yes." Fishing a chip from the bag, she divulged a few details about Nick's glorious physique, mesmerizing eyes, and his instant friendship with Norman.

"You ask him out yet?"

"No."

"Why not?"

"You're seriously asking me this?"

"Yes!" hissed Kim.

"Because I'm planning on leaving town—"

Kim threw a chip at her. It bounced off her elbow and fell to the floor. Norman pounced on the fallen chip, momentarily abandoning his new bone. "That's been your excuse for too long, Allie. That's why you've pushed away any man who's tried to say more than 'hello' to you."

"I've dated."

Kim laughed. "Going on two dates with a guy doesn't count."

"I've been on a bunch of dates." Allie took another swig of pop. "Just none too recently. I don't see the problem, either. I'd rather wait until I'm settled somewhere else." The oven timer beeped, giving Allie a much welcome excuse to get up.

"After we overeat cupcakes, we're going out."

Laughter sputtered from Allie's lips. "Where? To the *one* bar in town?"

"Do you think this new, sexy doctor would be at Marley's?"

Allie thought about it a little. "I don't know."

Remembering that Nick had inquired about the hardware store last week, she added, "Maybe he's home. Lives in Doc Herb's old place."

"Bring the jar of frosting to the table. And a knife," Kim said. "It'll be dark soon, so we need to be ready."

"For what?"

A devious smile spread across Kim's lips.

"We're going to get caught!" hissed Allie. Checking over her shoulder, she wished some evening walkers would spot them. And possibly save them the more humiliating certainty of Nick catching them peeking through his windows.

"Relax, Al," said Kim. "Right now we're just walking to the track field. Just going for a stroll for old times' sake." She scanned the area briefly. Allie did too. The school building to the right was dark. "Plus, no one's around anyway."

"And if Nick catches us?" Allie knew she'd never be able to look him in the eye if that happened.

"We'll say we're looking for Norman."

Allie shook her head as they turned toward the track. "Bad idea. They're best buds now. He'd probably try to help find him."

"Then I'll pretend to call your sister, who tells us Norman went home on his own. Seriously. You read all these books, Al. You should be good at making up excuses to spy on hot guys."

She nudged Kim. She'd noticed a lone black car parked outside the tiny school gym. "I bet Alex Rowe is working out." Allie dipped her chin to the only place in Willow Creek to work out. "Ed said he's back in town for a few days. Something about a case."

"Stop trying to distract me." Kim glanced at the Charger. "You know I've seen Alex in his birthday suit. Even if it was an accident I got trapped inside that locker after that football game."

"How could I forget?" A lightning bug zipped by Allie's nose. "It's all you talked about for weeks."

"No one's around," Kim whispered so loudly she may as well have been shouting. "Let's make a dash for those trees." Before Allie could object, Kim took off running.

Allie, left with no other choice, caught up with little effort. *Sometimes there are perks to being a record-setting sprinter.* "You're not getting the first peek through his windows." She passed Kim, sprinting far ahead down a dimly moonlit trail through the trees.

It'd been years since she'd taken off in a full-blown sprint or felt the thrill of competition. She'd suppressed the exhilaration that speed made her feel for so long, she'd forgotten how much she loved it.

Allie slowed as the trees began to clear. The back of the giant farmhouse came into focus, a light on. *Nick's home.*

"I think that's the kitchen," Allie called over her shoulder, panting.

Kim had since given up the run and was walking down the trail a few dozen yards back. Hugging the last tree that would give Allie cover from the glow of the brightly lit window, she poked her head around it.

Nick stood facing the window, stripped of his shirt. From her hiding spot, she could see defined muscles along his arms and chest. *You can't be real. No real man looks that good with his shirt off.* Nick walked around an island, revealing the towel wrapped around his waist. He stopped, facing the window. She ducked back behind the tree.

"Do you see him?" Kim called, just feet away now.

"Yep." Allie dared another look. He reached his arms above his head, stretching. The towel fell from his waist. Her jaw dropped at the sight, his beautiful body more glorious than her lusty dreams had imagined.

Nick spun around, bending over for his towel.

"Is this great timing or what?" Kim crowded Allie. "I am in love with that butt."

No longer facing the girls, he wrapped the towel around his waist and walked out of the kitchen, moving into a darker room, out of sight.

"You okay, Al? You look a little flushed. Surely you've seen a man's butt before?"

Allie tried to form words, but they failed her. Her insides tingled with desire. *Nick, completely naked!* Had her legs not been so heavy with shock, she might've sprinted to the back door, ripped that towel away, and tackled Nick.

"Oh my god!" Kim's hand clamped down on her shoulders. "You saw his man-snake, didn't you?"

The odd name eased some of the sexual tension pouring through Allie's veins and she laughed, long and hard in the shadow of the tree's trunk. "Is that what you call it?" She slid down along its bark, plopping herself in the dewy brush. "A *man-snake*?"

Kim laughed too, louder and more obnoxious than Allie. "You're the romance novel expert. What should I be calling it?"

Despite her best efforts to form an answer, Allie's uncontrollable laughter sucked all oxygen from her lungs.

Crossing her arms, Kim said, "I think man-snake is perfectly acceptable."

Suddenly, the trees lit up around them, like a giant

spotlight was trained on them. The back porch light blared bright. Nick had thrown the door open, towel still wrapped around his waist.

Kim grabbed Allie's wrist. "We gotta go!"

Chapter 7

Saturday morning, Nick's arms ached, as though he'd carried giant boulders up and down stairs all night long. His morning run could wait. He considered switching off his alarm and rolling back over.

As he drifted, Allie's eyes, the deep, dark color of melted chocolate, were there, waiting for him at the track field with Norman. In his fuzzy half-dream, she wore gym shorts that showed off her long, beautiful legs. Smiling seductively, she lured him with a crooked finger. Her hands gripped the hem of her tank top. The white material lifted, revealing inch by inch of smooth, tanned skin.

The buzz of Nick's snoozed alarm shot him clear out of bed. Irritated, he threw the covers off. He thought he shut it off, realizing he must've hit the wrong button.

Rubbing the sleep from his eyes, he wondered what had conjured such a dream. He'd been in Willow Creek just two weeks. It'd be months before he felt ready to consider dating again. After a cold shower, Nick decided to skip his morning run and head straight for the barn. Anything to get his mind off Allie Jordan.

Hours later, he surveyed his progress with satisfaction.

"Hi, Dr. Bryant. Nick."

Wiping the sweat from his forehead with a rag, he looked over his shoulder and down to foot of the ladder. A blonde in snug-fitting clothes that accentuated her perfect figure held a dish covered with a dishtowel.

Another one.

"I'm Rachel. I met you at Wilkerson's last week."

Nick stepped down from the ladder and wiped his dirty hands against his jeans. "Yes, I remember."

"I just wanted to welcome you to Willow Creek. Thought you might like something for dinner that you didn't have to cook yourself. How about a break?"

He cast a longing glance at the barn. The east wall was half scraped. He wanted to finish it and start the last side before nightfall.

"For dinner?"

Rachel laughed. "In Nebraska, we call lunch *dinner.*"

His stomach started to rumble. He wasn't sure what was underneath the dishtowel, but its aroma floated up with the breeze. He hadn't eaten since last night. "That's very kind of you."

"It's nothing," said Rachel, her smile dazzling. "Just a simple casserole I whipped up."

Nick thought most men would walk blindly through traffic to see that smile up close. Most men, but not him. Her unannounced presence was a little off-putting. *Probably because of that stupid dream.*

"I hate to impose, but some cheese spilled over." Rachel lifted a couple of fingers from her cupped grip of her glass dish. "Mind if I rinse my hands?"

Taking the dish from her, he allowed Rachel to walk in front of him, up onto his porch and through the front door. He pointed. "First door on the left."

"I've always been curious about this house. You know, hardly anyone in town's been inside." She slipped into the bathroom and closed the door behind her.

This casserole was the first Nick had received already cooked. The rest had come with cooking instructions. He slid the hot dish onto a potholder, leaving it on the counter while he washed his own cheese-splattered hands.

"I see I'm not the first one," Rachel said as he turned off the faucet.

"I've been very fortunate." He was a little embarrassed by the number of empty casserole dishes stacked on the counter, waiting to be returned. He didn't mention that he still had another half dozen in his freezer. "Can I get you anything to drink?"

"Oh, no thanks."

Nick filled a glass with iced water for himself, then led Rachel back to the living room, hoping to walk her straight toward the front door. Instead, she darted for the fireplace mantel, running her fingers along its intricate wood carving. "This is beautiful, Nick."

"I can't complain."

She glanced around the room, ready to debate that statement. He intercepted.

"I've got plenty of renovations on my list. The hardwood floors need sanding and staining. The wallpaper needs to come down. Brass light fixtures need changed out..." Nick let his voice trail off, hoping the small talk would satisfy her enough that she'd leave without him having to ask.

Spinning toward him, Rachel adjusted her necklace. The one that dipped into her exposed cleavage. "I hope you'll be living here for a really long time."

"That's the plan," he answered, hoping it didn't sound like a lie. He felt panic rising in his chest. *Why's she staring? Does she know?*

"You've got the town quite stirred up, Nick." Her blue eyes locked on his; the scent of her perfume hung heavy in the air, like she'd used half the bottle. She swaggered toward him.

"How's that?"

"Well, let's say I'm a little surprised there isn't a line of single ladies standing outside your doorstep. They're all quite taken with you." Rachel bestowed another of her sensual smiles. "In fact, I'm surprised there aren't women lined up outside prepared to leave their husbands for you."

Nick was supposed to laugh, but he could do little more than force an insincere smile. "I don't know what to say to that."

"You're the most exciting thing to show up in Willow Creek in years."

Not caring to see where this little cat-and-mouse conversation was intended to lead, he decided it was time for Rachel to go. "I need to get back to work on the barn. Thank you so much for the casserole."

She nodded, but her feet weren't moving toward the door. "I couldn't have our new doctor starving."

"I'd invite you to stay for a bite, but I need to keep working."

"Of course." Rachel smiled, though it didn't quite reach her eyes. "If you'd ever like to return the favor, my number is on the bottom of the casserole dish."

"You don't want me to cook you dinner," said Nick. "Road kill burned black would taste better than anything I could make."

"I don't mind going out, either."

He let her close the front door behind her.

Deciding he needed some iced water before returning to more scraping of paint—maybe even a bite of casserole since she'd been kind enough to drop it by hot—Nick returned to the kitchen. *Anything to buy some time in case she's lingering in the driveway.*

He slipped out the back door, cursing the burst bulb as glass crushed underfoot. *Damn this house.* Until now, he'd forgotten about the gigglers from last night. He wondered who he might ask about any kids prone to sneaking around at night. He'd have caught them himself had the back porch light not shattered when that breaker blew.

The last thing Lesley Jamison wanted to do on a sunny Saturday afternoon was drive one hundred fifty miles to the Lincoln Correctional Facility to see her pathetic excuse for a son. His first year in prison, she hadn't visited him at all, deciding he needed to learn his lesson the hard way.

He wrote letters and sent countless visitations forms, begging her to come see him because no one else would. Even if his father had the ability to visit, Lesley was sure Rich Meyers wouldn't have gone within a hundred miles of the jail.

The second year of Travis' sentence, she decided he needed some forced guidance. *Tough love.* The prison allowed inmates to advance their education during their sentences, so she enrolled him in an online community college. Her infrequent visits ensured he maintained passing grades. Travis would catch enough flack when he returned to Willow Creek, but Lesley wouldn't have the town calling him a dead-beat with no ambition.

He'd once been a model citizen, respected for working hard and honorably. How could Lesley know Rich's departure would take such an ugly toll on their son?

Transformations didn't happen overnight, but eventually she'd make certain Travis regained his favorable reputation. It was a nearly impossible endeavor in a small town, but Lesley had beaten the system years ago; Travis could too. *Even if I have to shove him forward each step of the way.* As long as he kept up his grades, she kept up on her bribes to shorten his sentence.

Behind a pane of smudged and pitted glass, Travis slouched in a cramped, dimly lit room, his folded hands resting on the surface of a crooked metal table. His sullen eyes wore a blank stare. *Five years in the Pen would do that to a person.* The sandy-colored crew cut hair was his father's, but the gray in his eyes was hers. When Travis was first sent to prison, he'd been lankier. Now, he was solid muscle.

Once the visiting guard closed the door behind her, Lesley took a reluctant seat on the cold metal folding chair, setting her worn purse on the dusty floor. She'd learned quickly not to bring or wear nice things during her visits. They'd only get ruined.

"It's been two months," Travis growled.

"Nice to see you too." She craved a cigarette, but she'd have to stop at a gas station on her way out of Lincoln. "I've been busy." Her lighter, which she knew to leave in her car before entering the facility, had been confiscated during the search and pat-down.

"You're always busy."

"Someone's got to run the town." *And blackmail a hacker to remove you from the parole hearing list.* Lesley crossed her legs, straining to keep the waistband of her jeans from rubbing against the dirty underside of the table. "You ready for your parole hearing?"

Travis tilted his head down toward the table, lifting

his eyes to meet hers. "I thought you took care of it."

She shook her head in disgust. "I took care of getting your hearing moved up by almost a year. The rest is up to you." She leaned forward. "You haven't gotten into any trouble, have you?"

He shot her a look that would've chilled anyone else to the bone. "I haven't fucked up, if that's what you're asking."

"Well, then, you've got nothing to worry about. Just make sure you acknowledge that you were in the wrong. That you've learned from your mistakes." She glanced at her watch. "Your hearing is no time to get arrogant. If you don't convince them you're sorry for what you did, there's nothing I can do. They'll leave you locked up to finish out your sentence."

Travis fidgeted, a telltale sign that he was nervous. She waited, letting him sweat it out. "Is the old farmhouse still standing?"

"Sure," she answered, swiping a careless hand through the air. "What would you want with that old thing? It's a pile of rotting boards."

"I've been doing some volunteer work, building houses," he told her, his voice small now. Like he expected to be mocked. "I'm going to need a place to lay low. I could fix it up."

Lesley barked a laugh.

"It'd keep me busy. Out of trouble."

That had her attention. The last thing she needed was Travis with too much time on his hands.

She studied him from across the table. *How much does he know?* But there'd been no witnesses the night she buried Rich's body.

Travis had always seemed fond of the old farmhouse. He'd worked construction before going to jail. Seemed to genuinely enjoy it. *Maybe tinkering with that pile of rubble will keep him occupied.* "I suppose I could make Mort hire you at the hardware store," she mumbled.

"That asshole hates me." He shoved a hand through his hair. "He'd never hire me."

"You let me worry about that. Remember who owns most of that store." She dropped her forearms back on the table. She had enough blackmail on her pathetic ex-brother-in-law to last her a decade. "You're sure you don't want to stay in Lincoln? Wait a couple of months before coming back? You know they'll have to notify that twit."

A furious fire flared in Travis' eyes; his fists clenched. She refused to acknowledge or encourage those feelings. "Maybe I should ask them to move your parole hearing back to its original date if you're going to get out and cause trouble. Why can't you just leave Allie

Jordan the hell alone?"

"I won't bother her," said Travis, his cold gray eyes meeting hers. "I'm tired of waiting."

"And just what else do you have to do but wait? You're the dumbass who ran around with her. If she'd stayed home that night, you never would've been caught."

Travis stared at his hands. He had no rebuttal.

There'd be no notification worming its way into Allie's mailbox. She'd seen to that earlier this week. Easy enough to accomplish when she possessed enough dirt to ruin the nice postmaster's comfortable life. But Lesley had learned all she needed to know just by bringing up Allie. Just as she suspected, her son was still hung up on that stupid girl.

As a matter of principle, Lesley herself had always despised Allie. But any spawn of Pam Jordan's was cause for inexcusable hatred. After all, it was Pam who had stolen the only true love in her life. *Marc Jordan was mine!* Until Pam entered the picture. As a result, Lesley had no choice but to let Rich Meyers knock her up.

"Last I knew, the old house didn't have heat or electricity," said Travis after a lengthy silence had elapsed. "Makes sense to fix it up before winter."

She shrugged, indifferent. But she felt a small pang

of admiration for her idiot son. He'd figured out his own place to stay. *One that'll keep him hidden from everyone in town.* "You're not to come into Willow Creek for any reason other than work. You'll be out of sight. Working in the storeroom only."

Travis nodded, his eyes locked on the table.

"If I catch you within the city limits for any other reason—even to buy a bottle of water—you can expect your parole officer to show up and haul your ass right back here."

"Fine."

"If I catch you within a mile of Allie Jordan, I'll escort you back to jail myself." She knew Travis would only be able to restrain himself from seeing her for so long. She'd have to drive Allie out of town—make her existence in Willow Creek so miserable that she'd pack her bags in the middle of the night and run out on her own.

It'd be the only true chance Travis would stand at starting over. At not screwing up.

"I'll have someone run out to the house this weekend, make sure the well still works. If you're good, I'll send an electrician out there in a month. Everything else is your responsibility once you're out. If you want to fix up that pile of rubble, that's at your expense."

A flash of hatred shot through Travis' eyes. Spite.

She shoved her chair back. *The ungrateful lout expects me to fund his renovation project.* "I'll know if you screw up your parole hearing. So don't."

"Or what?" Travis stood too. He'd always towered a few inches over her, even in her three-inch heels. But he'd never had so much muscle before. Had she not been his mother, she might've been a little intimidated. He taunted, "You can't send me to jail when I'm already here."

Typical. "Then I'll see that your precious farmhouse burns to the ground."

Chapter 8

Norman stood to the side of the deck swing, staring at Allie through her paperback. She dropped the book in her lap, realizing she couldn't recall a single word from the last three pages anyway. "No fooling you about what day it is, is there?"

An enthusiastic bark confirmed her suspicions. Norman expected a walk to the track field. She spotted his leash through the sliding glass door, piled on top of the fridge.

"I can't face him, Norm. Not after last night." Images of Nick, stark naked, flashed through her mind like strobe lights. It wasn't that she minded the visual, but how could she possibly look him in the eye without remembering his sculpted chest or his...his—*man-snake*? Allie erupted in a fit of giggles at Kim's odd nickname. Norman took it as his cue to smother her with sloppy licks.

She jumped up, dodging an excited dog for the kitchen.

"I have a better idea."

Half an hour later, Allie pulled into her mother's driveway on the opposite end of town. She noticed, as she did every time, how much better the house looked than it had years ago, before her father died. It'd been their project together back then, a pale, paint-chipped gray home, shutters broken or missing, the scraggly yard overgrown with weeds.

Norman paced the backseat of her little car until she opened the door and folded the driver's seat forward. Then he shot like a bottle rocket, sprinting toward her mom's large backyard.

Allie waited for her dog to circle the lawn a few times, studying a pristine navy blue shutter set against resilient white siding. Marigolds and white impatiens lined the sidewalk. She recalled the fixer-upper the house had been before her sister was born—the outdated kitchen with garish orange countertops, the pressed wood paneling throughout, the mildew-stained bathtub. In pink. Her parents had purchased the property with a complete remodel in their plans.

But after her dad's death, Pam snapped. With all

renovations complete on their own home, she used the insurance money to buy the house Allie now lived in. Her mother read every book, watched every YouTube video and HGTV show she could find on home renovations. Pam would call flipping a house every year a hobby. Allie called it borderline obsession.

Norman burst back around the corner, thudding up the stairs and posting himself outside the front door. From the living room couch, a home decor magazine in her hands, Pam called to Norman who darted inside, sniffing the air in search of the gray cat.

"Norm, give it up. She doesn't want to be found." Pam set her magazine on the arm of the couch to pet him.

"He'll search for that cat five years after she's gone." Allie closed the door behind her. "Amanda still in bed?"

"Where else? That girl sleeps most of her life away."

Knowing she had time, Allie fell into a cushy blue recliner. She watched a commercial about a home design competition, trying hard to force images of the very naked doctor from her overactive imagination.

"I heard your butterscotch chip cookies were a hit at the Legion bake sale," said Pam.

Allie nodded. "That's nice."

She looked up when she felt her mom's eyes boring into her over the hum of commercials. "You seem a little distracted, Allie. Something up?" Pam didn't give her a chance to answer before she began speculating. "I heard Ed fixed your gutters, so you can't be here asking me to replace them."

"I wouldn't ask you to do that," said Allie. "But yes, they're fixed." Leaning forward, she was about to push herself out of the recliner when her mom's next question stopped her.

"What do you think of our new doctor?"

"He seems nice." *Did I mention I almost broke into his house and tackled him last night?*

"You heard he's single?"

Allie eyed her mom. "Hasn't every woman in this town over the age of twelve?"

"I hear there's a line." Pam laughed. "Guess that means you better hop on that if you want a chance." She eased back against the plump upholstery as Norman took to sniffing the baseboard for the elusive cat. "Otherwise you might miss out."

Allie lowered her head, hoping her wavy hair would hide the lust surely filling her eyes. "And why would I do that? I'm leaving in less than a year. Guessing the town wouldn't be too happy with me if I took him away, now would they?"

"Then why wait a year?" Pam reached for her magazine. "Don't you think you're pushing the timeline a little?"

"What are you getting at, Mom?"

Thumbing through her magazine to the page she'd left dog-eared, Pam said, "I can't figure out why you're stalling. Why you've put your life on hold."

"My life isn't—"

Pam ignored her. "Your entire plan revolves around a parole date."

Allie felt her cheeks starting to warm. She hadn't expected to defend herself this morning. "More time to save money."

Pam laughed. "You don't even pay rent. What have you been doing with all that money?"

Standing, Allie decided to go upstairs before an argument broke out. "Mind watching Norman? I'm going to steal Amanda for the day."

"Better make sure she's off."

"Off?"

"Didn't she tell you? She got a job in Norfolk. At the mall."

"Amanda? Since when?"

"A few weeks ago. After the state track meet." Pam's eyes scanned an article as Allie slipped into the next room. Behind her came, "Good luck rousing her from bed."

She was tempted to ask more, but she'd get that

information out of her sister later today. She'd bring it up when they were a safe distance away from Willow Creek—and dangerously tempting doctors who liked showing off their sculpted, very naked bodies through curtain-less kitchen windows.

"Norman, would you like to say good morning to Amanda?" Norman's ears perked. The dog jumped up and trotted ahead of Allie toward the kitchen. "Let's go upstairs and wake Amanda up."

"No fighting!" Pam called from the couch.

But Allie had already flown up the stairs.

Amanda's door stood ajar, allowing Norman to wedge his nose into the crack and swing it open. He charged inside, his long black tail swatting everything in its path. Most of Amanda was buried beneath a messy array of mismatched blankets. Within seconds, Norman's wet nose smeared most of her face before she had the chance to object.

"Norman!" gasped Amanda. He paid little mind to the severity in her tone, knowing she'd soften up. He licked the hand that tried pushing him away.

"Good morning, Sleeping Beauty." Allie stood in the doorway, arms folded.

"What time is it?"

"Almost nine." She fought the urge to laugh at Amanda's makeup-smeared scowl. "It's Norman's doing, really. I didn't even have to encourage him this time." A blue sequin from last night's top was glued to Amanda's cheek. "Should teach you to leave your door open."

"It doesn't close all the way."

Allie was the one who was a neat freak, never allowing clothes or dog toys to be scattered on any floor in her house before she crawled into bed. Even the romance novels in her closet were stacked with precision. Amanda, on the other hand, couldn't care less if her floor was even visible. *Messes only concern her when she runs out of clothes.* Trying to ignore the mass of clothes blanketed on the floor, Allie said, "Get up."

"No," Amanda moaned. She reached for the nearest article of clothing, chucking a balled up T-shirt at Allie. "I'm sleeping."

"You've slept enough. Not my fault you decided to party hard last night."

"Go. Away."

Norman took the words as some sort of challenge, hopping onto the bed. He burrowed under the comforter, eliciting a squeal out of Amanda when his cold, wet nose came into contact with her skin.

"You can stay in bed. I'm going with or without you. But Norman stays."

Amanda groaned again, shoving at Norman's head. Her attempts to push him out of bed only rousing his playful instincts. "Norman!"

"I guess I'll go shopping without you." Allie reached for the doorknob. "I was just hoping my sister would help me pick out some new clothes."

Amanda shot up in her bed, a couple of blue sequins zipping through the air. "You're shopping? For fashionable clothes?" Norman's tail thudded against the slanted ceiling. "You're not my sister. What have you done with Allie Jordan? She's twenty-three, super boring, and a cheapskate."

Allie grabbed an abandoned pair of jeans hanging from a desk chair and threw them at Amanda. "Fine. This old, boring cheapskate can go to the mall without you."

"I'm coming!" Amanda threw the covers off the bed, revealing tanned legs dusted in more sparkling blue sequins. "After a shower."

Slamming the passenger side door, Amanda shot a considering gaze at Allie. There was no way her sister could refuse a challenge, so she shouted, "Race you!" And took off across the asphalt.

At the clothing store entrance, she panted, her hand first on the door. Allie'd been trapped in the parking lot by a minivan that failed to yield. When she stepped onto the sidewalk, Amanda said, "You're supposed to be the sprinter."

Allie narrowed her eyes. "I wasn't racing you."

Inside the store, Amanda immediately hid her face in a rack of jeans. She regretted her thoughtless words the second they shot from her mouth. The two of them didn't always get along, but there were a couple of sensitive topics she knew not to mention on purpose: Travis Meyers and sprinting. And one had stolen the other from her sister.

The Travis Tragedy, which had happened when Amanda was only twelve, drove her crazy. Back then, everyone told her she was too young to understand and for years, she bit her tongue.

Growing up, the excuses got so old that she finally stopped asking why Allie would ever date a guy who could shoot her. *Why choose a guy who'd caused you to attend your senior district track meet on crutches?* And she'd never asked her how it felt missing her opportunity to secure a full-ride scholarship to a handful of colleges.

"I'm going to look for something in the corner." Allie walked toward the store's clearance racks.

Amanda didn't know why she bothered. She'd occasionally find some gems at giveaway prices herself, but not often. Allie's wardrobe was drab enough to bore old people. The clearance rack probably wouldn't do her any favors.

Watching her older sister shuffle through a rack full of hideous shirts, Amanda wondered what had sparked this shopping idea. It wasn't often they went to the mall together. And never at Allie's suggestion. She'd considered asking why, during their hour-long drive, but Allie had cranked up the radio. A sign that conversation wasn't welcome.

Giving her sister space, Amanda scoured through a rack of tank tops. Her cell phone buzzed in her purse, but she ignored it. *Brenden Carter, you can wait.*

She grabbed four tops from the rack, deciding it was time to make amends with Allie. After all, her sister had been nice enough to get her out of a boring day. She'd planned to sleep past noon since it was her day off, because once she was up, her mom would put her to work. Probably make her mow their acre yard. Not a task she welcomed, considering the riding mower was out for repair.

Amanda held up a sundress with soft pink petals and dark reds and browns sprinkled about. "This would look cute on you."

"Are you kidding?" Allie fought a laugh. "How often do you see *me* in a dress?"

"You can't knock it until you've tried it on," Amanda countered, standing her ground. "Besides, a little change might be just what the doctor ordered."

She knew Allie hated wearing anything that showed her scar, but it was time she leapt over that hurdle. Even Allie couldn't deny that her physique was perfect for cute skirts and sundresses.

"If I showed up to work in that, Lesley would have me in her office for questioning before lunchtime."

"Why?" Amanda wondered why her sister had immediately thought about work, instead of wearing the dress for a girls' night out or a party.

"She'd probably think I was trying to seduce the new doctor." A grunt of laughter escaped her big sister.

"I haven't seen him yet, but that just sounds disturbing." Amanda assumed any replacement of Doc Herb's would be older than the Stone Age.

Allie pulled out a red T-shirt, holding it away from her body. "He's not sixty-five, you know."

Amanda eyed the hideous shirt, and bit her tongue. *Put it back, Allie. It's cheap, red, and* not *your color.*

"Where have you been the past couple weeks, Mandy Bear?" Allie asked. "In a black hole?"

"Working. Why?"

Allie shoved the ghastly red T-shirt back on the rack, much to Amanda's relief. "Willow Creek is all worked up about the new doctor. It's all anyone's talked about for a week."

"Fifty-five is still too old." Amanda shot a smile at her sister through a rack of sundresses, hoping she'd finally made up for her earlier thoughtless remarks.

Allie was smiling. She opened her mouth, on the verge of saying something more. But then her lips closed, as if deciding against it. Sometimes Amanda really hated how distant their relationship felt.

Like her sister didn't trust her.

Not that Allie trusted many people. But if she trusted her, Allie would've fessed up to what happened that night she got her scar. The *whole* story. Not just the rumored version flying around town. The one about Travis dragging Allie to a robbery and shooting her when she tried to get away.

The town's theories on why Allie ended up with Travis that night were all over the place. Amanda couldn't escape the conjecture. Some said he'd kidnapped her. Others claimed she was his accomplice. But those were all just rumors.

"You probably shouldn't wear it to work, you know," Amanda added after a few minutes of searching silently through the clearance rack. "Not every boss is as cool as mine."

"How is that working out for you?" Allie asked.

"Having a job?"

Amanda shrugged, pulling a couple of dresses off the rack to try on. "It's not as bad as I thought it'd be. I get a killer discount on clothes. And some other discounts around the mall." As eager as she was to divulge all the details of her new job—the one that would easily fund her half of a California vacation—she knew Allie was trying to change the subject. "So about this dress…"

Allie sighed. "Where would I *really* wear it?"

"Maybe on a date?"

Amanda suspected her sister hadn't been out on a date in months. But maybe a wardrobe update would help her *get* a date. She wasn't sure how much her sister actually shopped. Allie seemed as reluctant to spend money as Amanda was to save it.

"Maybe," said Allie finally, her gaze locked on the dress from the other side of the rounded sale rack. "But what would I wear with it?"

She likes it? Amanda was almost too stunned to respond. Darting for a rack of belts, she pulled out a braided one that matched the brown in the dress still in Allie's hands. "This will totally make that outfit."

"I guess I could try it on."

"Here." Amanda shoved the belt into Allie's arms. "Try it on now. Before you change your mind."

She followed her sister to the dressing room and waited outside the stall. She had half a dozen selections to try on herself, but wasn't going to miss her sister in that new dress. Allie could look like a million dollars and still find some reason to talk herself out of buying anything.

Amanda pulled out her cell phone. *Another* text from Brenden. *How many times do I have to tell him I'm* not *going out with him?* So what if he was the hottest guy in her class. And the nicest. And he looked great in those football pants. Brenden didn't fit in her plans to take off to California next year.

Shoving the phone back in her purse, refusing to respond, Amanda asked, "Will you still be in town for my graduation next year?"

It'd probably be the last time Amanda would see her sister for at least four years. Even if she was successful in getting Allie to California once, she didn't think she'd get her there again. "Or are you moving to Oklahoma before then?"

"Oklahoma?"

She smiled, knowing she was pushing Allie's buttons. "North Carolina?"

"Not funny."

"You didn't answer my question."

"You know I let you win, right?"

"Wait, what?"

"The race."

"But you said—" As her sister opened the dressing room door, Amanda forgot their argument. "Al, that looks great!" She was a little envious how Allie's figure really added sass to the cute outfit.

"Whether or not I'll be at your graduation depends."

"On what?"

"If Travis is eligible for parole." A look of hesitation hung on Allie's face. "You don't think it's too much?"

"I think it's perfect. You look *hot*," Amanda said. "It's not too scandalous or skanky if that's what you're worried about." Before Allie could add a financial objection, Amanda added, "It makes your body looks great. And it's on sale."

"Well that's good. Guess those cupcakes didn't do too much damage." Allie scrutinized herself in the full-length mirror beside the bench Amanda sat on. As she turned to the side, Amanda saw the demeanor on her sister's face change. Her eyes were locked on the scar on her left leg; stretching from below the kneecap to the top of her ankle, it was nearly a foot long. The mark reminded Amanda of one of the slides from the board game Chutes and Ladders, the way it indented Allie's calf. But it wasn't the eyesore her sister claimed.

She'd never asked Allie how a bullet wound caused

such a long scar.

Amanda hopped up from the bench. "You can hardly tell that's there. The color really draws attention away from it." Putting her hands on Allie's shoulders, she added, "With a pair of pantyhose, it'd be invisible."

Doubt hung in Allie's eyes.

"You'll look so gorgeous that no one will notice anything else."

"I don't have any shoes to go with this."

Amanda smiled. "I know the perfect store. Just a couple of doors down."

At the shoe store, Amanda followed Allie one aisle over as she scanned the displays, just able to see her sister from the shoulders up. She debated before spitting out the daring question: "Have you given any more thought to what I said?"

"About?" Allie's focus was on the plethora of shoes, especially sandals.

Amanda rolled her eyes. "About California," she snapped a little harsher than she intended.

"Why do you think I'd need a vacation?" But the usual firmness wasn't there this time. Amanda could sense Allie wavering.

"Just think how fun and relaxing it could be." Amanda pushed a shoe closer to her side of the aisle. "We could literally spend all day on the beach. Doing *nothing.*" She figured her sister would be reading. She was always reading a paperback, though she certainly liked to pretend she wasn't. Amanda had caught her countless times shoving books into couch cushions or in drawers. "And you know Mom would watch Norman."

Allie shrugged. "Maybe." She picked up a pair of flat sandals, studied them, then put them back. "It takes money, Amanda."

It took restraint for her not to throw a shoe at her sister. *Of course traveling takes money.* But she was sure Allie had plenty of money stashed in her savings account, considering she lived rent-free in a house their mother owned. "Do you like these?" Amanda held up a metallic silver-heeled sandal.

Allie gave a dismissive glance. "That's a little over the top."

Sighing, Amanda set the sandal back on the shelf. She'd take a maybe over a no as far as vacations were concerned. For now.

It was still early in the summer, but if they didn't plan to take a trip soon, Amanda would be tied up with early volleyball practices. Missing more than one of those two-a-days was grounds for being kicked off the team. Coach Jamison was rumored to be the toughest coach in the state. Amanda was sure she was the toughest in the country. Tough meaning cruel.

Unforgiving. Impossible to please.

"You got quiet." Amanda felt Allie study her. "What are you really up to?"

"Nothing," said Amanda. "Just deciding how many pairs of shoes to buy today."

Allie held up a pair of stylish flip-flops. "These are more my style."

No heels today. At least the sandals had crystal beads along the straps.

Sitting on the cushy blue ottoman, Allie asked, "Where in California do you want to go?"

"LA. Hollywood. Beverly Hills."

Allie stood and then paced, her eyes on her feet. "I like these." Plastic beads jiggled with each step. Amanda waited, but Allie didn't say anything further about their vacation.

A three-inch pump sat in her hand. It took every ounce of restraint for her to set it back on the shelf. She wanted to chuck it at her sister. "You need to be a little more open to this idea. Don't you want to scope out a couple of places you might move to next year?"

The smile washed away from Allie's face, replaced by an emotion Amanda couldn't quite pin. "I guess you've got a point." Allie set the flip-flops back in their box. "But I don't plan to move to Hollywood."

Amanda almost said, *You don't plan to move at all.*

But that'd start an argument. And they still had dinner and an hour-long drive ahead. At least her plan to scope out her own future in California was starting to fall into place. Even if it was happening at a snail's pace.

Chapter 9

"We've got our work cut out for us today, ladies." Dawn Hammond, the Director of Nursing, placed a checklist on the desk between Suzy and Allie. Each neatly written item uniformly bullet-pointed. "Today's Dr. Bryant's first day with his own patients. Since the downtown office won't be ready until the end of the summer, all of his appointments will come here instead."

Had Allie not known how seriously Dawn took her position, she might've let the woman's magenta-hued scrubs mislead her, patterned as they were with little bunnies.

Unlike the many nurses and ward secretaries that Dawn was in charge of, she did not engage in small talk or idle gossip. She simply executed orders. Dawn's former military experience shone through in the way she wound her plain brown hair in a tight bun and precisely pressed those bunny scrubs.

"The Board wants our front desk to keep track of his patients. They'll check in here, fill out any necessary paperwork, and so on."

The Board always meant Lesley. Allie had figured that out within her first two weeks of working at the hospital. Dawn probably had too. But saying *the Board* felt a little less irritating.

Suzy asked, "There's no one from the downtown office to do all this?"

"Not anymore." Not the type to elaborate on matters she considered irrelevant, Dawn said no more. She thumbed through the stack of papers tucked under her left arm. "Here's a list of appointments today. They'll begin arriving around eight-thirty. Dr. Bryant has a full day."

"What about walk-ins?" Suzy pushed her sliding glasses to the bridge of her nose.

"Direct them to Lesley. There aren't any more available appointments this week. Dr. Bryant is completely booked."

"Is that all?" asked Suzy.

"No," answered Dawn. "Someone will need to escort these patients to the exam rooms."

"By someone, you mean either me or Allie," Suzy said. "But Dawn, if one of us has to show every appointment where to go, we're going to be hurting until the floater gets here. Is it really necessary to walk them down the hall and through those doors? We don't even have a second floor."

"Lesley's orders," Dawn said, leaving no room for further debate. "I don't care how you ladies decide to handle it, but it has to be done." She shuffled through the stack of papers, apparently looking for something else. "All paperwork *must* be filled out completely before they are escorted to the exam rooms, understood?"

Both secretaries nodded.

"Good." Dawn took a step toward the nurse's station, but stopped as she pulled out a piece of paper from her stack. "Also, we have a surgery tomorrow. Start making phone calls."

The morning zipped by. While Suzy manned the constantly ringing phone, Allie spent most of her time handing out and collecting patient forms and escorting patients.

"My arthritis is acting up again," said an elderly woman wearing a visor the color of a grape Laffy Taffy. The petite woman everyone called Aunt Ruby peeked over her shoulder as Allie escorted her down the corridor. Convinced the coast was clear, she confided,

"Nothing I can't handle. I really just wanted to get a better look at our new hunky doctor."

"Aunt Ruby!" With her lunch break nearing, Allie had heard that confession from most of the older female patients, some old enough to be Nick's mother.

"I brought him my special runza casserole, you know."

"Don't go breaking his heart, now." Allie had her hand on the exam room door handle. "Okay?"

"I can't make any promises." Aunt Ruby winked at Allie as a nurse took over and closed the door.

Allie spun around to leave and nearly collided with Nick. She had just enough warning to stop a few inches short of his chest, but not enough to keep images of his naked body at bay.

He smiled, weakening her knees. "You're getting your workout today."

She ducked her head, allowing her wavy hair to cover her flaming cheeks. She'd managed to avoid him all morning, but now she was trapped in the narrow hallway. "You're a popular guy. They're all coming to see you."

Reaching for the chart on the exam room door, Nick said, "I *am* the doctor."

It was imperative that Allie look at anything but him. Her eyes locked on the door to the janitor's closet.

Stop imagining him pulling you into the closet, Allie! "Phone's ringing off the hook. I gotta get back." She tossed him a quick smile, then flew down the hallway toward the safety of the front desk.

The moment Allie plopped into her rolling chair, Suzy shooed her off on a lunch break. "We have a quiet spell. Hurry up and eat something now before the afternoon rush starts."

Allie carried a plate of spaghetti and garlic bread from the hospital kitchen to the old, secluded break room. A fancier break room with lockers, granite countertops, and a cappuccino machine lived in the hospital's new addition, leaving this room for Allie to claim as her personal reading space during her breaks.

It wasn't such a bad place, she thought as she set her food on her usual table against the far wall. It never had been. Sure, some of the chairs sat crookedly and the tabletops looked as though a three-year-old had taken a butter knife to them. But with the new addition, replacement of this furniture would never happen. It was better not to complain; complaining might find this abandoned break room transformed into a storage area.

Looking over her shoulder, Allie retrieved a hidden paperback from the top shelf of the room's lone coat closet. She managed to spend five pages with her latest friends, Danica and Jason, who were attending a mutual friend's wedding, before her peace and quiet was shattered. Forcing her to shove the paperback beneath her thigh.

"I see why you like this place." Tray in hand, Nick closed the door behind him. "Mind if I join you?"

"Sure." She stared at her untouched spaghetti, afraid to meet his eyes again. "I didn't realize you even knew about this room."

"Diane tipped me off."

Allie smiled, quietly wondering if she should thank the cook later or chew her out for interrupting her lunch-break reading time. Of course, that would require admitting she devoured romance novels like they were nuggets of rich, decadent chocolate.

Nick slid into the chair across from her. "I hope I'm not interrupting?"

Spinning spaghetti on her fork, Allie replied, "Nope."

She realized how cold she sounded, like she didn't want him in the same room. And other than him interrupting her humorous adventure with her newest characters, she didn't mind his company. *If only I could stop picturing him naked.*

"I see you've got quite the fan club," Allie finally said.

He worked at sucking in a loose spaghetti noodle.

She couldn't help it. Her eyes kept finding his lips. Nick smiled. "I should've brought all those casserole dishes with me. I'd have been able to return most of them already."

"Those little old ladies have spoiled you. As long as you stay in Willow Creek, you may never have to cook again a day in your life." *I give up on clothes. At least his man-snake is below the table.*

Because she couldn't keep her eyes off his lips, she watched them bend into a frown. If she wasn't careful, she was going to crawl across the table through two plates of spaghetti just to fix that frown. "You are staying, aren't you?"

Nick bit into a piece of garlic bread and chewed slowly. "That's the plan."

"That sounds rehearsed."

His eyes stared at his plate.

She felt the irrational pitter of panic in her chest. *Stop it, Allie! This is ridiculous.* "You've only been here a couple of weeks. Surely it's not such a bad place?" His right hand sat palm-down on the table. She fought the irrational urge to cover it with her own. "If it helps, I can tell the little old ladies to lay off the casseroles."

When Nick smiled, Allie relaxed. "Please don't call them off. I can't cook to save my life."

"They wouldn't listen to me anyway." Allie's watch

beeped. "I need to get back to the front desk." Scooting back her chair, she realized her book still sat sandwiched between the hard plastic seat and her leg. She couldn't stuff it back in the closet without him catching her.

"Thanks for sharing your table." Nick dabbed his garlic bread in spaghetti sauce. "I *want* to stay in Willow Creek."

"Good." Shoving the book beneath her tray, she decided she'd have to sneak it up front. "Bye, Nick." Allie blushed, knowing of all places, this was not the one for informalities. She wanted to correct herself, but all she could see was Nick sitting at the table—sans clothing. *Kim, I'm going to kill you!*

"See you later, Al."

Chapter 10

Looking for something sizzling that'll suck you in and leave you gasping for air? Then WITHIN TEMPTATION *is your story! Ashlyn Waters has been a spoiled brat most of her life. She's used to getting her way and everything she wants. She's the type of character you'd like to reach through the pages and wring her neck. Then the incredibly dreamy Gavin Sanders enters the scene, seeking employment as a groundskeeper. The moment Ashlyn lays eyes on Gavin, she wants—*

"Hey Al, you back here?"

Allie jumped in her comfy backyard swing, her laptop teetering on her legs. "Amanda, you've got to stop scaring me like that!" Norman barked once for emphasis.

Setting a stuffed tote bag on the wicker table, Amanda fell into a padded chair across from her. "I brought you something."

Allie eyed the romance novel on the swing next to her. Luckily, it was facedown so her sister couldn't see the cover's half-naked woman wrapped around a bare-chested man. She'd had a tense enough day at work, having been slammed that afternoon. Patient escorts, bombardment of extra forms, and answering phones that had mastered the ability to ring off the hook.

The only thing that had eased the chaos was the memory of her lunch break, recalling how her stomach had somersaulted with butterflies when she'd shoved open the door with her elbow, leaving Nick behind to finish his spaghetti after he'd called her *Al.* Now Amanda was disrupting her finally quiet evening. "What did you bring?" Allie asked, hesitation lingering in her voice.

First, Amanda extracted a bottle of Dr. Pepper from her tote. Beads of condensation covered the plastic label, reassuring Allie it was nice and cold. Perfect for this humid summer day. Had it not been for the layer of clouds holding the sun at bay, she would be writing her blog post on the couch, in air conditioning.

"I brought some info on our California trip. I thought it might help us figure out how we want to do this." Amanda plopped a bundle of brochures and printed papers onto the table. "I even researched some prices on hotels and stuff."

Allie clicked save on her unfinished document before closing her laptop. "Why are you so eager?" Twisting the lid off her pop, she added, "To go to California?"

"I want to see a little bit of the world before I die. Is that a crime?" A snappiness that hadn't been there before emerged. "I keep hearing these cool stories about places people have traveled to. And I want that. I don't even have *one* to tell. Not one, Allie. You know I've never gone on a vacation."

"You've—" But Allie cut herself off. Amanda had hardly been old enough to remember their dad before he died. Any vacation she'd gone on, she'd have been too young to remember. After that, family vacations had ceased entirely. *Never time for them with Mom's long list of renovation projects.*

"Exactly."

She saw a lot of her dad in Amanda. Marc Jordan had loved traveling, though he'd always be rooted in Willow Creek. They'd taken family vacations, sometimes twice a year. Allie had been to Mount Rushmore, the Grand Canyon, and Niagara Falls, all before she was eight years old. But Amanda had only been three when he passed away. She hadn't remembered that trip to Niagara Falls at all.

"I'll think about it," Allie said, this time sincerely, holding back on the *It'd be more feasible if you'd picked somewhere cheaper. Like Kansas City or Denver.* "I'm just worried about spending too much."

Amanda bit her bottom lip. Allie jumped in before her sister could say something nasty that she didn't mean.

"I know it's hard for you to understand, Mandy Bear, but I have to have a good amount of money saved for moving expenses. I have to put down a deposit, pay movers, rent. And all of that will happen before I even have a job. In today's economy, that could take months."

Instead of the understanding she expected to see on her sister's face, Amanda did the opposite, staring blankly at the shed in the back corner of the yard. Then it came. "Why do you *have* to leave, Allie?"

"We've been over this." Her fingers curled around the edge of the swing. "I don't want to be in town when Travis gets out."

"What's so bad about running into Travis Meyers?" Amanda's outburst caught Allie off guard. "I know he's a jerk who caused you a lot of grief. But why are you letting him force you to move away from your home? Your family?"

"It's hard to explain."

"Why? Sounds to me like you're running away." Amanda eyes narrowed into slits, daring her to deny it.

"Am not."

"Are too!"

"You wouldn't understand," muttered Allie, studying the wood planks of her deck.

"I am going to scream!" Amanda hopped up from her wicker chair, yanked her tote bag onto her shoulder, and snatched the half-full bottle of Dr. Pepper from Allie's hand. "I've heard that lame excuse since I was twelve. I'm almost the same age now as you were when it happened."

"Amanda—"

"Tell me, Allie, what wouldn't I understand? How about why you even dated a jerk who didn't think twice about *shooting* you? That's what I really don't get!" Amanda flew inside, the echo of the front door slamming seconds later.

Norman leaned against the empty chair, his head tilted in confusion.

Abandoning her book and her laptop, Allie hopped off the deck in search of her dog's tennis ball. Her backyard wasn't big enough to accommodate a Frisbee. But at least the ball bounced, bringing a whole new level of fun for Norman.

"I used to fight that way with my younger brother."

Allie startled and spun to face her neighbor. Despite the number of times Ed poked his head over the top of the tall privacy fence, she was always surprised. Feeling obligated to defend her outburst, she said, "I'm not running away."

With a twig caught in his ball cap and dirt-smudged nose, Ed was a comical site. "Didn't say you were."

"Need a break, Ed?" Allie asked. "I'll get you a beer."

She left the door open as she searched for her bottle opener. She heard Ed tromp up the few deck stairs and set himself down on the top riser.

"My little brother Eugene had a knack for pickin' fights with me," Ed called through the open sliding door. "I swore that boy sure knew how to set me off. Enjoyed doing it too."

Allie propped the bottle in a coozie, popped its lid off, and returned to the deck. Norman sat on the steps, Ed scratching behind each of his ears.

"The summer I turned seventeen was the best summer of my life." He tipped his bottle toward his lips, taking a longer-than-usual pull. "It was the summer I met Marianna."

This'd happened before. Ed loved bouncing from story to story. She usually sat quietly, allowing him to stare out into the small yard and talk without her pointing it out. He seemed happy reminiscing. She wasn't going to interrupt.

"Course, our first meeting didn't go so well."

Allie hadn't yet heard how Ed met his wife. He told many stories about their happy years together, but he'd never opened up on how they got together. Not wanting to conjure up sad memories of his late wife, she had never asked. But now she sat at attention, her back propped against the deck post.

"See, I was ridin' down our old road on my motorcycle. Eugene—he was twelve then—ridin' with me. We were arguin' about something trivial. Chores or baseball or something meanin'less. I took my eyes off the road, seemed like just a second. Didn't see Marianna up ahead, walkin' along the side of the road until she screamed and leapt into the ditch."

"Oh no!"

"Oh, yes. No one was hurt, but I rounded back to check on her just to be certain. She was already marchin' down the road, wouldn't talk to me. Refusing any help. A scratch on her leg, but otherwise she looked okay. But I felt bad. I was goin' to make Eugene walk to town. Give Marianna the ride."

"She didn't accept, did she?"

Ed laughed his low, hearty rumble. "She cussed me out good. Called me all sorts of names I'd never heard a lady use before. Told me and my brother she wouldn't get on my motorcycle if I paid her a million dollars."

"How'd you win her over?"

Adjusting his ball cap, Ed said, "Hold your horses there, young lady. I'm gettin' to that part." After another swig of beer, he continued. "For weeks, Eugene kept tellin' me I should do something about Marianna. Take her flowers or ask her out on a date. Said she was perfect for me."

A happy sigh escaped Allie. *How romantic. Just like the book I'm reading.*

"But of course, all my pigheaded self remembered was all the rotten names she called me, and how adamantly she refused my help. She hurt my pride, and I wanted nothin' to do with her. But Eugene wouldn't drop it."

Slowly, the connection fell into place for Allie. Ed hadn't wandered off topic at all.

"You think Amanda knows something I don't?"

Ed shrugged. "All I'm sayin' is what's the worst that could happen? Maybe this vacation plan of hers might not be so bad."

The worst? We get mugged, lose all our money, and have to hitchhike back to Willow Creek.

Ed readjusted his ball cap and finally lost the twig he'd snagged on it. "Would it be so tragic if for a week, you stop worrying so much? That maybe you just have fun?"

"But the cost—"

"Sometimes," said Ed before emptying his bottle with a last sip, "we try harder to convince ourselves most of all." Ed stood, then bent forward to give Norman a pat. "You talk about leaving so much, Allie, that I wonder how much of that talk is to convince *yourself* you're really going."

Lesley only stepped foot inside her ex-husband's hardware store when absolutely necessary. Despite that she owned fifty-one percent interest since the divorce, she hated thinking of it as hers. It did make her quite a bit of money, but only after she'd demanded all the prices be raised. She'd insisted they were increased discreetly, by pennies at a time so people in town wouldn't notice.

Failing to acknowledge the cashier—some pathetic high-school girl Mort insisted was bright and talented— she burst into his office without so much as a knock.

On the verge of fifty, Mort Meyers wore a large bald spot on the crown of his head, centered in his dark, graying hair that made him look a decade older than he actually was. As Lesley shut the door, he hurried someone off the phone, promising he'd call them back.

"What do you want?" Mort never feigned happiness when she showed up unannounced. He reached for a can of chew, tobacco flakes spilling onto the disarray of papers scattered across his desk.

"That's no way to greet an old friend." She'd never liked her brother-in-law, even before her husband had decided to screw the cleaning girl on their three-thousand-dollar antique dining room table. A cleaning girl Mort had referred to them.

"You haven't answered my question."

She debated whether to remain standing or sit in the dust-covered chair opposite Mort. "I need a favor." She remained standing. "Why else would I come here?"

Mort pursed his lips and reached for the empty water bottle next to his grease-stained keyboard. "I haven't heard from my brother in five damn years. Why the hell would I do his ex any *favors?*"

Lesley knew he didn't miss being in Rich's shadow. Mort hated his older brother. He felt he'd been cheated out of the majority interest in the hardware store, and he hated him for relinquishing ownership to Lesley during their nasty divorce instead of selling him that crucial two percent.

"Because if you don't do this favor for me, I'm going

to do a favor for your wife."

Mort spit disgusting black liquid into the clear bottle. "What are you talking about?" He sat up straighter in his chair, his fingers tapping the bottle.

"You're going to hire my son to work in the warehouse."

"Hiring is my responsibility. My decision. Says so in the agreement." Mort eased back into his chair. "Besides, that shit's still in jail."

"Wrong. He's out on parole, as it were." She finally took a seat in the dusty chair. She could go home and shower when she was done. *I might have to burn this outfit.* "But you're not allowed to say a word to anyone about that."

"Why the hell should I let him within a mile of this place? He'll just steal me blind. Merchandise. Probably cash from the register, too."

"He needs a respectable job to get integrated back into society." Lesley crossed her legs. "If he steals, press charges."

"So you want him to move heavy boxes and sheets of plywood around?"

"It'll build character."

Mort folded his arms across his chest. "No." The slight waver in his voice made Lesley smile triumphantly.

"I think you're mistaken." She stood, leaning across the desk toward Mort. "But all right. There *is* a little video I think your wife would be very interested in viewing."

"What are you talking about?" Mort's voice dropped to the lowest it'd been since she stepped into his office.

"You think that girl *wanted* to have sex with you?"

His eyes grew wide, his face draining of color. "We didn't—"

"Doesn't matter," she said. "The camera tells a different story."

The girl in the video had been easy enough to bribe to do her bidding. Offer a starving college student enough money, and they'd do just about anything. Even with men as disgusting as Mort.

He pursed his lips together so tightly that Lesley thought they might get stuck that way.

"Travis will start Monday." She pushed off the desk, reaching for the grimy doorknob. "I don't want this getting all over town, either. You and I are the only two who know. If I hear a rumor floating around, I'll be paying Betty a little visit."

"How do I know you're not bluffing?" Mort challenged.

Releasing the disgusting doorknob, Lesley yanked her cell phone out of her purse and pushed play on a frozen video. The sounds alone were enough to shut Mort up. "I can ruin your life with one click of a button. If you think I'm bluffing, then you're as stupid as your brother." With that, she slammed the door behind her and walked out of the store with her head held high.

Chapter 11

Meyer's Hardware Store sat a block north of the main highway. Nick couldn't have missed it if he tried. Along with the lumberyard, the massive building consumed most of the block. Pulling up to a parking spot, he ran through his mental checklist of items he needed to buy. "If only things would stop breaking," he muttered, tossing open the truck door.

Within a month of moving to town, his to-do list had grown obscenely long. He needed to repair the deck railing, replace several kitchen drawer pulls, half a dozen light bulbs, and the seal to the kitchen faucet, which had decided to fail the night he swore he spotted teenagers in his backyard. Plus he wanted primer for the barn, one fixer-upper project he actually enjoyed.

The past couple of weeks had been a blur. Nick

hadn't expected a full schedule of patients so quickly, but he wasn't one to complain; he hadn't been so booked that he couldn't dedicate the time he wanted to each patient. He genuinely enjoyed meeting the interesting residents of Willow Creek. Even those faking ailments, like Aunt Ruby and her "arthritis".

Approaching the entrance, he noticed a sign near the door advertising lumber. Once inside, he first scanned for painting supplies. He glanced toward the front counter, but saw no one behind the register.

Walking through the aisles, Nick noted the seemingly odd prices for hardware. Eighty-four cents for a paint-stirring stick? A dollar fourteen for two dozen woodscrews? He shrugged it off when he found the aisle with primer. He decided to start with one five-gallon bucket. Eighty-one dollars and sixteen cents. *Huh.*

"Can I help you?"

The unexpected question jolted Nick. Luckily he hadn't picked up the bucket yet, or he'd have dropped it on his foot. When Nick spun around, he noted a balding man propped on a stool behind the counter. "Just getting some primer and a few other things." The man wore a faded John Deere T-shirt, a tan vest hanging loosely over it. A name tag pinned to the vest. *Mort.*

"Need any brushes? Rollers? Paint stirrers?"

As eager as Mort seemed to be at throwing out

suggestions, he failed to move from his spot behind the counter. When Nick came close enough to lift the heavy primer bucket onto the counter, he caught a glimpse of a heavy belly hanging over worn jeans. "Nope, got all that. Mind if I leave this here while I grab a few more things?"

Arms folded across his chest, Mort nodded.

Gathering the assortment of items he'd need for his planned repairs, Nick carried his purchases up to the counter.

As Mort rang it all up, Nick caught a glimpse through a cracked door to a back room. Had he not been paying attention, he might've missed the wisp of a shadow altogether. He couldn't explain why he suddenly felt on edge.

"Don't mind him." Mort waved a hand toward the door. "He's new."

Nick felt a little relieved that he hadn't imagined a ghost, but unease still hung in the air. Handing Mort his credit card, he waited for the grueling process of a little machine to dial out authorization for the charge.

The front door jingled, and in walked Allie Jordan, her chestnut hair gathered into a ponytail, wisps of loose, curly strands framing her face. A worn pair of jeans with holes at both knees hugged her long legs. Nick felt his heart rate pick up a couple beats.

"Hi," he said, probably smiling like an idiot.

She tucked a loose strand of hair behind her ear. "Hi."

It'd been almost two weeks at the hospital since he'd seen Allie in anything more than passing. He'd enjoyed their quiet lunch in the old, rundown break room that one time. But he'd been avoiding running into Allie since then, afraid she was already onto his secret. Afraid she might see that staying was only optional for him. "Working on a project?" he asked.

"I owe my neighbor a new screwdriver." She slipped into the tool aisle. "My deck ate his last one." The top of the shelves were low enough for him to still see her, her warm, brown eyes and beautiful smile.

Neighbor? The pang of jealousy that struck Nick felt irrational. Yet, he turned back toward Mort, hoping to conceal his reaction. He'd been in Willow Creek less than a month. He still had to survive two months of his probationary period before he knew if the town would accept him as their permanent doctor. Plus, his divorce hadn't yet finalized. So why couldn't he stop sneaking glances at Allie?

"Here you go." Mort handed back his credit card.

Nick caught another movement from that ajar door in back, a man peeking over a stack of shipping boxes. Scruffy blond hair escaped the brim of his ball cap. But the guy wasn't looking at Nick. He was looking past him, to where Allie now stood. Approaching the counter, she ducked her head, digging in her small purse. In a flash, the guy in the back disappeared.

Taking extra time to replace his credit card in his wallet, Nick waited for her to pay for her screwdriver. He couldn't explain his sudden urge to protect her, but something about the man in the back room had him feeling uneasy.

Nick held the door open for her. "Thanks," she said as she stepped through. "You're really doing it?"

He sent her a confused look.

"Painting that old barn."

He laughed, lugging the five-gallon bucket toward his truck, two bags full of hardware and parts slung over his other arm. He'd refused Allie's offer of help at the counter. Stupid, he knew, with the luck he'd been having. "I guess things don't really stay quiet here for too long."

"It's a small town. Everyone knew within minutes after you decided to start scraping off the old paint."

He set the bucket down before disaster could strike. Last thing he needed was to break his foot or spill paint over both of their vehicles. After tossing the bags into the passenger seat, Nick heaved the bucket into the back of his truck.

Allie opened her car door, her fingers resting on the roof.

Does she want to say something else?

"Have fun painting."

He yearned to prolong their moment. Even considered asking her out, against his better judgment. "I will." Through the window of the hardware store, he caught another glimpse of the guy in the baseball cap peering at them from behind the counter. "I hope I'll see you at the track this weekend?"

"We'll see." The flirtatious flare in Allie's eyes looked promising.

Setting a plate in the kitchen sink beside another empty casserole dish, Nick was about to change into older work clothes when his phone rang. He debated ignoring it. The last thing he wanted was an argument with Miranda. He loved his sister, but she was pushing his buttons lately about his moving back to Georgia.

He had no clue what the long-term future held. And Miranda starting their last conversation with, "Sixty-four days," wasn't helping. *Sixty-four.* The number of days before he'd have to make a decision about his future.

Here in Willow Creek he was comfortable with the shorter version of any future. A version where he didn't have to face a failed marriage, a cheating wife, or the crumbling of all his dreams. His hopes were high that the town was accepting him as their doctor, if his full patient load was any indication.

On the fourth ring, the possibility that the hospital might be calling forced him to pick up the receiver.

"Still got my old number I see," said a male voice on the other end. It took a moment to register who was calling.

"Herb. How's it going?"

"Just checking up on my old house."

"It's still standing." Nick decided to omit everything he'd managed to break since he arrived. Like the legs that snapped on the rickety end table from the mere weight of a box of woodscrews just an hour ago.

"Good to hear." He heard the light chatter of people in the background and guessed Herb might be calling from his Daytona Beach bar. "Heard you've been keeping pretty busy there."

"Checking up on me, Doc?" A bead of sweat trickled down his neck. Despite the refreshingly cool day with a northern breeze, he was uncomfortably warm.

"You were my personal recommendation. You know I have to make sure they're treatin' you right."

It shouldn't surprise him that Herb would check in. Or that he probably had spies sending him reports. Nick yearned to ask if Herb had heard good things. *Or anything bad.* "I've gotten half a dozen marriage proposals," he finally admitted. "Mostly repeats from Aunt Ruby and her friend Abigail."

Doc Herb laughed deeply. "It's a wonder you have any peace and quiet."

"Well, the casseroles have slowed down a bit. But I don't risk starving any time soon."

Nick heard him mumble something to someone else. "Any troubles with the house?" Herb asked, sounding rushed now.

"No." But if he didn't stop breaking things, he'd have no choice but to make an offer. "Nothing I can't handle." He certainly didn't have the heart to tell Herb what a mess of things he was making. If he didn't stop blowing breakers, he'd probably have to hire an electrician to redo all the wiring too.

"Great." Herb cleared his throat. "Well, if anyone bothers asking, you bought it free and clear."

"Of course." Nick poured himself a glass of water. "I've been meaning to ask about the old barn." He paused, expecting something on the other end, but only silence filtered through. He continued without prompt. "I hope you don't mind, I decided to repaint it."

"Glad it's getting done. I've been meaning to do that for years, but never got around to it."

"I didn't know you made furniture."

"Well, we didn't really talk much about me, did we?"

Nick thought back to the solitary night at the sports bar. He only remembered rambling on about his life and his current problems. Had he even asked Herb about his experience as a doctor in Willow Creek? It'd been a little foolish not to. He might've risked showing up to a twisted town straight out of a horror movie. "Guess not."

"I haven't used it in a couple years."

Herb's voice tapered off, and Nick decided it was not the time to ask why not. "Mind if I do? I mean, I don't build furniture, but I like to refurbish old pieces."

"By all means."

"Thanks."

"Any troubles from the ex?"

In Florida, Nick had voiced concerns about moving to Nebraska before his divorce was finalized. Dana liked feeling in control, like she always had the upper hand. If she found out Nick had left Georgia without telling her, she might throw a kink into the proceedings out of spite. "Not so far."

"Good. Good." An awkward silence fell over the conversation. "Hope you decide to stay," Herb finally said. "Willow Creek could really use a good man like you."

Out at the barn, slapping on white primer with a roller, Nick kept repeating Herb's last words to himself.

In general, he liked the town of Willow Creek. He'd heard a couple of rumors: folks suspicious of his reasons for giving up city life and a city-sized salary for this small town. But he'd handle that tomorrow in the newspaper interview. He'd rescheduled with the local editor twice already, and he couldn't put it off any longer. She'd threatened to schedule a doctor's appointment if that's what it took to book a few minutes of his precious time.

"One thousand and thirty-six comments?" Elbows anchored into the booth table, Kim looked up from her smartphone. "Allie, are you seeing this?"

"I try really hard to read them all. Even the bad ones. But it's getting a little overwhelming."

Kim watched Allie casually sip Dr. Pepper through a straw, like the number of comments on her latest blog post was commonplace. As though keeping her fans happy created a slight dilemma rather than a huge opportunity. *Why can't Allie see that?*

Kim reached for another piece of bread but found the basket empty. *Where is that pesky waiter?* The one who was supposed to bring more delicious garlic bread without having to be flagged down. "Al, you haven't even looked into this, have you?"

"Into what?"

"You're lucky the garlic bread is gone. I'd throw it at you." She reached for her strawberry lemonade, emptying the cup. "Did you think any more about making your blog a thing? A thing where you can make a little money."

Allie shook her head, eyes locked on their empty bread basket.

"I'm about to go back in the kitchen and give that waiter a piece of my mind. Did you see him? He was just standing behind the bar, flirting with that bartender. We've been out of garlic bread for ten minutes!" She wasn't normally so snappy. She'd worked enough in the food industry to know that waiters could be spiteful if they felt unappreciated. She'd blame her mood on her dad tonight.

Taking Kim's smartphone from her, Allie stared at the screen with a look that said she'd lost her puppy and sighed in what seemed to be frustration. "How can I possibly read all these comments?"

Pushing around ice cubes with her straw, Kim tried to force the argument with her dad out of her mind. He'd never understand why she, the only sibling in her family who hadn't joined a branch of the military and left Nebraska, didn't want to run the family business in Willow Creek.

"I mean, I love that there's so many," continued Allie, oblivious to Kim's distress. "It's great to know so many people out there love these books as much as I do. And I'm sure it really boosts sales for the author."

Kim's head snapped forward. "Allie, did you just hear yourself?"

"Would you ladies like some more bread?"

"You *are* still here." Kim smiled sweetly, squeezing every ounce of sarcasm she could into her ridiculous grin. "We thought you'd gotten lost. Yes, more bread. And strawberry lemonade."

Once the young waiter walked away, Allie sent Kim a scolding look from across the table. "You should be nicer," she warned. "He might spit in our food."

Kim ignored her concern. If their garlic bread showed up with a loogie, she'd make sure they not only walked out of there with a free meal, but a couple of future meals as well. She wasn't one to put up with stupidity. She'd spent her college years as a waitress and could spot a lazy server in an instant. "How do you pick which books you read?"

Allie shrugged. "It's a toss-up, really. I get some at the used bookstore here in Norfolk. They're usually only a dollar." She fidgeted with her straw. "Others I get for free or almost free online. I read those on my computer." A boy in a red Cars T-shirt whisked past their booth, beating his parents to their table. "The library donates their worn-out romance novels to me and they order the new ones I don't want to pay for."

"So you read both new books and titles that have been published for a while."

"Yeah. I don't really have a preference."

"Historical? Contemporary? Rom-Com?"

Allie rose an eyebrow.

"I know, I know. I'm not supposed to know so much about your precious genre." She took her phone back from Allie. "I did a little research. Which may or may not have included reading a couple of your beloved novels. Or a couple dozen." She grinned.

The scrawny waiter returned with more bread, and Kim reached for a piece before the basket even made it to the table. "Food should be out in a few minutes."

Allie's other eyebrow arched as well. "A couple dozen?"

"It was research," Kim snapped, inspecting the warm piece of garlic bread and then shoving a bite of it in her mouth.

"I'm not against any type of romance. If the book looks promising, I read it." Allie reached for a piece of garlic bread. "The great thing about being anonymous is that I can literally read anything I want from sweet love stories to crazy erotic ones."

Kim's jaw dropped open. "You read erotica?"

"Sometimes." She didn't miss the crimson blush rushing into Allie's cheeks. She wanted to tell her not to be so damned ashamed of something she loved doing. But Allie intercepted. "The thing is, if I don't like a book I read, I don't post a blog about it."

"You wouldn't want to hurt anyone's feelings."

"Exactly. I imagine a lot of work goes into writing a book. I'm not about to bash an author's efforts."

"Know anyone who can build you a website?"

Mouth full of bread, Allie shook her head. Swallowing, she asked, "Why would I need a website? Don't those cost a lot of money? A blog is free."

"You can host your blog on your website."

"That still doesn't answer my question."

"If your blogs are really helping boost author sales—which I'm sure you can prove in the comments—don't you think that's something they'd see as valuable?"

Allie eyed Kim across the table. "When did you become an entrepreneurial expert?"

Kim waved away the question, sending breadcrumbs flying. "You should offer your services to authors. Offer to read their book—one they have to provide you—and then write a blog about it."

"How does that make me filthy rich? I can't charge money for reviews. That's unethical."

The waiter delivered their entrées, taking away their glasses for refills. For several moments, they ate in strained silence. Kim's grandmother's favorite saying popped into her mind—the one about horses and water. She decided she should never be given a horse to lead. Best friend or not, she'd shove its face in the trough rather than deal with all this back-and-forth crap.

Halfway through her rib eye, Kim asked, "Have any authors reached out to you?"

"A couple."

Which probably means like twenty-five. "And you just read their books for free?"

Allie nodded. "The ones that looked good, anyway. I did turn down a couple. One had more spelling errors on the first page than I could count. And the second lost all its tension by page five."

"Think about this," suggested Kim. "What if you had a website where you shared your blog—same blog so you wouldn't have to change a thing about that—and then a section where authors could go to submit requests for you to provide advertising on your website? A place where you set terms and price for *that* service. The review part could be a free bonus. Put up a disclaimer that you'll post a review on your blog at your discretion."

"Terms?"

"Make them provide you a copy of the book. Then you could include your fee for advertising space."

"How much could I charge for that?"

Kim shrugged. "I don't have *all* the answers, Allie. But if you made five dollars, you'd be making more money than you are now. And you'd be paid to do what you love."

"But what if no one wants to pay for it?"

"It may be slow at first," she admitted. "But you have the content to back up your price. I mean, a few hundred people are probably going to buy that last book you read. That's marketing. And right now, you're doing it for free. You could offer to provide a direct link for purchasing that book. Maybe offer the author space to talk about themselves and what they write. If a book is listed on your website, you're already backing that book and that author. They will get sales from it. Guaranteed."

From the growing light in Allie's eyes, Kim could tell the wheels were finally beginning to turn. "I think you're onto something."

She threw both her hands up in the air. "Hallelujah! I've only been telling you this for months now."

Swirling a fry in ketchup, Allie said, "You can't tell anyone."

Kim looked up from her plate. "Allie, you shouldn't feel the need to keep this a secret. Just because there are people who think it's not socially acceptable—"

"Please, Kim." The pleading in her eyes was enough to make Kim bite her tongue. She didn't know for sure what the hesitation was about, but she'd bet her next month's rent that it had something to do with Travis Meyers. He was the reason Allie sought out those books in the first place.

"I won't say anything." Kim dug her fork into a pile of loaded mashed potatoes. "Yet."

Chapter 12

When Nick emerged from the trees behind a storage building west of the school, his first sight was Allie hovering in a squat, waiting for Norman to reach her with his Frisbee. He'd been avoiding the track during the times he knew she would be there, but his lusty dreams hadn't calmed any. There'd been many cold showers as of late. A necessity. And self-gratification when those cold showers failed.

Gray yoga pants hugged Allie's lovely legs despite the already sticky humidity and rising temperatures. He couldn't recall a single time he'd seen her in shorts. Watching her several unsuccessful attempts at stealing the Frisbee from Norman's clenched teeth, he couldn't help but notice the grass stains on her white tank, streaking the sides.

The dog emerged victorious from the furry rumble. "Well, if you don't want me to have it, that's okay," he heard her say. "I'm sure you can figure out how to throw it on your own."

She crawled to her knees. Norman tilted his head and dropped his Frisbee. Allie darted, snatching it back just a second before the dog figured out what she was up to. She jumped to her feet and launched it for him again.

"I see Norman's awake."

"Hi, Nick."

He'd hoped to talk to her for a few minutes first like a perfectly calm, normal person, but at the sight of her smile and the grass stain across her collarbone, his heart started pounding. He blamed inappropriate dreams on his impulse to tackle her. To pin her to her blanket and—

"Morning run?"

Her voice snapped him from his fantasy. He nodded dumbly and asked, "Will you two be here for a bit?"

"Yeah." She watched Norman charging back with the clenched Frisbee wobbling in his teeth. "This is only round one. Norman naps in between."

"Norman does?" he teased. "Not Allie?"

She shot a playful glare in his direction, causing him a tight swallow. "He won't chase me around the track, will he?"

"Not unless you grab his Frisbee," she answered, looking toward the overcast sky. "Better hurry, though. Rain is coming."

Nick felt his tight muscles loosening after the first two laps. Though tempted to wrap up the run short of his usual two miles, he couldn't cheat himself in front of Allie. Each time he caught sight of her, he sped up a little bit; some weak attempt to impress her, no doubt. Funny how easy it was to feel fifteen again.

The run wasn't having the effect he'd hoped. He kept imaging inviting Allie to shower with him afterward. "Maybe I should go straight home," he muttered on lap number three.

By the time he'd run two and a half miles—that extra half mile just as useless as the rest of the run at ridding his lusty fantasies—Allie was curled up on her blanket with another book. Norman lay sprawled out in the grass nearby, asleep on his back. The dog didn't budge as he jogged up to them.

"Thirsty?" She held up a full water bottle. In the mix of things this morning, he hadn't remembered to bring anything to drink.

"Thanks." He plopped down in the grass next to Norman, giving her space to hide her book. He was almost going to let it pass today, but he couldn't help himself. "Still reading that fascinating mystery?" At her blush, he laughed. "Relax, Allie. I knew that's not what it was the last time."

She looked up from her paperback, guilt written across her face. "You did?"

"I've never read a mystery that had a shirtless man on the cover."

Nick watched her cheeks turn beet-red. He thought she'd be smiling, but it appeared she might cry. Seemed a little odd that she'd feel *that* embarrassed over a romance novel. "I'm just giving you a hard time, you know."

She shoved her paperback in her tote bag.

"Hey," said Nick, lifting himself off the grass and scooting next to her on the blanket. "I didn't mean anything by it." He bumped her shoulder with his. Good thing he was drenched in sweat, or he might be tempted to touch her, to reassure her. Might pull her into his arms. *Start kissing her neck...*

Allie managed a weak smile.

"I think it's great that you read, Al. I know a lot of people who couldn't be forced to pick up a book." *Like Dana, for example.* "Is it some sort of secret?"

"Kind of."

Interesting. He wasn't ready to let this go. "Why?"

"It's a long story." Norman let out a yawn, then

flipped upright to stretch.

"I'm in no hurry."

"Some other time, Nick."

When he met her pleading eyes, he wavered. *I'm helpless. Those damn begging eyes.*

Norman spotted his Frisbee and snatched it up. A second later, he dropped it in Nick's lap. "Okay." He hopped to his feet and launched it across the field. He tried to watch Norman, to keep his eyes off Allie on the blanket, burying her paperback at the very bottom of her bag like she worried it might fall out.

The dog raced back, dropping the Frisbee at Nick's feet again. After the red disc went soaring through the air, the wind carrying it to the opposite goal post, he decided to end the awkward silence. "I've finished priming the barn. Now I get to buy actual paint."

"What color?"

Nick shrugged. "Haven't quite made up my mind. I know red is typical. But it's not just a barn. Doc Herb had a woodworking shop in there."

Allie nodded. Obviously, that wasn't a secret.

"But what other color do you paint a barn?" he asked and reached out his hand, pulling her to her feet. He forced himself not to focus on how soft and delicate her fingers felt against his. Irrational tingles skittered up his arm.

"Red's still a safe bet, since you're in Cornhusker territory."

"True. But I'm thinking I want something a little more neutral. I hardly noticed that barn at all and I like that. I like that it's tucked between those trees." Norman trotted back, eyeing both Nick and Allie as if debating who should get the Frisbee next. He dropped it right between them.

Shedding the unnecessary sunglasses and tossing them onto her blanket, Nick looked from Allie to the Frisbee, an eyebrow raising, a playful challenge in his eyes.

She dove for the Frisbee, clasping it first. She fought Norman and won, but Nick was right behind, arms wrapped around her on the ground, gripping the Frisbee so hard he thought he might crack it. Norman barked a couple of times during the excitement as Nick and Allie rolled on the ground, but her grip on the Frisbee was firm.

For Nick, it didn't help that his body distracted him, wrapped around hers as it was; or his brain, imagining gripping her instead.

Almost out of breath, he rolled to a sitting position, pulling Allie up in front of him. It took him a moment to remember that she wasn't his wife or even his girlfriend. He let go of the Frisbee and dropped his arms behind him, leaning back.

She looked at him over her shoulder. "You gave up a little sooner than I expected."

What he wouldn't give to kiss her right now. They weren't touching anymore, but he still felt the heat resonating from her skin and knew to stand up before he found himself in an embarrassing situation.

"You're a lot stronger than I expected." His eye catching a morning jogger off in the distance, he hopped up from the cool grass. Extending his hand, he said, "I forget that people live around here."

Norman charged back and dropped the Frisbee.

"Extra nosy people," added Allie. "But I'm sure you figured that out after your little newspaper interview."

"Ah, yeah." He remembered how personal the questions had gotten. Where he'd grown up. If he had family back in Georgia. *Ever been married?* That'd been a fun one to dodge. Luckily the newspaper editor, Sue, was flirting shamelessly. Might've been wrong, but he threw her off course by complimenting her appearance. Sue had all but offered to marry him by the time they'd finished. "You read it?"

Allie nodded. "Front page news."

"Really?" He felt a tiny drop of rain bounce off his arm.

"Well, the paper's only six pages long. Still, it's not

easy to make the front page."

Norman gave up on his Frisbee and plopped onto the ground next to her blanket. Allie followed suit, leaving Nick with an internal debate. Sit and visit with her or go home like he knew he should?

But he couldn't bring himself to leave. So he resumed his seat on the grass, a safe distance away, and told her, "I should go paint my barn."

"I told you, it's going to rain." Her words were playful, not guarded as she'd been the first time they encountered each other.

Norman, still on his belly, crawled toward Nick and placed his head in his lap insisting on a rub between his ears. Another, heavier drop smacked his shoulder. "What do you think about beige?" he asked, ignoring the scarce droplets and the darkening sky. *There's time.*

"Beige?" repeated Allie. "Yeah, I think that'd look really nice. It'd keep the barn more or less blended. At least, I think it would. I've never seen it up close."

Was that a hint? "I like that. Maybe with white trim."

"Don't buy your paint in town, though," warned Allie. "Lesley keeps raising the prices. She thinks people don't notice, but they do. It'll be cheaper to drive to Norfolk. Much cheaper."

"Lesley?" repeated Nick. "As in—"

"The one and only." She ran her fingers through the cool blades of grass. "She took everything from her ex, including the hardware store. He ran it with his brother, Mort. The guy who was there the other day?"

He nodded, following so far.

"Lesley owns more of it than he does, actually. She sets all the prices."

"Why?" asked Nick. Steady sprinkles splashed his exposed arms. "I mean, why does she have to raise the prices like that? Shouldn't she want to keep them low so people will shop there?"

Now Allie was the one to sit back on her hands. But now her breasts were—Nick had to look away or he'd surely act on his masculine instincts. As it was, he'd have to excuse himself back to his house soon. Take another cold shower.

"People like Lesley Jamison..." Allie trailed off, her eyes searching across the field toward the row of houses along the road. "They run this town, Nick. Some of them are wonderful. Best you could ever meet. Take Aunt Ruby, for instance. She may not hold any position of power anymore, but she's got influence from having lived here her whole life. And she uses that for the good of the town."

"But some don't?"

"Some people get a little carried away with that

power. They seem to thrive on making others suffer." Though Allie wouldn't meet his eyes, he saw sadness trapped there. Something that warned him what she was saying was maybe from personal experience.

"I get that," he said. "I knew someone like that, too."

"Yeah?"

Am I really ready to talk about this? He waited for a sense of dread to slam him in the chest, but when it didn't come, he relaxed. It felt right to tell her. "I'll tell you a secret," said Nick. "One they didn't print in that article. But on two conditions."

Turning to give him her full attention, she lifted a brow. "What's that?"

"One, you can't tell anyone. Not even Norman. You'll need to cover his ears." Allie giggled, her true smile returning. He liked that one very much.

"Two?"

"And two, you have to share one with me. Something no one else knows." He hoped she'd open up about why she felt so ashamed of reading romance novels.

He wasn't looking forward to sharing his past, but it'd be nice to have someone to confide in. Miranda had called *again* last night, leaving a message on his machine. One that told him his sister wasn't giving any breathing room. Whether he wanted to or not, he'd have to confront his past eventually.

Allie nodded. "Okay."

He took a deep breath, hoping his secret wouldn't send her running. "Technically, I'm married."

She laughed, like he might be joking.

Nick lowered his brows. "Allie, I'm telling you the truth." He swallowed as the light left her eyes. "It's more a legality than anything at this point." He shifted his gaze to the grass at her feet. "I left Georgia because I caught my wife cheating on me."

"That's—I'm—"

He looked down the track field. "With my best friend." The words came easier than he expected with only the fluttering blades of grass to watch for a reaction. "The paperwork's been signed. I'm just waiting for it to be processed. Hopefully it'll all be finished within a couple months."

"First off, I'm really sorry, Nick. I can't imagine any woman married to you not appreciating what they had. And second off, why are you keeping that a secret?" She stared at her bottle of water, fumbling it again. *She's nervous.* "So what if people know you're *almost* divorced?"

He turned to face her and shrugged, hoping the gesture came off as nonchalant. It'd not be wise to tell her *all* of his secrets. Not when it could jeopardize his staying in Willow Creek for the long haul. "I don't want to answer questions about why I left." He tried to look away as she twisted the cap off her water and brought the bottle to her lips.

His restraint at keeping his hands off Allie was weakening, especially since the truth hadn't caused her to hop up and run away. "You're the first person I've told about it here. I guess part of me thinks that by not talking about it, that part of my life will just disappear."

"I get that."

"You do?"

"We've all got things in our past that we'd like nothing more than to forget."

"Your turn to—" A crackle of thunder caused Norman to jump up, cutting him off. In the next instant, the steady stream of cooling sprinkles transformed into heavy, blinding rain. Nick had to look away. Of all the colors she chose to wear, why had it been white?

"Norman hates storms," said Allie, gathering her things in her arms. "We need to get home before he really starts to freak out."

"My house is closer," he offered without forethought.

She looked away, toward the line of trees that provided a wind block for the football field. He knew she was trying to figure out the nicest way to turn him down. *Probably better this way.*

But then he heard, "Okay."

Running behind Nick through the wooded path from the track field to his house, Allie tried to keep from picturing him naked, the way she saw him the last time she ran down this trail. He certainly didn't make it easy, swaggering in front of her like he did. She'd seen both sides of his glorious and very bare body.

"If you want," he told her, rushing through the back door, "I can loan you some dry clothes. Put yours in the dryer."

"Sure." She should've run when she had the chance. How could she expect herself to behave? Nick, once again, had chosen to make his morning appearance at the track in the middle of one of the sexiest scenes of her latest book.

Inside the kitchen, her eyes roamed the dated room. She'd expected Doc Herb to have an expensive, updated home. One with granite countertops, shiny hardwood floors, and maybe even a marble fireplace. Instead, the kitchen, though spacious and boasting an island, sported pale yellow Formica countertops, worn vinyl flooring, and appliances older than she was.

"It needs a bit of remodeling," Nick said as Norman

shook himself and droplets flew in the small mudroom off the kitchen. "But nothing I can't handle."

"You and my mom would get along great."

"Your mom?"

"She renovates houses for fun." Norman discovered a rug beneath the small dining table in the corner of the kitchen. After trotting in circles, he settled into a ball, his chin tucked into his tail. "Hope you don't mind him? He's a little damp but he'll stay put." She eyed the muddy paw prints on the kitchen floor. "And I'll get these cleaned up."

"Don't worry about it. I'll get it later. Would you like a quick tour?"

From the doorway of the kitchen, she spotted the staircase. One side opened to the gigantic living room. If the tour included an invitation into his bedroom, what would she do? He'd just admitted to being married, yet she heard herself answering, "Sure."

The house was every bit as large inside as its exterior suggested. The kitchen, living room, formal dining, guest bathroom, and an office area all offered enough space for a crowd of people. Allie wondered if Doc Herb had entertained earlier in his life, when his wife was still alive. She'd heard that Doris was a very social creature, used to heading all the events in Willow Creek.

"Upstairs is a little messy," warned Nick. "Still have a lot of boxes to unpack."

Until she eyed the first spacious bedroom crammed so full of boxes there was no room to walk inside, it didn't hit her that Nick might leave Willow Creek. She remembered their conversation in the break room of the hospital last week. The one where he hadn't answered her question about staying. "That's a lot left to unpack."

"I've been busy with the barn and fixing things around the house." Instead of meeting her eyes, he continued down the hall toward the back of the house. "There're two more bedrooms beside my own, but they're pretty empty."

Her heart began to beat in her ears as they approached Nick's bedroom. If she didn't want to make a fool of herself, she needed to wait in the doorway.

"This is the master." He widened the door, allowing her to see inside. "The bathroom up here is the only thing in the entire house that's new." He looked about to encourage her to take a peek, then walked across the room to a dresser. Digging through a drawer, he pulled out an Atlanta Braves T-shirt and a pair of sweatpants. "Hope these are okay until your stuff dries."

"Yes, thank you." Slipping by her in the narrow doorway, his chest brushed against her arms, stopping them both. Her breath hitched. His emerald eyes held a fire of desire. "Can I change in here?"

"Actually," said Nick, "I need to jump in the shower quick."

She swallowed. *An invitation? I accept!*

"The dryer's downstairs, on the other side of the kitchen. If you want something to drink, help yourself. Give me a few minutes, I'll be down to join you."

"Okay." She turned away, embarrassed how she believed he'd actually invited her to shower. "Don't suppose you have any Dr. Pepper?"

He shook his head. "Sorry."

"Water it is." She scurried down the hall. What she wouldn't give to have her cellphone handy right now. She could call Kim, ask if throwing away her sensible reasons was the way to go. Or if it'd be better to keep her hands off of Nick. *Kim would say go for it.*

At the end of the hallway, she slipped off her tank top, noticing that her sports bra was also soaked through. *Guess I'll have to go without one for a while.*

Finding the dryer in a small room tucked in the opposite corner of the kitchen, she tossed her damp clothes inside. Studying the ancient knobs for a few seconds, she selected a setting, and the contraption hummed to life.

She returned to the kitchen and watched Norman's body rise and fall beneath the corner table. "You certainly made yourself at home." He didn't stir now that the thunder had ceased. She made her way to the cupboards—the only high-end feature of the kitchen, they looked to be hand-carved—and found a glass.

From her tote, Allie dug out her romance novel. *Might as well get some reading done.*

She'd finished chapter nineteen when she heard the creak of Nick's door. She did what she could to calm her heavy breathing, but the image of Nick naked was making her come undone. Glancing toward the staircase, her eyes widened in horror. Her wet sports bra lay on a riser halfway up the staircase!

Shoving her novel inside her tote, Allie sprinted from the kitchen. Catching sight of Nick at the top of the staircase, she rushed to snatch her bra before he saw it. But she was just a second too slow and instead collided right into him, knocking him backwards. Losing her balance, she fell on top of him. "I'm sor—Nick, are you okay?" *Crap, I broke the new doctor!*

Crushed against his chest, Allie felt the rumbling of laughter. "I promise I don't have the Frisbee."

Their faces inches apart, her gaze kept falling on his lips. *Say something witty.* Anything to distract her from the heat of his body pressed against hers. "Sorry, I—"

He followed the path of her gaze to her foot. Where her damp sports bra dangled over the edge of the stair tread. Heat rushed to her cheeks. She tried scrambling off him, but he'd clasped her elbows. She tucked her head against his chest, allowing her wavy hair to hide her face.

"Embarrassed is the last thing you should be." His low voice traveled hot against her ear. "Worried is what I'd be if I were you."

Lifting her head, she parted her lips to ask why. But the moment their eyes locked, she knew she was helpless to fight the inevitable.

One of his hands tangled itself in her hair, the other cupped her cheek, both pulling her face to his. Somewhere in the back of her mind, Allie knew she should fight this. Knew she was supposed to keep her distance so nothing distracted her from leaving town.

The sensation of his lips meeting hers forced all reason away. Dizzy pleasure washed over her. The uncomfortable staircase faded, giving way to a more pleasant sensation. Hot, roaming hands. Nipples tightening beneath loose fabric. Urgency growing into desire. Nick's tongue traced the inside of her lips, begging for entry.

The buzzer of the dryer startled her. His deep laughter made her desire too powerful to deny. She crushed her lips against his, wrapping one hand around his neck. Her other sought the hem of his T-shirt, desperately wanting to feel his bare chest. A chest that had plagued her dreams for weeks.

Again the buzzer sounded. Lights flickered. In the kitchen, the shattering of a light bulb elicited a squeal from Allie. Norman's loud barking echoed.

Nick groaned beneath her.

"What happened?" she asked.

"Just something else to fix." He lifted her from him, setting her to the side. Bringing his foot toward him, he lifted the wet sports bra, now dangling off *his* toes, and handed it back to her.

Instead of blushing, Allie giggled. "My bad."

While he swept up the shattered glass, she ushered Norman out of the kitchen. "You should have someone look at your wiring."

Nick emptied the contents of his dustpan. "It's crossed my mind."

Floor free of hazards, she retrieved her still-damp clothes from the dryer. "And you might need a new dryer. I think this is wetter now than it was before."

His body folding around her from behind, Nick groaned against her ear. Dizziness washed over her again, her body growing limp. Lips trailed gentle kisses along her neck.

The phone's shrill ring made Norman bark again. "You've got to be kidding me." Nick spun Allie around, kissing her deeply, ignoring the phone.

"Don't you have to answer that?" she asked between kisses. "Might be an emergency."

"Not my weekend on call."

The call rang through to an answering machine. "I see you're avoiding my calls," a voice echoed throughout the living room. "Don't think I'm not counting down every single day left before you come back to Georgia. The kids want you to know you're at fifty-nine."

Kids? She shimmied out of his embrace. "You *are* going to leave." She pushed around him to grab her tote.

"Allie, wait."

"Why?"

"It's not what you think."

"Really?" She held the back door open for Norman. "Because it sounds like your *wife and kids* are expecting you home in two months." The door slammed behind her, and she sprinted home through the rain.

Chapter 13

Wednesday night, Allie shoved open her front door and dropped her jacket and purse at the foot of the entryway bench. She patted Norman on the head a couple of times, but was too worn-out to give him his usual dose of attention. Her fingers ached from two solid days of typing policy letters. She had even avoided Ed sitting on his front porch reading a newspaper.

Yesterday Allie and Suzy had been griping—privately, they thought—about escorting the same patients to the two exam rooms. Lesley, a shiny black coffee mug clenched in one neatly manicured hand, had appeared out of nowhere, plopping a thick overflowing manila folder on the desk next to Allie. The folder looked like it had been run over by a bus in a hurricane, one thick blue rubber band holding it together.

With a sour smile on her face, Lesley looked directly at Allie. "These are policy letters from Dr. Rowe's old office. Most of these are ripped, written on, coffee-stained, and Lord only knows what. Retype them with Dr. Bryant's signature block. Leave them on my desk once you finish. I want to make sure they're still relevant before I waste the busy doctor's time."

By what Allie could only consider dumb luck, Lesley hadn't been sitting in her office when she left the neat stack on her shiny, granite-topped desk. *I can only imagine Cruella's malicious smile as she hands over another folder, twice as thick.* It was enough to make her lose her appetite.

"I don't want to think about work," moaned Allie as she plopped down on her recliner. Sliding her flat black shoes under the coffee table, she knew she'd have to move them before she went to bed. Norman felt anything left under the coffee table was fair game.

An untouched packet of printouts taunted her from atop the low table before her. She'd yet to look over any of the information her sister had dropped off about California, despite her little chat with Ed about pushy siblings. Her latest romance novel didn't entice her tonight; the main characters were arguing, anyway. Instead, Allie reached for the TV remote.

During a car commercial, her front door burst open.

Norman hardly lifted his head. "Are you actually watching TV?" Amanda teased as she fell on the couch next to Norman's spot. "I never thought I'd see the day when my sister would choose TV over reading or being boring."

"Ha ha."

"Wow, someone had a rough day," said Amanda, eyebrows drawn.

"You might say that."

For a moment, the two sisters watched a commercial about car insurance, though neither was paying attention to the nagging advertisement. Amanda absently rubbed Norman behind the ears, putting the dog into a state of ecstasy.

"Have you looked through the info?"

Allie should've expected as much. *Why else would Amanda be here?* Any other normal teenager would be hanging out with her friends on a summer night. "I've glanced at it."

"Liar!"

Too tired to stop the pillow aimed at her, Allie leaned to the side. The pillow hit her in the shoulder. "That's mature."

"Just a little California sunshine, Al. That's all I ask." Amanda hopped up from the couch and stormed into the kitchen. She returned with a Dr. Pepper for herself, but none for Allie. The can of pop looked so enticing, but she wasn't sure she could get out of her recliner tonight. *Maybe I'll sleep here.*

"I haven't been neglecting it on purpose." That was the truth. But how did she admit that her free time had been spent reading romance novels, writing blogs, and sketching a plan to make Kim's expansion idea into a reality? Not to mention her mission to avoid Nick at all costs. "I've just been busy."

Cracking open the can, Amanda fell back onto the couch. "Doing what?"

"Amanda! Try not spilling pop all over my couch." But she couldn't even summon the energy to admonish her properly.

"I didn't." Amanda slurped a drink.

A TV show Allie didn't recognize started up again. Three people were in a dark little room with cement walls and a cold metal table. One man was being questioned about a murder. She flipped the channel. *I don't need any prison-related shows, thank you very much.* "I'm working on a project."

Amanda folded her legs, tucking them beneath her. "What kind of project?" She reached for the blanket laid across the back of the couch.

So much for being boring. "A website idea." Amanda didn't seem too technology-driven. Maybe that'd lose her interest.

"What would you need a website for?"

A yawn escaped Allie—a long, obnoxious one, startling Norman from his near coma. "I didn't say I *needed* one."

"Oh, stop it, Allie. Don't make me throw another pillow." Amanda sent an icy glare across the room that should've sent shivers down Allie's spine.

Instead, she yawned. Again eyeing her sister's cold beverage.

"I don't know if I'll need one. It's just an idea I've been working on. That's all." She forced herself to her feet. The more she watched her sister sip her Dr. Pepper, the more she craved one.

"It's not one of those stupid pyramid things, is it?" Allie heard from the living room, as she opened the refrigerator.

A sigh escaped. She didn't want to keep playing this charade. How bad could it be to share her secret with one more person? It was Amanda, after all. *Maybe we'll bond over it.* She sputtered a laugh at the thought, trudging back into the living room with her can of pop. She headed straight toward her DVD tower and pulled out a romantic comedy. *Better than these stupid crime shows.*

"I happen to have a little hobby," said Allie, sliding

the DVD into her player. "But if I tell you, you're sworn to secrecy."

Amanda gasped. "Are you into *porn*?"

Allie wished she had something to throw at her sister. But her Dr. Pepper was her only option, and she wasn't about to part with her precious beverage. "Yes, Amanda. I have an obsession with porn. Midget porn specifically."

"Oh my—hey, *not* funny!"

She grinned as the horror on her sister's face turned into a scowl. "You brought it up." As the DVD played, the TV screen flashed through previews of movies now three years old. Allie sank back into her recliner and flipped up the footrest. Once she wrapped a blanket around her legs, she added, "But no, it's *not* porn."

"Then what?"

"Promise you won't tell?"

"Sure."

"If you do, I promise I will never take a vacation with you. Ever. Anywhere."

"Jeez, Allie. I promise."

Here goes nothing. "I write a blog."

Amanda laughed. "That's your shameful secret? It must be a really scandalous blog. Do you blog about porn?"

"What is it with you and porn? No!" Already Allie

wished she could backpedal. But she'd come this far. "I blog about books I read."

"You've got to get out more, Al. If you're paranoid people are going to think you're crazy for blogging about books, you haven't been socialized enough. I didn't realize how serious this was. Maybe you should move to a city now instead of waiting a year."

Ignoring the comment, which frankly she didn't care to think about tonight, she pointed out, "I blog about a certain kind of book."

"Oh my God, is it that high fantasy stuff? Does my sister play Dungeons and Dragons?" Amanda's eyes were wide, like she was actually afraid Allie might be into nerdy books.

She rolled her eyes. "Romance novels, you dummy!"

"Oh." Amanda stared at the TV screen. "That's seriously your big, controversial secret? That you blog about romance novels?"

Allie nodded. "Well, a *lot* of them."

"Okay." Amanda shook her head, likely disappointed that she hadn't revealed something more shocking.

Allie was a little offended and decided to drive home her point. Hopping up from the recliner, she said, "C'mon." Norman jumped from the couch and followed. At her bedroom doorway, Allie looked over her shoulder.

Amanda still sat on the couch. "Well, come on."

Flipping on the light, Allie held her breath. *What am I doing? She's going to think I'm nuts.* She stood by her sliding closet door, fingers curled around its handle. Only one other person had ever seen inside.

"What's this about?"

"Brace yourself," Allie said. Then, before she could talk herself out of it, she shoved her closet door open. Instead of clothes, shoes, or linens like most people kept in their bedroom, every inch of the eight-foot by three-foot space was filled with neat stacks of books. Some hardcover. Most paperbacks. The tall columns disappearing into the closet's recesses.

Amanda just stood, gawking. "Wow."

"I write at least two posts a week. Sometimes three." She felt a little lighter now that she'd shown someone other than Kim. Her shameful secret didn't feel quite so scandalous anymore. Maybe a little crazy, but at least not so controversial. "I haven't read *all* of them. The ones on that side"—Allie pointed into the far corner—"I've read. The ones I probably won't read again are all the way against the wall."

"There have to be hundreds of books in here, Allie. Maybe even a thousand."

"Yeah." Allie shrugged.

Amanda leaned against the dresser. "Why did you

need a website again?"

"Kim thinks I do. It might help make a little money if I offer authors advertising."

Amanda snapped out of her daze. "Why would they pay to advertise on your website?"

"I guess I have a handful of blog followers. Authors might find that valuable. You know, because I already have an audience who reads my posts on a regular basis." She yawned. "And some of them make comments that suggest they're going to buy books I wrote about. So I might be able to do something like offer those authors a chance to have their titles listed on my website with a link to buy them."

Amanda pushed off the dresser. "Interesting." Norman lifted his head, following her pace.

Allie still felt a little unsure about it all. But for the first time in so long, she was finally excited about something. Truly excited. Even if her exhaustion masked enthusiasm.

"Can I see it?" asked Amanda. "This famous blog?"

Allie bit the inside of her lip. The only other person she'd ever shown was Kim. Showing Amanda meant making that web address not so anonymous anymore. But she'd already shown Amanda her closet. *What the hell?* "Let's go start the movie. I'll get my laptop."

Allie drifted in and out of consciousness as the movie played. But she'd seen it enough times to have memorized most of its lines, so waking up to watch random intervals didn't faze her. She expected to be chastised by her sister for being old or lame, but Amanda seemed sucked in to Allie's laptop screen.

"Al, these are great! I mean, they're really, really good."

"Thanks." She felt sleep flow through her again; she let her head fall back against the pillow Amanda had thrown earlier.

"I don't even read romance novels, but you make me want to start."

Allie's eyes fluttered open to find her sister engrossed in the laptop screen, her long ponytail falling across her shoulders. "Mmm."

"I'm serious. I want to borrow a couple of these. You make them sound so fun and witty."

Allie yawned, her eyelids blinking to keep from falling shut again.

"Kim's right. You could make money." Amanda scooped up a handful of neglected popcorn. "And you said a few followers? Try four thousand, two hundred and twelve." Amanda threw another pillow. It whisked overhead.

"You've got to stop throwing things at me."

"I know someone who can build you a website." Amanda yanked the popcorn from Norman's eager nose. "A good website. And he'll be cheap."

"He?"

Amanda wouldn't meet her eyes. "Friend of mine."

"How do I know he's reliable? Or good at what he does?"

Amanda typed in a web address, then shoved the laptop over to Allie. "He designed our school website."

She wanted to say she'd look at it tomorrow. But the site was unexpected, not boring or basic; quite the opposite. It was professional. Flashy but not overdone. Allie couldn't help herself. *Interesting.* She clicked through the different tabs, finding everything from sports schedules to online payment forms for lunch tabs. "This *is* really good. One person did this?"

"Yes."

"And you're sure you can convince him to build me one?"

"Yep." Amanda reached for a bag of chips on the coffee table. "I'll even help you come up with advertising packages. I have tons of ideas. Like you could have a daily deals page. And author spotlights."

"Hey!" snapped Allie, catching Norman's nose inside the chip bag. "How much is this going to cost me?"

Amanda heaved a sigh. "Always money with you." Before Allie could retort, Amanda added, "I'll get you a better deal than you could get anywhere else."

The old farmhouse was as glorious as Travis remembered it. The seven miles had calmed him after a frustrating day at the hardware store. *The paint needs touching up. And that broken railing. I could fix that.* The hole in the center of the front porch remained. Created when Allie had asked to go home early, before he was ready.

The house still held its timeless charm. The second floor featured a turret and a small balcony. *I'll fix that room up for Allie.* As soon as he finished with the master bedroom.

Pulling into the driveway, he studied the overgrown lawn. Pretty much a pasture now. *I'd mow it if it wouldn't draw attention.* He didn't need anyone, nosy neighbors included, in his business.

He parked his beater truck behind the house to hide it with the mature maple trees. It wasn't the same truck he'd had as a teenager. His mother had made certain she exchanged it for something unrecognizable, a dark blue Dodge instead of the red and white striped Ford. *Still, just as old.* It'd been too much to expect an upgrade.

The sun was sinking into the horizon. Travis grabbed two full bags of supplies, including the big cell batteries for his flashlight and lantern. He just needed to stay out of trouble for another week, and his mother promised to have the electricity restored. The knob and tube wiring would have to be completely ripped out and redone. *She cheaped out on me for everything else.* He didn't feel bad at all that it'd be more than she bargained paying.

Slipping through the back door, he set the bags on a card table situated in the middle of the kitchen. Most of the furniture he owned was upstairs. In the bedroom. It'd been his priority to make that room as livable as possible. His first week at the house, he'd slept in a tent inside the dining room.

Allie can live through a renovation as long as the bedroom and her special room get finished. He couldn't wait to see the look on her face when she saw what he'd accomplished. She'd be so proud.

When can I move in? she would ask the second she laid eyes on it.

Travis replaced the batteries in the lantern before

the sun slipped away completely. Mort kept him hidden in the back like an unwanted child. Kept him moving and unpacking pallets and stacking lumber till closing. He'd really like a beer after the pain-in-the-ass day at the store. He dug in the cooler for a drink, thinking on all that manual labor Mort couldn't be bothered to do if his life depended on it.

Mort and Travis had never gotten along, even when Travis' father was still around. *Mort's always been an arrogant, entitled asshole.* Resented his brother's family for their wealth. Resented that Lesley owned more of the store than he did, even after the divorce. *One day I'll inherit it and be Mort's boss.* That'd be a day he would treasure, when he could tell Mort what to do. Make him move around boxes of heavy tools. *Make him restack lumber for the hell of it.*

The lantern glow revealed a new patch of subfloor leaned against the wall in the kitchen. Material he'd had to pay for. The rest he'd managed to acquire, one or two sheets at a time, was upstairs. The entire second floor was ready for new flooring. The main floor would come last. But Travis had nearly been caught the last time he helped himself to a sheet of it. *Had to pay for that one.*

His parole officer Jed had caught him. The man had promised to check in a couple of times before he finally showed today. Travis thought at first that Jed was lazy, only checking in with him during their scheduled times in Norfolk. The meetings where Travis had to drive to see *him*. But Jed's game was more the element of surprise. Let the man cry wolf and you'd never know which time he was telling the truth.

But I plan to be the wolf, not the victim.

"You're not stealing plywood now, are you Travis?" Jed stood several inches shorter. Though Jed was in shape, Travis could take him. *I'm stronger.* But he hoped it wouldn't come to that. A life on the run didn't appeal to him. *One in Willow Creek with Allie does.*

"I'm fixing up a house," said Travis. "I pay for my supplies at the end of my shift."

Jed glanced at his watch. "That's about now, isn't it?"

Travis nodded. "Just about to head to the register."

Even if he hadn't been followed, Travis would've paid for the single sheet of plywood that day, just in case Jed decided to call Mort and double check. He had tucked his head further into his hat, hoping no customers lurked up front. His mother would have a conniption if anyone recognized him.

"You're lucky that mother of yours owns this store," muttered Mort, writing up the plywood at cost instead of adding the inflated markup Lesley tacked onto everything. It was brilliant, really. Just penny increases at a time, small enough that most people didn't really notice. And they'd pay a little extra for the convenience of not driving all the way to Norfolk.

"I'll be back tomorrow." Travis nodded at his parole officer, slipping out the back door to his truck parked behind the lumberyard. He knew he'd never get away with stealing all the materials he needed. His mother watched the books a little too closely for that. She'd expect to see the supplies that miraculously ended up in the house tracked in the store's inventory.

Lesley could be a micromanaging menace. But Travis had certainly helped himself to what he could. *It's not like she's hurting for money.* She could foot the majority of the bill whether she intended to sign the deed over to him or not.

He debated whether he should slip back into town for some additional supplies under the cover of darkness or crack open a beer and start on the sheet rocking upstairs. It'd been slow-going without electricity, working only until the batteries drained.

Beer won out. Travis carried a six-pack up the rounded staircase, the one that opened right next to Allie's special room. *She'll love the cone-shaped roof. She can do her reading there.*

In prison, he'd had the time to think and regret

giving her a hard time for reading those silly books. He thought she'd never forgive him for that. The memory of her tear-soaked cheeks as she watched her book burn had haunted him over the past five years.

But with her own room, with bookshelves filled, she'd have to set aside that anger. *She'll be thanking me for this special room the rest of her life.* Thanking him in many ways he couldn't wait to enjoy.

Sauntering through the landing into the master bedroom, he eyed Allie's picture tacked up on the wall above her side of the bed. It was like she was already here with him, even if he did have to lay low for a while.

Travis, come lie down on the bed with me, the picture seemed to say.

He swallowed the contents of his can and tossed the empty away. Sheetrock could wait. Right now, he had some lost time to spend with Allie's memory. A memory soon to be lying beside him in the flesh. To the photo, he said, "I've never stopped loving you, Allie. And I'll never let you go." Just like he promised as the troopers led him off in cuffs. Just like he'd written in his letter.

"You're mine, Allie, and you always will be. Don't you ever forget that."

Chapter 14

Even before the sharp rap on her office door, Lesley had foreseen a visitor. Glancing at the green marble clock resting on a shelf beside the door, she noted that Allie Jordan had gone home all of ten minutes ago. Crossing her legs and leaning back in her thick leather chair, Lesley called for Dawn, the Director of Nursing, to enter her office.

She struggled to hide an amused smile. Dawn, despite her hot-tempered glare, was hard to take seriously. Today she wore lavender scrubs with fluffy kittens in bright colors. Her happy patterned attire, short stature, and look of fire in her eyes reminded Lesley of a five-year-old about to throw a tantrum.

"Have a seat," Lesley said.

"No thanks," said Dawn. "I need to talk to you about

an incident last week."

Lesley's hand clasped her shiny black coffee mug with a gold saber paw print. Portraying the image of supporting local school spirit at all times was important. One never knew who might stop by.

"You mean the week you were absent?"

Restraint held strong in Dawn's narrowed eyes and pursed lips. Her hair, pulled back in taut military precision without one strand out of place, made Lesley wonder if the tight bun gave Dawn headaches. But she of all people knew beauty and a good image did not come without pain or sacrifice.

Dawn's cheeks turned a light shade of pink. "You skipped over the chain of command."

"You weren't here."

"Suzy's in charge of the ward secretaries in my absence. You completely undermined her authority."

"She never spoke up," Lesley said, her voice still calm as Dawn's escalated.

If Dawn's stance was supposed to intimidate, it was a useless tactic. Even from her chair, Lesley felt a foot taller. Her confidence came from years of never backing down. She'd do whatever it took. Always had.

Dawn's hands flew to her hips. "You didn't exactly give her the chance."

"And you know this because you were there?" Lesley

challenged.

But Dawn wasn't deterred. If there was one person who would stand her ground when all odds were stacked against her, it was Dawn Hammond.

"I trust my employees to be honest with me."

"*Your* employees?" The pesky woman made this too easy. A smirk cracked through Lesley's tough demeanor. "I didn't know you were promoted to hospital administrator." Lesley could see Dawn's military background seeping through. Her mindset mirrored that of a high-ranking soldier.

"My responsibility is to look after both the nurses and the ward secretaries." Lesley was impressed; *Dawn's defense is unfaltering.* Usually she had people in tears by now.

"What would you like me to do?" Lesley inhaled the wonderful aroma of Kona, and sipped her expensive coffee.

"This is my courtesy complaint," said Dawn. "If something like this happens again, I'm going directly to the Board." With that comment, Dawn dismissed herself, shutting the door just soft enough to avoid it slamming.

Lesley laughed, long and hard. Dawn's threats were empty.

Unlike her own. Lesley had enough to blackmail

every Board member—material that'd last her decades. Their positions were simply formalities. They knew Lesley Jamison made the rules. *They'll comply, as they always have.* Like when she implemented the new fraternization policy.

A crisp stack of letters had sat in the top tray on her desk since Allie dropped it off the week prior. Now that Dawn had confronted her, Lesley grabbed the stack and dropped it in the black ceramic trash can beside her desk. She'd never needed those policy letters retyped. Doc Herb's secretary had emailed clean copies to Lesley a week before his downtown office closed.

What I need is for Allie Jordan to realize she isn't welcome in Willow Creek. The week of terror she'd forced on Allie during Dawn's vacation was only the beginning of her plan to drive the pesky girl away. Most importantly, she needed Allie to flee town with her tail tucked between her legs so she'd not plan on coming back. It was the only chance Travis had at reviving his reputation.

Nick stood back from the dresser, a sense of accomplishment beaming through him. It'd been years since he'd invested any time restoring old pieces of furniture. He'd revived something abandoned. Something unwanted and discarded as useless was now beautiful again.

The six-drawer French Empire dresser had been painted over twice. Once black, another coat lime green. Some teenaged fad no doubt. It'd taken two nights just to strip the old paint and another to sand the dresser smooth. He'd enjoyed picking out new hardware and just the right stain, a darker color that'd complement the cherry wood. The coat of varnish needed to dry overnight. Tomorrow this beauty would be ready for a new home.

"Now, what am I supposed to do with it?" he wondered aloud, reaching for a rag. A thought struck him as he tossed the dirty rag into an empty basket. *Maybe Allie would know.* He inwardly groaned. He'd been trying for over a week to explain the message on his machine to Allie. "Miranda, you had some timing," he muttered.

When he'd come to retrieve his clipboard from the front desk, Suzy would mumble that Allie was on break or off delivering papers to the opposite side of the hospital. She hadn't taken her lunch in the old break room again. And he hadn't been quick enough to cross her path while she escorted patients to the exam rooms.

The barn didn't have running water, so he retraced

his steps to the house to rinse off his hands. He may not have Allie's phone number, but it might be in the phonebook. He'd like a chance to apologize. An excuse to hear her voice.

"Not listed." That seemed odd, considering how many other names he'd been able to locate in the short three pages that covered the entire Willow Creek area. Even Allie's mom, Pam, was listed. Rachel Jamison. Lesley. Ruby Rowe. Doc Herb was still listed with Nick's number. Luckily no one had figured that out yet.

He received a couple of marriage proposals weekly at the hospital, mostly from women old enough to have raised him. But still. It was nice not to have them calling too.

That's when Nick spotted the *Willow Creek Journal* on the kitchen island, hiding beneath the odd assortment of bills and solicitations. The black-and-white photo of him in his lab coat consumed half the front page. He read the first few lines. Typical things— his name; where he'd come from; where he'd pursued his medical education.

About to toss the paper off to the side, he caught an interesting line. *"Our newest citizen of Willow Creek comes with a big house and no family to fill its many rooms."* Nick shoved the paper away, shaking his head. *Might as well hang a huge blinking sign above my house inviting every breathing female.*

"They'd never print that kind of thing in a city newspaper," Miranda had commented the following evening when Nick told her about the laughable photo shoot he'd endured at the local park. "But that town wants you to stay. And they're eager to marry you off." He ignored the contempt in her voice.

"Could be worse," he told her.

"How?"

"They could've dug into my past. Figured out that I'm still legally married. That'd be scandalous in a town this size. Headline news for sure. I'm just happy they're trying to marry me off instead."

"Just promise me you won't go falling in love with some local girl before the divorce is final? I want you to make up your own mind."

Nick laughed, dodging Miranda's request. "No you don't. You want me to choose what you want." *Falling in love?* Nick shook his head. *What does that even mean anymore?*

The noise level on the call was quiet for once. Josh, Miranda's husband, had taken the kids to a baseball game. "It's not like it's a horrible choice to come back home to family."

Nick thought about asking if Dana had called her again since he left. She'd made an occasional habit out of pestering Miranda. He'd never been happier to have an older sister that turned to Mama Bear in a heartbeat. Outside of the meetings with lawyers, Miranda had kept Nick from having to see Dana since that awful encounter in his bedroom.

But asking about Dana would only make Miranda think he missed her. And he didn't. In fact, he hardly thought about her at all.

He heard a popping noise. No doubt the cork popping from a bottle of wine on the other end. "Drinking alone?"

"Actually, I've got a date with Johnny Depp," Miranda answered. "And a couple glasses of chardonnay before the kids are back tonight."

"Don't let me keep you," teased Nick.

"Talk to you later?"

He returned to the barn, proud that it now boasted a fresh coat of exterior paint. He had set out an old rocking chair that needed attention next. But instead of beginning with it, he crawled up into the loft.

With a little work, this loft could be a nice getaway spot. One where women with their casseroles hinting at marriage proposals couldn't find him. He'd not spent much time upstairs while working on the dresser, but it held an odd calm about it with nothing but a smattering of trees out one window and the sunset out the other.

He could lock the barn door from the inside and the rest of the world would fade away.

Four states away, Miranda was three glasses into her bottle of chardonnay when the doorbell rang a half dozen times. The obnoxious jingling nearly threw her off the couch. *Who could be bothering me at eight o'clock on a Wednesday night?*

She had a right mind to ignore the irritating doorbell abuser. Might be some religious group wanting to convert her. *Would she like to talk to them about becoming a member of the Holier Than Thou Church? No she would not, thank you very much.* Not with Johnny Depp in his sexy pirate hat luring her to stay on the couch.

But the ringing wouldn't stop.

Miranda set down her glass, careful not to slam it against the table. She'd broken a stem once before, when Nick had still been here and could stitch up her hand. Hard for him to do that from fourteen hundred miles away. She'd tried not to push him on the phone tonight. Thought maybe if she laid off the pressure to come home that he'd decide it on his own. But he didn't have to listen to Hallie and Joey asking where their

Uncle Nick was. Why he hadn't been over to the house.

"I'm sorry, but I'm not interested in joining your—" Miranda's words froze when she spotted Dana on the other side of the door. "I should've stayed on the couch," she muttered.

"Hi, Miranda." Dana smiled her gentle, almost genuine smile. Except she didn't have one of those reserved for kindness. No, the woman's only genuine smiles were reserved for her malicious intentions— seducing a husband's best friend, for example. "It's really good to see you."

"Go away." Miranda tried slamming the door, but Dana's unusually strong arm stopped it halfway.

"I just want to talk to him." Tears pooled at the corners of her eyes. Tears that might be real. Hard to tell with a woman who was so great at faking every emotion. Including love. "Please."

"He's not here." Again, Miranda went to shut the door, only to be stopped. "Do I need to call the cops?"

Dana took a step back, like she'd been slapped. "I don't deserve that."

Good. Let her squirm.

But instead of hurt, anger boiled in her startling blue eyes. Eyes that turned most men into instant idiots. They'd forget their own names if they stared too long. It wasn't enough that Dana possessed blonde hair in a perfect curl that brushed her shoulders, or a body most fitness instructors would envy. No, she had to have those eyes that'd set any man she desired in a helpless trance.

"You can leave now. Without causing a scene." Miranda kept her voice calm, collected. Despite her urge to scream and throw dishes.

"Not until you tell me where my *husband* is."

Miranda bit the inside of her lip to keep from retorting. If she made any mention of the divorce that was nearly finalized, Dana might do something stupid. She had to stay cool. Nick would never forgive her if she screwed this up for him. She was beginning to see why he'd needed to get far away. Not that she liked it any better. "I told you, he's not here."

"Well, where is he?"

Miranda shrugged. She hoped she looked indifferent. But with the wine in her system, she wasn't so sure of herself. "Why do you think I'd know?"

"Because he tells you everything." Dana nearly spit the words at her, as if she were a venomous snake. She hated not getting what she wanted. Of course, growing up with enough money to run a small country could cause a woman to feel a little entitled.

"Not *everything.*"

"This isn't over. I *will* find him." Dana spun around

and flew down the stairs of Miranda's covered porch.

"Tell him the divorce is off."

Chapter 15

As Norman watched from the doorway, Allie scoured through her bedroom's smaller closet—the one *without* the stash of novels—pulling out most of its contents. Piles of shirts, tanks, jeans, and capris now covered her bed, while a dozen pair of sandals littered the floor in disarray.

As usual, Amanda burst through the front door without so much as a knock. Allie kept scouring her closet for the right outfit. She'd become complacent with her sister's unannounced appearances.

Amanda called from the living room, "You aren't ready yet?"

"You *are* a little early, you know," she called back. She hadn't gone to the Summer Festival with Amanda in years. When she'd asked what had changed since she'd decided it wasn't "cool" to hang out with each other, Amanda's response wasn't flattering.

"Who else am I supposed to go with? Tammy's in Florida." Contempt had coated Amanda's words. Another hint as subtle as a gunshot that Allie hadn't made a decision about the California trip.

"You don't have any other friends?"

Amanda had shrugged.

"Not even the one who's building my website?"

"He's not really a friend. More of a...website guru."

Allie didn't press that one.

Falling onto the bed, Amanda said, "Why don't you wear that cute sundress you bought when we went shopping last?"

"You don't think that's a little too much? I mean, it's just a parade." Even as she asked, she knew it was the perfect outfit to get Nick's attention. Make him regret lying to her about that alleged almost ex-wife and kids. The bigger issue was that wearing this dress meant she'd be showing her ugly scar.

"The dress is, like, casual country." Amanda dug through the first pile of clothes, throwing garments in every direction. "Where's the belt?" Norman grumbled when a coral tank landed on his head.

"Fine. I'll wear it."

Amanda eyed the dangling sales tags on the dress.

"Were you *ever* going to wear this?"

"You're one to talk about what to wear. How did you get out the door without Mom demanding you change?" In her skintight purple tank and denim miniskirt, Amanda would get all the attention she wanted and a bunch she didn't.

"Never mind that. Throw that on and let me do your hair."

One hour and a can of hairspray later, Allie grabbed Norman's leash. She'd let her sister talk her into makeup as well. Though she usually wore a bit of mascara, she rarely wore more than that. Amanda had insisted smoky eyes went perfectly with her red, pink, and white dress.

"Off to the festival?" Ed, rocking in his swing, hollered from his covered porch.

"We are," said Allie. "Aren't you coming to watch the parade?"

Ed waved a dismissive hand through the air. "I'll roam downtown for the fireman cookout later. Heard they're grillin' steaks this year." He ruffled his newspaper. "Glad to see you two gettin' along. You young ladies stay out of trouble now, you hear?"

The two sisters and Norman set out on the hot afternoon walk toward the festivities at the local park. Cars lined the streets of the surrounding blocks since parking near the city park wasn't allowed during the Summer Festival. People packed the grassy one-square block, only about half of them Willow Creek residents. The town typically doubled in size for their annual summer event. Several blankets covered the park's area near the main road, where the parade would pass first.

"We should've brought chairs," Amanda said as they found a small shady space against the thick trunk of an oak tree.

Further from the road, Allie spotted a dunking booth, some sort of water balloon challenge, and next to the park's fenced pool, a petting zoo with a couple of miniature ponies, one goat, and even a llama.

To begin the parade, the fire department drove down the route, tossing out candy and spraying eager kids from their truck's fire hose. Norman tugged at the leash again, just as excited as the kids to chase after the candy. "You might be spoiled, but you're not *that* spoiled."

"Talking to the dog, I hope."

"Kimmie, you made it!"

"Well, I *did* have to call in sick at job number two." Kim snatched a Jolly Rancher off the curb and joined Allie and Amanda in the shade. "But I couldn't pass up this opportunity."

"What opportunity?" Amanda asked, glancing back

and forth between them.

"Don't give me that *I don't know what you're talking about* look," scolded Kim. "If you don't point out Dr. Gorgeous to me, I *will* hunt him down on my own, and I promise my way's a lot more embarrassing. I haven't gotten a good, respectable look at him yet."

The floats, sponsored by local businesses, rolled down the road next. The first was a giant black saber-toothed tiger, the town's school mascot. Behind that float, the local minimart had their employees dressed as a snow cone, a popcorn box, a fountain drink, and a hot dog.

"You're not missing much," muttered Allie.

"What are you talking about?" Kim posted her hands on her hips. "Did he—"

"Allie, dear, so good to see you." Aunt Ruby placed her hand on Allie's forearm, interrupting just in time to save her from answering unpleasant questions about Nick.

Aunt Ruby's bright green visor was as cheerful as the woman herself. Allie smiled. "Great to see you, too!" She wondered if there'd be a bridge game tonight, after the festivities died down. Aunt Ruby was famous for her late-night get-togethers that were likely not card games at all.

"I have a couple of apple pies at the bake stand."

She peered around, then leaning close to Allie, Aunt Ruby whispered, "You best get one before they're sold-out. Don't tell anyone, but I added quite a bit of rum."

"I'll do that." Allie patted the woman on the back before Aunt Ruby caught sight of another friend and whisked herself off. Her short little legs scurried halfway across the park, as though arthritis had never been an issue at all.

"Look at you, Miss Small Town America." Kim shook her head. "That right there is why you don't want to leave, Allie."

"Because an old woman *likes* me?" Allie sucked in a sigh. The last thing they needed was to argue today. It'd been a couple of weeks since they'd seen each other or really talked. She was excited to share all the details about her upcoming website with her, such as the different advertising packages Amanda had helped her create.

"How much did you bake for that little fundraiser?"

When Allie didn't answer, Amanda took the liberty. "Three pans of mint fudge brownies, two batches of blueberry crisp, and three dozen cupcakes. We delivered it all last night."

"Face it, Allie. You *belong* here. You can't…"

Kim's lecture faded when Allie caught sight of Nick walking down the street toward the park. Her heart nearly leapt out of her chest. Tingles flooded her body. Apparently time hadn't dulled the thrill that memory of their kiss created. *Stay mad, Allie. He's just going to leave and go back to some family in Georgia.*

"Did you even hear what I said?" Kim was certain not even a tornado would catch Allie's attention now that Dr. Gorgeous had stepped into the picture.

Amanda leaned in and whispered loudly, "I think she's distracted."

Kim followed Allie's eyes. "Is that what Dr. Gorgeous looks like with clothes on?"

Watching him walk toward the park across the candy-covered street, Kim stared in unashamed awe. *He's straight out of those ridiculous romance novels Allie obsesses over.* In his tan slacks and short-sleeved dress shirt, Nick seemed slightly overdressed for such a casual outdoor event, but no one seemed to mind. In fact, every woman within a fifty-foot radius had taken a moment to cast looks of approval. "I think I prefer him without clothes," Kim murmured.

"I recognize him from the picture in the paper," said Amanda.

Luckily one sister is still free from the clenches of a

trance, thought Kim.

Amanda added, "That's the new doctor."

"You have good taste, my dear," Kim said to Allie, patting her back. "I could lick chocolate off that!"

"Wh—what?" stuttered Allie. "No, I don't—I mean, I'm not—"

"You read that book too?" Amanda asked.

A little startled by Amanda's recognition of the melted chocolate scene from *Delicious Desires,* Kim asked, "Since when do you read romance novels?"

"Since I read Allie's blog a couple weeks ago. Didn't she tell you?"

Kim turned, prepared to demand Allie fill her in, but she noticed several women around her suddenly distracted, sneaking glances and trying to hide smiles. Some politely shoved each other out of the way. Others threw discreet elbows.

But even when Dr. Gorgeous was staring at the ground or blankly into the crowd, Kim could tell he was constantly fighting the urge to look at Allie. And despite Allie's firm attempts to ignore him, her eyes kept falling on the doctor.

"Do you see this?" Kim whispered to Amanda. "We might need a garden hose, just in case these two decide to act on primal urges that aren't appropriate for public eyes."

"Hardly," mumbled Allie, turning her back on the pack of vultures surrounding the man. "Let them have him."

Stealing what little attention Allie had left for her friends, the doctor stepped up from the curb and onto the grass, headed in their direction. Kim watched him seeming to act casual, pausing to say hello to others before he approached Allie. Trying not to act like he was a moth and Allie a lighthouse beacon.

With Nick ten yards between them, Norman jumped up, his tail wagging.

"Your *dog* knows him?" Apparently Allie hadn't told her sister near as much as she'd told Kim.

Allie shrugged. "Nick offered us shelter when the rainstorm happened. And dry clothes..."

Kim eyes went wide. "Say what?"

"Did you guys do it?" Amanda jumped in.

"What? No!"

"But you kissed, right?" added Kim. "You totally did! Allie Jordan, you've been holding out on me! I demand details." But Allie was no longer responding to demanding questions.

A few yards from them, the doctor was again cut off by a couple of women, Rachel Jamison being one. The man was polite, noted Kim. *It takes a well-mannered man to stomach Rachel.* She looked sweet and as innocent as a puppy with her big blue eyes. But Kim, like every other girl who'd played volleyball in high school in the last seven years, knew better.

"Poor guy," said Kim. "Already victim to the vultures of this town and he hasn't been in the park more than five minutes."

Ms. Jamison was the toughest coach at the school. She rarely gave compliments to even the best players, but dished out insults like the crabby Lunch Lady only too happy to scoop a sloppy helping of mystery meat onto every student's tray. Even the football players were happy they had a more compassionate coach, and Kim knew that was saying something.

"She just doesn't quit," muttered Allie.

"Do I detect a hint of jealousy?" Kim asked, not expecting an answer. Ms. Jamison was gorgeous and only a few years older than Allie, probably about the same age as the doctor. With her wavy blonde hair and cute little khaki shorts showing off her petite figure, she caught more than a few eyes.

But it seemed Rachel was only interested in the doctor. Kim wanted to drop kick her. Besides the fact that she was prolonging Kim's official introduction with Dr. Gorgeous, Ms. Jamison had made all three of their lives a living hell in high school when it came to volleyball.

"So why aren't you two officially a couple yet?" Amanda asked, probably noticing like Kim, that the doctor kept sneaking glances through the vultures.

"Yeah, Allie," Kim chimed in. "Why is that?"

"Because he's a jerk."

Kim studied Allie. *This is news.* "The way you keep undressing him with your eyes doesn't seem to agree with that statement. What did he do?"

"Doesn't matter," muttered Allie.

"He *is* single, right?" Amanda asked.

"For now."

Kim picked up another Jolly Rancher from the ground. *Grape. It'll have to do.* "Because you intend to do something about that, right?"

"I'm leaving in less than a year. No point."

"You need to stop clinging to that pathetic excuse," said Kim. Allie had no other plans, and even though she talked often about leaving Willow Creek, she changed her mind once a week about where that somewhere else might be. *She's only planning to leave because that dipshit will be out on parole for a week; two weeks tops before he lands his bony ass back in jail.* "You're lucky we're in public." Kim sucked in an outburst building in her chest. "Or I'd scream at the top of my lungs at your stupidity. I love you, Al. But sometimes you're really frustrating."

"But—"

Wearing a pair of faded jeans and a Cubs T-shirt, Alex Rowe stepped into their little circle, looking almost as sexy as his older brother. For years Kim had allowed Allie to believe that Alex was the man she'd crushed on in high school. Easier than explaining she'd had the hots for Evan, a man ten years older than her. *A little awkward to be fifteen and half in love with a twenty-five-year-old.*

"Hello, ladies," said Alex, shoving his hands in his pockets. "How's everyone doing today? Enjoying yourselves, I hope?"

"Great," Allie answered, but her attention was still distracted by the overabundance of interest the doctor was receiving from the town vultures.

"Alex! I didn't know you were back in Willow Creek," said Kim.

"I'm just here for a short while," he answered. "On a case, actually." Alex was a special investigator for the state patrol. Normally such a dangerous, sexy job would make him irresistible. But Kim had gone through a law enforcement phase herself. "Anything juicy?"

Alex laughed. "Yeah, right. You know I can't talk about it."

She shrugged. "Had to try."

Again, Allie seemed to have zoned out from the

conversation.

"Hey Allie," Alex said. "Are you doing okay?"

Kim and Amanda exchanged looks. *Does Alex like Allie too?*

"Huh? Oh sorry. I was watching the parade."

It took all Kim's restraint not to tease Allie about what the last three floats were. They'd rounded the corner now, out of their sightline. Kim would bet her car Allie hadn't been paying a lick of attention.

"Just wanted to make sure you're doing okay. Thought you might've left town by now."

"Everything's great."

"Glad to hear it. Let me know if you need anything."

"Look, here he comes," announced Amanda.

Was everyone but Kim oblivious to the territorial gaze in the doctor's eyes? Like Alex might be overstepping his bounds. *Good,* thought Kim. *Let him think he has a little competition. Maybe he'll up his game a little and get Allie to realize she wants to be with him.*

The doctor looked relieved, breaking free of the vulture ring.

"Hey, Allie."

Allie refused to look him in the eyes. "Hi."

It took a moment before he acknowledged anyone else in the group, starting with Amanda. "You must be the athlete I've heard so much about." It took another moment before he faced Kim. This man was more distracted than a sixteen-year-old at a car dealership. *Apparently that kiss has stayed with more than just Allie.*

"This is my best friend Kim," introduced Allie after an awkward silence. "And this is Alex Rowe. He's a detective."

Kim did a double-take at Nick. She could've sworn his face paled. The men exchanged handshakes, and Nick instantly turned the topic to baseball. Kim zoned out as the two compared teams and players. *Does he have something to hide?*

"There's a game on in a couple of weeks while the folks are on vacation. Cubs are playing the Braves. Supposed to be a good one," Alex said, addressing the group. "I was going to invite you ladies out to the house for baseball and a bonfire. Nick, you're more than welcome to come."

"Sounds like a good time."

"I've got to find Hannah, my little sister," Alex explained to Nick as he turned to leave. "She's supposed to be playing soon. Basketball tournament. Game's on at five." Again, the sports talk was aimed at Nick. "Allie knows the way if you need directions." Placing a hand on Allie's shoulder, he added, "Let me know if you need anything, okay?"

Nick's eyes narrowed at Alex's friendly touch. Kim fought the urge to jump up and down. As it was, she had to squat down to Norman and rub his ears to hide her gigantic grin. *So, Nick is jealous.* If all went according to plan, Allie'd be living out one of her steamy romance novel scenes with him tonight.

"Allie, can I talk to you for a minute?" Nick's voice was gentle, yet she still refused to meet his eyes. Kim nearly shoved her toward Dr. Gorgeous. "Please?"

"I don't know—"

"I'll watch Norman." Kim yanked the leash from Allie's grip. "We'll take a quick walk around the block. Find the poor guy some water. C'mon Amanda."

Allie finally drew her gaze from the bulging tree roots. She'd agreed to talk to Nick—against her better judgment—but what he said made no sense. "What are you talking about?"

"It was my sister. On the answering machine."

She laughed, but it sounded harsh, even to herself. "Of course it was." Kim and Amanda hadn't gotten far. Even in a dress and flip-flops she could catch up with them in under a minute. "Does that lie work on every woman you seduce?" She tried brushing past Nick, but he blocked her path. She collided with his chest.

"Miranda's my older sister. She wasn't happy I moved away."

"You just expect me to believe that?"

Nick shoved his hands into his pockets.

Dress pants, thought Allie. *Why does he have to look so good in everything?* "Look Nick, even if that was your sister, why did she say you're moving—"

Nick reached out, gripping her forearm. "Please, keep your voice down." She wanted to be angry, but genuine fear washed over his emerald eyes as he scanned the area. Every couple of minutes, their conversation was interrupted by someone passing, saying hello to one of them.

"Obviously we can't talk here," said Allie as she spotted a small huddle of elderly ladies making a beeline for Nick. "I have to get back to Norman. I'll be at the sand volleyball tournament tonight to watch Amanda. Starts at eight. That's your one and only chance to tell me the *whole* truth."

Chapter 16

At the park, Allie vanished into the crowd despite Nick's best efforts to keep track of her. He'd have to wait until tonight to explain Miranda's inconvenient message.

When he arrived earlier, he had spotted her in her sexy sundress that flaunted her bare legs the moment he passed the giant lumberyard float. He'd intended to walk right up to her. To spill the truth about the message right away. But within seconds of stepping off the street, he'd been bombarded with more potential casserole donors.

If the humidity wasn't smothering enough, half a dozen women immediately gaggled around him. A couple of them he recognized. Amy, with a sprained wrist from a couple of weeks ago, no longer wearing her brace; and Daphne, whose little boy, Max, broke his leg falling from his tree fort.

And then there was Rachel Jamison. Her blue eyes held a kind appearance, but he'd not been fooled. Despite her sweet words, he didn't miss the arrogance in her smile, as though she considered herself to have already won him as her prize.

"Nick, how great to see you again. I hope you're enjoying yourself," she'd said as he approached. He hadn't missed the wide eyes of the other women as Rachel called him by his first name. Apparently that was considered impolite. Scandalous, even.

"Hi, ladies." He addressed the group. One by one, he acknowledged the ones he knew by name, then was introduced to the others. Had Allie not been standing twenty feet away, he might've stood a chance at remembering these new names.

"You've missed out on all the good stuff," one woman said, holding up a ribbon for 'best dessert'. *Donna? Darcy?* He didn't remember.

When a man about his own age stepped up next to Allie, he felt irrational pangs of jealousy. An emotion he hadn't felt since he was a teenager. He politely excused himself from the crowd around him and made straight for Allie before anyone else could stop him.

When Allie first mentioned Alex was a detective,

Nick had felt a little sick to his stomach. It wasn't outside Dana's realm to hire a private detective to spy on him. But the longer he'd stood in that little group following the parade, the more he was certain that Alex was here only to talk to Allie.

A group of older women had interrupted his private conversation with Allie, but a part of him had actually been relieved. She had every right to be upset, but her voice traveled in the crowded park. If even one person overheard, he could blow his chance in Willow Creek. Tonight, he'd insist they take a walk away from the crowds... and he'd tell her everything.

Moments after her departure he was inundated with friendly hellos and compliments on his newspaper article—like he'd written it himself.

"Quite a bit different in Willow Creek than the noisy city, huh?" an elderly woman, Edna, asked, shaking Nick from his reminiscence. She'd been by often—proposed to him no less than three times. Once per visit.

"Quite different, yes."

Suddenly, an ear-splitting scream tore through the park. He immediately recognized it as a child's cry of pain and instinct shoved him through the crowd and toward a boy lying on the ground, near the jungle gym. The boy clenched his arm. Nick could tell there'd been a break.

In an instant, everything else disappeared. He became Dr. Bryant, instinctively calming the boy. He carefully checked for bleeding or any break in the skin. Finding no puncture wounds, Nick ordered, "Someone get ice. And tape. Edna, your newspaper. Roll it, okay?" Gently, he elevated the boy's arm above his heart.

"Is he going to be okay?" The boy's mother sobbed from the sidelines.

"He's going to be just fine," Nick said, his even voice meant to reassure her, his eyes never leaving the boy's. Tears streamed down the kid's cheeks, but the initial shock was over. "What's your name?"

"Tommy."

"Hi Tommy. I'm Dr. Bryant." Nick talked to Tommy as he taped the rolled up newspaper around the boy's broken arm. "Your job is to keep this bag of ice on your arm, okay, Tommy? We're going to take a quick ride."

They made it to the hospital easily enough via police escort. Tommy no longer cried. Instead, he chatted about his pig, the one he was preparing for the county fair. And his mother had calmed too, other than to scold Tommy. "I told you those monkey bars were dangerous."

"But Jared dared me to do it. I had to." Tommy ducked his head as Nick wrapped his arm.

Nick bit back a smile at the mother's scowl. He

imagined it to be a lot like Miranda's reaction should one of her kids break a bone over a dare.

In the middle of instructions, the exam room door burst open. "What happened?"

Tommy's father filled the doorway. Nick could see the resemblance right away in the shape of their eyes and upturned noses. He waited while the parents hashed out the story and Tommy received another scolding, this one a little harsher than the last.

"I'll need to see him in three days, once the swelling has gone down so I can cast it," Nick instructed.

"Of course. And thank you, Dr. Bryant." The mother smiled, genuine gratitude in her eyes. "It's lucky you were at the park. I probably would've called an ambulance."

"They'd have shut down the whole festival if my wife had any say about it." The father finally smiled, the panic and anger gone from his eyes. "Thank you, Doc."

"Glad I could help." Nick hoped he wasn't smiling like an idiot. It just felt so *good* to make such a small difference. If the incident had happened in Savannah, the chances of seeing the family again were rare. And they'd probably not recognize each other crossing the sidewalk.

But here in Willow Creek, Nick would remember

this Tommy for years to come. And how, instead of sobbing all the way to the hospital, he'd rambled on about Ernest, his prize-winning pig.

"I'll walk Tommy back to the park." The wife kissed her husband on the cheek and slipped out of the room.

"Let me buy you a steak, Doc."

Nick turned down the offer. He longed to go home, shower, and change to make sure he wasn't late to the volleyball game. But he quickly found that his polite refusal came across as disrespectful. Turning down a steak dinner at the Firemen cookout didn't seem wise. Not if he wanted to make a good impression on the town.

The sun slipped slowly toward the horizon as a whistle announced the start of the semi-final sand volleyball game. Allie, Kim, and Norman had been huddled around a picnic table in the shade for over an hour. Allie wondered if Nick had changed his mind.

As the sky darkened, so did her hopes. Maybe giving Nick an ultimatum had been too harsh. Especially if it really was his sister on the machine.

Kim would yell some bout of encouragement every now and then at Amanda's team, but Allie did little more than clap for the points they racked up. To make matters worse, she couldn't stop thinking about Nick talking to Rachel earlier.

It sent a surge of possessiveness through her veins. *Do I really have a right to be jealous?* She and Nick weren't together. *Rachel will still be in town long after I leave. Maybe the Ice Princess is a better match for him.* The thoughts kept circling: closer to his age, a respectable teacher and, according to most of the town, a great catch.

"You're worried he won't show, aren't you?"

"I think I got too caught up in all of this. I have to stop pretending there's something between us; that we're together."

"Stop it," said Kim quietly but sternly. "Don't sit here moping, because you know you're spouting bullshit. Every moment I've seen the two of you within a hundred yards, I can tell you're *both* thinking about that kiss."

"You can?"

"Oh, come on, Al. You two have been sending 'get me naked' eyes across the park all day long."

"What should I do?" Allie wondered aloud. "I don't want to get hurt. It'd be dumb to walk into something that'll just break me when I leave town."

Kim reached for her bottle of Mountain Dew. "Then

give him a real chance, Allie." Unscrewing the cap, she added, "Just be careful. You know this town. People are thirsty for good gossip. Rumors might have you winding up three months pregnant, forced to marry him."

"What are you saying?"

"I'm saying don't ruin his reputation if all you want is a little friction between the sheets." After a swig, Kim asked, "Have you told him you're planning to move?"

Allie shook her head. *Guess we've both got our secrets.* She expected Kim to lecture again, but instead, the two watched the remainder of the first set in silence. Norman had even fallen asleep. Dark shadows fell across the park, while orange lights above the sand volleyball pit flickered to life.

"Maybe we should have signed up to play," Kim said, breaking the long silence between them. "We could've knocked out Coach Jamison." She laughed. "You were a great setter, Allie."

"I thought you didn't play volleyball," came Nick's southern-rich voice from behind, the sound of him sending shivers throughout her body. He slid into the small space between Allie and the end of the bench, hidden by fallen shadows. Norman jumped up and trotted around the table to say hello.

"I used to." Allie held her breath. Heat resonated from Nick's entire left side. She stared at his folded hands on the picnic table, remembering how they'd felt against her cheek, her neck, her back. *Focus, Allie. You're still mad at him.* "I was beginning to think you weren't coming."

"Tommy's dad insisted he buy me a steak at the Firemen's cookout. That set me back a little."

"What do you think of our little town festival, Doc?" Kim asked. "And your celebrity status?"

"Not a big fan of the attention," he replied. "But what little I caught of the other things, the parade and the car show, nice."

"Doc Bryant?" Nick stood automatically; apparently he'd been summoned. "Darrel Handy."

Allie wasn't sure, but Nick's gaze seemed to ask for permission to leave. She nodded. *Guess we can talk later.* He waved a short goodbye and walked off with the postmaster.

"Cheer up, Al. He'll be back."

"Did I ever thank you for your ingenious idea?" asked Allie, feeling desperate to discuss anything else. "About the website and the advertising?"

"You're going to do it, then?"

Allie nodded. "Some boy half in love with Amanda is building it right now for, get this, a hundred bucks. And he's offered to maintain it for free."

Kim laughed. "I bet that's not as free as you think.

He just wants an excuse to be around your sister. And if free is the price, then he must be crazy about her."

Filling Kim in on the details and Amanda's enthusiasm to help, Allie stole a sidelong glance at Nick. "What's the score?" She'd like to know how much time she had before the game ended and they were forced to part ways. How much time he had to straighten out their misunderstanding.

"Amanda's team's up by three." Kim leaned back against the table. "If her team wins this round, they're probably playing Coach Jamison's team in the finals."

"What I wouldn't give to see the Ice Princess's team clobbered by Amanda's."

"Did you see that last serve?" Kim was laughing obnoxiously. "Your sister knocked that girl backwards!"

"I wouldn't want to be on the receiving end of a volleyball Amanda last touched," said Allie. "She knocks people over all the time."

"Are you planning on staying for the championship game?" asked Kim, yawning. "There's still one more semi-final game to play. The one the vulture is in."

"You think Amanda would be upset if I took off?" Allie's eyes followed the dimly lit path between her and Nick. He'd escaped the postmaster's longwinded conversation, but now one of their local farmers was engrossed in some topic or another, trapping Nick.

Would he even notice if I left?

"I have to leave soon. I have to drive back to Norfolk tonight."

"You're not going to stay?"

"Can't. Sorry."

"It is getting a little late, isn't it?" It'd be better this way, for Allie simply to go home and crawl into bed with a good romance novel. No heartache if she and Nick never picked up where they'd left off.

"If Amanda's team scores on this serve, they win." Kim basketball-tossed her empty pop bottle into a nearby trash can. "Do you need a ride home?"

"No," said Allie. "I think I'll walk."

Cheers erupted from the winning team. Amanda ran up to the picnic table, high-fiving them both and hugging Norman. "Did you see that last spike? I hit that guy right in the face. I know that sounds mean, but he was being a really big jerk to my whole team. I call it karma."

Kim turned to Allie and laughed. "Did I ever tell you how much I like your sister?"

Amanda dug in a nearby cooler for a bottle of water. "We have a pretty good team, but we have our work cut out for us in the finals." She chugged half the bottle in a matter of seconds. "You guys don't have to stay, you know. Gonna be a late game, and Norman looks sleepy."

"Are you sure?" Allie was grasping at excuses to stay, hopeful that Nick might come and sit back down beside her.

Amanda shared a knowing smile with Allie. "You've got blog followers to keep happy." Like she'd been let in on a huge secret. "I'll call you tomorrow and let you know if we win." She took another gulp. "Or if I don't call, you'll know why."

Following Kim away from the volleyball pits and into the darker areas of the park, Allie felt an irrational twinge of panic. When she halted suddenly, Norman growled. Low and quiet, but enough to set Allie's heart rate off the charts.

"What's up, boy?" Kim asked him. Allie's eyes were busy scanning the unlit area around them.

"Everything okay?" At the sound of Nick's voice, Allie relaxed. It'd probably been a shadow. A shadow that could belong to any of the dozens of people still hanging around the park for more volleyball and then the midnight swim.

"Yeah," said Allie finally.

Kim threw her arms around Allie. "Don't do anything I wouldn't do," she whispered. "And let him walk you home." When Kim pulled away, she said louder, "I'll call you tomorrow."

"Are you coming back to town for the baseball

game?" Allie asked.

Kim tossed a careless hand behind her. "We'll figure that out when I have more brain power. Nick, you'll see she gets home safe? I'm sorry, but I don't have room in my little car for everyone."

"I'll take care of her." Nick turned to Allie, his face half cast in shadows, his green eyes drenched in desire. Allie swallowed. How was she expected to stay mad when all she wanted to do was pull him into the shadows and roam her hands over every inch of his body?

Chapter 17

Rachel Jamison knew she'd have her work cut out for her as she watched the trio from the picnic table get up and slink out of the park, as though they could hide unnoticed in the shadows. *Let Allie have her fun*, she thought. *It won't last long.*

Earlier in the afternoon, she felt Nick's eyes slip beyond her to that pesky girl. But she also recognized the interest in his eyes, surely reserved for her. Either way, it wouldn't be long—just as soon as Lesley implemented her new hospital policy—before he felt desperate to divert the attention he and Allie were receiving. Sometimes her sister's meddling worked in her favor.

"You ready?" nudged a teammate. "We're up."

Rachel gave her a devious smile. This game would

be a joke. She'd save her energy for the finals, when Allie's irritating sister would be on the other side of the net. Maybe she could scare her off the team too. Although it was a little much to hope for. Amanda fought back, unlike Allie. She didn't suffer the criticism. Instead, she took it out on the line drills and spikes. Amanda could hit the ball hard enough to send girls somersaulting backwards.

Allie was a much easier target.

If Rachel had learned one valuable lesson from her sister, it was that you had to be willing to do whatever it took to get what you wanted in life. A future with the local doctor appealed to Rachel very much. Dr. Nicholas Bryant would be hers by the end of the summer. Of that, she was certain.

Two blocks from the park, the buzzing of locusts and soft chirping of crickets filled the night air. The further he and Allie walked from the volleyball tournament, the calmer Nick felt.

While chatting with a local farmer named Archie on the way to find Allie, he heard a low, rumbling sound he hadn't been able to place. The air had felt thick and uneasy, as though lightning might strike at any moment.

Finding her near the swings, he realized the noise he heard was only Norman growling. Once he reached Allie, the dog quieted and the odd tension in the air dissipated. He didn't care that his abrupt departure surely worked against him meshing with the locals as a dozen heads had turned to watch him trot after Allie. He only cared that she seemed safe now.

"I met your neighbor at the steak cookout."

"Ed?"

"Yeah." Nick explained how they ended up at the same table. He left out the part about Ed grilling him like a father might have. Despite the intimidating encounter, Nick felt better knowing Allie had someone like Ed in her life.

"Ed's great," she said, pushing her hair off her shoulders, and revealing a neck Nick very much wanted to trace with his lips.

He swallowed. *Get this out of the way.* "Like I mentioned earlier, my sister Miranda was the one who left that message on my machine." Allie didn't so much as turn her head, so Nick continued. "She took me in when I caught Dana with my best friend. I stayed with her family for almost nine months. I'm not sure I could've continued functioning as a doctor had it not been for her. She and her chaotic family kept me sane."

There, he'd said it.

She continued giving him the silent treatment. He kicked at a loose rock and watched it skitter ahead. "Look, I met Doc Herb in Florida almost three months ago. Complete coincidence, but meeting him is how I ended up here. Everything in Georgia reminded me of my failed marriage." Nick watched Norman tug against the leash. "I wanted to get as far away as I could. All I've ever wanted as a doctor is to remember a patient's name when I pass them on the street. To remember that Tommy Johnson has a prize-winning pig named Ernest."

Though her eyes stayed locked on the street ahead, he spotted the faintest smile across her lips.

He took a deep breath. He'd bottled so much of this inside for the past six weeks he didn't realize how liberating it would be to get everything off his chest. "I'm on a trial period. I have three months to prove I'm a good doctor. Prove I mesh well in town. If I don't fit the bill, I move back to Georgia."

Allie turned her head at that.

"I'm not allowed to tell anyone because it could cause a little panic if people knew I was such a flight risk."

"But the message—"

"Miranda thinks I'm mostly waiting out the divorce

to be finalized. She doesn't think I'll want to stay after it is."

"Do you?"

"So many things have gone wrong since I left Georgia. You wouldn't even believe the list if I told you the half of it. Like the breaker blowing and frying my dryer? I thought it was all a sign I was supposed to leave. But there have been a few things that have gone right."

Allie looked away. "Oh?"

"Like helping Tommy. Discovering a woodworking shop in my backyard. Befriending a German shepherd who doesn't want to tear off my limbs."

Allie giggled.

"Meeting you."

"Nick, I—"

"So, I think I've let you off the hook long enough," Nick said, interrupting her before the conversation became too awkward.

"What are you talking about?"

"You owe me a secret." It was time he found out once and for all who'd made Allie ashamed of her reading. He'd like to punch that person in the face. He yearned for her to overcome her shyness at the track or in the old break room. Even just enough to let Nick see the covers.

"Something no one else knows?"

"Yeah." His eyes dropped to her loose hand. The one closest, not holding a leash. He yearned to take it in his own, but worried she might pull back like she'd been doing for weeks. "I think you at least owe me one after all the secrets I just shared."

"I've almost tipped a cow."

Intrigue hit Nick before disappointment. He wanted to press her for something deeper than a cow-tipping story that sounded cliché for a Nebraskan. But curiosity won out. "Almost?"

Nick shouldn't have looked at her in that moment. Her eyes locked with his, a look that made his blood rush. Had they not been in the middle of town, he'd have kissed her.

"Out in the country, there's an old haunted house." Allie's words were nonchalant. Like it was commonplace to talk of ghost stories. "One night, Kim and I parked a half mile away and trekked through a cornfield. A caretaker lives on the other side of the road, so we had to be sneaky. But I'd always been curious whether the rumors were true."

"What does this have to do with cow-tipping?"

"Quiet," she scolded, her eyes playful. "My secret."

He threw up his hands in surrender, fighting his inner urges to pull her into the shadows and kiss her until her toes curled.

"Well, the house was boarded up. The barbed wire fence around the yard, turned out, was more for keeping cows in than keeping us out. A small herd found us pretty interesting. Ended up chasing us onto the porch. We saw headlights shining from across the road and knew we had to do something to create a diversion. And then we saw a few cows in the corner of the pasture, sleeping near the barn.

"It was reckless, thinking back on it now. It was in the opposite direction of the car, but we snuck through the trees anyway, and a few cows followed."

Allie paused, peering over her shoulder. Instinctively, Nick followed her glance but saw nothing. "It takes a lot of strength to tip a cow. Neither of us had tried before, and after two solid shoves, it woke up pretty pissed-off. So not only did we have an angry farmer with a shotgun on his way to investigate, but an outraged twelve-hundred-pound cow, too."

"How'd you get away?"

"I've never run so fast in my life." Allie grew quiet, looking down at the ground as if she knew she were lying but unwilling to admit why. "Kim and I barely made it to the fence before the herd reached us. The leg of her jeans actually got caught. Somehow, we yanked it off about a second before a spotlight shone along the fence."

"So, this is what you small-town folks do for entertainment?"

Allie shrugged. "We make the best of what we can."

They'd reached the end of the road. Straight ahead, the track field waited. Turning east, Nick felt the night coming to a close, something he couldn't let happen. "I take it you didn't get thrown in jail?"

Allie looked away. "No."

Did I say something wrong?

She changed the subject. "Rumor has it you've finished painting your barn."

If we walk through that dark field to the tree line, we might just get to my place without anyone noticing. He wasn't concerned, but Allie, the way she kept glancing around, seemed worried someone would spot them. "Did the rumors mention I've been fixing up the loft too?"

She had a funny expression on her face, as though she was imaging something grungy. "I've never been in a barn that didn't have a bunch of hay and field mice. And bugs. I can't imagine what you'd want to fix up in an old, dirty barn."

"Then I have no choice," said Nick. "I'll have to prove you wrong."

She glanced over her shoulder again. No one was

about, and houses around them had darkened windows. If anyone was spying, well, what did it matter?

Visibly relaxing, she gave him a suggestive smile. "Good luck."

Turning down the dark road beside the track field, Allie and Norman followed automatically. In seconds, they'd be in dark shadows. Safe from prying eyes.

What am I doing? Allie knew she should go home. Knew she should turn around right now before they reached a point of no return. If she followed him to the barn, she just might fall too far. Too far to turn back.

She unclipped Norman's leash; he'd stay close by. They cleared the thick row of trees on the west side of Nick's house.

"It's a little bumpy through here." Nick secured her hand in his. The warmth of his touch had her entire body responding. Every nerve tingling. This was her last chance to turn around. To run. But the thought of kissing him again pushed rational thoughts toward whispered silence.

He dropped her hand to open the padlocked door. She turned away, hoping he wouldn't sense disappointment. Just because she was thinking inappropriate romance novel worthy scenes didn't mean he was. He'd been talking about his furniture restoration projects, the loft. Maybe he just wanted to show them off.

But once inside, they passed a beautiful cherry wood dresser without him so much as pointing it out. He headed right for a ladder on the opposite wall.

"This is gorgeous, Nick." She couldn't help herself. The dresser looked like it belonged in a magazine. "Did you do this?"

"Yeah." He slid his hands into his front pockets and she forgot all about the dresser.

Most men she met would've been rambling about their accomplishment given the first opportunity, but Nick seemed too reserved to brag.

"What are you planning to do with the furniture you fix?"

Nick shrugged. Norman circled the open area, spotting a folded blanket in the corner. "Sell it, probably. Ready to come up?"

She lifted her eyes up the length of the ladder to the floor above. "You promise there's no mice?"

"Maybe one or two," he teased, hands already on the rails. "Follow me. Unless you're afraid?"

The small challenge left Allie unable to do anything but oblige. She scurried up after him. He waited at the top to guide her to solid flooring. His strong arms pulling her to safety; she let herself fall against him.

She'd have stayed there, against his chest, had he not pulled her away from the gap in the floor. Stretched wide enough to be a manhole, a person might fall straight down to the floor below. He gently released his arms, his touch fading.

But Allie's skin tingled with sensation.

"This isn't what I expected." She studied the maple paneled walls. "It doesn't look like a barn loft at all." In one portion of the open room, an architect's desk stood like a podium. On the opposite wall stood built-in cabinets and a small refrigerator.

"Not so worried about mice now, are you?" With only the light of a dimly lit bulb dangling above the desk, the shadows cast mysteriousness over Nick. Something she'd read about in way too many novels.

Norman chose to bark from below just then.

After hollering down to the dog, Allie asked, "What's behind the door?" She approached the single door set in the middle of the back wall—a wall that extended only ten feet or so, then stopped. The weak light spilled across the top of the wall, then into the open space between the prow roofline. *Another room.*

Nick studied the door so intently she expected it to open all its own. "A little lounge area," he replied. He ran a hand through his dark hair, unruly from the windy walk from the park. "Would you like something to drink?" He walked to the mini fridge. "I've only got bottled water. And some Gatorade."

She really should leave the door alone. She grinned. "Let me guess, are you hiding a dead body in there?" She put the subject behind her and neared the mini bar. "Water's good." Nick handed her a bottle, their fingers grazing. Electricity pulsed through her body. *Does he feel it too? Or have I read too much?*

"It's just not finished, is all."

She had forgotten all about the door until Nick's eyes trailed back toward it.

"Too unfinished to show me? I mean, you brag about this loft being so great—"

Nick grabbed her hand, leading her to the door. "It's a work in progress." He threw the door open, allowing Allie to enter first. A blanketed mattress sat on a wooden platform in the middle of the room. She swallowed, forcing herself to focus on the other details. The maple paneled walls—half of them stained, half of them sanded bare. A rocking chair in the corner that didn't look like it'd support a starving cat. The windows on either side—one overlooking sunrises, and the other, sunsets.

Allie rushed to the west-facing window, setting her

bottle of water on a wobbly corner table. "It's beautiful from up here. Look! You can see the town. And hundreds of lightning bugs."

Nick came up behind her, the heat of his body engulfing her through her thin sundress. Reaching over her shoulder, he pushed the window open. "It's a little stuffy in here. Probably smells like varnish."

She hadn't even noticed.

Music seeped in through the cracked window. "The street dance. If only I wasn't—"

"What's wrong?" Nick whispered against her ear.

The words struggled to free themselves from the clenches of her stomach. She released a deep breath. *I have to tell him the truth.* "Nick, I… It's only fair you know…" It didn't help that he hadn't moved from behind her, his fingers caressing her bare arms.

"What is it, Al?"

"I'm—I'm not staying in Willow Creek." *There.*

"Mm-hmm." His lips were so close that she felt the vibration of his words against her back. "Ed told me that."

"He did?" As much as she longed to look over her shoulder, she couldn't bring herself to turn around. Hot breath tickled her neck. "You don't care?"

"Let's just say Ed and I had a nice chat."

Warm lips grazed her shoulder, slowly making their

way up her neck. When teeth lightly tugged on her earlobe, she gasped. "Will you dance with me, Allie?"

She spun into his arms, resting her head on his shoulder. Music from the street dance downtown filled the empty space around them. If Ed and Nick had talked earlier that evening, it could only mean one thing—that Ed approved. And if Ed trusted Nick, she could too.

As one song faded into another, Allie said, "It was my high school boyfriend."

"What?" Nick pulled back a little, but she kept her head lowered against his chest.

"He caught me reading my favorite book at a party. *Sweetly Scandalous* by Lillian Caywood." She waited for Nick to laugh at her, but he only spun her in slow, silent circles, so she continued. "We were at a bonfire, out in the middle of nowhere with some of his friends that I didn't like. They drank too much beer and things got rowdy. So I took a flashlight and curled up on the tailgate of his truck.

"I'd read three chapters before he even noticed I was gone. But when he wanted to show off by jumping over the bonfire and I wasn't paying attention, he wasn't happy. He ripped the book from my hands—" She had to take a break because a tear fell. Then another. "Told me only desperate middle-aged women read those pieces of trash."

"Allie, what that—"

"He ripped it out of my hands and threw it in the fire." Tears streamed down her cheeks. "He's the reason I hide the books I read. I've had enough chastising from him to last me a lifetime. I don't need anyone else mocking me."

She felt Nick's muscles tense beneath her touch. The dim light bulb flickered. "That's the secret I should've shared earlier. It's just, I've never told—"

"Shh." His hands caressed her back. She'd never felt safer than here, wrapped in his embrace. She knew from his gentle, protective touch that he'd never try to destroy something she loved. "You didn't deserve what he did to you." The words were barely above a whisper, but she didn't miss the sharp edge. "He didn't deserve you."

As much as she tried to focus on the slow country music floating into the room mixing with the scent of varnish, another heavy tear fell anyway.

Nick lifted her head from his shoulder, a warm hand cupping her cheek. His thumb brushed away the next tear before it escaped her cheek.

She hadn't realized she'd been staring at his lips until they lowered, meeting her own.

Every nerve tingled, and desire flooded her body.

Desire she'd bottled since the day she'd first seen Nick playing with her dog. Desire she'd shut out after their first tumble on his stairs.

Desire that'd been dormant for years.

Within seconds Nick had her pinned against the boxy mattress platform in a passionate kiss. Hands cupping her bottom, he hoisted her up in one swift motion, placing her on the raised mattress. It was easier to kiss him from this height. She could hardly keep track of her own hands, much less his. She only traced the hot sensation roaming restlessly from her neck and down her arms, traveling all over her back.

Every kiss, every touch, felt so right. So natural. So incredible. She never wanted to be without this.

Nick pulled back from her, just enough to look her in the eyes. "It's been torture waiting to kiss you again." His intense gaze was intimidating. Allie felt that he could see everything about her in that stare. All her secrets, all her fears and dreams. "Even more so with you in this dress. Allie, do you have any idea what you do to me?"

Both hands roamed to the sides of her neck; he drew her closer. How a man was capable of using his lips so perfectly was a mystery she never wanted to solve.

A soft moan escaped Nick's lips as her fingertips flicked the top two buttons and found his firm chest.

She wanted to memorize every inch of his skin, and her first touch made her heart pound in her ears. She felt defined muscles, hot skin. Her hands trembled as they slowly undid the remaining buttons. Nick helped his shirt fall to the floor.

It had been years, and her body ached for Nick as it had never ached for another man. She kissed his neck until he lifted her onto the bed and slowly crawled on top of her. The moonlight streaming in through the window along with muted strains of music revealed his magnificent physique. Allie swallowed, lost in the ecstasy that Nick was about to make love to her.

Sliding his hands up the length of her legs, her dress bunched near her waist. Her breath hitched as he ran his hand over the hideous scar on her calf. Mortified, she tried to pull her dress back down. Eyes hot, he caught her hands and pulled them over her head.

He hadn't paid any attention to her scar.

His lips crushed against hers, his tongue demanding entry. One hand slid a dress strap off her shoulder. Releasing her wrists, both of Nick's hands cupped her breasts. She moaned in sheer delight. Her legs wrapped around him, pulling his body closer to hers. Revealing how strong his desire was for her.

Nick traced kisses from her neck to her collarbone.

His lips forced the front of her dress lower. He was only inches from her erect nipple. A loud beeping echoed through the room.

"*Nooo*," Nick groaned. One hand inched away from her, reaching for his waistband.

"What is it?" A surge of frustration coursed through her. *Is he really checking his phone right now?*

"On call this weekend." Nick cussed beneath his breath. "I have to go."

"Now?"

He sat back on the bed and handed Allie his phone. "I save that obnoxious beep for hospital calls."

A text message: *Possible concussion. Come immediately.*

"Oh."

"I bet that sister of yours knocked someone unconscious with one of her Hulk spikes. Be sure to tell her I said thanks." He held her face between his palms and kissed her.

She wanted to tell him she'd wait right here until he was done. But that'd sound too eager. And Ed would know if she didn't make it home soon. He'd worry. Maybe even enough to call her mom.

Nick slid his shirt over his shoulders and fastened the buttons. "I'll give you two a ride home."

Staring at the floor was easier than meeting his

eyes. She couldn't be upset that he was being a good, responsible doctor. After waking Norman, Nick locked the barn. A long kiss lingered on her lips. Walking to his truck, Nick pulled her to him and whispered, "We *will* pick up where we left off."

Chapter 18

Seeing Allie at the park with that doctor trailing her had almost been enough to send Travis over the edge. It'd not been hard to figure out she had something going on with the new doctor. Even from the back room of the hardware store, he heard people buzzing about it.

Now, Travis crushed an empty pop can in his hand as he watched Allie from the concealment of his old truck. *Doesn't she know she belongs to me?*

In the park, it had required every ounce of restraint he had to avoid stepping from the shadows, even though her dog looked like he might cause some damage. Besides, the house wasn't quite ready. The staircase needed repairing, and he'd only started building the bookshelves for her special reading room.

Five years in prison had been tough, but he'd kept a

single photo of Allie in her little track uniform and short shorts that had brought him much pleasure in such a miserable place. *Pleasure she's about to give someone else.*

Almost three weeks he'd waited, Mother insisting he not let anyone know he was around. Especially Allie. *Stupid.* He only kept his distance so Lesley wouldn't bulldoze the house. A house that'd be ready for Allie to move into in just a few weeks.

Watching Allie and the doctor slip into the shadows under the trees, he figured she had simply gotten confused about who she belonged to. Forgotten the dreams they made together at the old house. Forgotten about his letter. But once she saw those dreams realized, she'd come around.

Approaching headlights blinded him. He quickly reached for his grease covered sweatshirt from the floor and tossed it over the gun lying in the passenger seat. If he was caught with a firearm, no more parole. He'd be sent right back to finish the remainder of his sentence. He would do anything he could to ensure he never went back again.

Fighting temptation to wait in the school parking lot until Allie left the doctor's house, he'd started his truck. He needed to finish the trim upstairs and continue assembling bookshelves. Lesley was adamant that no one in Willow Creek know he was back until the right time. And if it wasn't for her, he wouldn't have a job or any money for the house. But she had yet to disclose what that *right* time was and that irritated him.

His surreptitious visits to his mother's house were rare, limited to the cover of darkness to prevent neighbors from spotting him. But they'd been a waste. Mother didn't leave stray cash around like she used to. The hardware store job had been the only means for scoring a gun. Well, the job and his access to the register.

Driving away, Travis began plotting the night he'd surprise Allie. *I'll question her, oh yes. Need to know why she thinks she can spread her legs for another man.* But once they were through with questions, he'd make sure she understood that she belonged to him. That if she cared at all for that pathetic doctor's life, she'd prove it with submission.

He closed his eyes for a brief moment, savoring the fantasy of her soft, warm body pressed against his beneath silky sheets. Her legs spread for *him*.

When he opened his eyes, he didn't have time to swerve to miss the mailbox at the edge of the road. "Shit!" The truck smashed against the wooden post, sending splinters flying into a neighboring yard.

Travis sped off before anyone in the house came outside to see what happened.

Rachel Jamison tried to hide her smile as the nurse took her blood pressure. She was amazed how easy it was to fake a concussion. Of course, being Amanda Jordan's volleyball coach had its advantages. She knew what buttons to push to get that girl to spike the ball hard enough, making the audience in the dimly lit park think the hit had actually knocked her unconsciousness.

A volunteer EMT from the audience knelt beside her within seconds and Rachel struggled to play the role of an unconscious victim. *A lot like pretending to be dead in a movie.* The idea of being a famous actress had always had its appeal. But now even more so that she had played such a convincing role in front of a concerned audience.

"Do you feel drowsy at all?" asked the nurse.

"No, not at all. Wide awake, actually."

"I'd let you go now if I could, but the doctor needs to clear you. He's on his way. I'll just be down the hall if you need anything. There's some juice here on the table."

"Thanks." Rachel reached for the tiny cup. She was

quite thirsty from the game. After all, she had to make sure her team was far enough ahead to win before taking the hit, and that effort left her quite parched.

She stared at the zigzag patterns on the light-colored wallpaper, following them with her eyes, feeling a little like she'd won an Oscar. As the minutes poured by like molasses, she tried hard not to think what Nick might be doing at that very moment. She knew she'd interrupted his night with Allie, whatever that entailed.

Did he invite that twit over for a drink? She shook her head. She refused to believe he would allow someone like Allie Jordan into his house. That would set an expectation that wasn't fair for the poor girl. *It's not like doctors marry secretaries in this town.* In Willow Creek, doctors married accomplished women with careers. Business owners, head coaches, teachers.

Rachel nearly felt sorry for her in that moment. Allie probably thought she was in love. Rachel had learned that lesson at the age of fifteen. The sooner people realized that being in love was just an over-romanticized idea blown way out of proportion from sappy movies and ridiculous books, the better.

When the exam door opened, Rachel shook herself from bitter memories. She may not believe in love, but she could certainly imagine a future with this handsome doctor. "Sorry it took me so long to get here," said Nick, practically falling into the room.

"I haven't been waiting long."

Rachel reached to her temple, near the red imprint with giant volleyball textured stripes. She blinked feverishly and started to sway. Nick immediately went to catch her, his hand warm against her thin jersey. He'd be good in bed too, she surmised. They'd be companionable and have a decent sex life. What more could she expect out of a marriage?

"Have you been drinking fluids?" he asked after she was steadied and his hand fell away.

"I had a tiny cup of juice," she said. "I think I'm fine, Nick." Rachel stood and instantly fell back onto the table, with the assistance of his strong arms.

This is almost too easy.

This time he was closer, his face nearer hers. In fact, if he leaned in just a bit further, they might kiss. Rachel looked up in feigned innocence. "I guess I could use a couple minutes and a cup of water." She parted her lips, licking the bottom one just slightly. She caught the flicker in Nick's eyes that told her he noticed.

"You'll need more juice," Nick decided.

"Can't the nurse—"

He paused in the doorway. "Be right back."

Rachel sat up straight. "Dammit," she murmured. It seemed that she'd not interrupted in the nick of time.

That Allie Jordan had cast some sort of spell on him in that short absence from the park. It'd not stop her, but it'd make her efforts more challenging.

"Here you go," said Nick once he returned. She reached for the cup he offered. "Hope you like apple. It's all we have left. The kiddos drank us clean out of grape juice."

She swallowed the juice quickly. "Thank you." But he acted as if he hadn't noticed when she limply held the cup for him to take back. She was forced to set it on the tray next to the exam table. "How soon can I go home, Doc?"

Nick flipped through her chart. "I don't think you sustained any injuries that are concerning."

"Just one good blow to the head from one of your high school players, I hear," said the nurse, reentering. "Your sister's on her way."

Rachel suppressed a groan. Since she was five, Lesley had never let a day go by without reminding her how lucky she was. Lucky that someone was willing to take care of her since their alcoholic father was only good for bringing home a paycheck and loose, sleazy women. Tonight would certainly be no different.

"Great," said Nick with a little more enthusiasm than Rachel cared for. "Avoid any strenuous activities. No volleyball for a couple of days. Don't drink any alcohol tonight. Make sure your sister keeps you awake for a couple of hours." Nick rambled more about what symptoms Rachel and Lesley should be on the lookout for.

"I think I can manage," said Rachel, about to attempt to stand again. She hesitated. Hopefully the nurse would leave them alone.

"Can you escort Ms. Jamison to the waiting room, please?" Nick asked the nurse.

"Of course."

Rachel abandoned her final act of weakness when Nick slipped through the door and left. *Yes, Allie Jordan has bewitched him tonight.* Time someone shed a little light on Allie's scandalous past. Already, a plan began to formulate for Rachel to set things right.

Chapter 19

"If you were desperate to see me," Nick teased after closing the door to the exam room, "you didn't need to schedule an appointment, you know."

Allie kicked her legs nervously from her seat atop the exam table. "I'm sure you're expecting a marriage proposal like you get from the rest of your female patients. But you won't get one from me."

"No?" Nick scribbled on a chart. "Why's that?"

"I'm not that easy."

He scanned his notes. "Says you're here for birth control pills." Nick sent a wicked smile her way.

Allie blushed. She'd made this appointment weeks ago, only intending to refill an old prescription, before she knew little more about the new doctor than rumors lent. From now on, it'd be a thirteen-mile drive to the neighboring town for things like this.

"You have to stop doing that," said Nick.

"What?"

"That shy, blushing thing. You have no idea what that does to me."

She relaxed. Knowing she wasn't the only one forcing herself to stay calm, it was nice. Her fingers curled under the edge of the exam table, holding herself back from jumping into his arms and kissing him, an urge that overcame her every time she watched him walk by. "So what do I have to do to get you to approve my prescription?"

Nick took a deep breath, his entire body tensing and then releasing. "That's a dangerous question." His eyes darkened, making him seem less like a doctor and more like a lover.

Allie'd read a romance novel like this once. One where the heroine had a little fun with her situation. *I think I'll have some fun, too.* "Doctor, do I need an oral exam?"

Nick's head shook.

"Breast exam?"

He groaned.

"Should I remove all my clothes, Doctor?"

"You're lucky the nurse is due back any minute." Scratching a signature on a prescription pad, Nick ripped the paper off. "Or you'd be getting a thorough physical."

Allie swallowed.

Shoving the slip at her, Nick stood closer than he had since he'd entered the room. "Tomorrow night, the answer to all of those questions will be 'yes'."

A cloud of dust kicked up behind Allie's silver Cavalier as she turned off the highway and onto a gravel road carved into the gently rolling hills of corn, alfalfa, and bean fields.

Driving through the patchy gravel and washboards with Nick seated beside her, she knew if she didn't find a way to distract herself she'd likely end up in a ditch. It'd only been three nights since they made out in his barn loft, but she still had permanent images of a naked Nick trapped in her overactive mind.

She reached across the seat and rested her hand on his leg. "You never told me how you ran into Doc Herb."

"Met him at the bar he owns. I was, uh, watching the baseball game there."

Allie suspected he was omitting details, but let it drop. She merely wanted to keep herself occupied with small talk, not put him on the stand. The sun had nearly disappeared behind the horizon and soon the stars would be sprinkled across the sky against a half-moon. The last thing she wanted to do was spoil an emerging romantic mood.

"Are you sure you want to do this?" Allie still wondered how Nick had convinced her to take him cow-tipping. She could come up with plenty of romantic ideas that didn't involve parading through smelly pastures, navigating around cow pies. Like a moonlight picnic down by the creek, for example.

"It's one of those initiation things for Nebraskans."

Allie laughed. "That's your reasoning? If you wanted to belong, just wait until college football season. Show up to a game in red, and you're in. I promise."

"Not sure I can do that without my family disowning me." Nick chuckled.

"You know that the same farmer who used to chase me and Kim might pay us a visit tonight, right?"

"Part of the fun."

"If you say so." *What's sexier than a pursuit through a pasture with me probably tripping into a pile of cow poop?* Allie parked along an adjacent road, a quarter mile of tall corn separating them and the rumored haunted house. *We'll have to ride back to town with the windows open.* Not only would Nick not be interested in picking up where they left off, but he'd probably insist she hose off outside like a dog.

She didn't care. Leaning in to kiss him, she purposely pressed her chest against his. "You ready?"

The stars emerged one by one as she climbed over a hip-high barbed wire fence and led the way through an irrigation ditch into the cornfield.

Nick kept up with no problem. "Isn't this path a little wide? Someone might drive by and see us."

"I take it you've never had to detassle corn," said Allie over her shoulder. "If we take one of those narrower paths, our arms will be completely cut up by the time we reach the house."

Allie recalled the one summer she and Kim had decided detassling would be a good way to earn some quick cash. They'd been warned to wear pants and shirts with long sleeves, but with the unbearable heat they'd decided on shorts and tank tops. The edges of the long green leaves left slices on the girls like elongated paper cuts.

Tonight, Allie didn't worry about covering up. She wore jeans and tennis shoes. Her tight black tank selected specifically for Nick's viewing pleasure. She thought for a moment about forgetting the cow-tipping adventure, about tackling Nick to the ground. But making love in the dirt of a cornfield was about as romantic to her as rolling around in cow manure, so she trekked forward.

After nearly a quarter mile, she spotted a clearing up ahead. Behind a barbed wire fence—this one taller than the last, with wooden posts and rungs—stood a familiar patch of trees that hid an empty house. The last time she was here, every window and door had been boarded shut, as if someone was desperate to keep people out. Back then, the house had been illuminated by a bright street light. But tonight, the only light was cast by glow of the half-moon.

Nick came up behind her, wrapping his arms around her waist. "Are you sure no one lives here?"

"You see that over there?" She pointed into the distance.

"The blinking lights?"

"Those aren't lights. They're eyes."

"I thought all Nebraska country folk let cows roam around in their yards." He was teasing. Allie looked over her shoulder and kissed him quickly.

"Are you sure this is what you want to do?" she asked. "You do understand that I've never successfully tipped a cow."

"I don't think I can officially say I belong in Small Town, Nebraska without having at least *tried*."

The way Nick said *belong* warmed her heart. Any doubts she had about him wanting to stay kept fading.

"You know you can't really tell anybody about this, right? I mean, we could get charged with trespassing and a list of other things."

"Yep, got it."

Studying the tall fence, she concluded it was not electrically charged. For all the high school kids who came out here for the same reason she and Nick had, it was a little surprising that the old farmer across the road hadn't upgraded the security. *Maybe he likes scaring people off with his shotgun.* Protecting the property might be his greater purpose.

Clasping a thick post and planting her foot on a rung, she climbed the wooden fence. Once at the top, she hopped down on the other side, then propped her fists on her hips. "Your turn. Just be careful of the barbed wire. It likes to tear clothes."

Instead of scoping for nearby cattle, she fixated on Nick's body as he easily and effortlessly ascended the fence after her. He was wearing the jeans she recommended along with a worn T-shirt. She preferred this relaxed look to the more formal business apparel he wore at the hospital.

"What do we do now?" he asked.

She took a deep breath to focus on the task at hand. It wouldn't do any good to be distracted in a field full of twelve-hundred-pound cows, ones that would soon realize they had company. "Let's follow the fence down toward the barn," she suggested. "That'll keep us in the trees in case any of them get curious. I don't suppose you climbed trees as a kid?"

"Are you kidding?" said Nick. "Our backyard was full of them. I was in a tree more than I was anywhere else. My mom hated it because I had about twenty favorite spots, so I was never easy to find."

Allie reached for his hand and led the way.

"I'm surprised we haven't run into any cows," said Nick as they neared the two-story barn with chipped red paint. "I really thought they'd be mingling in the trees. Are they all asleep?"

Straining her eyes, Allie realized that the weak moonlight revealed an empty pasture for at least fifty yards in front of the barn. She began to sense something was wrong. "I know I saw eyes earlier." Bravely she stepped into the clearing beside the tree line. "Maybe they moved the cattle beside the barn."

"Looks like they forgot one." Nick pointed.

The broad-chested beast turned its head toward them, its eyes reflecting the light of the moon. But what made her heart begin to race were the arced horns on its head. "Uh-oh," she whispered. It suddenly made sense why the other cows were penned up separately. "That's a bull." She was no expert, but she knew cattle breeding usually happened in the spring. All other times of the year the bulls were kept separate from the cows.

As the bull started toward them, Nick asked, "Where should we go?" Even before he finished his question, the bull started to trot in their direction.

"In the barn." Allie yanked at Nick's hand, taking off at a dead sprint toward a man-door at the front of the barn. She crossed her fingers it was unlocked. She wasn't sure they'd have time to run in the opposite direction.

A few feet shy of the door, the bull began a full on charge.

Determined to break down the door if necessary, Allie practically fell into the barn when it shot open. Nick slammed the door shut and dropped a heavy wooden block to bolt it behind them. She was too relieved to wonder what they'd have done if that block had kept them from safety.

She shrieked involuntarily as a heavy thud rammed against the door.

"We should go up into the loft," Nick pointed out, "until he calms down. Just in case he breaks through that door."

"Good idea." She scanned the dimly moonlit area.

"Over here," said Nick. "I see a ladder."

Allie followed him up the rungs built into the barn's wall. Near the top, he reached for her hand and pulled her the rest of the way and into his arms. She was still panting heavily from the close encounter with the bull, and now in his embrace, she had little hope of catching her breath.

"Are you okay?" The warm breath that feathered her cheek was suddenly ragged too, but it didn't seem to be from their recent escape.

"I will be as soon as you kiss me." She lifted her arms around his neck and felt her body go limp as his lips trailed a line down her neck and onto her shoulder.

A warm hand gently shoved the strap of her tank top and bra down her shoulder. She backed up against the wall for support, lest she fall over from dizzy pleasure. Nick's lips hungered onto hers as she felt the other strap lower, followed by a cool breeze.

His firm hands covered her exposed breasts, massaging them, and she let out an involuntary moan. She wanted to beg him to make love to her here and now. She didn't care that the barn was most likely infested with spiders and barn mice, or that the most comfortable surface would be a bale of hay.

As his lips left hers, she sensed them hovering over her breast, then his tongue teasing her nipple. Her hands reached blindly for the bottom of his shirt, gripping its edge. Before successfully removing it, Nick's hands clamped down on her wrists. "Not yet."

With his teeth clenched around an erect nipple, she felt him slide his hands down her sides. Fingers feathered a caress above the top of her jeans. Allie moaned in delight, thankful the wall was there to keep her upright.

Nick undid the button of her jeans, sliding the zipper down. As his tongue ran along her collarbone, up her neck, along her jaw line, back to her lips, he eased a hand into her open jeans. The thin cotton of her panties the only separation between them.

Long, strong fingers pulled her panties to the side. "I love how wet you are, Al." The words made her shudder with ecstasy.

Nick stroked her clit, gently at first, but quickly it became more savage. His free hand pushed her jeans lower, off her hips. Allie gasped as a finger slipped inside her. Her legs about as sturdy as overcooked noodles, she gripped his arms to steady herself.

When he kneeled in front of her, she nearly collapsed. Jeans now around her ankles, his hot breath hovered, nearly making her cry out. Allie was already seeing a few stars when his tongue stroked her clit. His fingers slid in and out of her as his clever tongue worked its magic.

She gripped his shoulders so tightly she worried she'd leave bruises. Her body shuddered violently when she came. He wrapped his arms around her thighs to steady her.

Barely able to catch her breath, Allie watched Nick slowly stand, his desire for her evident, even through his jeans. She yanked him to her, managing to nearly remove his shirt when a bright light flashed in the window. At first, she was content to simply ignore it. But then panic struck. "It's the farmer."

"If we're quiet, he won't find us," Nick said, his voice a seductive growl. Allie nearly gave in as he suckled her exposed breast.

"He has a shotgun." Allie tried her best to sound firm. "He's known for being a little crazy. For firing off rounds when he thinks there're intruders." After a brief pause, she added, "And he'll find my car."

Nick froze, looking her in the eyes.

She nodded. "I don't want to go anywhere either, except over there in those bales of hay, but he's dangerous. And if he shoots and flattens my tires, we'll get in a lot of trouble."

The second Nick released her from his body and the wall, she yanked up her pants. Righting her bra and tank, she darted toward the window. "He's just unlocking the gate. If we go right now, we might be able to run back the way we came."

"And that bull?" Nick asked as he pulled Allie away from the window and toward the ladder.

Unsure of how to make any escape attempt sound reassuring, she didn't reply.

Nick said, "Follow my lead."

As if struck by a bolt of lightning, she dropped down the ladder to the first floor and lifted the heavy bolt locking the door. Nick inched the door open. To her relief, the bull was at least twenty yards away, more interested in the headlights at the far end of the property than the people he'd trapped in the barn.

"Now," whispered Nick." They shot out the door and toward the tree line along the fence.

At the first shotgun blast, Allie fought the scream that threatened to escape. She began to sprint even faster, relieved that Nick could keep pace. The two hopped the fence and dashed all the way to her car.

"I'm driving." Nick's voice was so adamant that she nearly gave in.

"No." She ran to the driver's side. "I'm a veteran at gravel road getaways. Get in the car!"

The keys rattled in her hand as she reached for the ignition. Another round fired—so close she knew the farmer was no longer parked in front of the cattle pasture. As she jerked the wheel toward the road, she caught a glimpse of approaching headlights.

"Hold on." She pressed the gas pedal to the floor. Her car shot forward with the force of a catapult. Too focused on outrunning the pickup truck in her rearview mirror she was careless about avoiding patches of gravel and her wheels spun as she lost traction. Many mischievous nights in the country with Kim had prepared her for this exact situation, leaving her confident they'd not end up in a ditch. She whipped the steering wheel strategically to the left, then to the right a couple of times until they reached the highway. She checked her mirrors again. Headlights no longer trailed them.

"Are you okay?" Nick asked once Allie slowed to the speed limit on the paved road. From the concern in his voice, she was sure he must think she was in tears. Instead, she turned to him and burst out in laughter.

"What a rush, huh?"

Nick cocked his head. "Anyone ever tell you that you run fast?"

Allie shrugged. "Maybe."

"Like, really fast."

She smiled demurely. "Runs in the family."

"Speed?"

"I may or may not have a school record, like my dad and sister." She hadn't talked about the high school track part of her life in years. She hadn't been able to face what Travis Meyers had taken away from her.

"What event?"

"Two-hundred-meter dash."

"Impressive."

"And four-hundred."

"Why—"

"—I hope you're not too disappointed that we didn't get to actually tip a cow."

Nick laughed, that low rumble echoing from his chest. "How many people can say they've been chased into a barn by a bull? This is the most fun I've had since I got to Nebraska."

"Glad I could show you a good time." It wasn't until she met Nick that she believed pleasure as described in her many romance novels actually existed. She'd lost her virginity to Travis, mostly as a way to prove he could trust her. But it hadn't been anything close to passionate.

And we haven't even done it yet!

"Hope that was mutual." Nick donned a seductive smile.

Travis always finished just as quickly as he started, concerned with only himself. Never giving her pleasure a second thought.

Allie turned a sharp corner down another gravel

road. "I want to return the favor." Half a mile later, she parked on a minimum maintenance road. Just a few yards beyond the tiny hill, her car would sit hidden in the darkness.

She unbuckled her seatbelt, kneeling in her seat to kiss Nick. Her short dating history hadn't given her more than a couple of comparisons to that selfish lover, no instances worth remembering. She'd never been so eager to express her gratitude.

Before she knew what had happened, she was squished in Nick's lap, the top of her tank top at her waist. The car didn't lend much make-out room, but she didn't care if her legs fell asleep. Just as long as he kept kissing every inch of her skin.

"Wait a minute," she said breathlessly. "I'm supposed to be showing *you* a good time."

"Oh, you are."

"But it'd be better if you stopped distracting me so much."

Nick's low laughter sent chills through her. She nearly had his pants unzipped when the blaring of headlights in the distance shook them from their passionate rumbling. Allie flew back into her seat, pulling her tank back into place as she scrambled. Her bra was a lost cause, tossed away in the backseat.

"No one's supposed to be on this road," said Allie,

panicking. She threw her little car in reverse and flipped around. The front of the car bottomed-out going up a hill, but she kept on the gas. No telling who was heading toward them.

Once back on the main gravel road, she sped back toward the highway to town.

An old blue truck tailed them back to Willow Creek until she turned down the road to Nick's house.

Sitting in his driveway, Allie sighed. "I'm sorry we got interrupted."

Nick leaned toward her, cupping her cheek in his hand. He kissed her sweetly. Deeply. "Don't be. I had a great time." He hopped out of the car and rested his forearm on the open door. "If I didn't have a full day of patients tomorrow, you'd be coming in. One of these nights we'll get to finish what we start."

Chapter 20

Allie let the flimsy screen door of her mom's latest fixer-upper project slam behind her. Pam Jordan stood on a ladder, twisting a screwdriver at a brass light fixture straight out of the seventies. "Allie, you're just in time. Come stand beneath this light. I need you to catch it."

"That's one of the ugliest fixtures I've ever seen," she told her mom, automatically lifting her hands to catch while Pam disconnected its wiring at the ceiling.

"You'd be surprised. I can probably get twenty bucks for this."

"You're kidding. It looks like a bunch of brass tubes with cheap candle flame bulbs. How does it even light up a room?" The wire from the ceiling dropped, allowing Allie to set the ugly fixture in the pile of items Pam was stripping from the house before she began demolition.

"Everything comes back in style at some point."

Yellow floral wallpaper and worn orange carpet made Allie doubt the validity of that statement. "I hope you got a good deal on this place. It looks like it needs a lot of work."

Her mom dismounted the ladder, shoving loose hair away from her face. Allie considered offering to help. It'd been months since she spent time working on one of her mom's flippers. Pam preferred to do most of the work herself. Any heavy lifting she got done by bribing high school football players with free pizza. But salvaging day was something Allie and Pam used to do together.

"Amanda told me you needed to borrow my hammer."

"Thanks, just set it down on that shelf." Pam pointed to a set of open built-ins that separated the living and dining area.

Allie deposited the tool and moved back beside her mom. "I have to check on Amanda soon." She chose not to elaborate that right now her teenage sister was at her house, alone, with a boy. Amanda's sort-of friend was building Allie's website, working out back-end details of the various advertising packages she had finalized just last night. "I can help for a little while, if you want."

"That'd be great. I need a hand getting the rest of the ceiling fixtures down. I think I can sell them all." Pam laughed at the look on Allie's face that showcased her obvious doubt. "They may be outdated, but they're in really good shape."

"I'll take your word for it."

Pam carried the ladder into the adjoining living room, plopping it near the ceiling fan. "I heard you and the new doctor are spending a lot of time together," Pam said, climbing up.

Turning away, Allie tried hiding her warming cheeks. And her ridiculously large smile. "We're friends."

"Friends?" Pam shook her head. The first screw from the fan dropped into her palm. "Sure, Al."

"What?"

"What are you going to do when you leave?"

Allie shrugged. "That's a long ways off, Mom. I have plenty of time to worry about that." Just because she and Nick had gotten a little carried away in a couple of different barn lofts didn't exactly lock them in for a wedding date.

"Hold your hands up." Pam eased the fan down to Allie. "I still think you're making a mistake waiting so long to go."

Allie started to regret volunteering to help; she bit

the inside of her lip. "Do you really want me to leave so bad?" When Pam didn't answer, she added, "Is it because you want a paying renter in my house? If it's such a big deal, Mom, I can start paying rent."

Pam managed to disconnect the wiring. "It's not that."

The fan teetered in Allie's outstretched hands. A dead fly rolled off a blade and dropped beside her flip-flop. "Then what?"

"I just want you to be happy, Allie. If you leave now, you can move somewhere you want to, not somewhere you have to."

"Move *now?*" Allie carried the fan to the pile of fixtures in the dining room. "I'm not leaving a whole year early. I'm not ready."

"Because of the doctor?"

Truth be told, that was a pretty big reason at the moment, but she refused to admit it. "We're just friends, Mom."

"Whatever you say, honey. You best go check on your sister before she gets knocked up on your couch."

"You knew?"

"Are you kidding?" Pam folded the ladder and set it against the faded floral wallpaper. "Your website is all she's talked about for days. That and the boy who's building it."

"I can come back over later." But really, she hoped her mom would turn down the offer.

Pam shook her head. "I've salvaged most everything I can. Go on."

Allie sighed in relief. She didn't need any further prying about Nick. She hadn't worked out herself what they were yet...other than eager to rip off each other's clothes.

"Your website is ready to publish," said Brenden Carter from Allie's living room couch. Allie and Amanda sat on either side of him. "If you're happy with it, that is."

"He can still tweak it after," said Amanda. "Right, Brenden?"

"Oh, yeah. Not a problem."

Tweak it. Allie tried not to pay too much attention to the exchange of demure smiles between her little sister and her sort-of-friend, Brenden. After the other night with Nick, she didn't know if she was witnessing the beginning of something between these two or if she was just wishing the whole world could fall in love.

"Publish my website!" Allie squealed in delight as Brenden pushed the final button.

"You're up and running."

"Let's try it out," said Amanda. "Allie, go grab your laptop. I'll use Brenden's and make a request."

Allie lifted her laptop from its usual spot. Excitement drained when she caught sight of Travis Meyers' letter. Dread swarmed over her. *What have I done?* She'd published a website. A website! Maybe her mom had been right, suggesting she leave town now. The entire world would soon know that she, Allie Jordan, was a crazy, romance novel-obsessed nut. They'd think she was desperate. Pitiful. A joke.

"Hurry up, Al!" called Amanda from the living room, snapping Allie from her spell.

Walking back to the couch, Allie forced away the negativity. If she needed any reassurance that she wasn't crazy, she found it glowing on her sister's face. Her tense muscles relaxed.

Even though it was a practice run, the first time she received an email request, she felt her insides tingle with excitement. *Someone can really request advertising on my website!* She suddenly wanted to share that news with the whole world. Maybe sharing her secret with Nick about Travis burning her favorite book had set her fears free. Released them into the universe never to be seen again.

"I'm going to post the blurb too. Let people know to

check out the new website."

"Allie, this is so exciting!" shrieked Amanda, hopping off the couch. Norman trotted after her toward the kitchen. Within seconds, she returned, three Dr. Peppers in hand. "I wish you'd let me post this on Facebook. Or at least let me make you a fan page that'd send people to your site."

Allie and Amanda had gone round about this very topic for weeks. It usually ended with Amanda storming off, upset that Allie wouldn't tell her *why* it was such a big deal that people knew what she did for fun. "Allie, it's what you *love* to do. You shouldn't feel like hiding that from everyone you know."

"Okay." Allie cracked open a can. "You can make a page."

Amanda's mouth dropped open. She sat frozen long enough to draw Norman's attention. He poked his wet nose at her jaw line. "You're serious?"

"Yes."

"Brenden, you were a witness." Amanda snatched his laptop from the coffee table, her fingers quickly navigating their way. "I'm making it right now. And you'll love it!"

Pushing himself up from the couch, Brenden set his pop on the table. "I have to run home and help with chores." To Amanda, he asked, "Mind if I get my laptop tonight?" She nodded, her attention already back on the screen.

"Thanks, Brenden," said Allie. "It looks great."

Brenden nodded, then slipped out the door.

With Amanda busy creating another social media account, Allie typed up her blurb for the blog—the one announcing her new website and the advertising opportunities she'd be offering authors. Before posting it, she decided to mention her fan page too. Might as well get it all out there at once.

"I'm so excited for you, Al! We should meet up with Kim in Norfolk someday soon and celebrate."

"Great idea." Allie wanted to share the details of her steamy evenings with Kim too. Just maybe not as many details with her little sister within hearing range. And maybe hold back the detail about the barn and that mind blowing orgasm.

"Just where the hell do you get off faking a concussion?" Lesley slammed the front door behind her. Rachel sat on the couch, calmly watching TV. Inside, she trembled. But she wasn't about to give her sister the satisfaction of detecting her fear.

"It's nice to see you too." Rachel slowly rose from the

couch and sauntered into her tiny kitchen, forcing each movement to be calm and collected. *Knew it was only a matter of time before she found out I was faking.* "Can I fix you a drink?"

The coldness in Lesley's eyes said that what she wanted was to rip Rachel's throat out, but she would never turn down a drink.

Rachel pulled out two glass tumblers from a cupboard as the TV went off. Swallowing her fear, she handed Lesley a couple fingers of straight Jack Daniels.

"You have some nerve interfering," said Lesley after a gulp. "You know I've got plans for that doctor."

Time to be brave. "Using him as a ploy to run Allie Jordan out of town is a poor plan." The flames in Lesley's eyes warned Rachel she better defend that claim. "You're going to ruin Nick's reputation."

"That's a risk I'm willing to take." Lesley tossed the remainder of her whisky down.

"Have you thought about the repercussions of humiliating a beloved doctor?" asked Rachel. "There's a good chance the whole town will turn against you. Travis doesn't stand a chance if they do. They've really grown fond of Dr. Bryant."

Lesley refused to meet Rachel's eyes as she whipped into the kitchen and refilled her own wide-brimmed glass.

"Everyone still gives you credit for finding him." Rachel sat on the armrest of her couch, crossing her legs now, having sipped her drink. "If I marry Nick, the town will have the both of us to thank for giving him a reason to stay. Permanently."

Lesley was too above admitting she might've overlooked something. But the way she studied her drink told Rachel that that thought was circling through her mind. "Do you have a better idea for getting Allie out of town?" she asked through clenched teeth.

Rachel took another sip, emptying her glass. "You managed to run your own husband out of town. It shouldn't be too hard to do the same thing to a young nuisance of a girl." She hopped up from the couch, reached for Lesley's empty glass, and headed back into the kitchen.

"You know I can't do that. I'm just lucky that Mort, the idiot, hasn't figured out why his dear brother never calls. Allie has too many people interested in her life. If she disappeared, there'd be a huge investigation."

Rachel's hand shook as she poured them both more whiskey. Marrying Nick meant she'd be free of Lesley's clutches. She'd no longer be a pawn in her blackmail games. When people got in the midst of her schemes, they died. She tossed down another drink. Lesley couldn't discover her real motive behind her desire to marry Nick or the plan would turn to dust.

Accepting the glass Rachel handed her, Lesley said, "I have another job for you."

Turning away so Lesley couldn't see the prick of tears at the edge of her eyes, Rachel managed only, "If Nick finds out, my chances of marrying him are shot."

Lesley tossed back her third whiskey, ignoring the plea. "I've got one Board member giving me trouble. His family is out of town next weekend. See to it he doesn't have any reason to fight me on the new policy I'm implementing, will you? You know what to do."

Setting her empty glass on the kitchen counter, Lesley charged for the front door. "That policy will help me fire Allie Jordan and run her out of town. And if you cooperate, I won't ruin Dr. Bryant's precious reputation while doing it."

After Lesley slammed the door behind herself, Rachel threw her empty drink against it, relishing the calamity of shattering glass. All her life she'd let Lesley control her, as though she owed her for taking care of her once Rachel's mother ran out on them. Ignoring the broken glass, Rachel retrieved the bottle of whiskey from the kitchen and took a direct swig. She hated the burn it sent down her throat... but at least the burn reminded her she was still alive.

Marrying the doctor was the only way to free herself

of the shackles Lesley had locked on her life. The house belonged to Lesley. The house their father had owned until he rolled his car in a ditch driving home from a neighboring bar one December night. He'd been banned from Marley's, but it hadn't stopped the drinking.

Being Lesley's sister hadn't made it easy for Rachel to make friends. Subsequently, she didn't have any. As much as she resented Allie Jordan, she envied her too.

One final swig and she put the bottle back in the cupboard above the refrigerator, too far out of reach when she only craved more. She'd never be like their father, though. Or Lesley for that matter.

Climbing the stairs, Rachel started to plan. "Sorry, Allie." If only she could manage to run Allie out of town before Lesley did, then she wouldn't have to worry about Nick's reputation. "I need him more than you do."

Chapter 21

"Allie, I didn't know you were a book blogger!" Jen, the floater ward secretary, exclaimed. She'd come in for half their shift to help during the busiest hours. She fell into her chair between Suzy and Allie, tucking a short strand of jet-black hair behind her ear. "And I definitely didn't know you liked to read romance novels. Wouldn't have guessed you'd be the type."

Allie smiled. She'd forgotten about the Facebook page Amanda created until she received a text a couple of hours ago.

257 likes on FB!

"Just a little hobby of mine," she said.

"I've been following your blog for months. Never knew it was *you!*"

"Really?" Why that surprised Allie, she wasn't sure.

She'd kept her identity a secret until yesterday. But she never dreamed anyone in Willow Creek would really pay much attention to things like romance novel blogs.

"Are you kidding? The day you wrote that review about *Forbidden Pleasures*, I hopped right in the car and drove to Norfolk to get it."

Kim was really onto something with this book sales thing. Allie figured she'd help authors by putting in a good word and allowing them to advertise. But for someone in Willow Creek to drive thirty miles to buy a book she'd recommended? Allie was astonished.

Another buzz of the cell phone. She glanced all around to make sure Dawn or Lesley weren't lurking. Then she stole a peak at the screen.

302 likes!

"I think it's great what you're offering the authors. It'll be good backing for them, having someone as popular as you recommending their books," Jen gushed as she made requested changes to the nursing schedule book that Allie and Suzy hadn't had time to get to. The hospital had been buzzing with activity since the first day Nick took on patients, and it hadn't slowed a bit. At least the escorting requirement had been dropped.

"Dr. Bryant, did you know that Allie is famous?" Jen beamed when Nick appeared at the counter, chart in hand.

Nick cocked an eyebrow. "Famous?"

Allie was certain he tried to tame his smile. But there was still a wicked twinkle in his eyes reserved for her. She glanced up, then returned her eyes to her computer screen. One of the last good looks she'd gotten of Nick was him kneeling before her. "I wouldn't call it that," she said.

"She's too modest. She's been writing a blog for years. Only yesterday, she revealed her secret identity to the world. It's a really famous blog, too."

Allie's cheeks heated. She'd planned to tell Nick this weekend, not expecting that anyone at the hospital would've caught wind of it yet. The swiftness in which the news spread was a little intimidating.

"Congratulations," said Nick.

"Thanks." *Jeez, Allie. Could you act any more like a bashful teenager?*

The foreboding click of heels threatened to ruin the happy atmosphere. Even Nick seemed to sense it. Tapping the counter, he said a bit loudly, "Send my next patient up in five, please."

Lesley stopped a few yards away to greet a patient's family. It never ceased to amaze Allie how the woman could appear to care and make people believe it. *Perfect time for me to go to lunch.* She pulled her latest read from her desk drawer. "I'm off for a bowl of chili," she announced.

As she slipped behind the desk, Lesley glanced in her direction. Allie felt uneasy tingles as those gray eyes followed her until she turned the corner.

Diane hurried around the kitchen, the lunch rush in full swing. "Help yourself, Allie. I'll write you down for a meal."

"Thanks." She scooped herself a bowl of chili, snatched a cinnamon roll and a packet of soup crackers.

The solitude the old break room promised called to Allie. She wanted to finish her latest read so she could post another blog tonight, a sample of her talent. It might entice an author or two to sign up for advertising.

The daunting click of high heels echoed in the hallway just as she reached the corridor to the old break room. Allie, eager to slip inside and avoid Lesley, arrived and stopped dead. Bright yellow Xs taped across the door prevented her entering the room. A hand written note taped to the door said "No Admittance".

"We've decided to close down that room," said Lesley with a smug smile on her face. "No sense in having two separate break areas, now, is there? Such a waste while we're hurting for storage rooms that don't require a trip to the basement."

Embers burned in Allie's chest. "Guess I'll eat in the other break room, then."

"You best not bring that silly novel with you, Allie. I'd hate to have to write you up."

"What?"

"Haven't you read your hire agreement? If you plan to read anything on breaks, it should only be material relevant to your position of employment. I'll let you put that book away this time. But don't let me catch you with one again or I'll be forced to give you a written warning. Too many of those and, well, you know what happens."

Allie'd spent the remainder of her day in a spiteful mood. Until settling in for the evening, she'd forgotten all about the website, focusing on overthrowing Lesley. *There's got to be a way to end Cruella's reign.* She had enjoyed imagining ways that Lesley could be fired. Run from town. Getting hit by a car had its appeal too.

Norman tilted his head from beside the dining room table as Allie cracked a Dr. Pepper before starting supper. "Don't judge me," she warned.

He hopped up, licking her forearm before heading outside.

She slid her chair back, about to change out of her stiff work clothes when she was drawn to her laptop on the table, buried beneath a few romance novels. One of them, *Forbidden Pleasures,* was the one she'd been reading the day she met Nick. The thought brought a smile to her lips.

"Let's see if my new website got any attention." A change of clothes forgotten, her email window popped up, coursing giddiness through her veins. The top email in her inbox was entitled "Advertising Request". She opened it, scanning the contents quickly. An author wanted to purchase the gold package on *her* website. And she'd attached a code to download her book for free in hopes that Allie would love it enough to write a blog about it.

After a quick reading sample, Allie replied to the email, hoping her excitement wasn't too obvious. *But it is my first author client!* She squealed internally. After pushing send, the screen returned to her inbox. Allie caught another email with the same subject line. Advertising Request. But it wasn't the only one. They were everywhere. She flagged each to separate them from other emails. "Twenty-two requests?"

Allie called her sister's cell, Amanda's snappy voice answering, "You stopped replying to my text messages!" Not so much as a "hi", just right down to the point.

"Rough day at work," grumbled Allie. "But that's not why I called."

"Did you call to see how many page likes you have now? Try seven hundred and sixty-two."

Her irritation for Lesley Jamison dissipated as excitement swept over her. "That's great, Amanda! And guess what?"

"You taught Norman how to drive."

Allie laughed. "No."

"You got laid."

"I wish," she muttered.

"Huh?"

"Never mind. Guess what?"

"I already did."

"The website worked."

"Yeah? Did you get a request?"

Allie's fingers tapped the table in rapid succession. "You could say that."

"Al, that's great!" Amanda sounded genuinely excited. "I'm sure in no time at all, you'll have a bunch of requests. Meaning you can basically be *paid* to read those books."

"I have a couple already," admitted Allie, hopping up from her chair to join Norman outside.

"Yeah?"

"Twenty-two, actually." Another ding, announcing a new email. "Make that twenty-three."

Allie heard Amanda spit something out of her

mouth. "Really?"

"Isn't it great?"

"That's awesome! We need to celebrate. Soon."

"How about this weekend? Maybe at the baseball slash bonfire thing?"

"I'm gonna pass. We'll figure out something else. I'm not really into baseball."

"I gotta check my other emails. Maybe make a spreadsheet or something. This is nuts!"

"Brenden will take care of setting up links and blurbs. But let me know if you need an assistant to track your authors. I know one that'll work for vacations."

With that crack, Amanda hung up the phone before Allie could add a snide reply. But truth be told, she felt like agreeing to the vacation on the spot. With this kind of extra income rolling in, how could she refuse to take her sister on one now? *Sitting on a beach all day, far from Cruella, and reading romance novels sounds pretty perfect.*

"Norman, how am I going to read all these books?" Maybe a vacation was the *only* way she'd get through so many requests. Though authors couldn't insist she write a post due to ethical concerns, Allie had promised to at least *read* each book if she received a free copy.

"I might need an e-reader," she mumbled as

Norman shot outside through the doggie door. Scrolling through the emails, she decided most of them seemed legit, like books she'd enjoy reading. One author even requested a blog takeover. *Whatever that is*, she mused. *I'll have to look into it.* The author even offered to pay for it outside of the gold package advertising. *Amazing.*

Allie stared at her laptop, wondering how many authors she'd have to sign up to equal her hospital income and benefits. *Health insurance will probably cost a pretty penny.* Norman flew back in through his doggie door, ball clenched in his jaw. He dropped it beside his water bowl.

Her cell jingled and she reached for it, still focused on the influx of emails. Another popped up as she answered the phone. "I'm going to need that friend of yours to post something on my website about a waitlist."

"You really are famous if you have a waitlist." It wasn't Amanda, like she'd expected. It was Nick. Allie's stomach was already filled with butterflies, but at the sound of his voice, they took flight, fluttering around in quick circles.

"Hi, Nick."

"I wanted to ask if you planned on watching the baseball game. At that detective's house."

"Alex?"

"Yeah, that one."

"I was planning on it." Norman lapped nosily, splashing excess water on the vinyl floor.

"I was wondering…" Nick's voice trailed off.

Is he nervous? "I had a great time the other night," she said. "Even if we got interrupted by a shotgun."

He laughed, low and sexy. She felt her stomach respond, just south of her belly button. "I had a great time too. Even if we didn't get to tip a cow." Nick sighed through the phone. A happy sound, she hoped. "I wanted to know if you'd come to that game with me."

"Sure." *Did he emphasize* with *or am I imagining things?*

"Pick you up around five-thirty on Friday?"

"Sounds good. Hope you don't mind if Kim rides along?"

"Of course." Nick paused. "Allie?"

"Yeah?"

"I don't want to wait until Friday to see you."

Good, me neither. "No?"

"Thing is, the casseroles have run a little low. And I can't cook a can of soup without screwing it up. I was hoping you'd come give me a cooking lesson. Tonight."

"What's on the menu?"

"Well, my sister emailed me a recipe for Mediterranean chicken. She said it's easy, but I think she was trying to sabotage me. Make me miss her cooking, or something. I already bought all the ingredients. Interested in helping me prove her wrong?"

"I'd love to."

Chapter 22

Nick stared at the array of ingredients spread across his kitchen island: tomatoes, garlic cloves, onion, white wine, fresh thyme, Kalamata olives, parsley. He knew Miranda had sent him the recipe on purpose. She wanted him to completely foil the meal, make it taste like burnt cardboard so he'd miss her even more. So he'd come back to Georgia.

Light rapping on the back door announced Allie's arrival. He felt his heart pounding harder in his chest. Last time they had a minute alone, she'd been missing most of her clothes. When she stepped into the kitchen, the scent of lavender filled the room.

He greeted her with a deep kiss. One that promised they'd finish tonight what they kept starting. "I hope I have everything we need." Nick watched Allie scan the counter, his eyes continuously slipping to tight jeans that hugged her beautiful long legs. "The chicken breasts are still in the fridge. Here's the recipe." He slid the printout along the counter toward her.

"I'm impressed." She leaned against the island. "You say you don't know much about cooking, but you found all the ingredients. Even the thyme."

"Well, I did have to ask for help," he admitted. "Especially in Wal-Mart." Stepping up behind her, he kissed her neck once. Her body shivered in response. He considered nixing the cooking lesson altogether and carrying her to his bedroom.

"Why did you drive all the way to Norfolk?" she asked, her eyebrow raised in amusement. "You could've found all of these things right here in town. Wilkerson's is small, but they have a good selection."

"And chance any number of women pressing me about a date?" He wished he were joking, but the women in town, especially the ones in serious pursuit, were relentless in their interrogations. "I didn't feel like breaking so many hearts tonight."

"Do you have a skillet?" Holding the printed recipe, Allie propped her elbows on the counter. "And some measuring spoons?" The way her body folded, her perfect ass popping out, forced him to walk around to the other side of the island.

He'd only started unpacking the kitchen pots and pans this week, but he managed to produce a shiny stainless steel skillet Miranda gave him before he left Georgia. "You're probably not going to use this," she had said, "but just in case..." There'd been tears in his sister's eyes as she packed him that box full of kitchen supplies.

Allie faced the ancient stove, one that looked as though it belonged in an episode of *Leave it to Beaver*, and studied the knobs. "First, we have to heat some oil and white wine before we add the chicken to the pan."

Hovering over her shoulder, Nick watched her measure out the liquid ingredients with shaky hands. Tickling her neck with his breath, he whispered, "Why?"

"The oil keeps the chicken from sticking. Heating it up helps thin it out so it covers the whole pan."

He tried to ignore the tremble in her voice. Knowing she still felt this nervous around him stirred something animalistic in him. Made him want to toss her onto the kitchen counter, vegetables and herbs be damned, and have his way with her.

"You can grab the chicken from the fridge," she suggested. "We'll need it in a few minutes."

He ducked his head behind the refrigerator door. When he emerged with the package of chicken breasts in hand, he caught Allie chugging from the bottle of white wine. If he didn't get her to relax, they'd end up burning the house down.

"Tell me a little bit about your family."

"What would you like to know?" Allie washed her hands in the sink. "You've met Amanda. She's my only sibling. And there's my mom, Pam."

He watched her scoop up chicken breasts and slip them into the skillet, knowing he'd have to talk about his family first. Help her ease into conversation. "I have the one sister—Miranda—the one who left that message. She's an older sister, though. Acts like one too."

Allie smiled at that, her shoulders visibly relaxing. So he continued.

Telling her about Miranda and her family felt easy enough. He rambled on about Sunday dinners, carrying his niece and nephew around on his back in the living room, how wonderful a cook his sister was. "I never went hungry. Even in med school."

He related how he'd come home for the weekends and Miranda would send him back with containers so stuffed full of leftovers that he thought he'd need duct tape to keep the lids on.

"Do you miss them?" Allie asked, her eyes extending kindness. Compassion. Something he'd rarely seen in Dana's eyes after they were married.

"Like crazy."

"We need to dice the onion and tomato, and mince the garlic."

Nick pulled two sharp knives from a drawer and handed one to her. "These won't look pretty once I butcher them, but they'll still taste the same, right?"

The chopping commenced, a shared endeavor, and he found talking about his parents came harder. His mom withering away one chemo treatment at a time— who'd have thought the very thing that rid the cancer had destroyed her lungs? "As her health declined, I spent hours in the library reading medical books, hoping I could somehow go back in time and fix it. But once the chemo reached her lungs, the damage was too far gone."

He hadn't meant to make her cry, but a fat tear rolled down Allie's cheek. He decided he'd save his dad for another day, regaling her with happy memories of his mother instead. Baking cookies when he was little, where she'd let him lick the beaters. Walking the streets of downtown Savannah. His mother cheering him on at his baseball games from the stands.

"Who fed you growing up, once your mother passed away? Was it your dad?" Finishing with the tomato, Allie turned toward the stove and flipped the chicken.

"My sister took over in the kitchen when my mother

started getting sick. Miranda's a wonderful cook, but she refused to share any of her secrets with me. I think it's the womanly pride in my family. Women are expected to be miracle workers in the kitchen, but men aren't allowed to witness the magic. Ever."

When Allie told Nick about her dad dying in a combine accident, he listened in empathetic silence.

"He was always helping people," she said, refusing to meet his eyes. She explained how she was eight when it happened, but the memories she described were vivid. Like they happened yesterday.

"My sister's a lot like him." Allie dropped chopped vegetables into the sizzling skillet. "At least in the ambition department. Also really athletic. She'll probably get a scholarship for any sport she wants. Something from our dad too. He still holds the school record for the boys' one-mile. Amanda followed in his footsteps, snatching her own school record this past spring for the two-mile."

"Sounds like school records run in the family."

Allie smiled at that, but it didn't reach her eyes. "What's that jar on the table over there?"

Nick didn't miss how quickly she'd changed subjects. "Seashells. My mom and I used to collect them when I was growing up. Each time we'd visit a new beach, we'd pick out the best one to add to our collection."

"I don't know how many seashells you'll get to add living here."

"I haven't added a new shell in years."

She cranked up the heat on the burner. "Can you bring over the tomatoes?"

He dropped them into the pan, standing so close he could feel the heat resonating from her skin. He checked the dial on the stove, contemplating turning it off so they could wander off to the bedroom. "What can I do next?"

"We'll need more wine. Can you measure out a cup?"

"I have a better idea," said Nick. "How about I measure out three?"

After pouring the wine into the pan, Allie turned the heat down low and set the timer on the stove for ten minutes. "We could start the green beans," she said, accepting his glass of wine. "But they'd be done way too early."

"Well, we do have ten minutes," said Nick. "I can think of several ways to fill that time. All of them include your body pressed against mine."

She sent him a challenging look.

He brushed a strand of hair behind her ears. "I can last longer than ten minutes, just so you know."

"I don't doubt that," she said, curling her arms

around his back and kissing him. "I don't want to be responsible for burning down this house of yours, so after dinner you can prove that to me."

"Okay," he whispered against her ear, his lips trailing kisses down the length of her neck. Hands slid beneath Allie's black tank top, pushing the material away from her waist, his fingertips feathering the firm skin around the waistband of her jeans.

Delicate, soft hands slid beneath the fabric of his shirt, slowly teasing it off.

When the timer on the oven beeped, he was missing his shirt. So was Allie.

"The chicken will burn."

Her body was trapped between his and the door jamb, and his desire was clouding rationality. "Let it burn." He undid the top button of Allie's jeans, a soft moan escaping her sweet lips.

Kicking her jeans to the side, she managed a few weak words between gasps of breath. "The burner... Let me..."

Standing in front of the stove in only her bra and panties, Allie tried desperately to catch her breath. She'd barely had enough restraint to keep the house from burning to the ground. Turning the ancient dial to off and removing the pan to a cool burner, Allie turned.

Nick stood, propped in the doorway. Her eyes kept stealing glances at the proof of his desire, the bulge of it evident through his mesh athletic shorts. She swallowed. It'd been years since she slept with a man. She'd all but given up once that stupid letter came.

"Something wrong?" He pushed off the wall, meeting her halfway.

Shaking her head, Allie reached her hands toward his neck, drawing his lips back to hers. Two strong hands lifted her. She straddled his legs, allowing him to carry her upstairs.

Still wrapped around Nick, Allie felt him kneel onto the king-sized bed. Gently, he lowered her against the mattress. Hot hands reached behind her back, expertly unclasping her bra. He tossed it across the room. A cool breeze from the cracked window swept over her erect nipples, causing a shiver. Nick laughed, his rumble low. "In a second, I'm going to make you do that for an entirely different reason."

Trapping her hands with one of his own, Nick's tongue teased a nipple, tracing circles around it. She yearned to touch him. *He needs to get rid of those shorts.* But he held her firmly in place. His lips hovered over her breast, teeth scraping against her skin. She let out a moan.

"Nick, please," she begged, her chest rising and falling. At this rate, she'd see stars before either of them lost half their remaining clothes.

"Please what, Allie?" With his free hand, he slid her panties off, tossing them into a darkened corner.

Might never find those.

"Please, make love to me."

Releasing her hands, Nick shoved off his shorts. After the quick shuffling through his nightstand drawer and the crinkle of discarded foil, he eased her legs apart with his knees. He entered her slowly, rocking in and out with a patience Allie certainly didn't feel, each slow thrust filling her more.

She was on the verge of begging when he cupped his hands on her hips, and with one steady thrust that caused her hips to arch, filled her completely. She let out an involuntary moan of pleasure. The wild look in Nick's green eyes told her that that single moan nearly caused him to come unglued.

Allie arched back, her head reaching a pillow, smiling when he moaned. "God you're beautiful." He pulled out until just the tip of him remained inside her.

He froze a moment, then buried himself inside her, sliding in and out in a desperation of yearning they'd both felt for the other for weeks now. Every smile, every simple touch, every good morning and look of longing since they met ran through Allie's mind while waves of pleasure swept over her. As her body started to convulse uncontrollably, she heard Nick moan loudly and thrust again, as though he couldn't quite get deep enough.

He gently collapsed on top of her, still nestled inside the pulsating heat of her. He kissed her once on the lips and then once on the neck. "So much better than chicken," he whispered, kissing her on the lips.

Chapter 23

Allie and Amanda were five miles shy of Norfolk when Kim called, announcing she'd been called into the radio station. "New Guy has measles. Do you believe that? Who gets *measles* these days? I'd ditch work, but my boss offered to pay me time and a half. Every extra dime helps unless I want to be stuck running a grocery store in Willow Creek someday."

Still in a good mood, and not wanting to waste the gas, Allie decided to head for the Dairy Queen for celebratory ice cream. Heaping Blizzards in hand, the two slid into a booth in the window-encased room where they could watch the traffic.

"So, you've been in a really chipper mood lately." Amanda scooped a mound of Butterfinger ice cream onto her spoon. "Word on the street is that you and Dr.

Gorgeous are kind of a thing."

Savoring a bite of chocolate chip cookie dough ice cream, Allie said, "That sounds accurate." Truthfully, they'd been too busy exploring each other's bodies to really talk about what they were. But Allie hoped to rectify that this weekend at Alex's baseball bonfire party.

Amanda pointed a plastic spoon at Allie. "Have you done it yet?"

Heat rushed to her cheeks "Mandy Bear!"

"I haven't seen you this happy in a long time." Amanda shoveled another spoonful into her mouth. "Or ever about a guy, really. I hope he's better for you than that jerk, Travis."

The air grew tense. Amanda rarely mentioned Travis. Or anything to do with that time in her life. Both her sister and her mom tap danced around the subject. Mentioning his name was something close to a mortal sin in their family.

"Allie, I think it's time you tell me what happened."

"Uh…"

"Not with Nick. I read enough of your books to fill in the blanks."

Good.

"That would just be awkward."

"Agreed."

Amanda stabbed her spoon into her half eaten Blizzard. "About Travis Meyers."

"I don't see why it matters." Without urgency, she chewed an oversized bite of gooey ice cream, ignoring the growing annoyance in her sister's expression as her face blushed an adorable bright rose.

For a few minutes, they ate in silence, Amanda's eyes focused on the traffic.

"That's it?" Amanda said finally. "You're just not going to tell me? At all?"

Had there been more than one customer in the restaurant, Amanda's outburst surely would've created a scene. As it was, the cashier at the front counter stopped mid-wipe.

"You're better off not knowing some things, Mandy Bear." It surprised Allie that her reason for refusing to talk about it had changed. She no longer feared reliving the trauma. "Why can't you accept that?" In fact, she couldn't recall the last time she had a nightmare.

"I'm not twelve anymore!" said Amanda with such exasperation that her entire body shook from across the table. "I don't know why you don't trust me to understand why you dated such a jerk. And stop calling me Mandy Bear!" Amanda edged out of the booth as if she had somewhere to go. But Allie held the car keys.

"It's not like that, Amanda."

"Then what *is* it like?" She stopped sliding, giving her sister a moment to come clean. "I hear these crazy rumors in school about that night, but you know how that is. It was so long ago that what people still say about it is so far from reality that it's ridiculous."

Allie fought the urge to ask what, after five years, people were still saying. Was Willow Creek so desperate for gossip that they'd cling to a story for years? Or was the story some sort of twisted legend, handed down from high school class to class? Her moment in thought caused Amanda to lose what was left of her patience and she flew out the side door of the restaurant.

After washing the sticky ice cream residue from her hands, Allie found her sister sitting on a parking barrier next to the locked car. *I hate to admit it, but tragedy never quite dies in a small town.* She shouldn't be surprised that people still gossiped about that night, even if they surely had the details skewed.

Approaching her sister at the slowest pace possible, she decided she had no choice but to tell Amanda the truth about what happened. And about what it had done to her life. It was better that her sister hear it from her, anyway. It was impossible to know just how outlandish the rumored story had become. "Get in the car."

The firmness in Allie's voice startled Amanda into

obeying. They drove in silence for several miles. Instead of sticking to the highways, a few miles from Willow Creek, Allie turned onto a gravel road.

"Where are we going?"

"Do you want to know or not?"

After a couple more turns, the old house came into view. It looked as it always had, though Allie was secretly hoping a tornado or fire had flattened it. She hadn't been here in over five years, yet she'd never forgotten the sagging covered porch or the little balcony with its cone-shaped roof. The worn white paint had chipped away a little more than she'd remembered.

"What are we doing here?" Amanda's eyes were glued to the windshield, much the way Allie's had been the first time Travis brought her here.

"You wanted to know." Allie led her sister around to the back of the dilapidated farmhouse, not surprised to find the kitchen door unlocked. The deadbolt had never worked properly. The hinges struggled to hold to the doorframe; only one screw in each still attached.

She stopped in the doorway, her heart rate taking off like a lightning bolt. For a moment, she wasn't sure she could do this. Maybe it was best Amanda never knew the truth. Brenden seemed like a nice guy, one who didn't have Travis' dark side. She'd hate to shed such a dismal light on young love.

"What's going on, Allie?" Amanda walked past her sister into a galley kitchen. The same dirty white cabinets lined both walls. A massive, deep sink ringed with rust stains positioned beneath a window overlooked the backyard. Gaudy floral wallpaper lined the spaces between the upper and lower cabinets.

"This is kinda cool. In a creepy way," said Amanda, her hand on one of the oversized silver drawer pulls.

"Don't open that." Allie hadn't meant to snap, but her nerves were fraying.

Amanda threw up her hands in surrender. "Afraid of spiders or something?"

"Or something." She took a few braves steps into the house, further toward the dining room, recognizing the mint green walls and oak window trim. A door to the right was closed; the bedroom Travis showed her on his eighteenth birthday. He had talked her into giving him a special present in the room that'd be his personal home office one day. Allie shuddered, leaving that door closed.

At the front of the house, a spacious room with a bay window was furnished with that same ratty couch. At least, Allie thought the olive green monstrosity was the same one she'd seen years before. She looked away, forcing aside the horrid memories the roughed-up couch held.

"What's upstairs?" Amanda asked, one hand on the railing.

Allie's stomach plummeted. *I can't do this. Not inside.* "Let's go outside." She led the way to the front porch, careful to avoid the remembered sagging spots and gaping hole. If she remembered correctly, there was a basement beneath the house. One she didn't particularly care to fall into.

Sitting on the steps, Amanda joined her.

"What's the story, Al?"

Amanda's question gave Allie a sense of gravity. "This is where Travis Meyers talked me into handing over my virginity. This is where he promised it wouldn't hurt. Where he swore he would never hurt me." Allie cracked open a Dr. Pepper she'd been carrying since they stepped out of the car. It shook in her hands, liquid spilling over the side of the can and onto the porch. "This was the first place he ever lied to me. Once he started, he never stopped."

"Let's go," said Amanda.

"Do you want to hear this or not?"

Amanda waited quietly.

"The first time Travis got physical, he pushed me down those stairs." Allie looked back over her shoulder. "The ones you were about to climb."

Buzzing locusts echoed in the air as the sun began

to fade over the horizon. "I didn't think anything of it at the time. I thought I'd somehow made him mad and that a small shove down four stairs was nothing. I landed on my feet. Didn't have any scratches." Allie finally took a swig of pop. "But it was only the beginning."

Five years earlier...

"Maybe you can drop me off at home. Pick me up when you're done?" The request didn't seem outlandish to Allie. Not when she watched her house pass as they sped down the highway. But they'd somehow been the wrong words to Travis.

Whipping the truck around and heading in the opposite direction of their alleged date, Travis said, "No, you're coming with me."

Allie fought back tears as they sped through Willow Creek. Travis hated it when she cried. Claimed it was a sign of weakness.

But she'd never known Travis to have a gun before.

A couple of miles from town, he jerked the wheel. She smacked the door as he turned sharply onto a gravel road. She swallowed a snide remark about his driving. When they'd first been together, Travis admired her candid honesty. Now he punished her for it.

As the old truck roared down the gravel road, she hesitated asking him anything. But he was acting differently tonight, more distant than usual. So she asked anyway. "Where are we going?"

"None of your damn business, that's where."

She watched the moonlight on the young crops from the open passenger window. The truck now rolled along at a snail's pace—another bad sign. Travis was always in a hurry. The more noise and commotion he caused, screeching his tires, flooring the gas every time he so much as left a stop sign, the bigger he smiled. He relished the disapproving looks and middle fingers. But tonight, she was sure the needle on the odometer hardly reached ten. She made the mistake of looking at the dashboard to verify her suspicion.

"You have a fucking problem?"

Staring out the dirty windshield, she debated which was worse—to answer him or to sit in silence. Either way, his reaction would make her cringe.

"I asked you a question," said Travis, his voice quiet but aggravated.

She knew he was trying to pick a fight. No matter how much she tried to avoid it, it was inevitable. She decided she might as well probe for what information he'd give. "I'm wondering if you're lost," she said, trying hard to keep the quiver out of her voice, hoping her stern tone would show him she wasn't afraid. "You never drive this slow."

"I know where the hell we are," said Travis, taking his eyes from the road long enough to shoot her an icy glare. His gray eyes were even more frightening with the glare of the bright moonlight reflecting there.

Turning into a driveway, Travis rolled to a soft stop in the shadow of a large barn—unusual considering he prided himself on making his friends smack their heads against the dashboard with his perfectly timed jerk of the brakes.

Travis had only pushed his door partway open, one foot still inside the dusty truck, when he turned to face Allie. "Get out."

"No." Her voice trembled. Any chance of standing up to him had just fled.

"You can get out on your own or I can pull you out— your choice."

"Why?" she demanded weakly. "It doesn't look like anyone's home. I just want to wait here."

The flash of metal in his sweatshirt pocket reminded her that he was armed. She didn't take the time to wonder where he had acquired a gun before jumping out her side of the truck. The moment her feet hit the hard-packed dirt, she felt the urge to run.

The full moon would never conceal her, though. And the farm place was small. Minimal places to hide. He'd catch her. The nearest neighbor was at least a mile away. And if he didn't want the chase, he had the gun. She didn't dare chance whether it was loaded.

Admitting defeat, she slunk around the back of the rusty pickup, slowing even more as she came within arm's reach of this stranger. The Travis she knew was not in those cold eyes. The Travis she knew had ambitions and dreams. He didn't share those with many people because he was afraid they'd laugh in his face. She never laughed, but that didn't seem to matter tonight. Ambitious Travis was gone and a monster was in his place.

With one hand in his sweatshirt pocket, the other clasped her arm like a shackle. His arm the chain that yanked her forward across the deserted driveway.

"Who lives here?" she asked quietly. She knew questions would anger him. She was hoping annoying him would win her a ticket back to wait in the truck.

She wouldn't, of course. She'd make sure he wasn't watching, but she'd slip onto the road and dash for the nearest farmhouse. If she only had a head-start before he realized she'd fled, she might make it.

But he muttered under his breath. "No one you need to worry about."

"I don't think they're home," Allie said.

"Nope."

"Then wh—"

He jerked her to a stop so violent, that if it hadn't been for his grip, she'd have toppled over on the patch of pavement. "You can shut up now, or I can break your jaw and shut you up myself." The fierce look in his eyes told her he was telling the truth. Right now she was sure a raindrop could send him over the edge.

Travis held her arm in his death grip as he fidgeted with the back door with his free hand, picking the lock. She hadn't known him to break into houses, but his swift, one-handed technique proved that he'd done this plenty before. She couldn't believe how blind she'd been—how wrong about him. The dreams he'd confessed to her—the things he wanted to accomplish—must have been lies. A man who aspired to be an FBI agent wouldn't break into someone's house.

"Get in there." He whipped her across the threshold like she was little more than a ragdoll. That iron grip never loosening, he pulled her around through the dark, obviously in search of something specific.

In the dimness Allie caught the red blink of a cordless phone charger on a sofa table. Part of her knew she was best off staying quiet and following. But another part of her felt danger and knew if she didn't try some different approach, something bad might happen. "Can you tell me what we're looking for so I can help?"

Seeming to mock her, Travis laughed.

Inside, Allie was thinking, *the longer we stay here, the better chance we have of getting caught. Let me help you so we can get the hell out of here.* Instead, forcing her best sexy smile, she said, "The sooner we find it, the sooner we can get back to our date."

Travis stopped abruptly and turned. His sharp glare sent shivers down her spine. Was that look debating whether he could trust her? "It's a hidden camera. About the size of a ring box."

Tempted to ask why, she caught herself. She was sure Travis would shove her into a wall if she questioned him. "Do you know what room?"

"One of the bedrooms," Travis said.

"We should try upstairs."

He was still staring at her, apparently caught off guard that she was helping rather than complaining.

Locking in the smile, she took a step forward. Her hand grazed his cheek and pulled his face down to hers. She didn't allow herself to consider how disgusting it felt to kiss him. He had to believe she was on his side.

It was her only chance of escape.

"I'll look upstairs," said Travis. "You check down here. See if there're any bedrooms."

"Okay."

He hesitated. "If you do anything stupid, I will make you pay." He pulled the gun from his sweatshirt pocket long enough for her to get a good look at it. A magazine had been loaded into it and she wasn't about to test it.

Her entire body trembled, but her smile held steadfast. "Don't be silly. One small camera coming up." She slipped away from him, into a hallway.

She waited only a few seconds after Travis trudged up the stairway before she grabbed the cordless phone off the charger and went in search of a room far enough away from the stairs to muffle the beeps. But before she could punch the last button, she heard his heavy footsteps crashing down the stairs. Forced to hang up, she tossed the phone onto a pile of dirty laundry on the floor.

"You called the cops," accused Travis angrily. There was blazing hatred in his eyes that she had never seen before, scaring her more than the gun half hanging out his sweatshirt pocket.

She shook her head. She wasn't going to admit she tried, especially since her attempt had failed. She hoped someone else had.

"You fucking bitch! I hear sirens!" He flew across the room so quickly that she had no time to react. He yanked her arm so hard she thought it would rip out of its socket. When she screamed out, he backhanded her across the jaw.

"I didn't call anyone," she squeaked, her voice panicky. Pleading. She tasted blood and felt a tooth dangle against her tongue.

"Then where the hell is it?" shouted Travis, shoving her into the sofa table with the empty phone charger. "It was here when I went upstairs!"

Allie buckled over onto the floor, feeling the table fold on top of her. She shielded her head, more from fear of what he'd do next than from the weight of the table. "I didn't do it!" She was nearly screaming through violent sobs.

And that only angered Travis more.

"I'm not going to jail for this," he hissed.

"Then why the hell are you robbing a house?" She threw the phone charger at his shin and tried scrambling away toward the kitchen around the corner. If she could just get a knife, maybe she could slow him down.

A hand clasped her ankle. "Bitch!" He pulled her toward him with ease. Travis flipped her over and crawled on top, pinning her to the floor. She felt the sharp jab of a table leg in her side, but he wasn't giving her an inch. "You don't run from me," he growled with possessive fury. "You will always belong to me. If another man so much as touches you, I will kill him. Do you understand me?"

Her head was turned away, her cheeks drenched in her own tears and blood. She refused to answer.

"Do you understand me?" Travis was yelling, but even his raised voice failed to drown out the nearing sirens. Red and blue lights flashed through the uncovered windows. Travis seized her chin in his firm grip, forcing her to face him. "Answer me, dammit!"

"Go to hell," she said with all the spite she could muster. And spit in his face.

His eyes grew wide. "You'll pay for that." Someone was banging on the front door. Travis jumped up and drew his gun.

When Allie tried to pull herself toward the couch, he kicked her in the stomach. She fell into a fetal position. "I'll make sure you never forget that you belong to me."

She screamed as the ear splitting echo of a gunshot filled the room. She felt a burning sensation down the length of her leg, but before she could look, another shot fired. Allie felt it pierce her skin.

As she wailed, Travis ran out the back door.

Amanda sat in stunned silence, wanting to ask what happened next, but not sure how. She'd heard some pretty awful things about Travis Meyers, what he was capable of. But his spiteful shenanigans like blowing up mailboxes with fireworks and uprooting street signs and stashing them at the cemetery seemed like child's play compared to the gruesome event that Allie had just described.

"They caught him half a mile down the road. He'd tossed the gun in some ditch," Allie explained, "So he really didn't have any way to defend himself when they tased him." She stood, her eyes still cast over the rolling field beyond the house. The sun was nearly gone now, soon it would be dark. "We should go."

Amanda followed her to the car. She couldn't help but stare at the staircase through a side window, sickened by the thought of things that had probably happened upstairs.

"Nick's not like Travis, right?" she asked as casually as she could manage once her sister backed out of the rutted, overgrown driveway.

"Nothing like him."

Pulling away from the house, Amanda felt like they

were being watched. *Typical for an old, abandoned house to feel a little haunted*, she mused.

"Did I fill you in on what you wanted to know?" She noticed Allie's eyes were locked on the road.

She couldn't help it. She still had one pressing question. "I just want to know *why* you ever dated him in the first place, Al. That's the part I don't understand."

"Travis wasn't always like that." Allie turned one corner onto another gravel road. Amanda felt a little dizzy with the zigzag pattern they drove. "He was a different person when we first started dating. Really popular, in fact. Had a good reputation in town for working hard. Being honest."

"What changed?"

"When his dad left town, he started acting weird. It was like someone flipped a switch."

Chapter 24

"You wanted to see me?" Allie closed a new screen door behind her and took in the new construction site around her. In just a week's time, Pam had stripped all the orange carpet and its pad from the living and dining room of her latest flipper project.

Dropping a large sheet of particleboard in the far corner, Pam said, "Hi to you too." She shimmied the board until it was perfectly aligned. "Do me a favor and step on the corner until I get a couple of screws in."

Allie obeyed. The whine of the drill smothered the weather forecast on the radio. One promising another hot, sticky Nebraska day. She longed to return home, where a stack of romance novels and refreshing air conditioning awaited her. "I don't know how you work with just a fan."

Pam shrugged. "I still have to repair some of the vents. No sense in using the AC if half the air's going to leak." Hopping to her feet, Pam disappeared through a side door. Allie poked her head through the doorway, discovering the one car garage where additional sheets of particleboard awaited, stacked against one wall. Pam wrestled in another, laying it beside the last.

"Why are you putting in new subfloor?" Allie asked.

"I'm going to try out this vinyl planking. An article I read said it's not very forgiving if you have any bumps in the subfloor. Safer to lay new." Pam lined the sheet next to the other and dropped in a couple of screws. "Allie, I hate to do this to you."

Allie folded her arms across her chest. *This can't be good.* "What?"

"I need to start charging rent."

"What? Why now?" She'd gone three years without paying rent. Sure she covered all her own utilities and maintenance, but her mom had never needed income for that house. It was one of the prime reasons Allie was allowed to live there.

"Look. I did you a favor three years ago. You needed a place to go. I gave you one. But now you've had plenty of time to save money. You're leaving soon anyway, right?"

"Well, I was going to wait until the spring." Allie

knew she sounded defensive. Leaving had been the last thing on her mind. She had months to decide where to go and *if* she still wanted to leave. "Maybe I'm going to stay." Facing her past last night with Amanda had shaken her up. She had a nightmare again, but woke up pissed off this time, not scared.

Kneeling, Pam looked up from the new patch of subfloor. "Don't be ridiculous, Allie. You won't be happy here if you're always looking over your shoulder." Before Allie could interject, Pam added, "You've been doing it for three years—ever since you moved back to save up your money. With Travis behind bars. How do you think you'll be when he's out?"

"So you're giving me an ultimatum? Move or pay rent?"

"Call it whatever you want." Drilling more screws into the subfloor, Pam drowned out any objections she might have.

During a quick beat of silence, Allie said, "I'll have a check for next month's rent by the end of the day." Then she stormed out of the house.

Petite Dawn Hammond stood at the front of the activity center room, climbing up to stand on a chair to be seen. The Director of Nursing's bright pink scrubs patterned with little rainbows were in direct contrast to her serious personality.

Three ward secretaries, a couple of cooks, the housekeeping staff, and most of the nurses on duty packed into the open room. Allie didn't see Nick. The rustle of conversation softened at Dawn's announcement, "Let's make this quick. Everyone take a seat."

Weaving her way through a gaggle of nurses, Allie scanned the room for Garfield scrubs. "Diane, do you know what this is about?" she asked, finding her favorite cook three rows back. "Doesn't look like our typical quarterly assembly."

Diane pushed back a long, loose bang. "Rumor has it there's a new policy or something." She reached for her steaming cup of black coffee. Allie turned away in quiet disgust. She'd force-fed herself caffeine in desperate moments lately. *So many books to read!* But no amount of hazelnut creamer could drown out that bitter coffee taste.

"What's this about, Dawn?" Suzy's question silenced the room. It was no secret that Suzy didn't care to be bothered with frivolities when the ward secretaries were slammed with paperwork for new admissions and dismissals.

"Just a few housekeeping notes."

Watching Suzy fold her arms, Allie tuned out announcements about training that didn't pertain to her. Though she tried to smother it, a yawn escaped. Lesley eyed her from across the room. *One daily Cruella glare down. Two to go.*

"I've been asked to discuss a new fraternization policy that the Board has implemented."

Chatter rose in the room.

"I bet this whole meeting is because of Doc Bryant," a nurse's aide, sitting in Snoopy scrubs in front of Allie, mumbled under breath. "Just another excuse for Lesley to flaunt her accomplishment at finding him. Telling us we can't pursue him."

Allie caught snippets of mutters about a waste of time. Emptying her coffee mug, Diane whispered, "They should've hired an older doctor. One who had gray hair and grandkids."

Allie felt her heart drop into her stomach.

Dawn raised her hands to quiet the room. "Ladies, ladies," she called. "And Aaron." She nodded toward the only man present. "The Board has concerns that justify this new policy."

Suzy shook her head, her glasses sliding to the tip of her nose. "I don't have time for this. I'm a happily married woman with children his age." Several side comments followed, the group rumbling with chatter.

Dawn sucked in a breath before hushing the room again. "Just so there is no confusion on the new policy, it states that dating anyone who works in the same small hospital is prohibited."

A few moans filled the room. Some in jest, others genuine disappointment. "How is that fair?" chimed one nurse.

Nick and Dr. Montgomery appeared in the open doorway, catching the tail end of the assembly. Allie tried to keep her eyes averted. It'd do no good confirming to the entire room that she and Nick were playing doctor outside the hospital.

"We have a limited staff. We can't afford distractions." Lesley jumped up from her comfortable seat. "Distractions that could cause *fatal* mistakes."

Dawn again silenced the room. "Let's not make this take all day. I happen to agree with the Board on this one. Our patients are our number one priority. It would be irresponsible for any one of us to compromise their safety."

"You're just saying that because you married a hotter version of Brad Pitt!" said a nurse.

A few laughs echoed.

"Can we get back to work?" asked Suzy, unfolding her arms. She'd been eyeing the door for a few minutes now. Allie knew she had a surgery to coordinate for early next week and was antsy to start making her calls. Because of its size, the hospital couldn't afford to house the different types of surgeons and specialists most surgeries required.

"After one last thing," said Dawn. "And this is the most important."

The room quieted. Lesley sat back in her chair, crossing her legs.

Dawn said, "Everyone must sign the new fraternization policy by the end of next week. You have one week to clear any existing relationships through the Board. After that, there'll be no exceptions. Failure to comply with this new policy is grounds for immediate termination."

Lesley sat back on her chair, a smug smile on her face.

"As I said," finished Dawn, "the care and safety of our patients comes first."

Armed with an unstuffed green bell pepper casserole, Rachel slowly walked up the front steps of Nick's house. She wanted to take it all in: the covered porch, the intricate brickwork, the lush green expanse of lawn, the feeling of superiority one felt while looking down at the town of Willow Creek from the only hill. She could certainly get used to this feeling. If nothing else, it promised security, safety from Lesley's power.

She pushed the doorbell with her elbow. Within seconds, Nick swung open the heavy oak door, excitement in his eyes.

Nick said, "Rachel." The slowness of his greeting confirmed what she already suspected—he was hoping, expecting, Allie.

"I'm not interrupting, am I? I just haven't had a chance to properly thank you for rushing to the hospital last weekend." When he didn't take the bait, she tried, "And I thought I might pick up my other casserole dish." By the end of her visit, she felt confident Nick would do everything he could to keep Allie as far away as possible.

He held the screen door open for her as she slipped inside, purposely brushing her arm against his. "Have a seat," he said, taking the dish from her and motioning toward the couch. "Can I get you something to drink?"

"Iced water would be wonderful." She looked to the couch, deciding she'd sit in the middle. When he returned with her glass, she patted a spot beside her. "How did you enjoy the Summer Festival?"

Nick, obviously debating whether he should even

sit, left enough space between them to fit a child. She reached for her drink and took a sip to hide her disappointment, discreetly tugging on the hem of her shirt.

He reached for his own water, his eyes passing a glance at the newly exposed cleavage.

I won't sleep with him right away. No, she'd go about this the proper way so the town of Willow Creek couldn't claim anything scandalous about them.

But she wanted him eager. That first time he'd be so overcome that he might forget to use protection, locking her future in place. She could already tell he was the type of man who accepted responsibility. Not such a bad strategy, considering it'd worked for Lesley all those years ago.

Nick set his glass down. "It was nice to see people outside of an exam room."

She hid her frown beneath her cup. Even if his answers hadn't been generic, the way he kept looking toward the front door told her she'd have to do something a little more drastic if she wanted to start winning his affection.

"Nick, I need to talk to you about something." She kept her tone purposely glum. "I don't want you to get upset, though." She paused, hoping he'd say that he wouldn't, but he just looked at her expectantly. "There's a silly rumor going around town. Surely you know how rumors can be in Willow Creek. This place sees so very little action that people take small misunderstandings and blow them way out of proportion."

"Do you have a point, Rachel? I have a busy evening ahead of me."

She didn't tell him that she suspected he was lying. "People are saying that you and that girl Allie Jordan are having a secret affair." Rachel put her hand up. "Now, I know there's no truth to it, but I wanted to let you know what's being said. They see you two spending time together and, well, that's all it takes to get the rumor mill started." She took another sip. "Someone at Wilkerson's even mentioned they saw you walk her home after the Summer Festival."

The expression on Nick's face was blank. She was annoyed at not being able to read into any potential reaction.

"I don't give any stock to rumors, or to the people who spread them."

She placed a firm hand on his knee. "I hope you don't think *I've* been spreading that rumor!" Leaning in so more of her cleavage shoved closer to his face, she widened her blue eyes so they seemed pleading. "I simply thought you'd want to know what the town is saying. You have an important reputation to maintain.

Something like this could tarnish your credibility."

Nick stood suddenly. "I hardly see how that rumor could cause any harm—unless Allie would be embarrassed by it. Is this about the new policy?"

"It's just that with her past, Nick..." Rachel stood, walking toward the fireplace, rather than the front door, then swung around. "The people of Willow Creek want to see you make a better choice." The small flare of emotion in his eyes told her he'd taken her bait.

"What are you talking about?"

She regarded Nick with just the right amount of hesitation—she really should've pursued her love of acting; she was so good at it. "She should be in jail, Nick."

He rolled his eyes and she knew she had to deliver the rest or he would kick her out.

"I don't know if you've heard, but Lesley's only son—my nephew—has been locked up for a few years. But he shouldn't be there alone. Allie was his accomplice the night he went to jail. Many suspect she was the reason they were robbing that house. But no one's ever been able to prove it. She agreed to testify against Lesley's boy in order to get all her charges dropped."

Nick's silence was exactly what Rachel had hoped for. She could see the wheels turning as he processed this new information. She was well aware that Allie didn't talk about her past with Travis. It was likely the subject had never been brought up in any of their conversations.

"Travis and Allie had quite the hell-raising reputation, too. Blew up a lot of mailboxes, used to supply minors with alcohol. *And*, word was, they used to trespass and cause all kinds of damage on dozens of local farms. All of these things he did because *she* wanted him to." Rachel began to pace, just slightly. Enough to show she hated dropping such unpleasant news on such a nice man on a Friday evening.

"Nick, you can ask around. Travis didn't always have that reputation. He used to work at the construction company. He had the strongest work ethic of anyone there. And that's saying something in this town." She took a step toward Nick. "Then he started running around with Allie, and well, *everything* went downhill. The town doesn't want to see you ruin your reputation over Allie Jordan. I don't want to see that. Nick, you're a great doctor. Don't let her change what people think of you."

Tucking a long strand of blonde hair behind her ears, she said, "You look like you could use some time alone." Again, she brushed against him as she walked by, leading herself into the kitchen. "If you don't mind,

I'll grab my casserole dish and be on my way." She smiled, confident that her touch had at least awakened his physical senses.

Nick called to her, "I'm sorry if I came off a little rude."

There it is. The apology she was waiting for.

"Nonsense." She spun around just before reaching the kitchen doorway, and Nick nearly ran into her. "I should've called first. You might've had company. I'm sorry to have turned your evening a little dismal. I just thought it was important that you know." Staring into his eyes, she read nothing. He'd be good at poker.

"Thank you for the casserole." Slipping past her and into the kitchen, he reached around the refrigerator, adding, "You'll have to tell me which one is yours."

Hearing the clanging of dishes, Rachel poked her head around the refrigerator, shocked to see at least ten casserole dishes stacked near the sink. *How many women think they're competing?* "The blue one."

Nick handed her a pristine dish. She smiled. It was nice to know her future husband didn't live like a slob or expect anyone else to clean up after him.

At the edge of the porch, she turned her head back over her shoulder, giving Nick a seductive look. "You do owe me dinner, you know."

Chapter 25

The sun hid behind a thick array of heavy gray clouds, promising rain before noon. Allie had hardly spread her blanket out on the green grass when another runner emerged. Someone from the town side of the track, opposite Nick's house. Rachel Jamison.

"Shit." Head tilted, Norman eyed Allie with concern. Maybe worried that a curse word had slipped out of her mouth.

In the weeks since Nick had made a morning run his routine, Allie had been surprised that more Willow Creek women hadn't suddenly taken to jogging. Of course, they'd have to get to the track before seven if they wanted to seem innocent.

It'd be too much to hope that Nick stayed home this morning, and avoided the head-on collision the Ice

Princess would certainly orchestrate. But running was something he did religiously unless the weather was bad. *Come on, lightning.*

Rachel jogged two laps in her cute little workout outfit. One that matched, with shorts so tiny they may as well have been underwear. *Where is this woman's dignity? Teenagers wear more clothes than that.*

"Sorry, Norm. We'll have to wait 'til she's done." She didn't know if Norman would chase after Rachel, but she secretly hoped he'd want to nip at her heels and scare her home.

She plopped down on her blanket and reached into her tote bag. She'd been feeling less and less ashamed about reading her romance novels lately. She pulled out a book, one overnighted to her by another one of her authors. She'd been reading entire books in two and a half days, trying her best to keep up with the flooding demands. Reading samples a chapter in length were enough to secure advertising. But she made it a personal goal to read every book for those marketing on her site.

Hardly past page five, she heard the grass rustling. She looked up, expecting Nick.

"You don't run?"

"Hi, Rachel." She wedged her finger between her book's pages. "I let Norman do the running."

"And you eat all those cupcakes," mumbled Rachel. "It's a wonder your metabolism hasn't slowed down."

Allie felt unusually bold today. "Did you come over here just to call me fat and lazy?" Ever since she'd spilled her secret about Travis burning her book, she'd been feeling braver. And a little less like letting people walk all over her.

"Actually, I came here to run." Rachel began to stretch, bending forward to reach for her toes. "Volleyball season starts in just a couple of weeks."

"You're the coach."

"And the example setter."

Allie shrugged. She was content to continue reading her book, regardless whether Rachel chose to flash her flexibility in her face.

"Why'd you quit, Allie?"

"What are you talking about?"

"Volleyball."

"Really?" Allie closed her book again. "You're asking me this after how many years?"

"It's just a question. No need to get so defensive about it. You were good."

"And you were a mean, coldhearted bitch of a coach." The words shocked Allie, coming from her own mouth. But she kept going. "You did everything you could to make my life miserable. I could *never* do anything right. I'd set a ball inches short of where you wanted it and you'd make me run suicides the rest of the practice while everyone else got to scrimmage."

"Not everyone can handle my coaching methods."

"Kinda hard when they're not fair. You weren't that harsh on everyone." She returned to her book, no longer interested in having any sort of conversation with Rachel. Enough bad memories had been conjured by the question to last a lifetime.

"You might've gotten a scholarship."

She laughed. "Before or after I was on crutches?"

"Your sister's that good. Better."

Amanda was the best player on the team. "Your point?" Most of the town knew she was too. And a scholarship would open a door for Amanda to go wherever she wanted. With her stats, most places would offer her a full ride. A recruiter would only have to sit through one game to realize her talent was unmatchable.

"I want to give Amanda that opportunity. Might even call in a couple of favors to make sure she gets good looks this season."

Allie didn't grace her with a response. *There's always a catch.*

"Of course, she'd have to make the varsity team for that to happen."

"You mean the team she's been a starter on since her freshman year?"

"That's the one." Rachel sat down in the grass, spreading her legs wide. Stretching forward down the middle, her chest brushed the grass.

"And why wouldn't she make it this year?"

Drawing her legs tight in a straight line, Rachel answered, "Well, that's actually dependent on you."

"Me?"

"Yes." Rachel looked over Allie's shoulder and smiled. Nick must be making his way down to the track. "You can give up this silly little crush you have on the doctor. You're not fooling anyone the way you're pining after him. It's kind of embarrassing, really."

Allie bit the inside of her lip to keep from exploding. This woman loved to push her buttons. Always had.

"I'll put it bluntly so there's no confusion." Rachel drew her legs in, knees bent outward, soles of her running shoes touching. "I know about the new hospital policy. So, you can either stop seeing Nick or your sister won't make varsity this year."

"Good morning, ladies." Nick stopped to pat Norman on the head, made small talk for a few minutes, mostly with Rachel, then took off on his run.

"If you don't want to do that," said Rachel as her calculating eyes followed Nick, "and you'd rather be selfish enough to let your sister's scholarship options vanish, then I'll make sure Lesley fires you. And you won't like how she does it. She does love making a scene."

Kim piped up from the backseat of Nick's crew cab, "Allie said there's a new dating policy at the hospital. Whatcha plan to do about it, Nick?"

Nick's grip tightened on the steering wheel as he stole a glimpse of Allie seated beside him. She looked like she wanted to bury her head beneath the seat. They had a few things to talk about tonight, after this bonfire was done. And not just the policy, either. But he didn't want her feeling abandoned now.

Undeterred by Kim's bluntness, Nick interlocked his fingers with Allie's. "I was planning to talk about that tonight." He squeezed her hand.

He caught Allie tossing a look over her shoulder that clearly said *thanks, Kim* with sarcasm.

"Good plan. I'm sure you two lovebirds will find a way around it."

Laughter escaped Allie. True, unfiltered laughter that warmed him. *How could this Allie be the same one that Rachel described? No way she should be in jail.*

"Turn down that road." Allie pointed out to him. "I think I see smoke from the bonfire."

Cars crowded the winding driveway, forcing him to park closer to the road. "I thought we were early."

Allie shrugged. "Alex hasn't been home in a while."

"He's a popular guy," added Kim. "When he does make it back for a bonfire, most of the town turns out."

"She's exaggerating," said Allie, no doubt noticing the look of horror on his face. Probably mistaking that horror for fear of crowds instead of his selfish fear of reputation.

"There's a good crowd, but it's mostly people our age," explained Kim. "We all grew up with him. Plus there's his extended family. He's related to half the town."

Kim hopped out as Nick pulled the keys from the ignition, leaving him alone with Allie in the long driveway. He nodded toward Kim as she walked away, "Allie, I was hoping after the game you and I could talk. Once we drop off your friend."

Allie smiled. "Sorry, she tends to speak her mind."

Instead of returning her smile, Nick looked off in the distance.

"Is something wrong?"

He leaned in, bracketing her cheeks in his hands. Lips crushing against her soft lips, he kissed her until shivers flowed throughout his body. Kissed her like he might never kiss her again before he finally pulled away. "Ready?"

Catching up with Kim, the three walked along the curving driveway in silence. Allie wore jeans and a navy blue tank. Nick knew she didn't follow baseball, but he was happy she'd decided to support his team. "But the Cubs are blue too," she had argued.

"Not *navy* blue."

A fire roared in the backyard. Three stacks of pallets sat along the wall of the garage, prepared to keep the bonfire going all night. On the side deck, a group of people gathered, chatting and drinking beer. Nick spotted the keg on a table near the sliding glass doors.

"I'm assuming you want to watch the game," said Allie. "We need to go in through the garage. There's a special man cave. I'm a little afraid to show you," she teased. "I may never get you out of there. Even if it's decked-out in Cubs gear."

The man cave Allie referenced was a massive room situated over the three car garage. As they climbed the carpeted stairs, they heard both cheers and boos from a safe mixture of fans from both teams. Tables along the back of the room sat overflowed with appetizers—bowls of chips and dips vied for space with mini corndogs, platters of cookies, and stacked pizza boxes.

From across the room near the big screen TV, Alex spotted the trio as they arrived. He jumped up to greet them. "Allie, Kim." He quickly hugged both. "Nick, right?" The men shook hands. Nick immediately reached for Allie's hand, securing it in his.

"Nick, it's the top of the second. Grab a beer and join us."

"Go on," Allie told him. "Kim and I will be outside."

He squeezed her hand before letting it go. "I'll come find you a little later." If reputation had been a concern earlier, he no longer cared.

Allie Jordan obviously wasn't that person Rachel described. Not anymore.

Once their plates were loaded with pizza, Allie led them outside near the fire. "You look a little unsettled," Kim said as she pointed to a pair of empty lawn chairs.

"Nick's jealous."

"Of Alex? Good."

"No Kim, not good. I don't need to go through this again."

Kim plopped down in an empty camping chair. "He's not Travis, Allie. Even I can tell that. And he has a right to be jealous."

"Excuse me?" Allie shoveled pepperoni pizza in her mouth, chewing slowly. She'd had enough of a jealous, possessive guy with Travis. He'd threaten guys who so much as smiled at her, even before his dad fled town. But she'd only been flattered until it was too late to recognize the signs.

"It's *Alex Rowe*. Remember the excuses we use to make to stay after school and watch his football practice? And whenever he was in town visiting his great aunt, how we'd walk by her place as many times as we could without being creepy. He's hot, Al. He's only gotten hotter with age. And he keeps eyeing you like you're a dessert."

"No, he doesn't."

"Well, maybe not dessert, but at least an appetizer. And it's what Nick sees too."

"Hey Allie." Alex stood beside their camping chairs, his shadow flickering in the firelight. "Can I talk to you for a second?"

Kim shot her a look that definitely said, *told you so*.

Just to prove Kim wrong, Allie set her plate in her chair and followed him. Odd that he wanted to walk away from the house, down a worn path toward the family barn. Once they were quite a distance from the other guests, Alex stopped them. "I'm really surprised you're still in town, Allie."

"Why?"

He cocked his head to the side. "With Travis Meyers out on parole—"

Her heart stopped, then took off at a gallop. "Wait, what?"

Alex's dark eyes grew wide. "You didn't know?"

"No. Are you sure?" Allie's heart raced in panic, the thumping deafening her ears. "He's not supposed to be eligible until next spring. Alex, are you sure you didn't mix him up with someone else?"

"I'm sure, Allie. How did you not get notified?"

"I—I don't know." Tears dropped before she knew they were forming.

Alex placed two firm hands on her shoulders. "You were supposed to get a letter in the mail. One that asked if you wanted to be present for the parole hearing. You're sure you didn't get one?"

Allie shook her head. "I—I—" Her shock was too much.

"Allie..." She let him pull her into his arms. The brotherly embrace was comforting. "Monday morning I'll help you take care of this." His voice growled, "I bet Lesley Jamison had something to do with this."

"How long has he been out?" she whispered into his chest.

"A month. Maybe a little longer." A gut-wrenching sob escaped her trembling body and Alex held her tighter.

"Haven't you been watching the website like I told you? Surely you saw his parole date post?"

She nodded her head into Alex's shoulder. "I check it every day. Have for three years. His name hasn't been on the list, Alex. How is that possible?"

"Not sure, but I bet I know who had something to do with that," Alex muttered. "Allie, do you have somewhere you can stay? Someplace safe? At least until I get that restraining order taken care of?"

"Yeah. I'll stay with my mom."

"What's going on here?" Nick's unkind voice cut through the dim night.

Allie pulled away from Alex's grip and ran to him, but he stepped out of reach. "Nick, I need to talk—"

"Save it, Allie. I've been here before." He turned and stormed off, leaving Allie to swipe at the tears stinging her eyes.

"Hey, asshole," called Alex. "Come back here. Unless you're too much of a coward."

Allie froze, afraid of what was about to happen. In the midst of these stirred emotions, Kim appeared at her side. "What happened?" she whispered. Nick came marching back toward Alex, enough anger in his expression to fuel an active volcano.

"Travis is out of jail," she told Kim, her quiet voice trembling, her tears renewing.

Nick and Alex yelled at each other, but she didn't comprehend their words. Her mind was a blur. "I think I'm going to stay with my mom for a while." She hated the idea of abandoning her little ranch home, but if Travis was out, he surely knew she lived there. Probably knew she stayed alone, too. *Damn you, Lesley.*

Tired of the argument, she stepped up, hoping to grab Nick's attention. She needed to leave. To go home and pack a couple of bags and get Norman. *Oh God, what if Travis hurts Norman because I'm not home?* The thought sent tremors through Allie.

"Nick, I need t—"

But that was cut off when Nick swung, knocking Alex off his feet. Kim screamed and rushed to Alex's side. "What did you do?"

Allie took an involuntary step back. Her blood ran cold. The similarities to Travis were all too much. "I'm going home." She made her voice go icy. "Now."

Kim helped Alex to his feet. He didn't challenge Nick again. The fire in Nick's eyes had died down "Fine. Let's go."

Allie only shook her head. "I'm not riding with you, Nick. Stay away from me."

Chapter 26

"It's a setup."

Allie laughed at Pam's serious demeanor. "A setup?" Falling into a recliner, she watched Norman disappear toward the kitchen in search of the vanishing cat. "Seriously, Mom. Come on."

"You know you only got the job in the first place because Lesley was gone and couldn't put in her two cents." Pam set her home renovation magazine on the coffee table with a slap.

Norman fumbled up the stairs. In pursuit of the cat, no doubt. "That meeting wasn't meant to keep people out of trouble. It was to give Lesley the perfect opportunity to fire you. There's nothing she enjoys more than humiliating someone."

Distracted by the TV for a moment, Allie fought a

sigh. The truth seeped in and she nodded.

"You know as well as I do that they'd never fire a good doctor. Not when we've been a year without one." Pam reached for her gray cat who'd emerged from his hiding spot behind the couch. She plopped him in her lap. "He'd be spared on account of need. You're the expendable one."

"Gee, thanks." Allie crossed her legs. "Why does Lesley hate me so much, Mom? I mean, I get that I was with Travis the night he went to jail. But *I* didn't put him up to anything. I begged for him to leave me out of it."

Pam sat back on the couch, reaching for a cup of lemonade. After a long drink, she stared straight ahead at the wall. At a family portrait when there were still four of them. Allie followed the trail of her mom's eyes.

"Lesley doesn't hate *you*, exactly."

Allie sputtered a laugh. "Really?"

"She hates *me*."

Allie'd been twirling a strand of curled hair around a finger, but dropped her hand at Pam's pronouncement. "You?"

"In her eyes, I stole the love of her life." Pam's eyes traveled back to the family photo inside its rustic frame. "Marc never did *love* Lesley. Just entertained a couple of dates with her before I met him at a party." She shook her head. "Your dad always had a way with trying to spare someone's feelings."

Allie dropped both feet to the ground. "Mom, what are you saying?"

"He was popular, you know? But not in that fake way that popularity usually works. He was a genuinely nice guy. Never mean to a girl who might be fawning after him. Even Lesley Jamison."

Her heart tugged, hearing those precious words. To confirm her dad was as great a man as her eight-year-old self remembered.

"Lesley didn't have the greatest life before she married Rich Meyers. Her mother left when she was young. Her dad remarried, had another kid. Then that wife ran off too. And for years, all those girls had was their alcoholic father. The man spent more time at Marley's Bar than he did at home."

Pam reached for her glass of lemonade again, the cat fleeing. "In high school, boys didn't really talk to Lesley. It didn't help that she was completely unapproachable. But she didn't trust anyone, which was understandable."

"Mom, I—"

"Hush. I'm not finished. It's important you hear this."

Norman marched back into the room, tail wagging

victoriously. He dropped a chew toy at Allie's feet and curled into a ball.

"The night I met him, I had no idea that Marc had taken Lesley on a couple of dates over the summer. I especially didn't realize he'd brought her to the party. Lesley wasn't the most social person. I hardly remember seeing her there at all. But your dad... He made a point to talk to everyone. Including me."

Allie hadn't heard this story. Had never really thought to ask how they'd met. "Love at first sight?" She assumed it might conjure sad memories. That they'd all end up in tears with her to blame.

"Something like that."

Pam stood, taking her empty glass with her to the kitchen. "Want some?"

She nodded, then scratched Norman behind the ears as she waited.

"Your dad and I dated all of our senior year. I went to all his football games, his Homecoming coronation. He was King, you know." Pam handed her a glass and sat back on the couch. "We were actually engaged by prom."

"You were?"

"Young and in love," said Pam with a careless wave of her hand. "We didn't get married until after college. But that engagement ring was enough to drive Lesley over the edge."

"What did she do?"

"Rumors have it she coaxed Rich Meyers. A bottle of booze and sex. A few weeks later, the whole town knew she was knocked up. Rich had no choice but to do right and marry her right out of high school. It was that or he'd have to leave town. Not something a man from one of the wealthiest families in Willow Creek was willing to do. Here, he had power and a name to back him. Out in the big, bad world, he was nobody."

Allie wondered what must've gone through Lesley's head the day Travis told her he was dating Allie.

"So, back to my original point. Be careful about the doctor. The whole town is already jumping to conclusions."

"Well, I won't have to worry about that anymore." Allie ducked her head, staring at the floor. "Nick and I aren't together. And now that Travis is out on parole—"

"Finally going to move?"

"Yeah, I kinda have to." Allie's words held less conviction than they ever had.

"But?"

"No buts. I'm going to take Amanda on her California trip. Use up my vacation time. Pack up when I get home."

"Where will you go?"

Allie shrugged. She hadn't browsed for a new city in weeks. "I'll figure it out on vacation, I guess." *Time to tell her about the website.* "I have a confession." Allie set her full glass on an end table. "I think I may've started a new business." She reached for her laptop bag.

Pam raised an inquisitive eyebrow. "By accident?"

"Well, I didn't think it'd take off like it did." As Allie booted up her computer and connected to the internet, she gave her mom the quickest version, "I have this blog where I've been writing book reviews for years. Kim suggested I link it to a website and offer authors a place to advertise."

"I've always known you like romance novels." Pam shook her head in amusement. "Just didn't realize you were a celebrity too."

"Amanda's friend made my website." Allie passed her the laptop.

"Ah, the famous website Amanda's been gushing about."

"I thought I might have one or two requests by now. But last count, I'm up to one hundred and thirty-two."

"Excuse me?"

"Yeah, a little overwhelming. Especially since I'm trying to read every book."

"You couldn't read all those books in a year if you tried." Pam looked up from the screen. "Could you?"

"I read really fast," said Allie. "But it'd be easier if I didn't have a job. I lose a few hours there."

"Then quit now."

"Well, it's a little early, Mom."

"Why?"

"It's still pretty new."

"You have enough savings to buy a house, Allison. You can afford a couple of months without income." Pam reached for her lemonade. "Don't you see? This is the perfect opportunity for you. You can quit on your terms. Go anywhere you want and still have income."

Allie tilted her head, watching for laughter. Or a smile. Or even her mother's smirk. "You're serious?"

Pam passed the laptop back to her. "Deadly."

Chapter 27

"Isn't this the life, Al?" Amanda propped herself up on her elbows, the sun tanning her back. Sand dusted her beach towel, but she didn't care. She was finally in California. Huntington Beach to be exact. "Sunshine, beaches, and hot guys without shirts?"

Parked underneath an umbrella, her sister had become a reading machine. Allie clenched a romance novel, blazing through books faster than Amanda could count. So far she'd finished one on the flight and another last night in their hotel room. And by the looks of it, she'd finish this third one within the hour.

"You should move to California." Amanda grabbed a handful of sand, allowing its silky texture to slip through her fingers. "*If* you're going to move at all."

Allie slapped down her book. "I *am* moving. Travis

is already out on parole. I should've never come back to Willow Creek. He'd never have caught me off guard if I'd just stayed gone."

As far as Amanda was concerned, the only damper to their vacation thus far was Allie's sour mood. Even the traffic that moved at a snail's pace or the necessity to get on the road before she was typically even awake hadn't bothered her in the slightest. "Cheer up, Al. He won't find you here."

Eyeing the nearly finished book, she debated whether now was the time to enlighten Allie about her decision to move to California after graduation. Maybe it'd go over better after they visited the UCLA campus. Or Hollywood Boulevard.

"What?" snapped Allie. "Why are you looking at me like that?"

Sighing loudly, Amanda sat up. "You know what I love about California?"

Allie let out a harsh laugh. "Can't be the traffic."

"Well, tomorrow we can ride the bus. I told you it was dumb to rent a car." She adjusted her floppy sunhat. "I love how nothing ever *stops*. This city's vibrant with life. I know we haven't seen much of it yet since we just got here, but trust me. Once we start exploring, you'll see what I mean."

"Doubtful," Allie muttered, opening her book again.

"There has to be something you like." Amanda stared, not allowing her sister to fall back into her novel. "Look around. Pick one thing. Just *one* thing, Al. And then I'll leave you alone."

Sighing, Allie shoved a bookmark in her book. "Okay." She scanned the area. "Well, it's not how *hot* this stupid sand is. Not to mention that it'll probably take all night to scrub it off my skin. Definitely not the bikini models. I bet they don't eat cupcakes."

Amanda glared over the top of her sunglasses. "Stop it."

"I like the palm trees."

"Why?"

"Because they look so relaxed and grounded. Like swaying in the breeze is their only purpose in life." Allie shoved her book into her tote bag. "I'm going to go cool off in the water."

Watching Allie speed walk to the edge of the ocean, Amanda sighed. It'd be a lot of fun to move to California with her only sister, but Allie would never be happy here. She'd never be happy anywhere other than Willow Creek. *How long will it take her to figure that out?*

Nick had secured the last screw at the base of the

new deck railing when he heard the slam of Aunt Ruby's Buick door. He'd been avoiding most people outside of the exam room. Even made a point to eat his lunch in the old break room, though he had to sit on an old filing cabinet to do so. He learned quickly how fast news spread through Willow Creek. Monday morning, he'd received enough disapproving looks to make a saint feel guilty.

"What do you have to say for yourself, young man?" Aunt Ruby, in her bright pink sun visor, posted her skinny arms on her hips.

He'd been dreading a conversation just like this one. The disapproving looks at least gave him hope that the issue would pass. But a confrontation, from Ruby Rowe nonetheless, wasn't good at all.

Standing, he faced Aunt Ruby. *Probably best to be honest.* "I let my emotions get the best of me."

"Well, I'd say! You punched a state patrolman."

He almost argued that Alex hadn't been on duty, but the fiery glow in Aunt Ruby's eyes warned against it. "It won't happen again."

"You bet it won't," said Aunt Ruby, poking a finger into his chest. For a petite woman, she packed a painful poke into that jab.

He knew an apology would be best, but he didn't want to promise something he might not follow through with. Alex had had his arms around Allie; no mistaking what he saw. How could he apologize for punching someone when it was justified? "I've never hit anyone before." He couldn't meet Aunt Ruby's glare.

"I find that surprising. My nephew's entire jaw is black and blue."

Of course Alex is her nephew. Nick stood in silence. No way to dig himself out of this one. He almost laughed at himself. He'd finally started unpacking his boxes. The ones that'd remained stacked in a spare bedroom. He really thought he'd passed the probation period with flying colors. Now he knew he'd screwed it up beyond repair.

"Just know that Herb *will* be hearing about this." Aunt Ruby whisked away, marching back to her Buick.

Nick hadn't stepped in a bar since his time in Florida when he'd tried almost anything to drown out the memory of catching Dana in bed with Neil. Since he'd been in Nebraska, he'd even been sparing on the alcohol. But tonight, he just felt like getting drunk. With Marley's bar within walking distance, the arguments for avoiding public intoxication were but faint whispers.

Hugged around the U-shaped counter sat several older guys who Nick assumed were regulars. A couple of them he recognized from appointments or the Fireman cookout. Mostly, they were strangers, and he was okay with that. He didn't feel like talking, anyway.

Not that they wanted anything to do with the man who'd punched Alex Rowe, Special Investigator. The state patrol's version of a detective. He may as well have decked a war hero. He just wanted to sit in the corner, drink, and pretend to watch the baseball game on one of the bar's three TVs.

After drink number two, he planned to swear off all women for the foreseeable future. He'd thought Allie was an exception. Sure, they hadn't talked about making their *whatever they had* between them official, but he had intended to do that very thing later, after the game. Once Kim was dropped off and he had Allie all to himself. That was before he caught her in the arms of another man.

He switched to beer, and finished off his first as the clacking of the rack and balls behind him announced the start to another game of pool. He ordered a second frosty bottle as the jukebox started up. *You've got to be kidding me.* AC/DC. The loathsome music of *that* day— the day he'd avoided confronting for months. *Even the same damn song.* But he was exhausted from outrunning his past, and no longer fought those horrid memories. He didn't have the energy or willpower to keep that horrible day at bay. As he drank, the nightmare poured in.

Nick had loitered in the driveway of their condo, imagining Dana pestering him the whole drive to tell her where they were going. She hated not knowing every detail. Trying to pull off any type of surprise for her was a chore that took rigorous and careful planning. And he was certain he'd managed the best surprise of her life. Their dream house was finally coming on the market, and he was the first to know.

She wasn't watching her favorite afternoon reality shows in the living room when he popped through the door, an odd skip to his step. Nor was she in the kitchen fixing herself an elaborate salad. He might've believed she was shopping, but her purse sat neatly on the kitchen counter. He peeked out the back door. Not sitting on the patio on her cell phone with a girlfriend.

He stood by the counter, staring blankly at her purse, wondering if he'd done anything the past few days to tip her off. The likelihood that she was in the bedroom awaiting his arrival was a far cry, but Dana was quite clever when it came to discovering surprises. Maybe she was posed naked on the bed, or in her see-through white negligee that he favored, her blonde hair tossed around her shoulders... The mere image made him ache, and before he knew what he was doing, he rushed up the stairs.

In the hallway, he heard AC/DC coming from behind the closed bedroom door. Dana loved to fool around to her favorite rock band, and if she was playing that, it meant she was in a happy, adventurous mood. He didn't think twice before throwing the door open.

He opened his mouth to ask her, "How did you guess the secret?" but instead he halted in the doorway as if he'd run into a brick wall. The air flattened out of his lungs and he suddenly couldn't breathe.

For months, he had blocked that image of Dana in his favorite negligee, mounted on top of his best friend. Both had their eyes closed, their mouths open. Dana's head was thrown back, long blonde hair trailing down her back, as she rocked to the beat of "Thunderstruck".

The music covered the sound of him opening the door, but it didn't smother the shattering of glass against the hardwood floor when the beautiful crystal vase with the pink roses fell from his grasp and crashed. He'd carefully carted those flowers throughout the house while searching for her, but now he barely noticed the splash of the water on his pants leg or the shards of glass that bounced up and caught his forearm.

Dana screamed and scurried to cover herself. Neil jumped up and clambered off the mattress, tossing Dana across the bed as he did. "Now Nick," he said, "I know this looks bad, but I can explain."

The images that followed Nick around through his careless Florida nights were that of Neil walking calmly toward him, completely naked and still hard for his wife. Dana scrambling to replace an escaped breast into her skimpy lingerie.

Nick wished the vase was still intact so he could smash it over Neil's skull. He couldn't believe the man he'd called his best friend since their first year in medical school was trying to calm *him* down over sleeping with his wife. Nick had openly offered their guest room when Neil was between jobs, not thinking, not suspecting that he would ever try to seduce his wife.

"I want you out of my house," he demanded. His voice was surprisingly calm, though rage burned ferociously in his chest.

"You can't kick him out," said Dana. She had a blanket wrapped around her body now, as if Nick were a stranger and not her husband. "He has nowhere to go." That was when he knew this hadn't been the first time.

"Of course we can't kick him out with nowhere to go," growled Nick. It was obvious whom Dana wanted to stay and whom she wanted to go.

He wouldn't make her ask. He turned and walked away.

At the bar a sturdy body fell into the stool beside Nick, shaking him from the gut-wrenching memory. Swallowing the contents of his third beer, Nick shoved the empty bottle toward the bartender, and prepared to walk home.

"Nick, right?"

"Officer Rowe."

"Alex is fine." Alex hailed the bartender, ordering a beer for them both. "Sit a minute."

The last thing Nick wanted to do was drink a beer with a man he punched. He took a closer look. He'd clipped the edge of Alex's jaw, but the bruise seemed to be fading. Not nearly as bad as Aunt Ruby had described. He'd apologize, but he wasn't sorry. He wished he'd clocked Neil when he had the chance.

"I think you and I got off on the wrong foot the other night."

Nick paused mid-reach to his beer. "Excuse me?" It

didn't make any sense, why this man was trying to make amends. But he'd helped Nick realize that Allie couldn't be trusted. Just like Dana. Better he find out sooner rather than later. He almost wondered if he should shake Alex's hand for that.

"You pack a pretty good punch, but I could show you a few moves for next time."

"Are you trying to be my friend?" Nick hopped off the stool, prepared to start for the door, full beer be damned.

The fierce look Alex turned on him made the hairs on Nick's arms stand up. "Sit. It's awfully rude to walk out on a free beer." If he started walking through town, what was to stop Alex from following him? Paying him back for the bruised jaw line? He obeyed, his other options limited.

"If you have something to say, get to the point. I'm not in the mood for bullshit tonight."

"You always lose your temper so easily?" asked Alex, taking a pull from his bottle.

Nick didn't answer.

"We can't have a doctor in town with a loose temper. Dangerous for patients."

He nearly mentioned he was packing his bags already. No point in staying in Willow Creek any longer than necessary. His three-month trial was almost up, anyway. He'd hand in his notice tomorrow and start boxing things up. Head back to Georgia like his sister begged on a near-daily basis.

"I'm a special investigator with the state patrol."

So Aunt Ruby poked into me. He gave Alex a look that said *want a medal?*

"But before I was, I had to do my time in the field. Spent a couple of years wearing a uniform, patrolling the entire northeast region, busting criminals and making arrests." Alex clamped down on Nick's arm when he tried to rise again. "Five years ago, I made an arrest that didn't make me too popular with Lesley Jamison. I hauled her son to jail after he shot Allie."

Nick fell into his stool, no longer fighting to leave. Leaning his elbows onto the counter, he began to listen.

"Don't know how much you know about the town history over this. About Lesley first divorcing her husband and squeezing every penny out of him before she ran him out of town with his tail between his legs." Alex's eyes stared blankly at the collection of liquor bottles behind the bar. "No one's seen him since. After Rich Meyers left, well, his kid's never quite been the same. Rumors had it he needed therapy, it messed him up so bad."

"He didn't get any, did he?"

Alex shook his head. "That asshole has been out on

parole for over a month. Allie didn't know until I told her Friday night."

"How—"

"Funny thing about the law," said Alex, taking a swig. "People with enough money and power always find a way around it. Allie should've been notified. Hell, I was surprised to see her still here a couple of weeks ago. She'd planned to jet before Travis Meyers was back in town. Before he decided to kill her this time."

Nick felt sick to his stomach. "You weren't luring her into the woods that night, were you?"

Shaking his head, Alex said, "Allie's a nice girl. Beautiful, even. But she's never been more than like a little sister to me."

Well, shit. "I feel like an ass."

"Yep."

"She's in California now. With her sister."

Alex nodded. The news of her vacation obviously had made its way around town. "Rumor has it she may not come back." He studied Nick. "You look a little under the weather there, Doc."

The idea of never seeing Allie again after the way they'd left things made Nick more than nauseated. He remembered all too well how she ran toward him when he caught her in Alex's arms. But the shadows had hidden her face. Hidden the tears he now realized had to have been running down her cheeks. "I only lost my temper because I thought you were trying to steal her from me."

"Why would you think a thing like that?" Alex flashed two fingers to the bartender. "Unless it's happened before."

Nick nodded, eyes glued to a baseball game he wasn't watching. "I didn't do anything about it last time. Just left."

"And ended up here?"

"Something like that." Nick eyed the new beer and wondered if he should stop. Would he remember how to get home if he had another?

"Relax, I'll give you a ride," Alex offered. "My little sister just got her license."

Nick didn't argue. He was too busy wondering how he'd make up being such an ass to Allie. Wondering how he'd keep her safe from some shit who should still be locked behind bars. "You don't live in Willow Creek, do you?"

"Nope. I'm in town on a case."

"Lesley's kid?"

Alex shook his head. "Not quite."

"Then what?"

"Can't discuss it."

Nick surprised himself at the blunt question that

came next. "It's best if Allie leaves, isn't it?"

Alex straightened on his stool. "Probably. Otherwise, she'll just be living in fear."

Nick's heart plummeted. Alex was right. If Allie stayed, she'd endanger her life. Ensuring her safety was the least he could for her. Not fair to ask her to stay when he was still dealing with the past he'd suppressed.

He picked up the fresh bottle from the bar. Not only did he have to *let* her go, he had to make sure she did.

Chapter 28

"Why didn't you just tell me upfront that you wanted to move to California?" Allie asked from across the rounded table. Forty stories up, she and Amanda sat in a rotating restaurant in the middle of downtown Los Angeles.

"I didn't think you'd come with me." Amanda poked at her tiny steak. "I thought you'd laugh."

As night fell and the sky darkened, Allie decided this was the only part of their trip she had truly enjoyed. The lit up skyscrapers were almost beautiful when darkness blanketed the rest of the city. There'd also been very little traffic tonight. *For once.* "Why would I laugh?"

Amanda shrugged. "I mean, it's a little ridiculous to think a recruiter from UCLA is going to show up at one of my volleyball games and offer me a scholarship. Plus, California is expensive, remember?"

"It is." Allie reached for her pop, taking a sip. "You'll have to get a job, even if you have a full scholarship."

"That's okay. You should move out here too. Wouldn't that be fun?" Amanda sent a cheesy smile across the table. "You could rent an apartment, and I could stay with you instead of in the dorms."

Allie expected her sister to burst out laughing, but she didn't. "I'm not moving to LA. Where would Norman run?"

"At the beach."

"After a three hour car ride?" Allie emptied her cup and slid it to the edge of the table. "You try tolerating a big dog when he's cooped up in traffic that doesn't move for that long. You'd be right back in Willow Creek after one try."

"I guess Nick might miss you if you moved out here."

Allie stabbed her filet with her fork. "Hardly."

"What happened? You two seemed really happy."

"Well, that was before he punched Alex."

Amanda's eyes grew as wide as saucers. Allie chewed on her steak. She hadn't realized her sister didn't know. Seemed like the entire town knew. "Nick thought I was making out with Alex or something. So he punched him.”

“Wow, Al. Just like Rance in *Forbidden Pleasures* when Bianca’s ex showed up. Except Alex isn’t your ex. Still, he’s pretty hot. I can see why Nick got jealous. But he *punched* him? How did you not drag Nick into the woods and rip off his clothes—”

“I think you need to lay off the romance novels. They’re filling your head with crazy ideas.” Sawing at her filet, Allie added, “They’re not reality.”

“Wait, you’re mad at Nick for that?”

She didn’t care to explain the whole scenario. Amanda already knew that Travis was back in town. That she’d be packing up her entire life in a matter of days once they returned to Willow Creek next week. Last she checked, Lansing, Michigan seemed a pretty good city to try out. Not too big, not too small. Not somewhere Travis would ever think to hunt for her.

“I think you’re being stupid.”

She took her time with the straw to stir her pop. “What?”

“Stupid. It means idiotic. Dumb. Ridiculous. Take your pick,” Amanda said. “Nick loves you, don’t you get it? He wouldn’t have punched Alex otherwise.”

At the icy glare her sister shot her way, Allie explained further, “You don’t understand, Amanda. Travis used to punch guys just for smiling at me. But that wasn't love. It was obsession. A hint of violence. Something I should've paid more attention to from the beginning. I was flattered at first, but then the shoving started—"

"Nick is *not* Travis, Allie."

As the waiter came to clear their plates, Allie realized it didn't matter anymore. She had to pack next week. Leave town. Amanda would be off the varsity team if she and Nick made amends. *Still haven't figured a way around the Ice Princess. Easier just to leave.*

The buzzing of her cell phone intercepted the uncomfortable conversation. "It's Mom." A close look at the text, and Allie scanned the restaurant for people she might possibly offend before swearing. "That bitch."

Amanda's head shot up, her fork clattering against the table. "What happened?"

"I should've known." Allie shoved her cell phone back in her purse. "Your two-a-day schedule got moved up."

"What?"

"The Ice Princ—I mean Coach Jamison decided today that practice starts this Thursday. Meaning we have to head home a few days early."

"That's stupid." Amanda picked up her fallen fork and set it near her spoon, readied for dessert. "I'm already out of town. I'm not cutting my California vacation short by even one hour. What's the worst she can do?"

"It's mandatory," said Allie, already calculating how expensive it'd be to change their flights. "Mom said no exceptions for anyone who wants to make varsity."

"I'm calling Tammy after we're done eating," Amanda said. "She's not supposed to be back from Florida until next week. She's the best setter on the whole team. I bet Coach won't make her catch an earlier flight."

"I'm sorry, Amanda."

"Why? It's not your fault my coach is a vacation-wrecking bitch."

Allie spit out her Dr. Pepper, luckily back into the glass.

"I'm not cutting my vacation short, Al."

The waiter delivered a chocolaty dessert for them to share; she picked up her spoon. "Don't be stupid, Amanda. If you want to come back here on a scholarship, you need to make varsity." If she was going to be giving up Nick, she'd be damned if her sister was going to sink her own chances of a volleyball scholarship simply to prove some stupid point.

The first night back from California, Allie's overstuffed suitcase lay unzipped and untouched on her bedroom floor. Norman grumbled, trying to get comfortable despite this obstacle. She sat on the edge of her bed, staring at her cell phone. *Should I call or save it for another night?* She needed to tell Nick she was leaving. That by the end of the week, she'd be gone from Willow Creek for good. At least explain what had happened with Alex so he wouldn't hate her memory.

She dug through her suitcase and found the seashell she'd brought back from Huntington Beach. The shell she found their first day in California. She remembered Nick's story about his seashell collection with his mom and thought it might be a good peace offering. "I'll be back, boy. Don't eat the coffee table." She pointed a stern finger at Norman. "I mean it."

Even from the street, Allie could tell that the house up on the hill was dark. Despite her instincts telling her to turn back, she continued down the lone road in her tiny car to Nick's house. Though it was after nine, he should still be awake. She shoved out any fear that Travis might lurk in the cover of darkness. *I'll just leave the seashell with a quick note.* If Nick wanted to say goodbye, he could call.

As she suspected, the back door was unlocked. She was in and out in just a couple of minutes. No point in lingering in the kitchen that conjured so many happy memories; those carefree days before Nick decided to express his jealousy with his fist. Allie shook her head. *Nick is* not *Travis. Nick is* not *Travis.* She closed the door behind her.

"Hello Allie."

Allie shrieked. "Lesley!" Of anyone who might've stepped from beside Nick's back door, Lesley Jamison wasn't even on Allie's list.

"Sit down, dear." The command hung in the air, heavier than the humidity.

Taking a seat on the concrete stair, Allie fought her desire to ask Lesley any of the many questions brewing in her mind. *Why is she here?* But her best option was to keep her mouth shut until she figured out Lesley's agenda. Still the questions circled. *What does she want? How long has she been waiting.*

"I don't have to remind you about the rules. You knew the consequences, so we won't focus too much on what you've done wrong. We're going to discuss what you can do to fix it." Lesley reached into the pocket of her sweater jacket and pulled out a pack of cigarettes and her lighter. "Smoke, dear?"

"No," said Allie. *The stupid policy! Cruella has an agenda.* She almost spit out that she and Nick weren't together. That Nick wasn't even home right now. *Keep your mouth shut, Allie. Wait this out.* It seemed an eternity that she waited for Lesley to retrieve a cigarette, light it, then slip the pack in her pocket.

"As I see it, you have two options." Lesley's words were calm and deliberate. "The first option is your best, I'm afraid. You'd be a fool to pass it up."

Allie stared at the long blades of grass growing flush along the side of the step.

"You can avoid the embarrassment and humiliation of me having to fire the both of you." Lesley took a puff. "Don't look so surprised. Nick works for me until his probation period is over. And it isn't."

"Why—"

"I have a replacement all lined up. Had one this whole time until Doc Herb called in a referral." Lesley blew out a nasty puff of smoke. "You'll hand in your resignation, effective immediately. I'll even throw in two weeks' severance pay. That should give you enough time to pack up your house."

Guess she hasn't heard that I'm giving a shorter notice tomorrow. "And if I don't?"

"Make no mistake, Allie. You're leaving town." Lesley puffed on her cigarette. "I have a job lined up for you in Boston. A friend of mine runs one of the smaller practices in the area. The pay is certainly more than you make here." Another puff. "Or could ever hope to make in this town. If you agree to go to Boston, Nick will keep his job. And his dignity."

She wanted to tell Lesley to go to hell. *She thinks she's forcing me to move.*

"You'll break this off with Nick. Tomorrow. If I catch wind of the affair once you've left, your job security *will* crumble. You should've known you two are in different worlds."

"What's the other option?"

"It isn't a great one, I'm afraid. I'll fire you both." Lesley was finished with her cigarette and flicked the butt into the grass. "You can deal with the humiliation of that however you choose. But consider how this town will feel about losing a great blessing of a doctor. One who arrived so miraculously in our time of need."

"You just said you had a replacement lined up."

"Oh, I do." Lesley stuffed her hands into her sweater pockets. "You should know by now that I always get what I want, Allie. And I want you to leave."

She was tired of being a puppet in Lesley's little game of town politics and decided to seize her opportunity. "I'll go."

"That's a good girl."

"But on *my* terms."

Lesley straightened at her boldness. "You think I'll cater to *your* needs?"

"I'm moving to Omaha, not Boston."

Considering Allie's request, Lesley nodded. "Fine."

"I'll need somewhere to stay. At least a two-bedroom with a yard. Fenced."

Lesley stood, turning away. When she turned back, her expression was blank. "Fine. But you're not to come within thirty miles of Willow Creek for at least six months. I don't care if your mother is on her death bed."

"Fine." In a couple of months it wouldn't matter anyway. Allie would quit her new job and find somewhere else to live. But for now, she'd take advantage of the blackmail arrangement. *Let Cruella's meddling work in my favor, for once.*

"Nick has a few secrets of his own, doesn't he?"

Allie stiffened.

"It'd be a shame if those secrets got out, wouldn't it?" A malicious grin spread across Lesley's face. "Best you head home. Start packing. I'll follow in my car so you don't go running into the sweet doctor's arms, now."

Chapter 29

"What the hell, Allie?" Kim slammed the front door behind her. "You're really doing this? You're really moving to Omaha?"

Allie steeled herself beside her suitcase. Kim wouldn't be pleased when she listened to her voicemail, Allie knew that. But she hadn't quite expected this outburst. "I don't know why that surprises you." She roughly shoved more clothes from her bed into her oversized suitcase. "I thought you'd be happy that I'm not skipping the state. Means I'll still get to see you."

"You're letting Travis control your life!" Kim appeared beside the bed. Norman scrambled from his cozy spot and darted for the kitchen at her stomping. "Stop running, Allie."

"What would you suggest I do?" She'd grown tired of

the constant harassment. Kim's demands. Would she never understand what Allie had gone through? Kim hadn't witnessed Travis turn from doting boyfriend to possessive monster, capable of shooting someone he claimed to love.

"Try taking a self-defense class. Get a restraining order!"

"I have one!" Allie slammed her suitcase shut. "It won't keep him away."

Kim marched into the kitchen, returning with the letter Allie kept hidden beneath her charging laptop. "Burn it."

"What?"

"You heard me. Burn this letter. Stop letting Travis win. Burn this letter and stay."

She refused to meet Kim's glare and instead began filling a box with a few romance novels she knew she couldn't live without. "You don't get it. There's more to all this."

"No there's not."

She considered telling Kim about Lesley's threat to reveal Nick's secrets. But she'd promised to keep them herself. *Not that it matters anyway.* He hadn't so much as called to thank her for the seashell, much less say goodbye. "I'm leaving, Kim. Today."

"You take Cruella up on her offer and we're not

friends anymore.”

The paperback slipped from her hand, dropping to the floor with a thud. “What?” Her heart slammed against her chest, and she could feel the blood draining from her cheeks. She didn’t want to believe Kim. They’d been through everything together.

“I mean it, Al.”

Kim had been the only friend that stuck out the entire ordeal with Travis, even when Allie had tried to push her away. *She’s just really pissed-off. She’ll come around in a couple days.* But the fire in Kim’s eyes begged to differ.

She could at least tell Kim part of the truth. “It’s not just Travis.” *How much will she see through this?* “Lesley more or less blackmailed me. I can’t step foot in Willow Creek for six months.”

Kim posted her hands on her hips. “Why?”

Returning her attention to the box she was loading, Allie said, “It’s the only way I’ll keep the job she arranged in Omaha. And the house.”

“Unbelievable!” Kim’s voice echoed off the walls. “She bought you out! She bribed you and you took it.”

“I plan—”

“Save it, Allie. I’m through. Through watching you cower in fear over something you can control. If you won’t stand up for yourself, then I don’t even get why we're friends." Kim stomped out of the bedroom. The front door slammed so hard Norman barked.

She'd been gone for nearly two weeks. Nick had to do something——anything——to keep his mind off Allie Jordan. And his punch still hung over him with all the disapproving scowls that many citizens reserved. It'd made shopping in Norfolk a must. But he wouldn't leave them without a doctor until the Board asked him to leave. As for missing Allie…

He'd thought her absence would get easier to adjust to. But it hadn't.

The seashell stared back at him from his kitchen island. He hadn't moved it since he discovered it late one evening after returning from Alex's place. Alex had been an unlikely ally. He hadn't expected to be watching baseball games with a guy he'd decked. But it was nice having at least one friend in Willow Creek.

The sight of the seashell had nearly broken him. He almost called her. Invited her over to tell her thank you. To tell her goodbye. The memento meant she wasn't mad at him. *Inviting her might've convinced her to stay.*

Something he couldn't let her do with a dangerous man out on parole.

Instead, he spent his time finishing the barn loft. They'd run him from town soon enough, but keeping busy helped keep his sanity at bay through all the waiting. He'd layered the walls with reclaimed wood he'd gotten from an old barn they tore down outside of town, a nice distraction. At a garage sale, he'd purchased a box of mason jars. He used them as lights he strung against the wall.

The best improvement was the new built-in daybed, including the new mattress. He'd tossed the old one out weeks ago when he suspected a mouse had worked its way through the cover. A mouse he remembered telling Allie that didn't live in his barn loft.

The Norfolk paper sat on the opposite end of the kitchen island, untouched. He grabbed it. Anything to take his mind off of all that might have been. He'd be back in Georgia within a couple of weeks anyway. Scouring the classifieds, he spotted an advertisement for an estate auction in a nearby town. Figuring he might find a piece of old furniture worth refurbishing, he grabbed his keys. If he hurried, he'd catch the tail end of the sale.

When he arrived, he found several cardboard boxes beneath tent covers. Only a couple pieces of furniture were left. Nothing he could do much with. He caught sight of Archie standing at the opposite end of the row, the farmer ignoring him with his head purposely turned away. Nick ducked his head in the boxes to see if anything might be worth salvaging.

Several old boxes sat filled with books, most with yellowed pages and a thin dusty film. Several shelves sat empty in his loft. He thought, *adding old books might give it charm*. Ridiculous, considering he'd be leaving soon, but perhaps the next doctor would enjoy the ambiance.

He purchased a box without really looking through it... until he made it home. There in his kitchen, next to the haunting seashell, he unearthed a book with a familiar title from the dusty box. It nearly broke him. *Sweetly Scandalous* by Lillian Caywood. "Allie's favorite." He wasn't certain how he remembered. But he knew without a doubt it was the right book.

He poured himself a fuller than usual glass of whiskey and tossed it down.

Slipping a bottle of merlot into her cloth tote, Rachel smiled. Her plan had worked quite nicely. It helped that Lesley had an agenda of her own to run Allie Jordan out of town. Helped more than she'd like to admit. But many things had played in Rachel's favor without her lifting a finger.

Verifying one last time that she had everything—marinated steaks, foil-wrapped potatoes, homemade fruit salad—Rachel reached for her keys. Tonight she planned to make Nick hers.

After Nick punched Alex Rowe at his bonfire, rumors had whisked around town. A few folks worried that if he couldn't control his temper he wouldn't make much of a doctor. But most found the story amusing. Who could blame Nick for his jealousy? Alex Rowe had quite a reputation as a heartbreaker and the good looks to support it.

She wanted Nick to know he had an ally. A small rumor had already swept through town that Nick might be returning to Georgia very soon. She intended to make sure that didn't happen. Whatever it took.

Dusk hung in the sky as she pulled into Nick's driveway. A dim light glowed from one corner of the house. She tugged her dark shirt a little further down, drawing attention to her cleavage in the red sleeveless top. "Show time."

The doorbell echoed inside; she frowned when footsteps didn't ensue. Nick's truck was parked in the driveway. She glanced toward the brick school building through the mass of maple trees. *Maybe he went for a run.* She rang once more, waiting almost a minute this time.

Rachel decided he wasn't home and reached for the doorknob. She knew her way around an outdoor barbeque grill better than most men, even though she'd intended to bring the steak and baked potatoes for him to grill. *A good way to boost his ego. Get him feeling nice and good about himself.* But with everything going on, he might prefer to simply show up and sit down to an already prepared home-cooked meal. One he didn't have to lift a finger for.

The front screen door hung half open when she caught sight of Nick emerging from the barn, looking distraught. Like he might need more than a little stroking of his ego tonight. *Might need to move up the plan a little.*

"Hi Nick," she called from the front porch, allowing the screen door to close. "I tried to call." It was a lie, but he'd been in the barn; he'd never know the difference. When he grew closer and she no longer needed to yell, she added, "Thought you might be hungry."

"I already ate."

Expecting his immediate resistance, she locked on her smile. "These are fresh steaks from Archie. He gave them to me for helping tutor his daughter. I certainly can't eat both of them on my own. I'd hate for them to spoil."

She watched his shoulders drop slightly, seeming to release tension. "I don't really do much grilling."

"Teaching is one of my specialties."

He stopped just below the porch. His expression held blank, but she didn't miss the dilemma in the gaze he fixed on the grass.

"I just wanted you to know you have a friend, Nick. If you punched Alex Rowe, I'm sure he deserved it." She bit her bottom lip. "I know not everyone feels that way, though."

Nick climbed the steps to the porch and held the door open. "Why don't you come in?"

Travis waited for the cover of darkness to slip into Willow Creek. He'd been outraged to hear Mort bragging that his own mother had driven Allie out of town. And because Lesley insisted he still stay hidden from the townspeople, he hadn't been able to find out where she'd gone.

He'd nearly gotten caught when Lesley woke for a shot of whiskey, stumbling through the living room as he snooped through her house last night for clues. But there'd been nothing. Not one single hint of Allie's whereabouts.

Tonight, he intended to comb every inch of Allie's little ranch house. He'd been keeping an eye on it, ensuring it hadn't been rented out to someone else. Odds were it'd sit empty until Allie came back. Oh yes, he knew she'd come back. Once he found her he'd give her no other choice.

The only decent spot in town to hide his truck was the far side of the school building. He was forced to park there, but the walk wasn't terribly far. Just a few blocks. Heavy shadows from mature trees hid him most of the way.

The glow from an orange streetlight washed over Allie's little front porch. The house would be locked and someone would spy him snooping around for a spare key. Instead, he hopped the locked gate to the backyard.

"Shit." *Back door's locked too.* He searched several minutes for a key, but Allie hadn't left one behind. *I'll just have to find another way in.* He stripped off his cotton T-shirt in the dark and wrapped it around his fist to muffle the noise. Punching the corner of a kitchen window, he reached his hand inside and flipped the window's latch. He swore when a chunk of glass clinked inside, bouncing to the floor.

A light came on next door and he shoved the window open and crawled inside. His knee caught another piece of glass as he rolled off something in the dark and closed the window.

Most of Allie's furniture still sat in the house. The kitchen counter looked bare to him, as did most surfaces. He stalked by the buffet table against the far wall in the kitchen, headed right for the bedroom. Searching around the room, he finally tore open the closet. "What the hell?" Hundreds of books sat stacked in Allie's closet. He shoved them out of the way, certain a clue to her whereabouts lay buried beneath all the books. They'd been important to her. Too important to leave behind unless she planned to come back for them.

A rattling echoed from the living room, Travis darted from the bedroom. Catching sight of a shadow through a curtained window next to the front door, he debated running. But the door was opening.

His sweaty palm covered his pistol.

"Who's here?" he heard an old man call out.

He waited in the shadow, hoping the old geezer would leave. He didn't want to do anything rash. *Close the door and leave, old man.*

The man's hand reached for the light switch on the wall. In the moment the light flashed on, Travis spotted the shotgun.

He didn't think. He just pointed the gun and pulled the trigger.

The old man dropped to the ground.

Chapter 30

"This has got to be one of the best steaks I've ever had." Nick leaned back in his chair, hands on his stomach.

"Nothing quite like fresh meat." Rachel slid from her chair, gathering their plates. "But I can't take all the credit," she told him. "You manned the grill pretty well for an amateur." Nick avoided her blue eyes. Eyes that'd do nothing but get him in trouble considering his two glasses of wine. *Almost three.*

"I know you hate rumors." After running water over the plates and setting them in the sink, Rachel turned around. Leaning against the counter, her breasts popping, she said, "But I heard one I really hope isn't true."

Nick stared at the table. *What now?*

"I heard you're leaving. Going back to Georgia."

Shuffling in his chair, he tried to form a reply. He considered lying. Even considered telling the truth. But words failed him.

"I hope you're not going to let a silly thing like punching Alex Rowe run you from town."

"You didn't have to deal with Aunt Ruby. I think that woman wants to stone me for what I did," he muttered.

"He's her favorite great nephew." She walked back to the dining table, but didn't sit. "Ruby Rowe's going to hold a grudge for a while. Then everything will go back to normal. You'll see." She reached for his empty wine glass and refilled it. He should object, but the alcohol was helping him let go. Helping him coast through just one night without feeling as though his world was crumbling around him.

"She was pretty mad." He didn't feel like disclosing the details of his probation arrangement, so he let the conversation die. "Rachel, thank you for dinner."

"You owed me." She smiled over the top of her glass. "So this makes us even."

Scooting his chair back, Nick stood. He wobbled once from the wine, but caught his palm on the island counter. Rachel's delicate hand held his elbow, her body inches from his own. Reason fled and the desperate desire to erase all his pain surged in. He'd be gone in a couple of weeks. No way he would survive Aunt Ruby's horrible report to Herb. Besides, Aunt Ruby wasn't the only one disappointed in his erratic behavior.

What's one more mistake?

He leaned in, his hand letting go of the island. Rachel closed her eyes, parted her lips. Then he stumbled, his foot catching something on the floor.

Bending over to retrieve it, he heard Rachel laugh. "You are a little tipsy, Nick. But so am I. Maybe we should…" Nick didn't hear anything else. Once his eyes locked on the seashell, the little note from Allie rolled up inside, everything else around him faded. Pain he'd fought down returned.

"Nick, are you okay?" Rachel held both of his arms as he stood, closing the distance between them.

"I need you to leave," he said as she pressed her body against his. He no longer felt anything but numb, his voice barely above a whisper. "Please."

"What? I don't understand."

"Please," he said, his voice rising. "Leave me alone."

Rachel eyed the seashell he had his fingers clamped around. The last thing he wanted was her figuring out its significance tonight. He'd already be battling memories of Allie. Regrets of letting her go. He didn't need Rachel making up some other derogatory stories on top of it.

"Thank you for dinner. But I need to be alone. Now." He removed her hands from his arms. "Leave."

Nick knew it was late. But the seashell and that stupid book had plagued him for hours.

Though he'd planned to walk, he felt sprinkles fill the air while stepping down his porch stairs. The overcast sky threatened a downpour soon. He smelled heavy rain on the horizon, so he hopped into his truck, and blazed down his road to town.

He wouldn't wake Ed up, but he'd knock if there was a light on.

Pulling alongside Ed's curb, he spotted the glow of a lamp through the front window and nearly chickened out. Nearly drove right on out of town just to get away. To clear his head. But if anyone would know what to do about Allie, he felt certain this man was key.

He knocked on the door and waited. The rustle of raindrops on the leaves filled the air as the wind picked up. Lightning flashed in the distance. He knocked again and listened for footsteps. *Maybe he's asleep in his chair.* Peeking through the front window, he didn't see any trace of him. Fear pricked his chest. "Ed?" Nick banged on the door. "Ed, you in there?"

The wind carried a garbled moan right to him, only it came from the east. His eyes snapped to Allie's house. Hanging off the front stair, he spotted a hand. "Ed?" He raced to Allie's house and found Ed sprawled out on his back, his chest covered in blood. "Ed, it's Nick." He fought down the fear of the old man dying on Allie's porch. Shoved it down so he could focus on saving the man's life. "Ed, I just need to grab my medical bag from my truck. I'm coming right back."

Sprinting to his truck, Nick whipped out his cell phone. "Get an ambulance. Now!"

He ran back with his bag, already digging out a dressing. "Ed, stay with me. The ambulance is on its way. But we've got to take care of this wound first, okay?"

Ed dipped his chin.

Blood bubbled on the left side of his chest. The worn Willow Creek Legion Hall shirt was stuck to the wound. Nick yanked a scissors from his bag and began cutting the fabric, leaving the stuck material intact. He watched Ed's lips, ensuring they weren't turning blue. Hoping that he'd been in time to keep his lung from collapsing. "Who did this to you, Ed?"

"Too dark," Ed wheezed. "Someone broke in."

Why can't I hear sirens yet? The fire hall was only a couple of blocks away. In a town this size, getting the ambulance out within minutes should be a cinch. "Don't worry. We'll get the bastard." He hovered the dressing over Ed's wound. "Ed, I need to you exhale and hold your breath until I say, okay?"

Ed tried nodding again.

Nick secured the dressing, leaving one side un-taped to allow air out. He wasn't convinced Ed hadn't already collapsed a lung, just hopeful. Sirens echoed as flashing lights invaded the dark street. "We're going to get you to the hospital."

"Call," said Ed, his voice growing weaker. He fought to keep his eyes open.

"Who do you want me to call, Ed?" Nick felt ashamed that he didn't know whether Ed Mullins even had any children living in Willow Creek. He remembered Allie mentioning his wife had passed away a few years ago. But she never mentioned kids.

"Allie. Call Allie."

The ambulance came to an abrupt halt in front of Allie's house. EMT's rushed out with a stretcher.

"Call Allie," repeated Ed, only moments before the emergency personnel descended.

"Dr. Bryant, thank God you found him."

Maintaining eye contact with Ed, Nick assured him, "I will."

Once Ed was stabilized in the hospital, Nick slipped out the back door. Miraculously there had been a surgeon staying at the local hotel, saving Ed a trip to Omaha. The rain had let up for now, but he could see ominous clouds building for another downpour. Driving away, he finally let out a deep breath—relief that he arrived in time. Ten minutes longer and Ed might've ended up in a mortuary cooler instead of his hospital bed.

At Allie's house he spotted Alex and a couple of other men through her now well-lit front window. Yellow tape blocked off entry to curious onlookers.

Knowing that Alex was going to be a few minutes, he decided to make the difficult call he'd been putting off. He'd avoided talking to Allie for weeks. And now, his first opportunity would be to deliver bad news. But she might know how to get ahold of Ed's kids.

Each ring made Nick's heart pound violently. His last memory of her wasn't a great one—she'd been crying. Another ring. A look of horror on her face at his repulsion. At his misunderstanding of the situation. Another ring.

Voicemail.

Not even a greeting. Just a generic female voice repeating a number.

"Allie, it's Nick." He took a deep breath. "I'm afraid I have some unfortunate news." His palms grew sweaty. "Ed Mullins was shot tonight. He's stable now and resting in the hospital. He asked me to call you. To let you know." Nick bit down on his bottom lip, debating if he should say more. *Tell her you miss her.* "Thought you might be able to notify any next of kin." He hung up the phone like it might explode if he didn't end the call.

Alex appeared on the small porch, talking over his shoulder to one of the men still inside. Nick pushed open his truck door and cut through the patch of grass toward the house. "Anything?" he asked, but Alex probably wouldn't be able to share details with him even if he had any.

Lifting yellow tape, Alex slipped off the porch toward him. "Nothing official." He scanned the area. "We found blood on a piece of broken glass. We'll send it to the lab."

"But?"

"But I don't need a DNA test to tell me who that blood belongs to. I don't think you do either."

"Meyers."

"I can't get a warrant until we have evidence. Keep an eye out for me, will you?" Alex tapped into his smartphone, holding up a picture. "Call me if you see this guy hanging around town."

"Of course."

Allie stared at her phone. At Nick's name on the screen next to "missed call". A tear fell before she even knew she wanted to cry. *Why would he call me now, after all these weeks?*

Norman grumbled from the end of the bed.

"I'm not calling him back." She tossed her phone aside and picked up her latest novel. Only sixty pages from the end, she had to finish it tonight. Her stack of requests grew daily.

A chime signaled; he'd left a voicemail. She dropped her book back in her lap. Norman looked over his paws at her as if to say *what do you want me to do about it?*

She picked up her phone, considered for a long moment that she might just listen to his pleading message and then refuse to call him back. But right before she pushed play, she switched off her phone. "Not tonight, Nick."

"What do you mean there aren't any flights

tonight?" Miranda paced the dining room as her husband set down his phone. "I have to get to Nick before *she* does. I have to leave tonight, Josh. It can't wait. Can't you call in one of your special favors?"

It'd been weeks since Dana last pounded on her front door. Until tonight. *Should've known no news was a cue for disaster!*

Miranda had just put her kids to bed when the doorbell rang. Dana stood on her porch with a smug smile on her face. "I found Nick *without* your help." When Miranda accused her of lying, Dana had shot back with, "Then tell me there's nothing special about a little town in Nebraska called Willow Creek."

"This is my calling in a favor." Her husband rose from the table. Laughing, he gathered her into his arms. "I'll do anything to stop your pacing. It's driving me crazy."

Most of the time Miranda hated how much being a pilot for a major airline kept him away from home. But tonight it came in pretty handy. Kissing her on the forehead, Josh said, "I know which flight she's on. There's no faster way to get to Nebraska than to follow her."

The tip of her head hardly reached his shoulder. "I've really mucked things up this time," she said into his T-shirt. "He'll never move back to Georgia now."

"Did you ever think that maybe he doesn't want to?"

She beat a fist into Josh's muscular chest. "Stop it." She hated it when he used reason to foil her illusions. "How could he want to stay in the smallest town in the middle of nowhere? There's nothing there for him, Josh. Just cows and cornfields. Did you know he even tried to tip a cow a few weeks ago?"

Laugher vibrated against Miranda's cheek.

"It's not funny!" she snapped. But she hid an emerging smile in Josh's warm T-shirt. "What sane person tries to tip a cow?"

"Did he say why?"

"No. Just said a friend took him—" She stopped mid-sentence, pulling away from Josh's vise-grip embrace. "I'm such an idiot. *Such an idiot!*" Marching into the kitchen, she uncorked a bottle of merlot and drank right from the bottle.

"Such a classy woman. That's why I love you."

"Nick's been happy the last few times I talked to him."

"That sounds downright awful."

"Shut up." She took another swig. She knew the wine would be better after a percolator, but there wasn't time. "He's been sounding different on the phone. Before, it seemed like he was just getting by. I thought he'd get sad as time went on, realize how much he missed home."

Josh leaned against the doorjamb. "But he's happy?"

"Yes. Too happy." She started to pace again, the enclosed kitchen not allowing her much space. "He's infatuated with someone. Has to be. He thinks he's in love. Josh, this is worse than I thought. Call again." Miranda tried to push past her husband, but his sturdy frame didn't budge. "Check one more time on the flights. There has to be one leaving tonight. Nick thinks he's in love, but—"

Two firm hands clamped down on Miranda's shoulders. "Babe, there are no flights tonight. And you can't jump to any conclusions until you get to Willow Creek and see what's going on for yourself."

"But—"

"I know you're his big sister, but Nick's not a boy anymore."

"But—"

"If you wanna play Mama Bear, do it on that cheating piece of—"

"Josh," she warned. Their kids may or may not be asleep.

"If you wanna get vicious, stop Dana from making a scene."

And just like that, the guilt crept in again. "Nick's going to kill me," Miranda muttered.

"Why?"

Failing to meet his eyes, she sighed. She hadn't exactly tipped Dana off. But she'd made an empty threat on the phone just a week ago. She mumbled her confession. "I told Nick I'd send Dana if he didn't make up his mind soon. His ninety days is almost up."

"That woman has enough money to hire a hundred private detectives to find Nick. You couldn't have stopped her, babe."

"Why do you always have to be right," murmured Miranda. "If Nick really has found someone else, do you think a crazy psycho woman showing up claiming to still be married to him has an opportunity to really sabotage things for him?"

"Yes."

Miranda frowned at Josh's firm tone. "Not helping."

"Which is why I've called in a favor to get you on the earliest flight out of here. Tomorrow."

"But—"

"Stop fretting. There's nothing you can do tonight that will make a difference. Unless you plan to call Nick and t—"

"Nope."

Josh wrapped his arms back around Miranda. "Let me take your mind off all this tonight."

"What are—" Teeth tugging on her earlobe quickly

made her forget what she was about to say. "I have to pack."

"I know."

"And sleep."

"We both know you won't sleep." Josh's hot breath hot against her ear had Miranda coming undone. It'd been a week since they had the bedroom alone. Whenever Josh was home, one of the two kids seemed to have a nightmare. "Let me take your mind off your worries, babe. Tomorrow you can conquer the world."

Chapter 31

Flooring the gas pedal, Allie darted around the tractor hogging half the road. "Move it!" She'd been driving well over the speed limit for almost two hours. Just a few more miles and she'd be back in Willow Creek. Norman barked at the farm machinery now in their rearview window.

Stupid, stupid, stupid. She'd broken first thing that morning and listened to Nick's voicemail. And read through the inundation of text messages from her family and old coworkers that she hadn't received while her phone remained off last night.

Nick hadn't been decent enough to stay out of her dreams. She'd seen no other way to shove him out of her mind but to face the mystery message.

And now Ed Mullins was in the hospital recovering

from a gunshot wound!

She'd considered warning Nick that Lesley might spill all of his secrets if she stepped foot in the hospital, but the message had only been about Ed. Nick hadn't so much as mentioned that he missed her. No hint he'd thought of her since that night Alex got punched. He could fend for himself where Lesley Jamison was concerned.

Willow Creek came into view. Just two miles away, the town spread across the flat landscape ahead. Allie drove faster, passing another car in the process. After dumping Norman off at her mom's house, she sped through town toward the hospital, blowing a stop sign and parking across two spots. She threw open her door even before her car was in park.

"Where's Ed?" She asked Suzy.

"Room Twelve." Suzy pointed out of habit. "Allie, are you sure—"

She didn't stay to listen to any warning Suzy might have. She dashed to the left for Ed's room.

His door was cracked. Inside, she caught sight of a nurse taking Ed's blood pressure and reading it off to someone.

"You're making a quick recovery. Blood pressure's even back to normal." Nick. That southern drawl had plagued her dreams for weeks.

She plastered herself against the wall, not wanting him to find her spying.

The daunting click of heels echoed from far away and grew closer. Allie caught sight of Lesley at the far end of the hospital, near the activity center. Her head was tucked in a folder. Allie had just enough time to fall into Room Twelve before Lesley looked up.

"Hi," she said, shutting the door behind her. "Sorry to interrupt."

"Allie, you came." Ed offered a weak smile from his hospital bed. She hated seeing so many tubes and wires. His true age shone through his hospital gown and pale complexion. She didn't like it one bit.

"Of course I came." She fell into a chair beside the bed and took his hand. "Ed, what happened?"

"Ed, I'll be back in an hour to check your blood pressure again," said the nurse.

Allie expected Nick to follow the nurse, but he stood. Unmoving.

"Someone broke into your house," Ed reported. "I went over to check it out."

"What? Ed, why would you do that?"

"I had a loaded shotgun." Ed narrowed his eyes and she instantly felt guilty. He probably didn't like her chastising him. "The bastard was ready for me, that's all. I couldn't see him in the dark. Lucky Nick found me or I'd probably still be lying on your porch."

For the first time, she dared to look up. Dared to meet Nick's emerald eyes. He had a tentative smile for her.

"Thank you, Nick."

The nurse ushered Allie out of Ed's room within thirty minutes. She didn't argue, just darted like a ninja to her faithful old break room. Even if it was a storeroom now. If Lesley caught wind she was in the hospital, she'd probably not think to look in the new storage closet to throw her out.

Grabbing reading material first thing this morning hadn't occurred to her when she heard that Ed had been shot. She could be stuck here for a couple more hours, and now she'd be alone with her thoughts. She wished for a novel to keep her busy while she waited for Suzy to deliver an update.

Sitting on top of a table, Allie tried not to let Nick Bryant trespass in her thoughts. Still, he shoved his way in. *How had he known to check on Ed?* She knew the two men had talked during the Summer Festival. And she'd brought Ed up in a few conversations with Nick. But she couldn't pin any solitary reason that he would go to see Ed, let alone be lucky enough to find him in time to save his life.

Despite the stuffiness of the storage room, Allie felt goose bumps rise on her arms. A truly alarming thought had crossed her mind. *Who broke into my house and shot Ed?*

A chill crept over her skin, twisting her stomach. *Travis.* And in that moment, as much as Allie wanted to hide out and wait for news about Ed, she knew she'd have to leave the hospital. *Go and find Alex Rowe,* her gut said. *See what he knows.* Even if this wasn't typically his jurisdiction, Alex had been in town awhile. He'd be more forthcoming with information than the stuffy old Chief of Police. *The one Cruella's got at her beck and call.*

Cracking the door, Allie poked her head into the hallway. Hearing voices, she ducked her head back inside. Still, the conversation carried through to her.

"Lab results should be back later this afternoon."

Alex is here! She wouldn't have to sneak around town to find him. She had no idea if Lesley had figured out if she'd come back, but if the woman hadn't yet, well, she would soon. Not much slipped by Lesley Jamison.

"You plan to arrest him?" Nick's growl surprised Allie out of worrying about *Cruella.*

"Once we have the affirmative results, I'll be able to get a warrant." Through a crack, she kept an eye on both of them, straining not to move as she listened. "First, we have to find him," Alex was saying. "He's kept clear of town since the shooting. No one I've talked to has seen him at all."

Nick ran a fast hand through his hair. "No one?"

"Hell, most people are shocked to hear he's out." Through the crack, Allie watched Alex check the hallway for eavesdroppers. "I've never seen something this big get by so many people. Someone had to arrange that."

"You think?"

Cruella. Always Cruella.

Allie let go of the door, and it sighed closed, before Nick caught site of it ajar.

She'd been thinking so deeply, it didn't dawn on Allie at first. *Are Nick and Alex friends? After Nick punched him?* She shook her head. She had to be in the twilight zone. She'd never understand the true nature of men. She supposed it had happened in *Forbidden Pleasures.* Rance challenged a man he hated to a jousting match and kicked the crap out of him, the same man he punched in jealousy. Then they ended up as best buds.

Time to grovel. She reached for the door again.

Even if Nick hadn't said so much as thank you for the seashell, Allie felt obligated to thank him for saving Ed's life. To let him know that she forgave him for his jealous outburst. Then, if Nick wanted her to leave, she'd head back to Omaha tonight.

It'd been necessary to take back-country roads to reach the doctor's house, but Travis couldn't risk detection. Crouching in the backseat of an empty car, he watched for Allie. Like the building was on fire and she'd rushed to save her precious books, she hurried into the hospital, not looking either left or right. It'd only be a matter of time before she and the doctor both ended up at his mansion on the hill. *And when she does, I'll be ready.*

Even though Travis knew there hadn't been any witnesses last night, aside from Ed himself, Mort had been pretty vocal at the hardware store this morning, warning him that the whole town was looking for him. "Better just head home today. I don't want any trouble here."

With the darkness and Ed's likely poor eyesight, Travis just had to lay low for a few days. He'd pick up Allie and hunker down at the farmhouse until the commotion died down.

Expecting to pick a lock, he was pleasantly surprised to find the doctor's back door unsecured. With ease, he slipped into the kitchen.

He'd hide upstairs for a while before making his presence known. Meandering through the kitchen, Travis helped himself to a beer from the fridge, careful to grab a bottle from the back of the lineup so it wouldn't be missed.

Tossing the cap into the stainless steel trashcan, he sauntered into the living room and straight toward the double glass doors. He threw them both open as he'd seen done in movies and waltzed out onto the vast deck that overlooked miles and miles of green corn and bean fields. From the very corner he could see half the town of Willow Creek, including the long lone gravel road to the house.

The very power he felt from the top of the only hill in town was intoxicating. He would have to ask his mother why she hadn't bought this house from Doc Herb when he moved.

After finishing his beer and discarding the bottle beneath some butcher wrappings in Nick's trash, Travis grabbed a second bottle. Then he took the stairs two at a time, scoffing at how dated Nick's house was. So unworthy of *his* Allie.

Of the four bedrooms upstairs, two were empty aside from curtains. Another room was half-filled with unpacked boxes. *Odd considering he's been in town almost three months.* The last room along the hallway was the master bedroom. It took all his control not to light a match and toss it onto the bed. Travis looked forward to reminding Allie she had no right giving herself to anyone else. She'd always belonged to him. *Always would.*

From the bedroom window, he caught an approaching black truck out of the corner of his eye and knew he'd have to hide.

About to hunker down in an empty bedroom, he spotted the barn through the open window. He'd heard how the doctor had been fixing it up since Allie left town. *I bet he takes her there.*

Slipping downstairs and out the back door, Travis darted for the barn. He'd wait there for the doctor to bring Allie to him. *Then I'll reclaim what's rightfully mine.*

Everyone wanted to thank Nick for saving Ed Mullins' life. It'd taken almost an hour to slip out of the hospital and back home. He had gone from villain to hero in less than twenty-four hours. The whole population seemed to want to tell him how lucky they thought it was that he had found Ed before it was too late.

Even Aunt Ruby and her friend Abigail had bantered about his heroic act.

"It's a miracle that you showed up, don't you think?" asked Abigail, placing a hand on Nick's forearm. "Divine intervention."

"It's a wonder none of the neighbors heard a gunshot," Aunt Ruby said.

"Well, who expects to hear a gunshot in Willow Creek? I wouldn't have thought twice about it, either."

"Dr. Bryant, we're both very grateful you saved Ed's life." Aunt Ruby placed a hand on his other arm, opposite the one Abigail had a hold of, and leaned in. "I'll be changing that recommendation of mine to Herb. We'd love for you to stay indefinitely."

Nick pulled a beer from his fridge. Up until last night, he'd been convinced moving back to Georgia was the only thing left to do. Now, in one unexpected turn of events, he'd found his place. Found a small town that wanted him to stay and be *their* doctor.

Why does it all feel so empty?

A honking horn jarred Nick. *If Rachel's here...* The last thing he wanted to deal with was Rachel Jamison.

He considered ignoring it. Just going upstairs and lying down. He hadn't slept much last night, with Ed in surgery. But he'd not known anyone yet to announce themselves with a honking horn.

Stepping out onto the front porch with a wide yawn, Nick stood with folded arms.

Dana stepped out of a red Corvette—he would have expected nothing less—in her four-inch heels and two-thousand-dollar dress. He'd been with her the day she bought it. Heard that laugh when he showed her the price tag. "Relax," she said, "it's only money."

For a moment, the slender blonde woman stood in the driveway, just staring through her sunglasses. He wasn't sure if it was at him. His suspicion was that she was quite jealous of the house. *She'd feel differently if she saw the wallpaper inside!* Nick waited for Dana to make her first move.

When at last she took a couple of hesitant steps toward him, Nick called out, "Why are you here?"

That stopped Dana in her tracks. She pulled the sunglasses away from her face. "You have some nerve to ask me that," she snapped. "Nicholas Bryant you get over here this instant. You have a lot of explaining to do, leaving Georgia without telling your *wife* where you were going."

At one time, he would've leapt off a ten-story

building to obey her. He'd always thought himself lucky to have landed such a rare beauty. A woman so sure of herself and in control.

It was amazing what a little distance, and time, did for his perspective. There wasn't much to the woman behind her expensive haircut, clothes, and jewelry.

"No."

It shocked Nick how good it felt to stand his ground—to face his fears. *Why have I been afraid?* Well, that really wasn't it, was it? No, he'd been afraid of what life would be like without her. *But now I know.* Life was effortless. Happier. *Well, happier aside from one missing piece.*

Dana marched as quickly as she could in her heels. Nick surmised she'd probably beat most women in a four-inch heel race, but only because she had the practice. Two steps below the porch, she stopped again. "I don't know where you get off telling me no," Dana pointed a perfectly manicured finger at him, "But I won't stand for it. Now let's go inside and get this mess straightened out."

"We're not going inside," Nick said, holding out his hand toward two cushioned patio chairs. "We'll sit out here on the front porch and talk. This is my house. Not yours."

"Don't you know anything?" huffed Dana, pushing

past him and sitting in the first of the patio chairs. "We're still married. Meaning it belongs to me too."

Nick fought the urge to announce he hadn't actually bought the house. He liked her jealousy. This was the kind of home they'd always talked about living in. One he'd been about to show her when he came home early from work and caught her riding his best friend like a mechanical bull.

"How's Neil?"

She plopped into a seat, apparently deciding it unwise to slap him.

"Don't make yourself out to be the victim in this," said Dana. "Deep down, I think you know why it happened. You know you pushed me away and practically shoved me right into his arms. But that's neither here nor there now."

"No?" Nick actually laughed at that.

"No." Dana maintained her perfect posture in the cushioned chair. He wondered what she'd think if he told her he found them at a garage sale. That they weren't new or even expensive. "It no longer matters. All of that is behind us now. Time for you to come home to Georgia where you belong."

"Why the hell would I do that?"

"Because the divorce is off. I had my lawyers rescind the papers."

Chapter 32

First thing this morning in the airport terminal, Miranda had pulled her sun hat further down on her head. She hoped it'd keep her mop of hair hidden. That donning reading glasses would make her hard to recognize.

She hated flying. Always would. Once they boarded, she had been able to relax. Dana wouldn't be bothered to scour the economy class for stragglers. That hadn't stopped Miranda from scanning every seat until she spotted the petite blonde seated in the forward section, wearing a beige designer dress that no doubt was worth more than Miranda's car.

It was early Saturday afternoon before the final leg of the flight ended and the shoebox of a plane landed in Omaha. Seemingly not fatigued at all from her first class ride, Dana rented a flashy car and sped out of town.

It'd been a chore to keep up, but Miranda had been cut a little slack when Dana chose the bright red Corvette. Miranda had to settle for a Focus and crossed her fingers that she could keep Dana in her sights. The Corvette was obviously for more than show—it was to make time.

She knew if her little blue car got pulled over for speeding, she didn't stand the same chance as voluptuous, blonde Dana for getting out of a ticket.

The red Corvette had disappeared halfway down Dodge Street in Omaha, hardly five minutes from the airport. With a rented GPS and cruise control set for five miles over the posted limit, Miranda set her course for Willow Creek. She might not get to Nick before Dana did, but she'd be there to keep him from doing anything rash. After an ugly argument that needed so desperately to happen.

When Nick would remember how he met Dana, the same dreamy vision clouded his senses, evoking the warm, sunny day in Palm Springs. Time seemed to stand still. "I bet I already know what you want." She'd said that the day they met, and now under this overcast sky, she said it again.

Nick always thought it had been fate that Dana knew his favorite beer was a Corona. But if fate really had brought her into his life, why hadn't it been kind enough to tip him off that his best friend would eventually steal his wife?

Staring across the porch at Dana, hearing her continuing to rant about how horrible their marriage had been, the realization hit Nick like a half-ton pendulum. Fate *had* warned him from the very beginning, but he had been too blinded by infatuation to notice.

"I hate Corona," Nick said.

That stopped Dana midsentence. He wasn't even sure what she'd been talking about. Something about shopping and dinner parties? Housework and cooking? He didn't know.

"I hate Corona. Always have."

Until his trip to Palm Springs, Nick had never cared much for Corona. He'd always leaned toward Guinness. The two beers were nothing alike. But since that day, Corona had been branded into his brain as his favorite beer.

"And it wasn't sunny. It was overcast. Looked like it was going to rain."

"Nick, what are you talking about?" At first, Dana seemed annoyed at his interruption. Now, there was a coating of fear in her voice, as if he was uncovering something she was sure would stay hidden from him forever.

Nick forced himself to remember the details he'd washed from his mind. Fate had warned him from the beginning, he realized. Fate had delivered all the signs that he chose to ignore. "That son of a bitch."

"Who?" Dana's voice shook.

"Neil. You and Neil slept together the night we met. You were together the *whole* time!" Nick shot up from his seat and stared pacing. "All this time you've been blaming me for a horrible marriage, and you've been with Neil since the night we met!" He felt like breaking something, but other than the patio furniture, there was nothing out here he could throw.

For once, Dana was speechless. The look of defeat in her eyes said more than she ever could. That look told Nick he was dead on. "Why are you really here? It can't because you love me. You've *never* loved me."

Dana swallowed.

"The truth would be nice."

"I don't get Daddy's trust fund money unless we've been married five years." Dana fell against her back of her chair. "Can't you just stick it out a little longer? Neil is gone. And I can be a good wife." Tears pooled at the corners of her eyes. But Nick had learned long ago that this woman could produce tears on demand. He saw through it all now, the desperation in her words. Tears from Dana couldn't be trusted.

"Figures it's about money." Nick stood. "Why, Dana? Why'd you marry me?"

"I don't know what you want me to say," she mumbled.

"Why didn't you just marry Neil and save me the trouble? Surely he'd stick around five years for a few million."

"I'll tell you everything," Dana murmured. "But first, fix me a drink."

"Where's Travis?" demanded Lesley, inviting herself into Mort's office. The hardware store had closed an hour earlier, but she had arranged for some overtime for her son—before she heard there was a warrant out for his arrest.

She'd like to kill Travis for breaking into Allie Jordan's house. Not much she could do if Ed remembered who shot him. Good thing the best lawyer in the county owed her a huge favor. It'd take the best to convince a jury that just because Travis had broken into the house didn't mean he'd shot Ed Mullins.

"I told him to stay out of town," said Mort, feet kicked up on the desk, his worn shoes scattering dirt smudges on the ledger books there. "I don't need anyone spotting him here after everything that's being said around town. Bad for business."

"I ought to fire you," muttered Lesley. She hadn't expected to inherit such a worthless brother-in-law, nor had she expected at this point in her life to have to deal with him.

Mort bristled, "I'd like to see you try."

"Really?" Lesley pulled her cell phone from her purse. She relished the worried expression that washed over Mort's face. Instead of explaining herself, she simply forwarded the saved video to Mort's wife. She'd divorce him so quickly after she saw it, he wouldn't know what happened. "Better pack your bags, Mortimer. Betty is pretty hot right about now."

"You coldhearted bitch!" Mort's feet dropped to the floor like cement blocks. "You didn't?"

"I always win. You know that."

Lesley turned and left the office, her deed forgotten. After confirming that Travis really had been sent home, she stormed from the store through the back door and hurried to her car. With her son on the loose, running from the law, and Allie Jordan defying her and parading back into town, she had a lot to deal with today.

Chapter 33

"I guess I understand better than I ever have," Nick said. "But I still don't know why you chose me." He twisted open another beer, then shut the fridge with his elbow.

"Neil knew about my money all along, even before it was mine," said Dana. "I told him, thinking I'd never see him again."

"So marrying someone like me who doesn't care about money kept someone like Neil from blowing it all?"

She nodded. "Something like that."

"That's the most selfish thing I think I've ever heard come out of your mouth," said Nick. "And there are some pretty selfish spotlight moments to beat." He took a swig of beer. "Why not just do a prenup?"

"Because, before we got married, Daddy didn't put any stipulations on my money. But then he met *you*. The son he never had." Dana tossed her arms up. "I didn't even know he rewrote his will."

"So this is *all* about money?" Nick growled.

She didn't answer. "I really expected I would come to love you," said Dana. "You are such a caring and selfless man. I never thought it'd be a problem. I saw stability with you, a future with kids, and a big house like this one—maybe a little newer—with a covered porch. I thought I'd grow out of Neil, just like I have."

His hand squeezed tightly around the bottle, and he turned his voice cold. "I loved you Dana, worshiped you, even. I thought I was the luckiest man that you loved me back. But it was all a show."

"If you'd been a little meaner like this in the beginning, you might've saved yourself a lot of trouble," Dana seemed unaffected by his harsh words. "Why Nebraska, Nick?"

He shrugged. "That's the opportunity fate handed me."

"Well, I'm certain you've had a fun go of it, playing small town doctor. But let's get serious for a minute. Your portion of the practice is still waiting for you in Savannah. Stick out this marriage for two more years, I'll let you walk away with a million. That's more than enough to get you set up, especially since Daddy paid off your med school loans. Some wedding present," muttered Dana. "Not a honeymoon to Fiji."

"No."

"Fine, three million."

Nick laughed. "You think I can be bought? You *cheated* on me and don't have a single regret over hurting a man you vowed to love for the rest of your life."

"You're being awfully dramatic." Dana rolled her eyes. "Fine, five million. But it's my final offer. It's time for you to come home."

"Come home to what?"

Dana took a gulp of her whiskey and Coke. "Neil ran off with a twenty-two-year-old last month." She set the empty glass on the kitchen island.

Nick hadn't expected that. But he couldn't allow himself to feel sympathy for such a cold person, no matter how much he once loved her.

"Come back to Savannah, Nick. Hell, I'll even try counseling. I'm willing to do whatever it takes. Just come home."

Allie knew stopping at Wilkerson's Grocery was a

risk. She'd even spotted Lesley's Cadillac at the back of the hardware store on her way here. Every time she heard the jingle of the bell over the door, she dove behind a stack of boxes to hide.

She intended to make a special dinner for Nick—an apology dinner—and had considered sending Amanda to pick up the items on her grocery list. But that'd require too much explaining. It was enough that her sister was watching Norman for the day.

Another jingle. Allie darted behind a display of cake mix boxes. *Where was this the day Rachel wanted to be a bitch? Surely all these carbs would've kept her away.*

"Hi," she heard a female voice call out to the woman at the register. "I was hoping you could help me find someone. Looking for Nick Bryant."

Allie couldn't quite make out what the other woman said in return, but she distinctly heard phrases like "local hero" and "Ed Mullin's life".

And in response to a question, "I'm his sister."

Poking her head around the display, Allie caught sight of a woman about her own height, dark brown hair slipping from beneath a white sun hat. Nick's sister turned, her eyes locking with Allie's for a moment before moving on. Very familiar eyes. At one time, Allie would have yearned to introduce herself to Nick's only sibling. She looked away, abandoning dinner plans.

"I suppose I could pick up a few things while I'm here," said Miranda. "I'm sure he's close to starving."

Allie slipped out the front door empty-handed. She'd have to head straight to Nick's house now. Try to reach him before this sister showed up. The one counting on Nick moving back to Georgia.

Waiting to turn onto Nick's road, Allie slowed for a red sports car speeding down the narrow lane toward her, a wall of dust lifting behind it. Allowing the Corvette to make its turn first, she caught a glimpse of a blonde behind the steering wheel. At first she thought it might be Rachel Jamison, but this woman's hair was too short. Not to mention, Rachel didn't own such a flashy car.

If Nick's sister's in town getting groceries, who could this be? Allie shook away the thought. It didn't matter. She just wanted to thank Nick for saving Ed's life, then she'd head back to Omaha. It wasn't any of her concern anymore.

Standing on the front porch, the door opened before she even knocked. "Hi, Nick. I was hoping I could come in for a minute."

"Of course."

She thought she caught a glimpse of a genuine smile, but if she had, it flickered away before taking hold. "I just wanted to say thank you." She couldn't help herself and threw her arms around Nick's chest, hugging him. His warm body felt so perfect against her own. "I don't know if I could live with myself if Ed hadn't made it." Tears dropped from her cheeks, bleeding through his shirt. She knew she should let go, but the selfish desire to memorize this feeling in his arms won out.

"Don't think like that, Allie." Wrapping one arm around her shaking frame, Nick tilted her head back till their breaths mingled. "No point in dwelling on horrible things that might've happened. Just focus on the reality that Ed is alive, and he'll pull through this."

"You're right," Allie whispered. The words she had rehearsed, words intended to finalize her departure, escaped. Eyes locking, she forgot about the world around them. In this moment, there was only Nick.

Lips hungered against her own. "I've missed you," Nick growled against her ear.

She pulled him closer, drawing the hem of his shirt from his waistband. "I've missed you too."

His lips trailed her skin, finding the pulse at the base of her neck. "Want to go upstairs?"

Her knees buckled as his teeth scraped her bare shoulder. "Mmm." *What am I forgetting?* "Wait!"

"What?"

"Your sister's in town." At that, Nick's eyes

widened. "You didn't know?"

He shook his head. "In that case, I want to show you something I've been working on in the barn. Why don't you go up to the loft?" Nick kissed her deeply. "I'll grab us a couple of drinks. My sister isn't going anywhere."

Grabbing two glasses and an unopened bottle of Chardonnay, Nick spun, taking a deep breath. He should send Allie on her way back to Omaha after all Alex had explained to him. Insist she leave now before anything happened. But he didn't want her to leave. *I can protect her.*

First, he'd have to tell her about Dana.

It took him two trips to carry everything from the house. He thought he heard a noise—a growl or something...*snoring?*—and paused before his second climb up the ladder, glancing around the shop area. When he spotted nothing unusual, he shrugged it off and continued to the loft. The door to the back room was closed. Two glasses filled, he knocked once but didn't give time for warning. When the door opened beneath his free hand, he found Allie hunched over a paperback. Crying.

He set the glasses down, swooping to her side.

"Allie, what's wrong?" Tears streamed in such rapid succession that he didn't know what else to do but draw her into his arms.

He let her sob for what felt like hours. When she finally pulled away, she wiped at her reddened eyes. "I'm sorry, Nick. I—I just..." Allie was staring at the copy of *Sweetly Scandalous*. The favorite book she'd told him her ex-boyfriend had thrown into a bonfire. And it clicked.

Nick reached for the book. "I didn't mean—"

"No." She grabbed the book back, hugging it against her chest. "I *love* it. It's such a thoughtful gift. It's a hard book to find."

Unsure what to do, he sat there beside her and waited. He hadn't meant to leave the book out. He'd intended to send it to her in the mail.

"It just brought back a lot of memories." Allie wiped tears with the back of her hand, then looked him in the eyes. "I've been too afraid to read it again."

Hers were puffy from crying, but she still looked beautiful. He wanted to kiss her. To help her forget her pain. Nick said, "I just thought—"

She rolled up one leg of her jeans, forcing him to look at a long, narrow scar. One he'd hardly noticed. "He gave me this."

Fury surged through Nick. He felt like smashing a

window. "*He* did this to you?"

"Five years ago," said Allie, her eyes locked on the scar.

And Rachel had tried telling him that *Allie* should be in jail too!

She rolled her pant leg back down. "I've only just started realizing how much he took away from me. When I saw the book, I just kind of lost it, you know? Like a wave knocking the wind out of you."

"I'm sorry, Al—"

"Don't be." Allie crawled up to her knees, towering a few inches over him. "Because of you, I've been slowly getting those things back. I was just a little caught off guard, is all." Tears no longer pricked the corner of her eyes. Eyes that were now the color of melted chocolate, and Nick was certain, filled with want. "I'm not going to run anymore. I'm going to stay and fight." She straddled his legs, cupping his face with both her hands. He could no more have stopped her than stopped breathing.

Allie's lips hungered onto his, more savage than any kisses they'd shared. She wanted to forget crying in front of him. To track down her all-time favorite romance was the sweetest gesture any man had done for her.

Nick wrapped his arms around her, tossing her onto her back against the new, fluffy mattress, new yellow pillows surrounding them. "You redecorated," said Allie between kisses.

"You like it?" He traced his tongue along her collarbone. She barely caught the mason jar lights strung along one wall before fading into complete ecstasy at his touch, his hands fumbling with the zipper of her jeans.

With trembling hands, she reached for the bottom of his shirt, sure she would rip it right down the middle if he made it difficult to get off. A soft dusting of sunlight illuminated his wondrous body. She ran her hands over Nick's hard muscles, yearning to touch every inch of him.

His hands slid from her shoulders, down her sides, then Allie felt them at the top of her panties. For a moment, she froze. *Is this what I want?* But there was such hunger in his eyes that she knew there was nothing she'd ever wanted more.

Warm hands fondled her breasts. Allie reached for the button on Nick's jeans. Her quivering hands fumbled only a moment before he yanked his pants down and threw them to the floor with the rest of their clothes. In the glow of the sunlight, Allie could see that he wasn't wearing anything underneath. She could see his desire for her, long and hard.

There was something animalistic about the look he gave her as his mouth covered one of her nipples, "Does this surprise you?" he asked when he caught her staring down at him in awe, at him sucking and biting with the edge of his teeth. Allie's knees shook. Nick cupped her rear, drawing her closer.

She gave a wicked smile. The best she could, considering how much she trembled with anticipation. Shimmying out from beneath Nick, crawling on top of him, Allie forced him on his back. She'd intended to thank *him*.

Gentle fingers stroked Nick's hard desire, teasing him with her softest touch.

"You're going to kill me."

She gripped his shaft with one hand, eliciting a moan. Leaning down, she took him into her mouth, teasing him with her tongue, light along his tip. She savored the taste of him, knowing she was no longer falling, but had fallen.

"Allie."

At the sound of her name, she lifted her head—and her hips and plunged down on him. She'd intended to take things slowly. To be seductive. To torture him until he couldn't take it anymore. But she lost control once he was inside her. His firm hands gripped her hips, rocking her against him until a wave of pleasure blinded her. Their worlds collided in ecstasy.

Travis startled awake, shaking his head as if from a daze. Pushing off a pile of musty blankets in a darkened corner of the barn, he again heard the noise that must have woken him. *Moans. From upstairs.* Standing, he wiped the sleep from his eyes. Feeling for the gun in his sweatshirt pocket, he knew what he had to do.

Then he spotted the ladder.

Chapter 34

The door burst open and Allie screamed, shoving herself against the wall of the barn next to the bed. "Travis!"

Travis wore an evil smirk. "What do we have here?"

Allie felt Nick tense beside her. Hardly thirty seconds earlier she had finished dressing. She touched his arm, and sent him a quick look, warning him to stay quiet. It'd only end badly if she didn't take control of the situation. *Please don't try to be the hero, Nick.*

The gun Travis held flailed in the air with his waving arms. "This place is crap. Allie, I finished your reading room."

Fighting to keep her voice upbeat, she slid slowly away from Nick and toward Travis. "Reading room?" She doubted Travis would shoot her. But the rage in his eyes didn't ensure Nick's safety.

"At the farmhouse." The gun pointed east. "I've been fixing it up. For us."

A smile plastered on her face, Allie fought to stay calm. "I can't wait to see it."

"I came to get you. We have to lay low for a few days out there."

"Why—"

She shot Nick a fierce look, frightened by the outrage in his eyes. *Doesn't he know he's asking to get himself killed?* She reached for Travis' arm. "Let's go." Nick's only true chance at survival was to put distance between him and Travis.

"Not until I've dealt with *him*." Travis shoved her aside.

Tripping over her own feet, Allie tumbled backwards onto the mattress. "He's going to pay for trying to steal what belongs to me. With his life." Nick was on his feet in seconds, ready to punch Travis. He seemed to give no consideration to the gun.

Inside, Allie's heart beat at an erratic pace. But outside, she kept a calm exterior, a survival tactic she learned with Travis five years ago. "Really, your jealousy is flattering. But Travis, he's nothing." She swallowed at the lie. A lie she desperately hoped Nick didn't believe. "I wasn't sure you were in town. Your mother kept it a secret, you know."

"That bitch thinks she knows best," muttered Travis, swinging the gun in Nick's direction, signaling him to back up.

"She's wrong." Allie stepped between Nick and Travis. In front of the gun. "But let's not let her ruin our day." She reached out trembling fingers, resting them against Travis' arm. Biting the inside of her lip, she forced herself to remain steady. "He's nothing, Travis. I only ever wanted you."

Travis' gray eyes locked on Allie's.

"Please, don't do something that might take you away from me again. He's not worth it."

"Fine." He lowered the gun.

Allie's tense muscles relaxed.

"I won't shoot him." Travis pushed her aside and marched toward Nick. With savagery and speed he swung the butt of his pistol against his forehead. An unconscious Nick crumbled to the floor. "But I don't need him calling anyone, either. Let's go."

Lesley drove along beside the school just in time to catch the sight of Travis' pickup rounding the corner from the doctor's private road. "What is that idiot up to now?" she muttered, pulling out a cigarette and tapping at the console lighter as she watched him speed out of town. Allowing him a head start, Lesley followed at a safe distance. His dust trail guaranteed her cover until they reached the highway.

One thing she knew was not to let her son know she followed him. He'd change his course just to spite her. If his current plans hadn't already reserved a spot for him back in jail, any revised ones certainly would. Lesley only hoped she'd beat any law enforcement officials to her son.

"That ungrateful little shit still hasn't learned how to appreciate the opportunities he's been given." And Allie Jordan was always interfering. Tonight, Lesley intended to make certain that she never interfered again.

As the miles flew by in a dusty blur, Allie had no doubt about where Travis was taking her. "I thought you had one more year," said Allie after several long minutes, filled with only the metallic skittering of rocks from under the truck tires. If there hadn't been a gun aimed at her abdomen, the drive might have been a little more familiar.

"Nope." Travis shifted gears and careened around a

corner. "You get time taken off your sentence for good behavior." From his smug tone, she knew he was very proud of that fact.

"Not *that* much time." Now that Nick wasn't in danger, she didn't feel like playing such a doting role. "Helps to have a powerful mommy, doesn't it?"

Travis shoved the gun a little deeper into her side. She held her breath. His finger was securely latched on the trigger, and she was unsure if it even had a safety. One solid pothole in the gravel might set it off.

It was one thing to be shot in the leg. Allie knew she was going to live after that incident. She thought that searing pain might cause her to lose her leg, but she never doubted whether she'd be alive when her ordeal was over. Having a gun shoved at her side was an entirely different matter.

Allie tried keeping calm, taking deep breaths and thinking of happier memories. Tried to keep insults to a minimum. The first distracting memory that flashed through her mind was the romp in the barn with Nick, before they'd been chased away by the farmer with a shotgun. She fought a smile. *Don't want to explain that one.*

Travis said, "I didn't break out, in case that's what you think." He tore around a corner, his expression blank. "I want to start fresh. Hard to do that as a fugitive unless you run off to Mexico. I didn't feel like eating burritos for the rest of my life."

The truck slowed as they neared the abandoned farmhouse.

"I hope you'll like what I've done with the place." Travis threw the truck into park and killed the ignition. "I've been staying out here, fixin' up the place just like we always talked about. I even have a special room, just for you."

She hardly recognized the house. The exterior showed a fresh coat of white paint. Even the navy blue window trim and matching front door was new. Just a few weeks ago, it'd looked like a dilapidated pile of rotting boards. *Oh God, what's going to happen to me?*

"I'm still working on the front porch," he told her, dragging her from the truck. "I'm going to have to rebuild it." He spoke so casually, as if Allie had only been away on a vacation. Not to mention the front porch needed replacing because he'd shoved her down so hard she nearly fell through to the basement.

"How long have you been out?" asked Allie, fighting to keep her horror out of her voice.

"A while." Travis yanked them to a halt, pride in his voice. "I've been working at the hardware store."

"So you stole all the supplies?

"What? No god dammit," Travis snarled. "Mort gives

me a discount because I work there. I get everything at cost."

She'd blurted the wrong thing. Travis' eyes widened with that crazy fire of his again. "Go straight to the front door. If you run, I'll shoot you."

Of course she'd contemplated running, since she knew where they were headed. At least two miles of open corn fields and gravel roads separated Allie from any help. Travis' family owned over twenty-five hundred acres of farmland. She might be able to lose him in a field since the corn was taller than she was, ready for harvest.

But she might lose her own way. And if that happened, he would hunt her down.

Until she had a better plan, her best option was to stay and play along with Travis' deranged fantasy. Her only hope was that Nick would awaken and recall the detail about the farmhouse—and tell Alex Rowe where she was.

"It's a work in progress, but you can move in tonight. The upstairs is finished."

Allie swallowed, turning her face away so Travis couldn't see her disgust. Would Alex would call a SWAT team in for backup? "I can't wait." She smiled. "I want a tour."

The crazy fire in Travis' eyes died down, and

happiness replaced it. "I thought you'd never ask."

Slamming her car door after parking in Nick's driveway, Amanda marched toward Nick, who was rubbing his head, wobbling. *Probably suffering from a hangover. Good!* "So, I ran into someone interesting at the gas station, Nick!"

"Allie—"

"You're *married*, Nick? Are you kidding me?"

"Allie's been—"

"Allie's been *lied* to!" yelled Amanda.

As she closed the gap between them, the front screen door slammed. "Who is *she*?"

Another woman Amanda didn't recognize stood on the porch, arms folded.

"I'm his sister."

Hand held to his head, Nick said, "Miranda, please—"

"And who might you be? You look a little young for my brother."

"Please." Amanda tossed a hand in the air. "I'm Allie's sister."

"Who is Allie?" Watching this other woman——Miranda——scurry down from the porch, Amanda caught the fire in her eyes.

"Seriously, Nick?"

Now within feet, Nick hollered, "Allie's been kidnapped! Travis took her." The hairs on Amanda's arms raised as she finally noticed the red knot on Nick's forehead.

"Who is Allie?" repeated Nick's sister.

He pushed past her into the house, returning with a cell up to his ear. "I don't know where he took her—Allie kept talking about a farmhouse." Amanda's heart dropped to her feet. She listened to Nick say, "I'm not making any promises. He has a *gun*. Alex, get your guys there yesterday."

Amanda felt sick. "Travis took her? To the farmhouse?"

"You know where it's at?"

Just then the flashy Corvette Amanda had encountered at the gas station sped up the gravel road toward them. Nick barely spared it a glance.

His gaze was focused on Amanda. "How do I get there?"

"You're not going after a kidnap victim!" Miranda commanded, grabbing Nick's arm and giving Amanda just enough time to slip toward the passenger side of his truck, unnoticed. "Nick, *who* the hell is Allie?" she heard his sister demand.

The sports car slid to a dusty halt, the blonde woman hopping out without setting the brake.

"Allie's the woman I love."

"C'mon," Amanda shouted. Her hand was already on the door handle. "I know how to get there." *We can have it out later. Once Allie's safe.*

Nick winced, a hand at his brow. "You're not going."

"You'll never find it! Way too many back roads!"

The new arrival pointed at Amanda and spat, "What the hell is *she* doing here?"

Amanda jumped into the truck, looking to Miranda. "Can you handle *her* until we get back?"

Nick slammed his door shut. Miranda didn't have a chance to argue as he shoved the truck into gear. Her head jerked back as Nick sped down the gravel road. She bumped her palm against the glove compartment latch, popping it open. "Don't suppose you brought a gun?"

"No time."

Chapter 35

The first time Travis invited Allie to see the abandoned farmhouse, she'd been thrilled; fascinated by the possibility of fixing it up the way her mom fixed up old houses. But she hadn't realized Travis had meant to restore it for *them*. For *their* future.

"I still have to put in the flooring downstairs," said Travis. "Just have subfloor right now, but at least it's supported. You won't fall through or anything."

"Where did you learn to do that?" Allie asked, plastering a sweet and admirable smile on her face.

"It gets boring sitting in a cell all day," said Travis. "They offered us community service, building houses for charity."

Despite his obvious mental issues, she was impressed that he had used his time locked up to learn something of value. For a moment, she forgot the gun he was holding. She wondered if Travis hadn't been painting just hours ago.

"I hung all new sheetrock," said Travis. "Painted."

The house reeked of the new paint, the walls a soft earthy green. The paint was still wet in patches.

"Trim is next," said Travis, waving his hand.

Beyond the narrow entry hall, the living room to the left had a fresh coat of paint and new subfloor. Spotting the same worn couch from Allie's previous visit, her stomach twisted in a knot.

"The water is running again," said Travis. "The pressure's really low, but at least it's clean."

She was certain that he had already spent several nights in this house. Weeks probably. *How's he been hiding, working in town without anyone noticing?* The town couldn't keep a secret if their existence depended upon it.

"I want to show you something," Travis said, pulling at Allie's hand. He yanked her up the rounded staircase.

"Do we—"

He ignored her. "That room with the balcony is for you, Allie. It's not finished yet. I have some bookshelves to finish puttin' up. But I wanted to give you a room where you could read."

Allie's stomach dropped. The bastard who'd *burned* her favorite book in front of her, belittled her for doing what she most enjoyed, was now...what? Trying to make up for it?

"We'll come back to that room later."

She looked longingly at the balcony, wondering if she'd be able to spot help on its way. *Or is help not coming?*

"Come on," Travis said, pushing her forward. "I saved the best for last."

Swallowing hard, she shuffled toward the once rickety, now reinforced door, and slowly turned the new knob. In the corner was a bed, two flat pillows, a nightstand with a lantern, and a worn picture of Allie in her high school track outfit pinned above the right side of the bed.

As much as she tried to stay in the way of the door, he shoved her forward with the barrel of his gun and closed the door behind them. "We have a lot of lost time to make up for."

"I know we're close." Amanda fought to hide her panic from her voice. She and Allie had only been to the house once.

"Are you sure this is the right way?" Nick asked.

There were abandoned farmhouses all over the country. It was hard to keep the roads straight. These country roads all had numbers. She couldn't quite remember the number she needed. *Was it something Road? 863, maybe 865?* They had just passed 861. "I'll recognize the turn."

"I hope so."

"Why didn't you mention you have a *wife*, Nick?"

He stared straight ahead, refusing to meet her glare. He growled, "Allie knows. Dana's supposed to be my ex by now."

"Did you mean what you said?"

"What?"

"That you love Allie?"

Not even a second of hesitation. "Yes."

Amanda squinted through the tinted glass, hoping to recognize a landmark——maybe a large tree or a dilapidated shed. "There!" she shouted as she pointed. "I recognize that windmill. Turn right at the next road. We're just a few miles away."

"I need another drink." Dana pushed passed Miranda, marching into the house.

"Excuse me?" Miranda whisked around, following her. "This isn't your house."

"Actually it is." Dana made it all the way into the kitchen, tossing open the refrigerator like she owned the place. "Community property laws and all that."

Miranda stared out the kitchen window. Why had her brother gone to confront that kidnapping lunatic without a weapon to defend himself? "Nick doesn't own this."

"Don't be ridiculous." Dana cracked open a Coke, grabbed a glass, and unscrewed the cap of the Jack Daniels. "Of course he does."

"Naïve was a good word for you," muttered Miranda.

"Doesn't matter, anyway. He's coming back to Georgia." She watched Dana dump too much whiskey into her glass.

"You changed his mind. Is that all you can think of right now? Not sending for an ambulance in case that maniac decides to *kill* them?" Miranda yanked a shot glass from the cupboard. "Why don't you use that expensive phone of yours for something besides your agenda for once?"

Swallowing half her drink, Dana ignored that. "He's coming around. I know it."

Grabbing the bottle, Miranda poured herself a shot. "I wish that were true. Believe me." She tossed the burning liquid down. "But I don't see that happening. He's a local hero, in case you haven't heard. Saved a man's life last night."

"He can do that anywhere," Dana dismissed.

"You think he's gonna give up the girl he's trying to rescue for *you*?"

That seemed to jar her.

"I've always known I took him for granted," mumbled Dana.

It didn't seem to be the right time to have it out with Dana. "Nick's the most loyal human being on the planet," Miranda said. "Except when he's given a reason not to be." There'd never be an ideal moment for this conversation, so Miranda kept going. "If you really care, you'll call off your army of lawyers and disappear from his life."

Dana's glass halted halfway to her lips. "He really does love her, doesn't he?"

"I don't know too many men who'd chase after a mentally unstable guy otherwise."

"You knew, didn't you?"

Miranda checked her cell phone for the fourth time. *Why isn't Nick calling me?* "Not at first. I could always tell Neil had a thing for you," she admitted. "I mean, even at your wedding he was constantly undressing you with his eyes."

Dana took another gulp.

"You thought your precious money would guarantee you happiness."

"I didn't have the money back then," said Dana. "Not until a few months after the wedding."

"It must be tough," said Miranda. "Inheriting millions. I mean, one day you're like everyone else. And then boom. You never have to work another day in your life. You could travel the world ten times over. Why did you target my brother?"

Dana didn't answer right away. Then she turned to face Miranda. "You try losing both your parents at twenty-two."

"I'm not a therapist," said Miranda.

"The last thing my mother said before she left on that train with her boyfriend was 'Don't be a slut, dear. It'll do no good for your reputation.' That was the *last* thing she said to me, at fifteen. Not 'I love you,' or 'Stay out of trouble.' "

"What's your point?"

"The money, it's always gotten me what I wanted." Dana set her empty glass on the counter. "And until this circus busted into the driveway, I just about had him."

"You're delusional," muttered Miranda. "I bet he told you to leave."

"Think what you want. But make no mistake, I won't be leaving Willow Creek until Nick agrees to come with me."

The idiot! Travis had mentioned his plans to fix up the old farmhouse. But Lesley hadn't anticipated him repairing it as some sorry attempt to win over Allie Jordan.

Digging through her purse, she reached for her lighter again, her knuckles grazing her gun. She hoped it wouldn't come to that, but if it were necessary... she'd bully her son back home. *If that doesn't work, a can of gasoline will.*

She had to admit Travis had revived the dilapidated little home. She let herself inside, her studied survey calculating exactly how much his renovation had cost her precious store.

A small moan escaped from up the stairwell, stopping Lesley's exploration. Rich had brought her here once when they were young; she knew what room was upstairs. She considered breaking up the escapade, but decided to turn her head instead.

Let Travis have his fun.

The couch in the living room was obviously used,

but it'd have to do. Dusting off a spot, Lesley sat and waited, purse in her lap. Ignoring a scream of "No!" she studied her nails instead. *I'll need a manicure after this.* She always did look better pointing a gun with a fresh manicure and bright red nail polish.

Chapter 36

Abruptly Travis pushed Allie across the room. She tripped over an uneven piece of laminate, landing on the corner of the mattress.

He threw off his hoodie, tossing it on the floor beside the bed. "Take off your clothes," he said with a hungry look in his eyes.

With every ounce of fight in her, Allie plastered on a shy smile. "It's been so long, why rush it?" She crawled backwards onto the mattress, maintaining eye contact. The excitement in his eyes told her she had him, at least for now.

He knelt, gun still in hand. Hovering, his knees trapped her thighs and he kissed her neck. Allie closed her eyes and purposely let out a soft moan. She hoped he'd focus on her encouraging noises and not notice her fingers edging toward the gun.

A hand slid beneath the leg of her jeans, bunching up the fabric to reveal her scar. "You're mine, Allie." He traced his fingers along her ugly mark. "Don't you ever forget that again. You got it?"

Forcing down the urge to kick the bastard between the legs for giving her that scar, Allie said, "I won't."

Next, Travis reached for the button at her waist.

"No!" she shrieked.

There was a flash of confusion on his face, she had to think quickly. "I mean, do you have a condom? With the house not finished, we're definitely not ready for kids."

"Good thinking." He hopped off the bed. "I have one downstairs."

Allie's heart sank when he took the gun with him. She thought about jumping out the window, but she'd likely break a leg. She cringed, wondering how far she'd have to allow things to go. *I have to get the gun.*

"What the hell are you doing here?" Allie heard Travis growl from downstairs.

She sprang up, re-buttoning her pants. She felt hopeful… until the confronted person spoke.

"I'm making sure you don't do something stupid enough to land you back in prison."

Cruella? This can't be good.

"We're doing just fine," said Travis. "Leave."

"Last I checked," said Lesley, "I own this house."

"Then what do you want?"

Allie froze in the doorway, her breath halted as she awaited the answer.

"I want to make sure you see reason," said Lesley.

"You brought a gun?"

"I see I'm not the only one."

Allie's heart dropped. They *both* had guns. Maybe her only chance was to roll down the roof above the covered porch and run. They'd be arguing for a few minutes, giving her a head start. But as she stepped forward, the floor creaked.

"Allie," Lesley called up the stairway. "Do come downstairs."

"What do you want with her?" demanded Travis. "She has nothing to do with this."

"She has everything to do with this."

"Up ahead!" Amanda pointed. "Behind that patch of trees!"

Nick stepped on the gas, throwing Amanda back against the seat.

"Slow down!" yelled Amanda. "Your best chance is

catching him off guard. He's crazy! He sees you tearing into the driveway, he'll do something impulsive." Once Nick eased off the gas, she added, "There's a rough road on this side of the trees."

The truck bounced as he drove onto the rutted dirt path and shifted into park.

"How long before Alex gets here?"

"He was in Norfolk. They're at least ten more minutes out." Nick reached for the door handle. "I'm not waiting."

"Allie's probably upstairs."

He read everything he needed to know in Amanda's pitiful expression. If that asshole raped Allie, Nick would kill him.

"Stay in the truck."

"No way." Amanda threw her door open and hopped out.

"He has a gun," Nick pleaded. He'd never forgive himself if Allie's little sister got hurt in the process. Good chance Willow Creek wouldn't, either.

"I know Travis better than you do. You *need* me." Amanda was halfway to the patch of trees before Nick had any further opportunity to object.

His only choice was to follow.

"Allie, hurry along," said Lesley, no doubt spotting her feet on the stairs. "I don't have all day now."

Not knowing what other choice she might have, Allie shuffled into the living room and stood in the doorway. She locked eyes with Lesley, but kept silent. She'd finally felt the ultimate freedom from this woman's reign of power over her. But a couple of guns quickly brought those feelings of oppression back like a violent thunderstorm.

"We need to straighten this little mess out once and for all," Lesley said. "Allie, tell Travis that your quick little trip back to Willow Creek was a mistake. That you're not back to stay."

Travis shot Allie a look of disbelief, as if her answer would make or break his world. And if she broke his world, he might shoot her. If she told Lesley the truth, they both might shoot her.

"He's done a marvelous job with the house," said Allie. "Don't you think?"

Travis smiled victoriously. Lesley's frown deepened. "Stop this fucking game. The charade is over." She stood up from the couch. "I fired her," said Lesley. "She had no choice but to move. You won't want her anyway. Her reputation is ruined."

"She's staying with me," said Travis.

"You'll be the laughingstock if you shack-up with her."

"*Why* is her reputation ruined, Mother?"

"Because I caught her leaving the doctor's house in the middle of the night. She violated our fraternization policy. If she stays, I will make sure the entire town knows. I have the evidence on camera."

"You're still blackmailing?" Travis shook his head.

"I couldn't well wait for you to get out," said Lesley. "And if this little tramp hadn't gotten you caught that night—"

Allie's knees shook as fury built in Travis' eyes.

"You've been blaming her for five years." Travis stomped one step closer to Lesley. "You even tried brainwashing me with your bullshit. But I know better now. Oh yes, I do," said Travis, waving his gun. "I told you I couldn't go that night. I told you I had plans."

"You were living under my roof. Your plans weren't a priority." Lesley put one hand on her hip, the other hung at her side, gripping her gun. "Catching the Hillsboro mayor with that college girl, that was the priority. He was a day away from a meeting with the hospital Board about a merger. If that had happened, I would've been out of a job and you know it."

Allie's eyes darted back and forth from speaker to gun to speaker. It was a little unsettling how unsurprising it was that Lesley had been blackmailing people for years. Setting them up. Brilliant, in the most awful way.

"I don't believe you," said Travis. "You knew what my plans were and were doing everything you could to fuck them up."

"You were about to make the biggest mistake of your life," argued Lesley. "Why on Earth would you want to get married that young? And to this tramp?"

Allie's eyes opened wide. She'd never have guessed Travis would propose to her that night. But slowly, the pieces fell together. She leaned her hand against the wall. It was the only thing keeping her upright. She understood that Travis meant everything he said about this house, fixing it up to raise a family. Had meant it for five years.

"I didn't want to see you make the same mistake I did," Lesley said.

"*You* called the cops," said Allie, barely above a whisper. "It was *you*."

Rage washed over Travis' face, his gray eyes growing cold. "It *was* you."

"Yes, I called the cops."

"That's not what I'm talking about." Hatred filled

each growled word as Travis steadied his gun, slowly pointing it at his mother. "I know what you did!"

"What are you talking about? Put down that gun, you idiot."

"You killed my father."

"You're crazy."

"I remember." Travis raised the gun a little higher. "I—I saw it. I watched you shot him in the head. You shoved him into a hole."

It all made so much sense to Allie. Why Travis flipped when his father disappeared. He'd witnessed the most horrific event imaginable. It must have been a little like PTSD, but until now she'd never been able to fathom what traumatic event would have caused such a reaction.

"You don't know what you're talking about," Lesley spat. "Your pathetic father left town because he didn't love you anymore."

Travis shook his head. The fire in his eyes was unfaltering. "I saw it. You killed him."

Allie took a couple of involuntary steps backward, never dropping her eyes. She wasn't sure running was an option, but at the moment she wasn't about to be caught in anyone's crossfire.

"I never—"

"Admit it," yelled Travis. "Admit it or I'll—"

"Fine!" screamed Lesley. "Yes, I killed your pitiful excuse for a father. He made a fool out of me, pummeling the cleaning girl in *my* house. I was the laughingstock of the whole town. He would've ruined the reputation I worked so hard for." Lesley raised her gun and aimed it at Travis. "I couldn't let that happen."

With a quick scream, Allie ducked. One of the guns fired.

Two more shots echoed.

Chapter 37

Two strong arms grabbed Allie from behind. She struggled before she realized it was Nick. *Nick!* Tears welled up in her eyes.

"Let's go!" Amanda waved to them from the open back door.

The three ran toward the tree line as a mass of state patrol cars surrounded the house, their lights flashing.

Amanda threw her arms around her sister. "Are you okay? No one's shot, are they? Please tell me they suck at shooting!"

Allie looked back toward the house. "I don't know."

The ride to Willow Creek was a long one. Nick sat in the passenger seat with Allie on his lap, his arms wrapped tightly around her while Amanda drove them to the police station.

Allie told Alex everything about the blackmail tapes and Lesley's confession of murder. Travis, a gunshot wound in his chest, was flown away in a helicopter to Norfolk. His chances of survival were minimal, they both heard. Travis had only grazed Lesley on her arm. An EMT wrapped her minor wound, and she was escorted to the station in the back of a police car.

One of the deputies mentioned something about self-defense or attempted murder. If Travis woke up, only then would they have a solid case for the latter.

Allie hoped it would be enough to get a warrant.

"Allie, you brave girl." Alex had hugged her against his chest like a big brother before leaving the scene. "You're going to help me solve my case." Eyeing Nick over the top of Allie's head, Alex said, "No need to punch me, Nick. Allie's statement will get me the warrant I need."

"Can you arrest Lesley?" Allie asked, hopeful.

"A warrant lets us search her house. And comb this

property for a body. I don't think she'll be able to bribe her way out of this one. Not on a murder charge."

"Rich Meyers is your case?" Allie asked. "You've been looking for him?"

"I work in the missing person's division, remember?"

It was almost midnight by the time they left the police station. Nick invited the small group, which now included Allie's mom, to his house. Thankfully, there were a couple of frozen pizzas in his freezer that Miranda had been able to bake, but now most of it sat on the kitchen island, untouched.

"I always knew Travis Meyers was bad news," said Pam because no one else was talking. "He was always getting into trouble. I was so relieved when he was hauled off to jail that I could've cried. I can't believe he's been in town for weeks without anyone knowing."

"I'm going to call the hospital in Norfolk," said Allie.

"You can't possibly care what happens to him now, can you?" Miranda asked.

"He needs help. He's mentally unstable and it's all his mother's fault." Allie grabbed Nick's phone off the charger. Dialing the number, she added, "Plus, if he dies in the operating room, Lesley has no eyewitness to testify against her."

Allie heard Dana ask Nick from across the room, "Can I please talk to you for a moment?" She tried to taper her jealousy. Nick had explained Dana's unexpected appearance during their slow drive back to Willow Creek. Amanda freely added her own commentary. *I'll feel a whole lot better when Designer Barbie heads back to Georgia and stays there.* Tonight, she just couldn't deal with Dana too.

Despite her adamant pleas, the hospital refused to update her on Travis' condition. "Stupid HIPPA laws," she muttered, falling onto the couch.

Seconds later, the front door burst open. Kim raced across the room and tackled Allie in a violent bear hug. "Oh my God, Allie! You're okay!"

Allie tried to reply, but words were choked from her in an unexpected lack of oxygen. She patted Kim on her shoulder, gently at first. Then harder.

"Oh. *Oh!* Sorry, Al. I'm just so relieved you're okay. I've been such an idiot. I'm so sorry I said all those things when you moved to Omaha. Amanda told me everything. I'm so proud you're staying, Al."

Allie was silent for a beat.

Kim huffed. "You *are* staying, right?" Allie caught the curious tilt of Miranda's head and her mom's stare from across the living room.

"Yes. This is where I belong."

Nick could feel strain in his eyes, on his entire face. He wanted to go to Allie to comfort her, but he knew he couldn't put off dealing with Dana any longer. The longer he let that go, the better chance Pam would start asking uncomfortable questions. He stood up and followed Dana to the back door, closing it behind them.

"I've made a call to my lawyers. The divorce will be final on Monday."

Nick braced, certain there'd be a catch. "What about your money?"

Dana folded her arms across her chest. "I haven't been completely truthful with you, Nick. Surprised?" When he didn't say anything, she continued. "Daddy *did* revise his will. If we stayed married five years and divorced, I got to keep all the money. That's why I wanted you to stick it out a little longer. But after everything that's happened tonight, I realize I can't stand in the way anymore." A solitary tear dropped from Dana's blue eyes. Perhaps the only real tear Nick had ever seen from her.

"I don't understand."

"If we *did* divorce before those five years, I'm obligated to give you ten percent."

"What?" Feeling overwhelmed, he stumbled a bit and actually fell against the back door.

"Daddy really liked you. Had a feeling I'd run you off." She took a deep breath. "So he made certain you'd be taken care of. On Monday, once the divorce is final, fifty million dollars will be wired to your bank account. Ten percent of what Daddy left me."

"You're joking, right?"

She shook her head and let it hang in shame. "I tried to buy you off because I wanted to keep all of it. But you don't deserve that. You deserve to be happy, Nick. Even if you hadn't had to put up with me."

"I don't want it."

Dana laughed. "I'm afraid you don't have a choice. It's a non-negotiable term. That's why it took so long for the divorce to process. My lawyers have been looking for every loophole imaginable. Daddy made sure there wasn't one. You have to take the money."

"Why the change of heart now?"

"I'll be honest. I had every intention of convincing you to come back to Georgia. Had even planned to stay here and play house if that's what it took. But then you walked through the door with *her*. She looked so frightened." Dana stood. "You didn't even notice me.

And it hit me how selfish I'd been." She kissed him on the cheek. "For what it's worth, I'm sorry for everything. But I'm happy for you, Nick. She's a very lucky woman."

Dana brushed off his offer to walk back through the house. "I'll walk around. Fresh air will do me good."

From the kitchen window, he watched as taillights faded at the end of his private road.

"I have a confession to make, Nick," said Pam as she slipped into the kitchen to lean against the counter near him. "I pushed Allie to leave Willow Creek. I was afraid she'd never be happy here. That she'd always be afraid of Travis finding her."

"I was afraid of that too. So when she left, I let her go."

"He can't hurt her anymore." Nick was grateful she kept her voice low so they'd not be overheard.

Stepping closer to Pam, he said, "I want you to know that I love your daughter. Very much."

"I know." She patted him on the shoulder. "No man would chase down an armed maniac unless he truly cared about the person in danger." Pushing off the island, she added, "When things calm down a bit, you should make sure Allie knows. But be patient with her." Without looking back, she returned to the small crowd in the living room.

Nick stole a couple of moments to himself. He

yearned to rush into the next room and insist that everyone except Allie leave. Yearned to hold her in his arms all night long and let her know just how much she meant to him. But he knew Pam was right.

"Hey."

Nick turned, spotting Allie in the doorway. "Hey."

"I'm pretty tired. I'm going to head home."

He bit back the urge to ask her to stay. "Okay."

"Tomorrow I'm going back to Omaha."

"Oh." His heart dropped to the bottom of his stomach. "I thought—"

"I need to pack up my place there. Get everything moved home."

A smile fought its way through his carefully blank expression. There'd be no future for him in Willow Creek without Allie here to share it with. "Need any help?"

She shook her head. "I need a few days, Nick. All of this has been a little overwhelming. Including Designer Barbie." Her cheeks turned red. "I mean—"

Chuckling, Nick said, "No, that's a pretty accurate description." He'd reluctantly give Allie the space she requested. He pulled her tightly into his embrace, and kissed her forehead. "I'm here when you're ready."

Chapter 38

"How's the local hero?" Doc Herb asked the next day during an early morning phone call.

Nick yawned into the phone, yearning for a cup of coffee after the long night he had. "I'm recovering."

"You've had quite the week, I hear."

Nick shifted. "You could say that."

"I've called to say that you passed. With flying colors. But I'm sure you knew that."

Nick yawned again.

"If you want the practice, it's yours. And the house. I can have my lawyer draw up the papers tomorrow morning."

The front door screeched open, announcing Miranda's return. She'd run to the grocery store to finish stocking his refrigerator with some "proper" food.

He wanted to accept the job on the spot, but he'd have to make his sister understand first. "Let me call you back later today, Herb. Okay?"

"Sure thing."

"I'm willing to bet you haven't had a decent breakfast in almost three months," said Miranda, dropping several bags of groceries onto the island. "I'm going to whip you up some bacon and sausage omelets."

Watching Miranda unpack the bags, Nick steeled himself. She reminded him of everything good he left behind in Georgia. Of the Sunday family dinners, his niece and nephew, his family. Could he give it all up to stay in Willow Creek? Now that Dana was truly an ex-wife and he was fifty million dollars richer... Nick shook his head. *Still can't wrap my head around that one.*

"Your probation period is just about up, isn't it?" she asked, reading his expression.

"Yes."

"So what are you planning to do, Nicholas?"

A week had passed since Travis kidnapped Allie, and she was finally settling back into her ranch home. The main area she had been avoiding was her closet. The one overflowing with books. She'd packed in such haste that her once neat stacks were now haphazard, wobbling towers.

She went to retrieve a full box from the living room when the doorbell rang. Before she could answer the door, Nick burst inside, halting when Norman barricaded him in the doorway. Those pesky butterflies were back, playing gymnastics in her stomach. She'd avoided him for the past few days, ignoring his calls and texts. "Norman, you can let him in."

"I know you asked for time," said Nick, approaching her with Norman right at his heels. "But I've given you about as much time as I can take, Allie."

Allowing him to follow her into the bedroom, she pushed the sliding closet door open and scooped up a pile of books from the box. "I'm still processing everything." *Allie, that's a lame excuse and you know it.*

"What are all these?" Nick reached around her into the closet, pulling out a paperback novel. "*The Tortured Temptress?*" He reached for another. "*Happily Ever After?*" He couldn't seem to help himself and grabbed another. "*The Heavenly Hero?*"

"Give me those." Allie yanked the books out of his hands. But Nick wasn't done. He reached in to pull out another, and brought down half the wall of what must have been three hundred romance novels. The avalanche of paperbacks engulfed their legs, causing both to lose their balance. Together, they fell onto the floor.

"This is familiar," said Nick from underneath Allie.

The urge to kiss him overwhelmed her. But hesitation won out. She scurried off him and stood.

Brushing off a pile of books, Nick jumped up. "You have to let the past go, Allie, or it'll haunt you forever."

Eyes locking, she knew he was right. Knew she was out of excuses to run. Dropping the handful of books she'd begun gathering, she whisked past Nick. Two shadows followed her to the kitchen. "You're right, Nick." Lifting her laptop, she grabbed the letter that'd stayed in her life too long.

"What's that?"

Allie dug through a kitchen drawer and secured a lighter. "My past." On the back deck, she lit the corner of the envelope. The one with Travis' return address from prison. Dropping the flaming letter into an empty trash can, she watched her past turn to ash.

"Feel better?" Nick asked as a drop of rain landed on his cheek.

For the first time in five years, Allie felt freer. Liberated. "Much." Raindrops sprinkled her arms.

Norman must have sensed the imminent rainstorm and rushed inside, leaving Nick and Allie alone on the deck. "What about you, Nick? Is your past still haunting you?"

Raindrops fell in heavy succession, dampening her hair and his. He shook his head. "My past went back to Georgia. Permanently." He brushed a wet strand of hair from her cheek. "All I see now is my future, right here in Willow Creek. With the woman I love."

Cupping her cheeks in his hands, Nick pressed his lips against hers like it was their first kiss. As rain poured, hands roamed, lips and tongues intertwined. Allie's shirt was halfway up her torso when a jesting voice shouted over the fence, "Get a room!"

"Sorry, Ed!" Nick called across the yard. Grabbing Allie's hand, he pulled her inside.

Shedding wet clothes, the wandering lips and hands continued as they moved through the kitchen. A wet nose wedged between them in the living room. Allie let out a squeal. "Norman!" Barking once, the dog offered up a few enthusiastic licks.

Nick laughed. "Looks like Norman approves."

By the time Nick led her to the bed, a trail of damp clothing littered the house. Wrapped in soft sheets, his arms and legs tangled with hers, Nick smiled down at Allie. "Do you have any idea—"

"What I do to you?" she teased, her eyes traveling between their bodies. "Because I think I have a pretty *big* idea—"

Lusty eyes locking with hers, Nick entered her at once, filling her completely. "Actually, I was going to ask if you had any idea how much I love you."

His words warmed her heart, just like so many happy endings in her romance novels.

"I love you too, Nick."

If you enjoyed this book, please consider leaving a review online. I read and appreciate every review. You guys rock!

Acknowledgements

To my early readers: Thank you for helping me see the heart of the story through all the extra words.

To my creative writing class: If any of you are reading this, I want you to know how much your objective honesty meant to me. I will admit I went home in tears after our first class, but I quickly realized that each of you only wanted to help me improve. You helped me grow thicker skin, and for that, I am forever grateful.

To Nicole: Thank you for the hours and love you poured into critiquing an early draft of this book—a very brave endeavor indeed. There is no way this story would be what it is without your help, the late night shop talks, and the constant discussions you were so kind and patient enough to provide for weeks and months on end.

Magen: Thank you for insisting I let you read an early draft. Your feedback and collaboration were essential to elevating the story to where it is today. Thank you also for proofreading the final draft—I hope you're okay being a proofreader for life!

To my critique panel, Nikki H., Nicki L., Audrey, Jen, Jules, and Melissa: Thank you all for sacrificing the time and energy to read and critique my novel. I value the feedback you provided beyond words. Each and every one of you helped me work through the kinks and flaws of the story to make it stronger and more cohesive.

To Nikki H.: Thank you for constantly letting me talk through ideas and changes with you. You were always available to bounce ideas off of, and I can't express how much that meant to me. I know my characters and my story are better off for it. I'm very grateful I sat down at that table next to you.

To Jules: Thank you for always being there when I had questions—and I know I had dozens. Maybe even hundreds! Your honest feedback was refreshing, and I appreciate that you didn't hold back on telling me what I needed to hear. Thank you also for holding me accountable to my writing goals. You've helped me realize what I'm capable of achieving if I only put my mind to it. I appreciate you taking the time to walk me through the different phases of publishing. Hopefully my infinite amount of questions has been helpful to you as well.

To Niecey: Thank you for answering my many, many questions about the publishing process. Your insight ultimately helped me decide that this was the best route for me to take. You have always been available for random questions and very helpful in recommending the right people and explaining things in depth.

To E.J.: Thank you for being the kind of editor that not only helps me craft a better story but helps me understand and grow as a writer. I have learned so much working with you and look forward to continuing to grow in the future.

To Brenda: Thank you for helping me polish this book and making it shine. You were an absolute pleasure to work with, and your constant encouragement really helped me feel confident about this book.

To Letitia: Thank you for creating such an amazing cover! I fell in love with it the first moment I saw it. You really understood my vision and then proceeded to exceed my expectations.

To my proofreaders, Magen, Barb, and Mariana:

Thank you all for being my second set of eyes.

To Michelle: Thank you for being the final set of eyes. And thank you for making this book look, well, like a real book!

To Brad: Thank you for building my awesome website! And thank you for constantly updating it with all my many requests.

To my parents: Thank you both for raising me to believe that I can accomplish anything I put my mind to. You've never doubted me as a writer, and that has meant so much to me. I love you both.

To my fans and readers: The amount of encouragement I've received for months now has truly humbled me. In those moments when I felt the slightest struggle, one of you were always there to convince me to keep going. Your excitement has been contagious in the best way. I hope each and every one of you enjoys reading this story as much as I've enjoyed writing it.

If I've forgotten anyone, it wasn't intentional. Every person who has had any amount of input or influence on this story will forever hold a cherished place in my heart. I cannot accurately express how grateful I am to have you all in my life. Thank you!

About Jacqueline Winters

Jacqueline Winters has been writing books since she was nine and had to sneak stacks of paper from her grandma's closet to write them. Born and raised in Nebraska, she has since spread her wings and taken flight to Alaska. She's a sucker for happily ever afters and loves dogs, hiking, and traveling. On a sunny Alaskan evening, you can find her curled up on her deck with her dog writing her next novel.

You can learn more about Jacqueline, read her blog, and stay tuned for upcoming novels by visiting her website at http://jacquelinewintersromance.com/.